To Kiersten,

May you d … e,
& may you pursue it with passion -
never stop being a Reader! ♡

KJ Madsen

Emospherica

The Destiny of Jasmine Blade

Part I

KJ Madsen

ISBN:
ISBN-13: 978-1482368871
ISBN-10: 1482368870

Paua Publishing

DEDICATION

For faith. And for family. But mostly for faith.

CONTENTS

	PREFACE	
1	THE BUBBLE	1
2	ESCAPE	18
3	BREEZES THAT BLOW	24
4	WIND IN MY SAILS	43
5	CHARLOTTE	67
6	NIGHT FLIGHT	80
7	HISTORY	85
8	FAMILY	100
9	SOUND WAVE	109
10	TESTING THE THEORY	122
11	IN TRAINING	130
12	TESTING	153
13	HOME SWEET HOME	171
14	THE OAK TREE	192
15	COUNCIL OF CARRIERS, FRAMERS & READERS	205
16	LOVE IS IN THE AIR	229
17	LIVE & LET LIVE	240
18	STILL FALLING	261
19	KISSED	278
20	TEAM WORK	283
21	MEETING OF THE MINDS	296
22	EMOSPHERICA	311
23	OUT OF THE FRYING PAN	326
24	INTO THE FIRE	339
25	ALL THINGS	347
26	A TIME FOR EVERYTHING	350
1	THE OUTFIELD	362

ACKNOWLEDGMENTS

Greatest appreciation to the following extra-special people:

Karl – husband and best friend extraordinaire,
Talman, Micah, Isaac, Amos & Samara – children in a trillion;
Family & Friends who have cheered me on (you know who you are);
Ruth Blaikie of Pea Pod Enterprises for her most excellent skills and encouraging words;
Aidan 'T-Bird' Turvey for grasping my imagination and imprinting it on the cover

"Poetry is the spontaneous overflow of powerful feelings: it takes its origin from emotion recollected in tranquility."

William Wordsworth

PREFACE

Within recent recorded history of the modern rock concert I guess I can't be the first girl to drown in a mosh-pit. But this seething ocean of untamed emotion has burst my last bubble, and I am sinking fast, totally out of my depth.

Please, dear God, let me see Levi one last time. I can hear his gravel voice graze my ears, his rough haunting lyrics sliding from the stage to where my broken body is holding out against the dark side of destiny. I have done everything asked of me, and failed. Spectacularly. It is time to face the facts: when you dabble in emotional warfare, love doesn't always conquer all, no matter what rock star you fall for…

1. THE BUBBLE

I LAY IN THE LONG GRASS AND GENTLY BLEW. The delicate soapy skin began to stretch, arcing toward the sky, and as it trapped my warm, soft breath it sparkled. With a light sigh I released it into the breeze, watching it rise en route to the sun and away from me, beautiful and free.

I have grasped all the scientific complexities of bubble-blowing. I know they have tension a bit like bubble-gum, and are just as explosive, which is why a bit of added soap coaxes them to hold their fragile form; then there's the spherical shape, surface area, and volume calculation that launches physicists into math heaven. But the simple theory is that blowing bubbles makes me happy. Surely there must be a way to inject my joy into the bubbles and spread the feeling around? I can't help but think I'm on the brink of a formidably momentous discovery and I can sense the physics nerd within me tearing her hair out trying to solve the puzzle, but just like the bubble the answer keeps floating away out of reach and out of sight.

Closing my eyes, I soaked up the early spring sunshine. This was one of the few places I could be alone; whoever else would choose to lie in the weeds behind the compost heap where old junk and garden waste pile up? Certainly not my parents, and definitely not my brothers – they are all far too busy. This is my domain and my solace: my faithful plum tree by the fence and my wild jasmine that throws itself over post and rail with wild abandon.

The vine is my namesake. Although everyone I know calls me Jazz, my full name is Jasmine – Jasmine Blade. My mom always told me that they named me after the heavy-scented spring vine that grew through the cracks in the floorboards in their first home back in New Zealand – luscious pink buds that explode into pure white stars as the heat of summer rises. "After four sons, we deserve a daughter who is tenacious and tough enough to withstand her brothers, but beautiful like her mother," Dad teased Mom after I was born, and he had planted the vine in my honor when we settled in Carolina. I think he forgot that the nature of jasmine is wild and very difficult to tame.

It's not like I didn't try to fit in; in fact, as far as teenage daughters go I think I'm pretty close to being a paragon of virtue. At seventeen I'm graduating near top of the class in physics and chemistry, which pleases my parents immensely, each claiming my scientific abilities as theirs. I'm average at most other things, and as for sport, I just like to run. Running seems to jog my brain, which every good scientist needs on a regular basis – it helps to "un-stick" me when I'm stuck and thrust me into the unknown recesses of my frontal lobe. I have all my best ideas when I'm out pounding the pavement – ideas on how to pay back my brothers for their never-ending pranks, ideas for experiments I'd like to try, or dreams about my future. Sometimes I feel like running in the same direction for as long as it takes for something to change. I don't want to sound ungrateful, but I'm a great believer in personal destiny, and I am itching for mine to begin.

As I lay in the stillness, hazy in the back of my mind was a memory that occasionally obtained clarity, but usually it just sits like a fuzzy photograph of people and places that don't look familiar but somehow feel important. As the sun reached the zenith of its spring warmth, a vague scent of jasmine opening to the heat wafted across my face, and I breathed in deeply. Tantalizingly, the perfume tickled my scent glands; the photo began to come into focus. I dared not move, for this was the closest the memory had come in years.

There were lots of jasmine flowers. The fragrant perfume grew stronger in my nose, and I realized that I was in the picture – not visible, but I felt for certain that I was under the wooden floorboards of the front porch. No one was looking for me, so I guessed I'd absconded from nap time and crawled into the cool space to escape the intense heat of the day. Now I remember! I was lying on sand because the house was near the beach! But where was the beach? And whose house was I lying under? In my mind I drifted to the shapes in the photo that I presumed were people. I heard a voice saying, "She must never know this! You must never tell her!"

And then another, shaking with anger speaks out: "How can you deny her destiny? There are those coming today to testify and seal their quests! You may not agree with her inheritance, but you cannot, must not, turn her into a sleeping beauty. We need her, we all need her!"

"She is not yours to need," someone else declared, "and if you try to stop us, I swear you will never see her again – never!"

"If that is your final word, then so be it," rejoined the angry voice, "and you will never see us again either! We will not abide your disloyalty, or your selfish actions!"

A soft cry sounded, and I looked down – I had scratched my hand on a nail, and it was bleeding.

Someone was calling my name. "Jazz-zzy!" It broke through my daydream and the picture fell from my mind, pulling me back into real time. My mother, Ashley, was the only one who called me Jazzy and I let her get away with it, although I outgrew any fondness for it years ago.

Ashley Blade didn't look half bad for someone who was now fifty and had survived raising five kids. Walking towards me she gave the impression that she descended from royalty – the straight back and square shoulders, long elegant neck and quiet eyes commanding attention. Her ash-blonde hair was confidently tucked into a tidy arrangement and her countenance exuded a calm demeanor within. Only those who knew her best understood that this was a survival mechanism, exercised to not scare people off. My mother lived life at a million miles an hour, and each quest for success required swift focus as she torpedoed from task to task, person to person, until complete domination was secured. Usually she juggled multiple quests with only the very occasional crash and burn.

"Dinner time! And don't forget that tonight we are sitting as a family – even Marcus will be here ... you are on dishes with Fale and we want the kitchen clean before 8pm because your father's new documentary is airing ... would you mind bringing the cat back in with you? She hasn't eaten yet today ... oh ... and one last thing: there's some birthday mail for you – it's on your bed, but you're not to open it until Saturday ... I think one of your brothers has brought you something crazy on the internet again – it's that sort of package ... walk and talk, walk and talk!"

And so it continued throughout the next hour. Mom wasn't really a non-stop talker; it was just that she never knew when she would find the time to communicate all the messages she had for us, so they all spilled out in one big monologue. Later, after dinner, she would settle into the evening having the satisfaction that her role as personal assistant, mailman, and answer phone service was complete.

Our dinner table was large. Dad had it made when he lived in New Zealand and then shipped it back to the States after he and my mom married. It had been crafted from native New Zealand heart Rimu, and no matter what the light was like it had a rich glow all of its own. I loved that table, we all did. With complete comfort it could accommodate fourteen people – even more when we were younger. Long benches had resided down each side, but once we got older Dad had ordered matching chairs – some with our names engraved on them. Some of our best family moments happened around that table and every now and again Dad would remind us: "*a family table keeps us stable.*" He had a saying for everything that man!

Dad was a Kiwi through and through. I loved the fact that he had kept his accent, even though he had lived in the United States for sixteen years. For a while he worked in Kaikoura on the east coast of the South Island of New Zealand as a young marine biologist graduate studying the giant sperm whales that are year-round Kaikoura residents. He was also collating data on fur seals, pods of dusky dolphins, humpback whales, pilot whales, blue whales, and southern right whales depending upon the season. His dream was to gather extensive data on the world's largest dolphin – the killer whale – as well as the world's rarest and smallest dolphin – the hector – with a view to creating television documentaries. That was when he met Ashley.

Ashley, too, was a young graduate, and having finished her college degree she set out to discover tastes from around the world, hoping to feed her latent passion for culinary delights. Kaikoura is a Maori place name that roughly translates "to eat crayfish," and that was the first meal they had together. To fund his studies, Nick (my dad) was working on a whale-watching boat for tourists, spotting the big mammals and answering questions from excited passengers. Ashley had taken the trip that day not because she loved whales, but because she couldn't bear to stay still for more than a few minutes, and Kaikoura was not, by any stretch of the imagination, a happening town. The rest is history and Mom still claims that crayfish is the best tasting seafood ever.

Nick jumped at the chance when fledgling New Zealand film makers approached him to direct a documentary on killer whales, and being on a tight budget, Ashley became the presenter by default. She discovered a talent she never knew she had and went from strength to strength fronting the myriad documentaries Dad had researched about the natural world, and in the last five years presented her own culinary show on the food channel – Mrs. Blade's Food Rave – a resounding success.

It's a pity Mom couldn't bring the leftovers home. Tonight was Chad's turn to cook (we all took turns in our house – at everything), and as much as he was my favorite brother, I wasn't that keen on tucking into the huge pile of macaroni cheese on the plate in front of me.

"Carbo load, Jazz! I'm planning a big run for us tomorrow; you won't be able to keep up!"

"Yeah right bro – in your dreams." I picked up my plate and scraped half of it onto his. "I may have to live with four boys, but I certainly don't have to eat like one!" And with that I took a spoonful of the stir fry vegetables Mom had surreptitiously added to the table.

Dad was distracted and my oldest brother, Marcus, who being twenty-four going on forty, was trying to engage him in conversation over some potential business venture he was looking at. The twins, Harley and Fale, were busy having a fork fight, stabbing at each other's plates to steal the crispy cheese bits. They were nineteen going on nine, and Chad was eating as if his life depended on it. It was noisy and chaotic, but we were all used to it; in fact dinner would be considered boring if it were any other way. Once dessert had been demolished (Mom had managed to scrounge some left-overs from her test kitchen after all!) we all sat and watched Dad's new doco on commercial Paua farming in New Zealand. The family loved to critique dad's work, and the lounge became even noisier than the dining room, until the carbohydrate overload finally took its toll and one by one we drifted off to bed. Another day of chaotic family life, I thought sleepily; some things never change.

The next morning as the early sun flew through my window and danced on my bed, the first thought I had was that today was a Day of Lasts. I couldn't help but smile. This would be my Last Time waking as a seventeen-year-old, my Last Entry through the gates of Carteret West High School – my Last Day of my Last Year at school. My smile grew.

Breakfast was a hurried affair in our house. Independence ruled the roost: Mom and Dad had usually left for the day already, so we each took care of our own. I, being influenced by a house of boys, drank milk from the carton then ate two slices of toast with Marmite – another New Zealand delicacy – rinsed the dishes, put out the cat, grunted at my brothers and left. When we moved to Beaufort, North Carolina, over fifteen years ago, my parents struggled to find a house big enough to accommodate us all. Mom jokingly suggested that Dad had better look for a hotel not a house, and that's when he stumbled across what was listed as "The Pecan Tree Inn." It was very old, circa 1866, but boasted beautiful private porches, gardens and courtyard, formal living and dining rooms, plus eight bedrooms, each with a private bath! The deal also included an adjacent vacant lot, which Mom and Dad were keeping for a rainy day. The estate agent touted it as "*A rare opportunity to satisfy a big need for a very large stately home in the Beaufort historic district.*" We had a big need for lots of space, so the fit was perfect. Well, nearly perfect. I would have preferred if we had been able to settle nearer Rock Hill or Chapel Downs where the schools were bigger and had more options, but I had grown to appreciate the old world charm of Beaufort. I liked the fact that Beaufort became big news when the Queen Anne's Revenge (Blackbeard's pirate ship), was discovered under twenty feet of water in the Beaufort Inlet in 1996. It's still underwater, and retrieval and restoration processes are halfway there – and Dad gets to write and produce all the footage for the National Geographic Channel, so he's in documentary heaven.

I gently twisted a trail of *Jasminum Polyanthum*, commonly known as pink jasmine, from the vine that wound its way over most of the nearby fence, and tucked it into my pony tail. It had become my trade mark over the years. It was not as common a species as the yellow Carolina jasmine, but my dad always said it reminded him of New Zealand, so we grew it everywhere. By the time I made it to Cedar Street, the jasmine had become my background fragrance, and Elle commented as I hopped into her car. "They should make jasmine into an ice-cream flavor just so we could eat it. Imagine capturing that smell in a taste … yummy!"

I laughed! Trust Ellie to come up with some crazy idea. She sat behind the wheel of her car all blonde and perky, her tiny figure immaculately dressed in clothes I knew every girl at school would soon copy. She wanted to be a fashion designer one day, and her quirky take on mainstream fashion had already proved its popularity. But things would change after today – we both knew it – and the ride to school was a silent one as we contemplated this Last Ride together.

Pulling up in the school car park we sat in her old VW Beetle, and I whispered, "It's crazy, Elle – four long years end today!"

Elle sighed. "You got it Jazz; one last day to go. Think I can make it through without getting detention?"

"Stay away from Matt and Sam and you'll be fine."

She laughed, and at the sound of the bell we made our way to class as I grumbled that I would not be sorry to leave the insistent ringing behind. I had never gotten used to the way it ruled my world, prodding me to conform. "Bells and timetables should only be used in mental institutions and prisons," I grumbled, but Elle wasn't listening, she was too intent on reading a flyer some senior had thrust into our hands as we walked through the packed hallway.

"Hey! A last day surrrr-prise! The student body have organized a band to play in the gym over an extended lunch break – cool! Let's go Jazz, let our hair down and all that."

"Our hair is already down," I quipped lamely, as Elle walked backwards in front of me, waving her phone in my face, blonde curls flowing over her shoulders, her little heart face fierce and determined.

"You will come, Jasmine Blade, and if you cause problems I'm going to text Eugene Tiller right now and tell him to come get you to dance down the front. I know he'd love that!"

I sighed. Being Elle's friend was never dull. I sort of let her carry me along on her waves of enthusiasm, cooperating enough to keep her happy and withholding enough to satisfy me. I was still keeping myself on a short leash, knowing that going my own way would come soon enough. Elle thought I already had plenty of freedom, but she just didn't understand. It wasn't about staying out past 10pm on a school night or no longer having to tell my parents where I was going every five minutes. The liberty I yearned for was holistic – mind, body, soul, and spirit. The chance to be unfettered for days – no months – on end, to dream endlessly, impossibly, to unearth mysteries and have time to draw conclusions before being rushed through life like it was an Olympic event rather than a meandering discovery. It wasn't that life was bad; it was just that it didn't seem to have really begun yet.

Elle had her cell phone out and was texting madly with an impish grin on her face.

"Oh no you don't!" I yelled, and grabbing the phone took off at a mad dash. I knew she'd chase me, but I also knew she didn't stand a chance, so I gleefully sped up, sprinting through the empty cafeteria, bulldozing over a junior or two as I reached the nearest exit. Flying across the grass, down the bank to the football field and under the stands I turned to look over my shoulder. "Ha! Not an Elle in sight!" I yelled gleefully. Gloating over my success I whirled around the next corner and screeched to a halt just in time. I found myself body to body with a boy, a hair's breadth away from being another crash test dummy. I could feel him through my jeans and could see a broad chest of gray shirt just centimeters from my eyeballs. Embarrassing! I raised my head and before I could help myself said "Knock Knock!"

"Who's there?" (He almost smiled at me through the grayest of eyes).

"Accident."

"Accident who?"

"Accident waiting to happen! That's me, huge apologies." It rushed out in a single breath. I was still mesmerized by his soft lead pencil eyes and unable to move, now even more embarrassed that I had repeated the old family joke out loud. What was I thinking?! I held my hands up in surrender, and he gripped my wrists firmly, definitely smiling now.

"What are you running away from?" He sounded mildly curious, and his voice involuntarily made me think of the sea. "Or more to the point, who? I might be able to help, you know. I used to be excellent at giving teacher's the slip."

I shook my head, trying to regain my composure. "And I might tell you, if you let me go. Who are you anyway? You're not a student here, that's for sure." I said belligerently. He held on for a few more moments, his thumbs firm on the pulse pounding in my wrists, then let go.

"I'm with the band," he replied dryly, thrusting his hands deep into his front pockets.

I raised my hand to sweep the escaping hair off my face,

and heard him draw a sharp intake of breath, as if something had startled him. I looked behind me to see if I had been discovered. No one. "What is it?" I demanded. "Do I have food on my face?"

He was looking down at my hands then back to my eyes and over my face with a sense of urgency, as if scouring for something hidden. His eyes raked in my disheveled hair slipping from its ponytail and suddenly spoke again. "Oh … ummm ... Jasmine."

"How do you know my name?" I should be getting impatient, but I wasn't; this was all too surreal.

"In your hair,' he gestured. "Jasmine," his gaze intensified.

"Oh." Reaching up I found the trailing spray of flowers I had tucked into my hair on the way to school. I shrugged my shoulders, bemused. "What of it?" I asked.

"It's…ahhh…very…Indie..." he began, then reached out and slowly grazed his fingers through my hair; the crumpled jasmine fell to the ground. Bending over, he picked it up and slipped it into the pocket of his jeans.

"Swap you," he said, and with that passed me a creased piece of paper from the same pocket. He half smiled, but it seemed as if he had already moved on. "Jasmine. Wild by name and wild by nature." And with that, he brushed past me and was gone.

I leaned against the graffiti wall with my eyes closed and in the silence felt it all over again: volts of energy behind my eyelids slipping away before I could capture them. How weird, I thought, a brief encounter with one stranger, and I want to dissect it, pull it to pieces and examine each second in minute detail. I must have Post Exam Stress Disorder. I needed to pull myself together, but I stayed there, motionless, until the final bell sounded and I had no choice but to head to class.

I managed to avoid Elle until lunch time by volunteering to scrub the benches in the science lab, then scoffed my sandwiches in the school office reception as I handed in text books and chatted to Mrs. Skelte for as long as I could, silently congratulating myself that the concert was well underway in the gymnasium and I was home free. But Elle, the consummate tracker, finally caught me unawares at my preferred water fountain next to the cafeteria.

"Surrender! I have re-enforcements! You are surrounded! Give yourself up and no one gets hurt!" Where Elle had got the megaphone from was a mystery, but before I could straighten up I was pinned to the wall by the hands of two faces I knew very well: Sam Aston and Matt Saben. "Jazzzzzz," Matt whispered in my ear, "you know you can't win."

"Yeah," joined in Sam, "last time you beat one of us you were five!"

"You wish!" I rejoined. "That's only 'cause you're too scared to take me on one-on-one; don't wanna be beaten by a girl!"

"Tough talk from the naughty kid who stole a cell phone and abandoned a friend! I think punishment is in order. What say you dear Elle?" Matt turned to look at Elle for instruction, who was standing there with arms folded trying rather unsuccessfully to look stern.

"Agreed." stated Elle. "As we discussed then; follow me."

I knew my fate was sealed and it would be futile to struggle. Ever since we had attended kindergarten Matt and Sam had made it their mission to turn me into one of the boys – as if it wasn't enough having four brothers. Matt was an only child who had adopted our family as his own, and Sam was, well, just Sam. He drove me nuts at times, but had always been there so I'd kinda got used to him. The two of them had been my personal body guards throughout school, unless, of course, they were the ones harassing me. I supposed that if this was the last time they could torture me, who was I to deny them that pleasure? But I would suffer in silence; no cries for mercy from me.

Before I knew it I was being hoisted into the air and onto my back. Matt had my shoulders and Sam had my legs and we were moving at top speed towards the gymnasium, with Elle leading the charge. Using my Converse sneakers as a battering ram, they barreled through the swinging fire safety doors straight into the ensuing mayhem. The noise was magnificent – garage band grunge intensified by the gym's dirty acoustic qualities – and despite my compromising position I felt an unfamiliar pull in the pit of my stomach, a sensation that for years I had subdued and shoved into the smallest recess of my mind, never giving it room to move. Oh! I wanted to dance. The music was heady and rough, like the waves at a wild surf beach, taunting me to test their strength.

"Incoming crowd surfer!" Sam yelled, and with that I was thrown to the mercy of the human waves.

Being the last day of school, everyone was dancing. The ground swell was growing as the crowd moved to the beat in unison. I didn't stand a chance. Like flotsam on the surf I was tossed from side to side and I could feel waves of warm hands beneath my back and my thighs throwing me higher through the wash of people. It was as if a force greater than gravity had me in its grip – I almost thought I really was in the water, staying afloat like driftwood. Now I actually felt wetness – was I imagining it? I could feel salty spray on my face and was moving so quickly to the crescendo of the song that everything was a blur. How far would this surge take me? I had surrendered to the pull of the tide and I no longer cared. Throwing my hands up towards the sky in a euphoric gesture, I felt the blood rush to my head and closed my eyes; death by drowning seemed timely and exultant. As I gave in to the sensation of the surf I dimly became aware that I was vertical again, and standing, of all places, on the stage. Someone was yelling "Thank you Carteret West High! Now for the last word here's Levi!" As the crowd went wild I opened my eyes to the same gray t-shirt, the same gray eyes, and an ocean of people stretched out before me. Without removing his gaze from mine, he began to sing:

The power of the wind and of the air
The feeling of my hand upon your hair
Last time I saw you, I thought I knew you.
The surging waves of ocean and of sea
Have bought you back alone right here to me
Last time I saw you, I swear I knew you.

My heart beat like the drums behind me and I trembled, locked eye to eye with a boy I did not know, but who seemed to know me. Every nerve in my body was hammering – was this a dream? His soulful stare deepened in intensity and I had to look away. With that he gave several resounding strums on his acoustic guitar and turned back towards the audience, belting out what I presumed was the chorus:

Last last time
It was a fast fast wine
And you had me had me had me
From the very first line
Be Mine

His voice was gravel under fast moving cars – intoxicating and dangerous. I was so busy trying to catch all the words that I ignored the pinch above my elbow and shook my arm. Seconds later both my arms were in a tight grip and I was being marched off the side of stage by two large men. I didn't even need to walk, as my feet were no longer touching the ground – literally – but not from the state of euphoria I was slowly emerging from. I was unceremoniously dumped in front of a girl who stood with her arms folded looking at me sardonically.

"I am so over you groupies!" she hissed. "You have no right to be on that stage, no right at all."

I recoiled at the venom in her voice and found mine, weakly saying, "Chill! It's just a prank some mates played on me. I'm no groupie!"

"Oh," she vented, "you are all the same – full of pitiful excuses, doing whatever it takes to get near him – and it's my job to tell you to stay away! Got it?" She stalked off, and the men thrust me out a rear exit, locking the door behind me.

Sitting outside I could hear cheering as the concert wound up. I closed my eyes and before I could stop myself, he was there in my mind. Above that gun metal gray t-shirt was a face etched with an emotion I couldn't identify. His hair was tousled and unaffected, shocks of brown and gold that fell where they liked. I had thought his eyes were gray, but now I wasn't sure; were they just reflecting the color of his shirt? They certainly had an ocean's depth and were filled with that foreign emotion. Over his t-shirt he wore a men's shirt, un-tucked, and op-shop looking dress pants, rolled up to reveal suede ankle boots - no socks apparent. I had never seen anything like him – a contradiction of styles and textures that seemed as comfortable on him as he was in them. What would Elle make of his get-up? And why had it magnetized me with such an overwhelming intensity? Boyish and scruffy, and yet... What was it about him that I couldn't place? Why was he affecting me like this? For some random reason a verse came to mind from the Bible my Grandmother had given me: "*a man's eyes are the window to his soul.*" That was it! I shivered; I had seen a man's soul.

The sky had darkened into heavy gray as I sat there, but suddenly streams of sunshine appeared through the cumulus clouds and a torrent of students spilled out from the gym. A group of girls drifted by and I overheard one telling her friend, "Levi was amazing – he is *so* my new hottie! You know I was right up the front looking straight at him, and he was *so* eye flirting with me the whole concert, I was just screaming and jumping and going crazy! I reckon he winked at me towards the end. Oh I could just die! Me and Levi couldn't keep our eyes off each other."

"He so looks like a rock star," chipped in one of the other girls.

"Yeah," said another, "sort of like an older and cooler version of One Direction. What are they called again?"

"Alien Potion," replied the first girl knowledgeably. "My older brother knows the drummer's brother's friend, and he says that they are totally out there and it's only a matter of time before they're on the world stage."

The voices faded and I thought about what they had discussed. I was no stranger to bands. My twin brothers Fale and Harley had formed a band just over a year ago when they turned eighteen. They started off by playing hot cover tracks for friends' parties – hence the name "Cajun Braves" – brave to imitate the hottest cover songs from a range of bands and styles. They had yet to develop their own brand of music, although I would call their niche market loud and proud head bangers; whenever they practiced at home I wanted to bang my head against a wall! But I was secretly quite proud of them. They had gigs most Friday and Saturday nights and had even played at the opening of the new underage night club in town.

I also knew all about the egos of musicians. Fale and Harley constantly filled the house with their perceived glory and boasted about all the girls that loved them. Perhaps this Levi was just the same, I mused, caught up in a big ego bubble, blowing hot air out from the stage and eye flirting with girls. I am such a sucker, I thought. That song was not for me; I didn't look into his soul, and I was wasting my time thinking about him for another second. That thought ended just in time, as Matt, Sam, and Elle had appeared beside me rescuing me from my introspection; I felt life flood back into my heart. Laughing, the boys flanked me and laid their heads on my shoulders.

"Here's our little surfer girl. Thought you were gonna need a lifeguard for a moment back there!" Matt crooned.

"Saved by the stage," mocked Sam. "You so looked like a stunned mullet!"

"Oh come on guys," interjected Elle, "haven't you tortured Jazz enough? I only wanted her to dance with me and instead I was stuck between you two head bangers. My shoes will never be the same again!"

As the friendly banter continued, I noticed the girl who ordered me evicted emerge from the gym. It was almost comical the way she was scouring the landscape, as if some latent groupie was going to spring out from behind the bleachers and catch her unawares. My smile faded as I saw Levi come out behind her and sling his arm over her shoulder. She turned and hugged him fiercely, and I could see he was laughing. It was all too obvious now – no wonder I had felt such animosity from her. I watched as the girl, so slender and tall with the blondest of hair, walked purposefully off to the car park. Sigh ... maybe blondes do have more fun. I was so engrossed in my train of thought I neglected to notice that my friends had begun to walk back for the start of afternoon school.

"You coming?" yelled Elle.

"I'll catch you up," I jested. "Just picking up the last pieces of my pride."

Poking out her tongue at me, Elle hurried off after Matt and Sam. I knew she had a soft spot for Matt – she just couldn't help herself. I slowly stood to my feet, trying to shake off the last vestige of discontent that seemed to have wrapped itself around my mind. Without conscious thought my eyes drifted over to the gym entrance one last time. And there he was – leaning against the door– looking straight at me. I couldn't tear my eyes away; it was as if there was an invisible laser that had fused our sightlines. Even from this distance I surely couldn't be mistaken ... could I? At what point does staring become socially unacceptable? When are you supposed to avert your eyes and break the connection? It was almost like holding your breath until you think you are going to pass out from lack of oxygen. This was not natural. Just at the point I could take it no longer, someone walked between us, and the spell snapped. The blonde girl reappeared and I ducked down as if to tie my shoelace, mortified. What was wrong with me? Did I have no self-respect at all? Now I was angry and all churned up inside again. *How dare he?* Tears welled up, blurring my vision, making me even angrier. *What on earth was wrong with me? Why is this day so strange? Why am I even reacting like this?* I savagely yanked at my laces and my hair fell like a dark shadow shielding me from the outside world. Rather than brush it back I let it comfort me, the familiar jasmine scent still clinging to the long heavy locks and I breathed it in, searching for the inner calm I needed.

The fragrance was still so strong! It never failed to impart comfort: memories of my mom playing Seals & Croft's "Summer Breeze' at top volume and dancing round the lounge with me; of hot still summer nights laying under the stars with a blanket of jasmine scent; of fresh jasmine-infused air buoying me on the way to school each morning. I could feel the intoxication that always came, and I opened my eyes, prepared again to face the world. There, at my feet, was a fresh trail of jasmine, cluttered with pure white flowers and a few remaining pink buds, flirting with me. I flung back my hair and jumped up, looking around wildly. He stood a couple of yards away, hands clasped behind his head, waiting for me to see him.

"It's a peace offering … for being kicked out. You know if you wanted to meet me again, you sure made it more difficult than it needed to be." The husky humor in his voice sent my pulse racing again, but I kept my eyes firmly planted on the jasmine. I could not, would not, look into those eyes. The arrogance of him, thinking I was that into him! I could feel the heat rising up my neck and flushing into my cheeks. "Yeah, whatever, dude." My voice sounded like a snap dragon as I finally looked up. "I know the drill. No invading the personal space of a wanna be rock god and all that! And," I continued angrily, warming quickly to my theme, "your band is average – not a patch on the Cajun Braves – not that you'd even know who they are your music taste is probably so limited!" My face stayed fierce, attempting to deflect the fast beating of my heart and I think it worked. The Grey Phantom (as I mentally named him) scowled, and his next words were clipped. "Ouch. I know them. And I even like them – pity I can't say the same for you."

Our eyes locked as we attempted to stare each other out, and I felt a strange swirling wind all about us, almost as if a storm neither of us had control over was about to break. A shrill vibration ended the bout, and I broke first.

"Saved by the bell," I muttered morosely, then added with a hefty dose of sarcasm: "Nice to meet you…not!" but the Grey Phantom had already stalked off, fists clenched around the now crumpled jasmine.

I mechanically bent down to pick up my knapsack, the knot in my stomach bigger than the broken strap digging into my shoulder.

2. ESCAPE

FOR THE REST OF THE DAY I COULD BARELY concentrate; there was no need to anyhow, everyone else, even the teachers, were the same. The year was all but over. There was only one thing I wanted to do, and that was to run. As soon as the Last Bell of the Last Day rang, I raced out the classroom door without looking back. I quickly texted Elle to let her know I wouldn't be catching a ride home, but that I would phone her later to make plans. The next text I sent to my brother Chad: "resQ me NOW plz xox." Once in the gym changing sheds I quickly changed, and as I laced up my runners my phone vibrated "Buzz Lightyear to Star Command! Come in Star Command!" I groaned. Matt must have been changing my ring tones again, but at least it meant Chad had arrived. Racing along the pavement I saw the familiar old red station wagon – or as Chad called her – The Wavy Lady, double parked. Speeding up, I flung open the door, threw myself and my bag into the front seat and in a single fluid movement Chad had rejoined the flow of traffic out of the school grounds. It was a sequence we had down to perfection; for at least two years we had been running together several times a week; it was something no one else in our family understood and for that I was most grateful.

"Where to, sis?" Chad grinned at me. "Celebration run for the last day of school ... hmm ... I'm thinking the wasteland. What say you?"

I was glad he had something in mind, because my mind didn't seem to want to work. I cynically replied, "Sounds perfect – swapping one wasteland for another."

"Says the brain box that hasn't wasted a moment of the last five years at high school; you're such a nerd, Jazz. Anyways, I want to show you something, something I've been saving for a day like today. Chuck us that drink bottle would ya?" Chad was into hydrating before running and the reminder was a good one. I hadn't had anything to drink since lunch. I gulped down some mouthfuls before throwing a vengeful squirt towards his t-shirt.

"Oops! Accident – so sorry bro."

"Ja-azz! Just remember, what goes around comes around!"

"Idle threats," I mumbled, and the revival I had experienced from his company dissipated. I just didn't have the impetus for banter this afternoon. Fortunately, Chad felt the same.

"Shut-up, OK? No more talk!" he said sternly, like he was my school teacher or something.

We drove the rest of the way without speaking. The drone of the engine and the crackle of the old radio provided enough noise to drown out any silence. Chad sped through Moorehead and after a few miles turned right and parked at the trail head leading down to the Neusiok. The Neusiok Trail is about twenty-two miles long and was named after an early Coree Indian tribe that lived in the area. It was the local Carteret Wildlife Club who became national leaders in the concept of utilizing public lands for recreation when they constructed the trail for recreational purposes only, cutting and pasting together a rugged pathway through the coastal forest landscape. The traditional start point is at the Neuse, a major fresh water river, which follows beach sand ridges, through stands of pine, various forms of hardwood forest, oak and maple, cypress swamp and cane breaks. The club constructed bridges to enable passage over the wetter areas, skirting swamp and wetlands, including bridging small stream crossings. It crosses several roads, making shorter runs possible, and showcases many forms of plant, bird, and animal life. The trail is contained entirely within Croatian National Forest lands, terminating on the salt water Newport River or Oyster Point to the south, and is nationally unique – the only hiking trail of its kind located almost entirely within a coastal forest.

Chad and I jokingly called it "the wasteland," only because if we ran the trail too far into the high heat of summer, we got bitten silly by the abundant wildlife, namely mosquitoes, ticks and biting flies, not to mention the tiny chiggers and "no-see-ems" (gnats). Today I almost wanted to run to the end – and back – with the mood I found myself in, restless and angry, with no apparent logic. We both leaned against the Wavy Lady, that faithful faded red surf wagon, and automatically began the series of stretches to warm up before we set out. It was a perfect sequence that never varied – a bit like my life really, up until today. Yes, I thought, today has unraveled the automated robotic life I have lived over the past four years of high school and I no longer feel in control – at least as much in control as I once was. I thought of the bubbles I had blown yesterday, so fragile and dependent on the winds that blew, and I remembered that their shape was held by tension and, just like my shape, my world had been held together by the tense routines of my life.

But what would happen if the tumultuous emotions I had felt today could be captured within a bubble, then burst through that elastic sheet? If I could create the right collision between emotions and tensions, thereby forcing a chemical reaction … there must be a way! My heartbeat quickened and my emotive responses morphed into analytical thought paths. If I could capture my emotions in a disordered or tense state, could I encase them? The answer was there! I could just about see it; this whole bubble phenomenon was going to make sense if only I could grasp this one last clue! Ping! Gone! All I could hear was the Black Eyed Peas getting their boom on.

"Chad, you loser!" I yelled angrily, pulling the earphones from my head.

"Get over it, sis." Chad didn't even blink. "Thought you needed waking up, that's all. You didn't even notice when I put your earphones on you. Off on one of your crazy genius moments again, eh? You gotta give that up sis, it just won't pull the guys y'know. By the way, I put together a new play list for our run today – hope that's OK. Wanted to try some new stuff, yeah?"

Last summer Chad and I had saved all our summer earnings and bought iPod Nanos and Nike+ running shoes. You put the sensor in your Nike+ shoe (there's a built-in pocket specifically designed for it under the insole), then connect the receiver to your iPod Nano. The sensor tracks your run and then sends the data to your iPod. As you run, it tells you your time, distance, pace, and calories burned, then it gives you feedback at the halfway point and at the end of your run. Chad spends a heap of time putting together play-lists for our runs; easy listening to start, building up to hardcore rock, and then mellowing out as we warm down. I love him for that – even though he makes me so mad at times. I just couldn't be bothered making the effort with creating playlists, but as we share pretty much the same taste in music, he keeps an ear out for new tunes and we experiment together.

"It's called 'Last List for Jazz', seeing as this is the last time I'll run with my kid sister as a seventeen-year-old." Chad was yelling over his shoulder, as he had already started out down the trail. I felt a little guilty for shouting at him. It was a bad habit of mine: shout first, get to the facts later. I defended it as a survival mechanism in a large family, but anger was also something I took a bit of sadistic pleasure from, and it was always getting me into trouble.

I was content to follow Chad, knowing he would keep a steady pace and check I was still within shouting range every now and then. I scrolled through the options, found the play-list, plugged the ear piece back in and put my best foot forward. Maybe I could redeem this strange day after all.

We had soon settled into a steady pace, and I could feel a light layer of sweat on my face. It felt good. The mix of music was just right, a middle tempo of tunes that were well known but not radio hits – just the way I liked it. Songs should be intelligent, I mused as I ran, or if they're not intelligent, they should at least conjure up some sort of emotion within the listener – fizzy happiness, or intense sadness, or overwhelming need. Yeah! I raved in my head, that's it: emotional intelligence; that's what songs need to connect us to them. At that moment Coldplay's "God put a smile upon your face" was playing and I sucked the lyrics into my soul, hoping to find the smile I needed. The rhythm had me and carried me along, and before I knew it we were three miles down the track and it was time to turn around. Chad was running back towards me and I could hear him singing along (very badly) to the Red Hot Chilli Peppers' "Snow" track. I ran to the next marker, did a U-turn, and began the journey back to the same tune.

The sweat was dripping down my spine now, and the reward of hard physical exercise started to elevate my soul. U2 came on to confirm this just in time. I grinned, wiped the sweat from my face with my sleeve, and picked up the pace slightly. The sky was darkening – not just because of the time, but also the huge black clouds that were rolling in off the Atlantic. I mulled over my preoccupation with bubbles and the formula I had been working on, hoping that my runner's high might jolt the equation into place. I had been working secretly on it for months, and had even done a science project into the properties of various types of bubbles and their applications. I hardly dared hope that one day I might crack the code. Over and over I put my brain through its paces, but as I reached the stand of long-leaf pine with their ghostly trunks, I still had nothing. It was as if I was caught in a dream with no end and no way out. A quick check of my iPod revealed around another fifteen minutes running left. I gave up trying to think and focused on the music. Jack Johnson was slowing me and I wasn't ready to mellow out and warm down yet. I manually clicked to the next song and promptly tripped up. I would recognize that voice anywhere, even though I had only heard it for the first time today.

If you have the time
I will grab the time
We will travel time
And tell the story we all want to know
So take my hand in your head
And show me your ways
The sand dune is rising
Your heart is surprising and I want to know

Where will love plant its face?
Where does hate find a space?
We are not so alone
We are not so alone
Brave in belonging are we

What was wrong with me? Why did I feel so illogical, so emotional and full of angst? Why did the Grey Phantom affect me this way? I had not let any boys get under my skin while at high school; I was too busy preparing myself for when my life would truly start, dreaming of being free, of finding a reason for my life on this earth. My brothers thought I had my head in the clouds, away with the fairies, and they were probably right. I had always felt different from other girls, but not this different. Any composure I had regained from my run was now in tatters, shredding itself with every pound of my feet, shriveling with every word, every beat, and then, of course, the rain came. I let the tears from my eyes mingle with the sweat from my pores and the wet drops from the gray clouds, and I saw those gray eyes, and rode the waves of emotion flowing from that gravel voice. The sweet pain grabbed me and I was undone. This was overwhelming emotion, and I did not have control. Rivers ran silently down my face, but in the darkness of the car Chad ignored me. He was good like that. We listened to Dashboard Confessional at full volume, and I felt every "emo" bone in my body.

3. BREEZES THAT BLOW

IT WAS SILLY TO THINK THAT TURNING EIGHTEEN would change everything, but for some reason I had thought it would. Over the past four years I had done everything that was expected of me (and more); not becoming distracted by youthful exploits any more than would stop me from being considered "normal," nor did I ever relax my guard too much, even when I was angry. You might call me a perfectionist or even driven, but it was more like I was in training, being shaped and molded by my subconscious. I sometimes felt a wild desire for freedom rise up, but I had disciplined myself to restrain it. Stupidly I had believed that at eighteen everything would somehow click into place, that the dormant hibernating wild jasmine would be coaxed to life by the scary thought of responsible adult life looming. Perhaps I had succeeded at restraint too well.

I had released the full floodgates on my eyes when Chad and I had arrived home last night; I hadn't let myself do that for years. It was a healing thing, crying, and I had blubbered all the way up the stairs to my bedroom, down the plughole of the shower, and into my pillow until sleep flew me away. I didn't even really know why I was crying, other than I fiercely wanted to. Perhaps it would purge me of all the conflicting emotions that were trying to rage out of control in my head.

I was kidnapped at 7.00 the next morning, the day I turned eighteen. Blindfolded, hoisted over shoulders and man-handled out of the house and into a waiting car, I was wearing baggy gray sweats and a t-shirt that said "bite me" across the front.

I struggled to get my face free, but it was the tantalizing smell of donuts wafting through the car window that provided the final impetus. Matt and Sam flanked me in the back, and Elle was in the driver's seat, busy giving an order through the drive-in window.

"You guys are too much! I'm not even dressed, and now I'm grumpy. Happy Birthday to me." I heard my voice, sarcastic and grumpy, verging on angry.

Matt turned to Sam. "That's code for I love you so much!"

"Oh you don't have to tell me," rejoined Sam, "I have the bruises to prove it. You're an animal, Jazz. I feel pity for anyone in the future that might kidnap you for real!"

Elle started singing Happy Birthday, and the boys joined in at the top of their voices. I slunk down in my seat, scowling, but the windows were all down now and I could see the smirking face of the drive-through attendant, as if she was enjoying my discomfort. As soon as we reached the beach I escaped from the car, and kicked both of the boys hard in the shins as they got out.

Elle backed away cautiously. "It was Sam's idea," she protested, and I had to grin, seeing the horror on her face that I might bruise her legs as well. I hugged her instead. We girls have to stick together. Matt got blankets, and we sat on the sea wall blissfully warm despite the cool morning air, drinking hot chocolate and scoffing donuts.

There are a few moments in life where you wish that time would stand still, and this was one of them. The early dawn yawned with a hopeful scent of fresh beginnings, and the ocean stretched out in front of us as mysterious as the future. The new light of day seemed to magnify and clarify nature's furniture, from the gull soaring overhead to the freshly washed sand beneath. A mood of contentment hung over us all, comfortable in each other's presence and the familiar Beaufort backdrop. Last night's tears now seemed distant and historic. Eighteen! I am eighteen! High school is over and my future can finally begin. My mind came alive with new hope and I smiled at my friends. "Thank you,' I whispered, not wanting to intrude on the stillness. The boys responded by putting their arms around Elle and I and we sat, each pondering our own hidden future, but together in the moment.

The rest of the day flew by in a whirl of presents, phone calls, and party preparations. After Elle dropped me home I found Marcus in the kitchen making my parents breakfast in bed. Marcus didn't really "live" at home anymore; he just stayed with us in between business ventures. The rest of the time he survived out of suitcases and hotels. Ever since he finished college two years ago he had barely stood still, and everything he touched always seemed to turn to gold. He had a natural talent for unearthing opportunities and then taking risks most sensible people didn't even dream of – and succeeding more times than not. But today it was all about me. I was pulled into the biggest bear hug ever, and squeezed until I squealed for mercy.

"You might be eighteen, but you'll always be a baby to me. Now grab that tray and let's raise the dead." Tradition dictated that we gathered as a family at the end of Mom and Dad's bed on birthday mornings for the official present-opening ceremony. Marcus kicked down each of my brothers' doors in turn and they stumbled into our parents' room in various states of consciousness. Once we were all draped across the bed and the kicking for possession of blankets and space had subsided, dad called for the first gift.

As usual, Harley and Fale had combined resources and they handed me a plastic bag.

"Happy Birthday Jazz! Sorry, no time to wrap it," smiled Harley through bleary eyes.

"Hope you like," added Fale, grinning widely. I was already suspicious; I had seventeen years of past birthdays to lean on.

"Thanks guys," I dubiously replied and gingerly opened the bag. Under the layers of tissue paper was a large-ish box, which, when opened, revealed rows of small glass bottles, each with its own unique stopper. Included in the box were instructions on how to make bubbles, and a series of pouches, each containing different colored sugar-like crystals.

"It's a 'Make Your Own Bubble Kit'," Fale enthusiastically pointed out.

"Yeah," Harley joined in. "We saw you blowing bubbles over the back fence and we thought you might like it. Hope you don't think it's too babyish?" I was basically speechless. Last year the twins had given me a bag of party poppers and an electric shock pen, so this gift was way outside the realm of my Harley/Fale expectations.

"Jazz?" Fale looked anxious.

"I love it – thank you!" I exclaimed, finding my voice. "You have no idea how perfect it is!"

Harley looked relieved. "You can even make the bubble solution different colors, and add flavors and perfume!"

"What will they think of next," mused Mom as I jumped up to give Fale and Harley a hug.

"I dunno," joked Dad, "but I hope it comes with a second cup of coffee!"

"My gift next 'cause I need to hit the road in a minute," said Marcus, as he lobbed a package airmail across the bed. A beautiful notebook and pen set emerged from the lime green wrapping. "The pens are Staedler – a drawing set in twelve colors, plus a writing pen with your name on it," Marcus enthused. "You can use the notebook to plan your next few years at college." I screwed up my nose at the word "college," but I was grateful nonetheless. I had always had a huge notebook fetish, and Marcus had become my main supplier. This year's fix was spiral bound and its cover depicted a flashlight artfully lying on its side photographed in black and white – obviously a book for bright ideas, I thought with satisfaction.

"Thanks M. You never fail to please as usual. I promise to

fill it with…girl stuff." I said out loud with a twinkle in my eye, and placed a resounding kiss on Marcus's cheek before he had time to dodge.

Chad quietly slid his present across the bed. "It's kind of what I wanted to show you on our run last night as a precursor to your birthday, but we didn't end up having time."

I flushed – there was no way I wanted to be reminded of the night before, so I focused on the gift. It was large and flat and wrapped in old sheets of Chinese newspaper that Chad had recycled from the local Asian supermarket. It looked kinda cool, but I quickly untied the aqua ribbon and tore at the paper. Inside was a photograph encased behind glass and surrounded by a recycled timber frame. The photo was of our Atlantic, but I couldn't picture where it had been taken from. What caught my eye was the long curl of a huge wave that was about to crash into oblivion, freeze-framed at the peak of its power. I shivered involuntarily. I loved the wildness hidden in an untamed ocean.

"You know the path that veers to the right towards the end of the trail we ran last night? Well if you follow it for around a half-mile, it leads up to a lookout, and this is where I took this photo from. See? You can just catch a glimpse of the tips of the pine trees in the foreground."

"Wow," I breathed, hugging him fiercely, "I never knew we were that close to such a wicked view. It's awesome, Chad. Thanks heaps!"

"Let me have a look," grumbled Dad. We all knew that Dad was disappointed with Chad. It was an unspoken expectation in our family that you went to college. Chad had dropped out of his final year at high school and had disappeared to the west coast surfing for a year. When he came back he got a job shaping boards for some old timer up at Emerald Beach and spent the rest of his time in the water. Only I knew the amount of time he also spent on photography and amateur film making; he was too sensitive to let the rest of the family know.

"Why, it's a lovely photo, Chad," came Mom's soothing words. "You've really caught the emotion and sensation of the surf. Very clever darling."

Dad just went "hhhmmmffh," and failed to see the hurt flicker quickly across Chad's eyes. "Now," Dad continued, "for the '*pièce de résistance*'. Firstly, as always, a piece of New Zealand."

Every birthday Dad gave each one of us a small token to remind us of our kiwi heritage. It was important to him that we stayed connected to the country of our birth, even though we were all now US citizens. The box was small and circular, and when opened, revealed a set of stud earrings made from Paua shell, which is like abalone, each in the shape of a koru. "The koru, dad enthused, "is a spiral-shaped design that is inspired by the New Zealand fern as it unfurls, bringing new life and purity to the world. It represents peace along with a strong sense of new beginnings and also the strength of family.

"They were selling them at the Paua farm I was researching down under," Dad concluded sheepishly, "so I didn't have to go far to find them."

"Just beautiful," I beamed at him, "simple and classic – and meaningful. Thank you, Dad." My arms wrapped themselves around his neck instinctively, squeezing until he started tickling me in protest.

"And now," broke in Mom, "a piece of home for you. Open this." I took the envelope curiously, wondering what Mom and Dad had chosen to mark the significance of my eighteenth birthday. Chad had been given money towards his car for his eighteenth. Inside were two further envelopes. I saw one had a college postmark, and I quickly flicked over to the other envelope first. Inside was a letter, penned by my mother. It read:

Dearest Jasmine,

As you know, we were all struck with grief when your grandparents died tragically in a car crash last year. It is not our intention to remind you of that horrible time now, but rather to share the gift that my parents left for me. Unbeknownst to all of us, Grandma and Pops owned a beach-front house at Emerald Isle, which they had rented out for years. On their death it was bequeathed to me in their Will. Your father and I know that you wish to have some time to yourself this summer, so we have decided to give you the use of it for two months to "go solo." The tenants have now left and we have furnished it in preparation for it to become our future family beach house. You can pick which months of the summer you would like it for, and it's all yours – food and electricity included!

Love from your very fantastic Parents

I looked up, my eyes shining, but before I could say anything, dad interjected.

"Open the other envelope first – the one with "open first" written on it – duh!" Oops – I was ahead of myself again. Enthusiastically I ripped open the number one envelope, forgetting it was from a college. It was actually from Duke University, and beneath the fancy letterhead it quite simply stated that a *"$20,000 per annum scholarship had been awarded to Jasmine Blade to matriculate in the science and math subjects of her choice at the said location, receipt of which is to be acknowledged forthwith with commencement in the coming fall."* A small note was attached saying, in Dad's familiar scrawl, *"We have accepted on your behalf – congratulations – please claim your prize holiday in envelope 2."* As I read it I felt the life suck out of me, but I kept a smile plastered on my face for appearances sake. Every part of me was yearning for freedom, and now this! University? Yes! One day. But now? Next fall? No way. I needed time; I needed space; I needed tomorrow with no strings attached.

We had talked about college, my parents and I. We had discussed options and timing, but now it was as if they hadn't heard a word I'd said. Surely I had made myself clear over the past few months. "I'm definitely excited about college, but I want a 'gap' year first to assess my options, to explore who I am and to uncover my purpose. I know it sounds stupid, but I feel like I have a life to discover, that my journey here on earth is more than just a science degree and a white lab coat," I'd said to them. Mom and Dad had nodded their heads in agreement, but advised that we should submit college applications anyway, as most were valid for more than just the following semester. I had gone along with them to keep the peace, and now look where it had got me: a $20,000 ticket to prison.

But it was my birthday, and they were my parents, and gratitude was called for. "I don't know what to say," I started – and that really was the truth!

"Say nothing now, Jazz. Look at the time!" Mom squealed. "Save it for later tonight. We have so much to do! Out, out, all of you, out! Thank you for brekky, Marcus; 'mwah mwah' to all of you, but out, NOW!"

We scurried back to bed or breakfast, knowing that family time was officially over, as Mom began her battle attack on her very long "to do" list.

Like I said before, the rest of Friday was about presents and phone calls and party preparations. Aunts, uncles and cousins came and went and called, and the family all pitched in to get the place ready. It was only intended to be a small birthday/graduation bash, but with a family of seven, small is difficult. By the time everyone invited a friend or two, obligatory relatives and family friends were included – and my friends on top, the numbers attending had swelled to around one hundred.

Dad was sterling. A daughter couldn't help but be proud of him; even now, in his fifties, his hair was still thick and dark, with only slight signs of gray around the temple. With a muscular build his physique showed only a hint of the relaxation that tends to accompany age and comfortable living. A stubborn jaw and laughter lines around the eyes gave him a boyish look, and he certainly knew how to act the part. He had everyone laughing as they set up the chairs and tables in the backyard, and strung lights from the trees, regaling them with tales from his childhood in New Zealand.

The afternoon sped by, and by the time the final canapé tray was laid out, the final glass in place and the final candle lit, guests were about to arrive and I had still not changed. I raced upstairs and briefly showered, wishing the evening was already over. As grateful as I was for my parents love and attention, escape to a lonely haven seemed more appealing right now. So many uncharacteristic things had happened to me in the last few days, and there had been no time to process them properly: the distant memory under the beach house that had resurfaced as I lay in the weeds; the chance encounter with the Grey Phantom that had knocked my equilibrium so badly; the polar-opposed gifts from my parents, one representing freedom, the other a prolonged, constricted existence –all demanded my attention.

I stretched out on the carpet partially dressed, trying hard not to succumb to the cloud of emotional and physical tiredness that hovered overhead. As I lay prone on my stomach, my eye caught the corner of a package poking out from under my bed, and I absently wiggled it with my toes until it came free. Of course – Mom had said something about a package on my bed the other day. I almost couldn't be bothered, but picked it up and gave a half-hearted tug at one corner of the cello tape. It came away easily, and soon I held in my hands three things: a key, a letter, and a photograph. I elevated the photograph up toward the fast-fading light, and there was the house and the jasmine vine from my memory, with two people sitting on the stairs leading up to the front door. Between them sat a small child. I turned the photo over and read: *Alistaire and Arabella Blade – with our Jasmine (summer, 1991*). I stared at the photo again, feeling a dim swirling begin in my mind, and the mists of time unraveling.

Just then the door flew open and I jumped, sliding the parcel's contents back under the bed. "I knew you'd need me," Elle announced as she bounced into the room. "You'd live in a cave and only come out at Christmas if I let you!" The mists rolled away and I smiled at her noisy entrance – so different from me; so exuberant, and loud, and funny. We were opposites in many ways; maybe that was our secret. She was vivacious, blonde, and tiny; I was sedate (outwardly anyway), brunette, tall, and curvy. Elle had thrust me to my feet and flung the chosen party dress over my head, zipping up the back in one swift movement. How did she do that? It certainly hugged the curves, I observed critically as I stood in front of the mirror.

"Oh come on, Jazz, you weigh all of one-hundred-twenty pounds – not exactly giant material. Those curves belong on you – show them off for once!" The wild sea green of the halter neck dress contrasted well against my olive skin, a feature I had inherited from my dad, along with my dark chocolate hair and hazel eyes, which were turning greener by the year. I gently threaded my new koru earrings in and left my hair down, allowing tendrils to wisp away and curl over my shoulders and down to the curve of my bare back. I clipped a sprig of fresh jasmine to my hair and I was done – not half bad for a girl who's grown up half boy, I thought!

Elle insisted on a touch of eyeliner and lip gloss and a light spray of perfume (not that I had any). "Well you do now! Happy eighteenth from me. It's called 'Angel,' and when I smelt it, I had to get it – so hope you like!"

Something about the friendship in her eyes made me laugh out loud, and I danced into the perfume mist as Elle sprayed it, feeling it fall on us like chocolate, and moonshine, and freshly cut flowers. "Thanks friend," I whispered and we danced down to the party together.

Now the sun had gone down, the back garden looked spectacular. The big old jacaranda trees that I often climbed to be alone were lit up like glow worm caves, and the music spilled out over the growing crowd, creating a real sense of occasion. Elle made the rounds with me, meeting and greeting and providing the right words when I ran out. Sam and Matt arrived late, and snuck up on Elle and me just as we were at the stereo choosing some new sounds.

"Chicalicious," Matt began, his eyes flicking from Elle to me, and back to Elle again. "You girls never fail to amaze us blokes. How long did this complete transformation take?"

Elle smiled and retorted, "As long as it will take for you to get us both a fresh drink."

"I can't carry four drinks," he complained. "You'd better come and help me."

"Matt, Matt, Matt," Elle crooned, "Whatever will we do with you, always needing my help."

"Watch it, baby, or I might not dance with you later."

"Oooh, I'm terrified. You don't dance; anyway, you just leap around like a crazy thing."

Sam and I listened as they walked off, their light banter

amusing us until we could hear no more. Sam leaned down and whispered in my ear, "But seriously, Jazz, you are looking pretty sweet tonight. You might even be able to drag me onto the dance floor!"

I flashed him a smile and placed my elbow on his shoulder to conspire his demise. "Oh yes, dear Sam, please give me a chance for some revenge for the other day. I'm sure I can think of a thousand subtle ways to embarrass you in ways you can only imagine!"

"But I just complemented you on how great you look! How cruel can a girl be? And I helped kidnap you this morning. I thought we were just letting bygones be bygones. Have a heart Jazz; you don't want to ruin your party, after all." Sam almost sounded truly worried.

"Well, there is that. How about you track down my drink, and you never know, I might develop a soft spot for you from across the crowded room and I won't have to seek revenge." I didn't mind flirting a bit with Sam – after all, it was my party, and I had not allowed myself to think of any boy as more than a friend during high school as I didn't need the distraction. And Sam was cute – at least I remember thinking that at kindergarten.

As he left to chase up the drinks, I looked around. Everyone seemed to be having a great time, so I figured it wouldn't hurt to escape for a while and draw breath. I scooped up one of the tiny plastic bottles of bubble mix we had left around for people to enjoy, and headed through the house to the front porch, away from the action.

I absentmindedly released the stopper and raised the wand, blowing gently. A shower of minute bubbles erupted in front of me, and I continued to create the soapy spheres as I walked into the dining room, enjoying the floating trail they left in my wake. Fale and Harley were sitting at the table with some mates, but I was too pre-occupied to say more than "Hey, everyone." Harley jumped up in front of me and I was brought to a sudden halt.

"Hey sis, enjoying your party? Umm…hope it's ok, but we invited a few extras – sorta involves band stuff. Didn't think you'd mind; we won't be long. I'd like you to meet ..." And I didn't hear anything else. Lounging at the table, on a chair that was etched with the word "Jasmine," was the Grey Phantom, and I'm guessing I looked more shocked than he did. In my house. On my chair. I felt like Goldilocks looking at the bear, only my hair was black-brown, and he looked more like a mountain lion than a bear.

I recovered in time to hear Harley finish with "...and that's everyone. Oh, apart from Bailey; here she comes now. Jasmine, meet Bailey, Levi's friend, Bailey, this is my sister Jasmine.' I automatically stuck out my hand, and Bailey gripped it briefly – very hard. "Hi," she said, just as briefly, but I don't think she recognized me. Sitting down next to Levi, she nudged him and said, "Right everyone, let's talk business. Please excuse us Jasmine." She smiled up – briefly again – dismissing me from the group. Marcus had joined the meeting, as he was the manager for Fale and Harley's band "Cajun Braves," and he smiled at Bailey (too big a smile, I thought) and raised his glass.

"A toast first! To being eighteen, and to future concert tours! Bravo!"

"Bravo!' echoed everyone in the room, the standard slogan for followers and fans of the Cajun Braves. I think my mouth moved.

I exited stage left and almost ran to the porch seeking haven in the bench seat swing my father had installed last summer. A soft ocean breeze began to cool the redness of my cheeks, and I closed my eyes letting it fan over my face while breathing in the saltiness of the air. I pictured the sea in my mind and heard the rhythmic crashing of waves as I rocked, to and fro, finding comfort in the steady movement. I would dive into the surf right now if I could, I thought. A sudden unplanned jerk nearly knocked me off my perch and my eyes flew open to find the other end of the bench now occupied. I knew without looking who it was, and I stiffened slightly, on my guard – for what? I don't know. I could feel him looking at me, and could only guess at the amusement in his eyes.

"I won't bite, you know," he started. I involuntarily

shivered at his voice; it was as distinctive as when I heard him sing. "I just wanted to apologize for gate-crashing," he continued stiffly.

I folded my arms defensively. "You don't have to be polite. I told my brothers they could invite who they liked. It's not as if they would want to hang out with me and my friends, I'm just the kid sister." I think I sounded a bit petulant, but I didn't care.

"Mind you," he continued as if I hadn't spoken, "you did crash into me down at the school the other day, then you gate-crashed my stage performance, and then you insulted my band and taste in music, so perhaps I shouldn't apologize."

I didn't give him the satisfaction of a retort, but glared at him through the dim light. Just as I thought, a musician with an ego – surprise surprise.

"But seeing as it is your birthday – is it actually today? I could overlook your current crash status ... I guess. Anyway, aren't you being rude – out the front while your party rocks on out the back?"

"It's actually none of your business, but seeing as you asked so nicely," I replied, screwing up my face in sarcasm, "I would prefer to be on my own with a book than entertaining crowds – unlike you," I finished with a flourish.

"So you do have an opinion. I take it you really didn't enjoy the concert the other day then? Or your part in it anyway." Was that a hint of sarcasm I detected in his voice too? I could feel my face flushing in the darkness.

"That," I enunciated clearly, as if to a simpleton, "was completely the fault of my friends. The concert was the last place I intended to be."

"Oh," he replied lazily, "that's a shame. I could have sworn at the time you were actually connecting with the music, if nothing else."

"That's not fair," I rejoined. "Music is different. It's a bit like reading: it provides an escape route, and it draws out thoughts and emotions, some you don't even know you have, let alone understand."

Levi looked over at me, obviously surprised. "You get that?' He continued without waiting for my reply. "I take it you're a Reader, then?"

"If you mean do I read books a lot, then yes, I do. That and music are my sanity." My eyes glazed over as I began to think my thoughts out loud. "It is in the pauses between the lyrics of a song or the words of a book that my emotions begin to read and create links that may or may not be there. I then see possibilities with an acute focus, and my mind flashes with ideas..." I suddenly remembered who I was talking with. "Far out, I probably sound insane – I'll shut up now." I slunk down on the seat, totally embarrassed. A change of subject was urgently required. "Anyhow, why are you out here talking with me? You should have picked up by now that I don't like you very much."

"Ouch. Again." I saw the Phantom wince mockingly before he threw me a conversation curve ball. "I dare you to spend a day with me before you make such a harsh call." He sidled over on the seat until his shoulder touched mine, and it was my turn to wince. His voice lowered. "I dare you to quit the snobby attitude and take up your namesake for the day – wild Jasmine."

I couldn't help myself. I slapped him. He was pushing all my buttons, and he knew it. In fact I think he was enjoying it. Up til the point where I slapped him at least.

"So…7am then? Meet me out front?" he was speaking to my back as I made a hasty retreat, but I could clearly hear the mix of amusement and challenge in his voice.

"You'll be waiting in vain," I muttered, and slipped quickly into the guest bathroom to cool down. Stupid boy band ego and dumb one-liners – "I dare you…" – whatever! I grumbled silently, trying to brush off the disturbing effect he had on me and returning to my party, which, I found, hadn't missed me at all.

Cleaning up in the kitchen later that night I finally had an opportunity to talk to both Mom and Dad at the same time without anyone else around. A large contingent from the party had decided to continue on to the small hours of the morning elsewhere, and had left around 11pm, inviting me to accompany them. I declined, using the excuse that it would be wrong to leave the mess for my family to clean, but promising to head out with them another night. Sam, Matt, and Elle were going to stay to help, but I pushed them out the door too, reminding them that I'd never stayed to help at their parties and fair was fair. Elle guessed something was up, but she knew I liked to process by myself before confiding in anyone, so she just shrugged, hugged me and left. The fact that Matt was going added an extra incentive not to stay behind. I didn't see when Levi left. I had spotted him talking to Fale at one point, Bailey hanging off his arm. I purposely turned my back, resolving to ignore any early wake-up call the next morning, if it came. He was obviously just goading me, I huffed.

There wasn't too much to clean, as the glasses had all been hired, and the plates were disposable, so after a general tidy around the backyard we focused on the kitchen, and I took a deep breath before I spoke.

"Mom? Dad? Thanks for the party and the presents. I love the earrings, and the summer at the beach house, but I'm not so sure about the university part. I sort of wanted to wait awhile before I decided anything."

"We know that, dear," Mom replied.

"But," dad interrupted, "this was just too great an opportunity to pass up. You know you want to go to college sometime, so why not now? There'll be plenty of time in the future to re assess your options. After all, a degree is just the key to many doors."

"I can't explain it," I argued weakly, "I have just finished years of hard work at school, and something inside me says to wait, to take time to allow a gap after a long chapter of life before starting a new one." I saw my parents exchange glances as Dad handed Mom a fresh tea towel.

"But there are three months of summer vacation before you need to start," Mom smoothly urged. "That is an ample pause in life, and with the scholarship you don't even need to get a summer job."

"You're missing the point, Mom. Haven't I always done everything you've asked of me, and now you're asking me to ignore the part of me that wants time out? I don't want to be limited by the summer break, where I have to plan timetables for the coming semester, a place to live, courses, and lectures to choose. I want to have the year stretch out in front of me with no commitments, no appointments, and no expectations. I don't expect you to understand, but I feel as if there is something out there waiting for me, and if I organize my world, I will miss it completely. It's not an experience or a career option, it's a life, and I'm not prepared to pass that up, not even for a $20,000 scholarship!"

My parents looked at each other again, as if sending an unspoken message. Both of them stiffened, turned towards me, and my father's voice was harsh.

"Jasmine, we are not going to let you throw your life away on a whim and a fancy that somehow you are more special than anyone else! We have given you every support over the past eighteen years, and that in the least should warrant your respect and obedience!"

"So it's a matter of obeying you now!" I could feel the temperature of my own voice rising. "I have always obeyed you! Well nearly always. Surely it's my life, my scholarship to embrace or decline?" I was just about shouting now. "I know you're disappointed in Chad, and you think I might go the same way, but you don't know anything! You're so intent on your own successes that you think that we all should have the same type of goals as you – to have busy crazy lives where there is no time to think, no time to plan, just years of pursuing status and money, and for what? So people are impressed? Well guess what, I'm not impressed, and I am not going to give in to this pressure to conform!"

Mom and Dad had stopped drying the dishes and were silently staring at me with shocked, yet desperate, looks on their faces. "You don't know what you're asking,' Mom whispered.

"Maybe we were too adamant, too controlling?" Dad

spoke to my mother with a question in his voice.

"Never," replied Mom. "You know what they expected, what they wanted. We couldn't, I couldn't..." I saw tears in my mother's eyes that I did not understand. It was as if they had forgotten I was there.

Dad took Mom into his arms and looked over at me, part in defeat, and part in anguish. "Go to bed Jazz," he sighed, "we'll discuss this tomorrow."

I made a hasty retreat, puzzled and shadowed somehow by a cloud of guilt that I didn't fully understand. Parents were such a mystery, I mused. But I wasn't about to let them emotionally blackmail me into submission; there was no way I was backing down. I slumped over my bed and stared at the floor, too tired to change, but too wired to sleep. Remembering the photo I had been looking at earlier in the evening, I pulled it out from under the bed, along with the key and the letter. The key was silver and quite old fashioned, but obviously a door key. It was on a chain that bore evidence of weathering, as if it had been long unused. On closer observation, I realized there was another key, very small and shiny and new – maybe for some sort of box, I wondered? I turned to the letter, and opened the crisp white folded pages. It began:

Dearest Granddaughter,

We are still entitled to call you this, although we have not been present as your paternal grandparents for the past sixteen years. Now we know you are eighteen, we are sending this letter to make a request of you. We will make this request once, and once only. Enclosed with this letter are two keys and one photo. The photo is to confirm that we genuinely are who we say we are, and the keys we will explain shortly.

We presume that you have finished your schooling and may or may not have your future mapped out. (I grimaced as I read.) *We agreed with your parents that we would maintain our distance and silence until you reached the age of independence, and then offer you the chance to become informed, should you so wish.*

If you are curious at all as to the meaning of your existence beyond that which you currently enjoy, and wonder about the prolonged silence we have endured as your grandparents, then you will follow the instructions enclosed. But be warned: should you choose to follow, there will very quickly come a time when you pass the point of no return. You may already know that of which we speak, or you may be guided by blind faith. But know this: the spaces in life and on paper exist to give our world and our words their true meaning. Tell no-one.

Affectionately yours,

Alistaire and Arabella Blade.

I turned to the second sheet of paper.

Instructions to the Reader:'

(Then there was a big blank gap)

1. Make your way to Charlotte International Airport
2. Use locker key to open B24861
3. Book and purchase next one-way flight(s) to Auckland, New Zealand
4. Text flight confirmation to +64 21 937 412 from the cell phone provided
5. Remove contents of locker and return key to customer service desk
6. Travel light and don't look back
7. Send the letter enclosed in the locker addressed to your parents prior to boarding the flight
8. Hydrate, try to sleep, and travel in silence
9. Make all connecting flights!

I had found my "Get-Out-Of-Jail-Free card," even though it seemed dramatic and far-fetched. I felt a small ball of excitement form in the pit of my stomach. It couldn't hurt going to the airport, could it – just out of curiosity to look in the locker? When was the point of no return, anyway? I didn't actually have to get on any flight, but how would I get to the airport? And what day? Surely flights to New Zealand were few and far between.

My mind worked over and over my options, and soon

enough a simple plan emerged. Satisfied that it would work, I was able to drift off to sleep to the sound of anything but Alien Potion in my head phones.

4. WIND IN MY SAILS

I WAS UP WELL BEFORE SEVEN. MORE QUESTIONS swirled in my head, but there was no time to ponder them now; I needed to think in the present tense only. Looking around my room, there was little I wanted to pack. My knapsack had a zip-off lower compartment, and I stuffed it with clothes. I kept on my trackies, but wore a pair of cut-off jeans underneath and pulled on two summer singlet tops. In the top compartment I loaded some toiletries, the notebook and pen set Marcus had given me, and, as an afterthought, my new bubble kit. I might get bored. Lastly, I grabbed a hooded sweatshirt.

Now, where was my passport? I tiptoed down the stairs, avoiding the three steps I knew that creaked, and into Dad's office. Which drawer? I closed my eyes and visualized back over the years to each time Dad returned from a trip. Not drawer – bookshelf! I located the brass box and bingo! All our passports were neatly stacked. Was it current? Yes! Jackpot – two years till expiry. I jammed the passport, keys, letter, and photo into my wallet, which was flush with birthday money given to me the night before. Excellent! Was there anything else? Cell phone, charger – oh research notes. I might get bored.

Next stop, Mom's laptop. I checked for flights out of

Craven County Regional Airport. There was one to Charlotte Douglas International Airport at 3pm, another at 7pm. Distance to County Airport: thirty-eight miles up the US70. Travel time: fifty-six minutes. Thanks Google Maps.

The time was now 6.50am – just time to scribble a note and leave it on the kitchen bench. "Gone out with a friend for the day – talk soon – love you all. Jazz." I could hardly call the Grey Phantom a friend, but never mind.

6.55am. Last check of my room. Anything else? No, I reminded myself, *"travel light and don't look back."* Oh – iPod. I slipped it into my pocket along with a nearby packet of gum. Downstairs again, I grabbed a green apple from the bowl on the bench and gently let myself out the front door, walking quickly down the entrance path to wait at the roadside. Sitting on the curb, I focused my attention and appetite on the apple: the color, the crispness, the sweet flesh … and I waited.

Just as I was contemplating eating the apple core in my hand, Levi drove up – on a Triumph – a Triumph motorbike. My brother Harley loved Triumphs – especially old ones like this – his walls were covered with them. That's the only reason I recognized it. It was aluminum silver and jet black –worn in like a favorite item of clothing, almost ready to drive into your lounge and make itself at home on the couch. I think it was love at first sight, and without thinking I bit right through the apple core I was still holding to my mouth.

He didn't say anything, just handed me a faded black leather jacket, military style, his size and smell, and a small orange helmet. I didn't say anything back, my heart hammering at my crazy idea of escape, so I just jammed on the helmet, threw on the jacket, slung my arms through my knapsack and mounted the bike, clasping the seat below rather than the body in front. He reached behind, pulled my arms around his waist and with a triumphant growl, we were off.

There is something about riding a motorbike that every human on the face of the planet should experience. Staring into the face of speed with no protective barrier invites recklessness and rebellion – a pretty good summation of my current state of mind. Wild abandon, once tasted, is a difficult drug to deny. All the senses are intoxicated simultaneously; the touch of the wind and vibrating caress of the road; the blurred vision intensifying colors and shapes; the brave taste of fear and adrenalin; the raw scent of body and bike, and the sweet sound of pure energy, growling to be released.

Despite the apprehensions I had hidden so well, I quickly discovered that I never wanted the feeling to end. All of a sudden nothing mattered except the moment. A bike hugs curves like a lover and eases over undulations like a soaring eagle. Euphoria comes in waves, increasing in intensity as each mile flies by. This was a new feeling, and I wanted it to go on forever. No past, no future – just the here and now, a warm, strong body in front of me to lean on, and the sensation of perpetual motion.

We were hugging the Ocean Highway, heading south west along the coast, whipping past the landscape as fast as the speed limit allowed, sometimes even faster. Beaches and buildings, trees and tennis courts, houses and highways all became a blur. After traveling for an hour, almost as an afterthought, Levi yelled back at me, "Over it? Feeling wild yet?"

"Dare you to drive to Charlotte!" I shouted into the wind, trying my luck, having thought earlier that if we headed north I would say, "Craven County Regional Airport – I like to look at planes," but because we were travelling in the opposite direction, the airport at Charlotte was an alternative option. Actually getting him to take me to the airport would have to come later, although I doubted he would take my request seriously.

Rather than show any sign of surprise or horror, his shoulders' shrugged, his hand tightened on the throttle and our speed increased again.

It was six hours drive from Beaufort to Charlotte, and my intention had been to fly in the sky, not along the ground. But we were heading that way, and if Levi loved the open road enough to take me even part of the way there, I was not going to complain; I was going to revel in it. I crossed my fingers for luck, wondering what Mom and Dad would say if they could see me now, then banished the thought completely.

After three hours had passed, the sun was well into the sky and I could no longer feel my legs. Levi guided the Triumph off the highway and down towards Lake Waccamaw, the traditional halfway stop on the way to Charlotte. He pulled up in the rest area about twenty yards from the lake and eased to a halt. I hastily unclasped my arms, and promptly dismounted – onto my bottom. As he pulled off his helmet I heard snorts of laughter and glared at him. I did, however, make use of the outstretched arm, shrugged off the jacket and helmet, and shook my head in true head-banger style to stir up my flattened hair.

"Having fun yet?" Levi offered.

I couldn't help but grin back at him, my mind picturing flashbacks from the last few hours. "OK, so I'm a speed freak, I confess. Give me a roller coaster, give me adrenalin, and I'm first in line. It fits with my temper. Are you surprised?"

"Not at all," he smiled, "although it was Jasmine 'the scientist' I thought high speed might appeal to: velocity equals distance over time."

I looked at him suspiciously. "How did you know about my geeky obsession?"

"Your brother Fale last night – I bet he's your worst nightmare. I found out all sorts of *interesting* things." He looked at me with an intense scrutiny.

I blushed, hating him, but hating me more. "A little bit of knowledge can be a dangerous thing." I mumbled, feeling his eyes on me but not daring to look up. By the time I did he was gone, jogging towards the small store at the other end of the rest-stop.

I didn't bother to follow, but rather stretched out flat on the grass and tried to relax every muscle in my body, not that they were cooperating. The sun was at just the right temperature, smiling down on North Carolina. I gently hummed the famous James Taylor song *"In my mind I'm going to Carolina..."* and let my mind relax instead.

I hadn't yet figured out why Levi had wanted to take me out, other than taking him at his word. Maybe I was just a new challenge for his ego to conquer. I may not have even gone had I not seen an impulsive opportunity to check the locker my long lost grandparents had mentioned; escape had never been so easy. The antipathy I had felt towards him was slowly converting to curiosity. I was so focused on getting away that I had avoided looking at him or thinking about the past few days or our conversation of the night before. When I closed my eyes I could picture him so clearly it was like high definition television – every feature was chiseled into my head; an indelible image that pounded with my heartbeat just beyond my conscious mind. I knew nothing about him, yet this morning I had no qualms about riding off on his bike into the unknown. Why the irrational behavior, the impulsiveness? It was so … Elle! Jasmine just sat at home biting her fingernails waiting for life to begin. Again I felt an overwhelming sense that I was slowly being moved outside my comfort zone, that somehow all the pieces of a puzzle I wasn't even sure I wanted to connect were coming closer together.

It seemed only minutes and he was back, dropping onto the ground beside me. I half opened my eyes and decided that the real thing was still better than the image in my brain. Those girls gushing about him after the concert were right damn it – he was gorgeous. His tousled head was bent over a brown paper bag, entirely focused on unpacking the contents. Surreptitiously I observed his face through my half-closed eyes. He had laughter lines around his eyes and a strong side profile, with a fine silvery scar traversing the side of his face from the edge of his temple past his left ear and petering out at the side of his jaw. Part of me wanted to reach out and trace it with my fingertip, but I didn't.

He looked over, and I guess my eyes still looked shut, because his gaze rested on my face. His eyes were topaz blue today, deep and rich, and I felt the urge to open my eyes fully to his, and see if the invisible soul connection I had felt on the first day we met had been imagined or not, but something made me hesitate, fearful of falling off a high cliff into a mysterious blue sea I could drown in. I rolled over and sat up.

"So what do rock stars eat for breakfast? Let me guess ... strong coffee and French toast with maple syrup?"

Levi looked sheepish. "Why settle for coffee when you can have a real caffeine hit? I bought us Red Bull energy drinks.

We've- still got a drive ahead of us. And to eat: bananas and some cinnamon buns – yum. Wish we did have maple syrup, now you mention it." He sounded almost glum.

"I have four brothers, remember, I'm not fussy when I'm hungry, but I'll pour some energy drink over yours if you're desperate." I joked.

We ate in silence for a few minutes until Levi abruptly asked: "Why did you come today?"

I answered with another question: "Why did you ask me to come?"

"I had to find something out, to give you something."

"To find out what?" I asked curiously.

"You'll see," he replied cryptically. "It's not for me to say."

"Well, if that's all you can give me I certainly won't be telling you why I came for the ride." I lifted my chin and I know he saw the challenge in my eyes.

"Fine then." His eyes oozed challenge right back at me and without a word he stripped of his shirt and jogged off towards the lake, down through the trees to the water's edge. I didn't even hesitate, stripping down to my shorts and singlet. I shoved everything into my bag and took it with me past the trees, dumping it by Levi's stuff, kicking it all under a nearby bush. He was already in the water, swimming at pace towards a pontoon about two hundred meters from shore.

I ran and dived, wanting to get my feet off the sludgy bottom as quickly as possible. The water slid smoothly off my skin and a touch of newly melted spring ice added to the trippy plunge. I began a freestyle sprint, determined not to be left behind. The pontoon was further than my estimation though, and by the time I reached out to haul myself up onto the warm wood, Levi was stretched out in the sun, like he had been there for hours. I was relieved to note he too had worn shorts under his jeans.

I lay on my back, not able to speak, my heart hammering from the sudden exertion, and not seeming to slow, due to the nearness of Levi's strong lean body. Here we were, in the middle of nowhere, unable to run, unable to hide. He was still so enigmatic. I had no idea why he was even here today, or why we were on this trip. It was all crazy, just crazy. I turned on my side, determined to confront him. As if in sync, he had rolled over at exactly the same time, and our eyes locked, this time only inches apart.

Without dropping his gaze, Levi whispered across at me, "Jazz, I have a message to give you, and I kinda chickened out last night, you were so…so…"

"Bitchy?" I whispered back, almost giggling at the ridiculous nature of our conversation and proximity.

"I was going to say stormy, but if you insist."

I glared at him. "So what's the message? And who's it from? And why the mystery?"

He pushed himself away and swung his legs over the side of the raft, seemingly in frustration. "Oh man, I'm making such a hash of this…I'm not saying that…it's just that…umm… It's not my role to explain everything, only my time to Carry you forward into the next stage of your journey."

"I don't understand," I blathered, thinking that this was all getting weirder by the minute and I hardly recognized myself in the words that slipped off my tongue. "I know something is happening, but I don't know what. It's as if my intuition and sight is slipping in and out of focus. I see clearly for an instant and then everything becomes fuzzy again. But you're not making any sense..." Our eyes were still touching when Levi spoke again, and this time there was no way I could take him seriously.

"Confusion," he announced, "is just a song, because often they don't make sense either. So rather than focus on what I can't tell you, let's just go with the moment. Come on, a line each," he urged mischievously. "Back and forth ... ummmm ..." He began to tap a steady rhythm on the rough wooden raft.

"You're joking, right?"

"*The time has come I know to carry you*," he began.

Obviously not, I thought, but compelled by the gravel of his voice and the strange wildness of the day thus far, I made a feeble contribution, not really singing, but keeping my voice in time with the beat: "*And read between the lines is what I'll do.*" It was uncanny, but I was sure I could sense the invisible fibers between our two lives beginning to intertwine, like woven strands of rope.

"*Tied up in a melody* …" he continued.

"*Wrapped up in the harmony* …" I added, still not giving in completely, but mesmerized by his eyes.

"*Unpackage me-e-e* …" Levi wound up the tempo and volume.

"Ummm ... *Set me free-e-e* …" now I was warming up … I think.

"*Unwrap my soul-oul* …" Damn! He was good at this.

"*Make me whole-ole* …" I just sounded like a caterwaul.

"Again, yell it, "he half said, half sang. "No one can hear you. *Un-package me*," he stood as he sang.

"*Set me free*," I yelled as I rose up beside him.

"*Unwrap my soul*," he unleashed the full measure of his voice.

"*Make me whole*," we sang together.

And with that I promptly pushed him off the raft, back into the icy water.

As he came to the surface he shook his head and yelled "What was that for? Guy trying to help girl here, you know!"

I knelt down at the edge. "That *may* have been the intent, but you've given me nothing other than 'High School Musical,' and, in case you've forgotten, I've finished with high school! I want answers! I still don't understand. I'm going to go crazy if you don't give me something more. Is this some big joke my brothers have put you up to? Are you just having some cheap entertainment at my expense?" I might have played along, but I wasn't going to be made a fool of.

He stayed in the water and crossed his arms over the side of the raft. With his hair plastered down, his cheek bones were more pronounced and his face held a haunted expression.

"Well?' I asked him fiercely.

He slowly kicked his legs in the water, making bubbles pop up to the surface. I watched them implode.

"You're going to find out soon anyway, I guess. May as

well be prepared ...” His brow furrowed as he searched for the right words.

“Well?!” I reiterated even more intensely, not giving an inch.

He sighed and looked straight at me. “Realizing that you’re not going to understand what it means and that you should never shoot the messenger, you’re a *Reader*, Jazz, a *Reader*.” His voice held a hint of reverence.

“A what? A *Reader*? What’s that? Someone who sits in a library all day? You’re not making any sense, Levi! And where do you fit into this? You’re making me more confused, not less!”

“Like I said, it’s not my place to explain it to you, and anyway, every *Reader* is different. That is your journey not mine. As for me, I am a *Carrier*. I have two purposes. The first is to wake the *Reader*. The second … is … well … I won’t know until it’s the right time. I know none of this makes sense, but it will, Jazz, it will.” He shrugged his shoulders self-consciously, as if he knew how stupid it all sounded, as if he had been told what to repeat and that there was nothing else he had permission to add.

“Trust me or not, Jasmine Blade, it’s your call. I didn’t really even want to pass on the message, you were so loathing of me the other day, but I really didn’t have a choice in the matter. Daring you to come with me was the only way I could think of to get under your skin and hopefully get you to come. There’s a package arrived in Charlotte I’m to give you to get you started. And that’s why we’re on this crazy trip…believe it or not.”

He struck out for the shore before I could respond. Sometimes they say questions beget questions. Maybe I shouldn’t have asked any. Now I had more than ever.

We changed behind separate trees and threw our wet clothes into the bag left over from breakfast. I felt slightly shy, suddenly not sure if I was doing the right thing. Maybe I should just get him to take me home. This Reader-whatever-thing was all a little weird for my liking. It wasn’t until we walked up from the lake that we realized that there was no bike, just an empty car park and an empty road. I stared at the tire marks in the asphalt with a feeling of dread.

Levi sighed. "Does that bike have a sign on it 'STEAL ME', or what?" He turned around towards me. "It's not the first time; it's the third. You think I might have learned by now." He sat down on the curb and pulled out his mobile phone. I numbly took out mine as well. Better text Elle and arrange a longer alibi.

I paused in my texting. "If it's been stolen twice before, how have you got it back?"

"I know exactly where it is," he replied, sounding resigned to a fait accompli. With that he walked away from me, talking rapidly into his handset. I couldn't make sense of anything he said; it was so clipped and fast. I gave my attention back to the message at hand.

Hey Elle - will ph. & xplain soon - can u tell olds I am stayin at yrs 2nite? long story x (send).

As I sat and waited for her reply, I realized that I wasn't as worried as I first thought. In fact, if anything, I felt deliciously free. No agenda, no hurry – no bike. I frowned. How were we going to get to Charlotte? Elle texted back - *all gd - ph me SOON! :)*

Levi rejoined me at the curb, his face changing from stern to slightly less stern as he stood over me.

"Up you get! Time to walk. Good will 'triumph' over evil – pun intended – and the bike will catch us up soon. All taken care of." I looked up at him with too many questions in my eyes, and he pulled me to my feet saying, "Jazz, Jazz, Jazz, sometimes you just have to look on the bright side, ignore the obvious and enjoy the company you find yourself in – in this case, me." He stayed facing me and began walking backwards.

"One foot in front of the other – come on – let's find some coffee." I stood and walked towards him, automatically opening my mouth to protest, but before I could, Levi jammed the last cinnamon bun into my mouth and grabbed my arms as I tried to fight back. I managed to lunge forward and deposit the sticky remains down the front of his T-shirt, using my face to rub it into a mushy mess. Laughing out loud, he promptly tripped me up, falling on top of me and grabbing the crumbs to rub into my hair. And there we lay in the dust, giggling and gasping for breath, a sweet tangle of sugary bread and bodies.

It felt as delicious as I thought it would and we stayed like that for a little longer than was completely necessary. When we finally stood I quickly marched ahead, tossing my hair and trying very hard not to look self-conscious. What was I thinking? I had no time for boys. The Grey Phantom had become more of an enigma than ever – who else had I ever wanted to punch, kick, torture until I got answers and kiss *(kiss)???* all in the same hour?

After about five miles we came to Hallsboro Township and gratefully entered Pete's Pit Stop feeling well and truly beat. Out of a need for normality, we had kept the conversation on neutral ground, and as we walked we had swapped iPods and spent the time scrolling through each other's music, enjoying the variety –although he had thousands more tunes than me – and sharing favorites. Usually you can learn a lot about people by the music they listen to, but Levi's taste range was so wide I gave up trying to put him in a box – maybe it was a muso thing. Me, I was easy: plenty of old stuff mixed with mainly rock and a bit of techno and emo. Levi cringed a few times. At my insistence, he finally shared a few of the songs he had written, yet to be properly recorded, and although I pretended to be cool, I was nearly weeping inside. His music was such a mix of wild and free melodies combined with honest, stabbing lyrics. *Could the real Levi please stand up?* I couldn't help thinking to myself.

The café felt cool and shady after our long walk, and after washing up it was a relief to be able to sit for a while. We ordered cokes and sat in a booth by the window, and although I kept an eye on him through my lashes, I avoided looking at him straight in the eye – it had become far too unnerving. It was obvious that Pete's Pit Stop doubled as the local Karaoke Bar in the evening, and being 2.30pm the crew was setting up the night stage.

One of the young guys kept glancing over as he moved microphones and plugged in leads, and it wasn't long before he hesitantly approached our table and mumbled at Levi "Hey, dude, aren't you that guy from Alien Potion? I saw your music video the other night. You guys rock, man!"

I looked at Levi with a new respect. Music video? I had no idea his band was at that level, but having heard more of their songs, I can't say I was surprised.

"Hey, thanks ...?" Levi paused, waiting for a name.

"Oh, I'm Jeff, Jeff Saunders. I work here part time on the evening shifts."

"Well, thanks Jeff. I'm Chris, and this here is my friend J …" He glanced over at me. "Jules," he said, winking at me.

"Good to meet you," Jeff enthused, barely glancing at me. "Hey, if you guys are hanging around, maybe you could do a song to start the evening off. Whaddya say, man?"

"Oh, I dunno," Levi paused. "Maybe. What do you think, Jules?"

I shrugged my shoulders. "Your call I guess. I'm just the passenger – I know nothing." I couldn't help the note of sarcasm in my voice.

"Tell you what," Levi turned back to Jeff, "how about you organize us a top notch feed, and I'm in, but it'll have to be early, 'cause we have places to go."

"You're on!" Jeff was so eager he took off to get menus before Levi could change his mind. I frowned quizzically across the table, not bothering to ask what I wanted to know.

"What?" Levi questioned. I glared witheringly at him, knowing he was playing games with me. "Ohhhh, the name thing. Now we both know you're a *Reader*," he said the word *Reader* in hushed terms. "The fewer people that know your real name, the better." He kept the tone of his voice light.

"What? Now you're telling me there are bad guys too? What gig is this *Reader/Carrier* thing? It's beginning to sound like a bad spy movie or something! More information, please!" Levi raised and lowered his hands above the table in a calm-down-you-are-too-loud kind of a gesture, but I wasn't buying it. Seeing Jeff approaching the table, I leaned over and whispered angrily, "I'm off to the rest room, but you better have that explanation when I get back. If I'm going to need an alias, at least you could let me choose my own –*Jules!?* What were you thinking? And, hang about; is Levi even your real name?"

I jumped up and stomped off, but not fast enough to miss Jeff saying, "Feisty friend there Levi, eh? Comes with the rock territory I'm guessing."

Levi just laughed. "She's a wild one, all right – very inspirational you know!"

I seethed. So I was a joke! If I wasn't stuck in the middle of nowhere I might choose to sneak out the back door and head home, but head home to what? Angry parents? Questions? Decisions? No thanks, I decided. May as well act cool and walk this out. My time to disappear was coming; I just needed to hang on and get to Charlotte. I used the phone outside the ladies' room to phone Elle, texting her first so she could stand by her home phone and answer before anyone else did.

"Jazz?" I heard her voice all excited on the other end of the line. "What's going on? I know you talked with Levi last night – I saw you on the porch. Does this have anything to do with him? 'Cause if it does I'll scream. He is the man, according to the talk around school last week!" She was so amped that I had to interrupt before I ran out of coins.

"Yes, Elle, I am with Levi, and yes he *thinks* he's the man, and we're on our way to Charlotte, but you can't tell ANYONE ANYTHING! It's just a joy ride and he gets to show off his motorbike. I'm, uh, going to visit a relative for a couple of days, but I don't want my parents to know where I am – I just needed to get away. They want me to go to college next fall and we had a big fight and ..." I was fighting to get the entire story out as fast as I could. "...I'm gonna send them a letter, and I'll write to you as well and explain everything properly, but please, please, please, can you cover me 'til then? So much to tell you, but no time!"

Elle always had my back. Her voice was soothing now as she replied, "Always, Jazz, you know that. Just make sure you explain soon, OK? Wish I could have this adventure with you," she ended wistfully.

"Many more to come, I can promise you that Ellie. Got to go. Love you long time."

"You too girl; you too."

Levi had already ordered for me when I returned, but I didn't actually care, eating was so far down my agenda at the moment. I had pulled my long hair back into a pony tail, and had put some face paint on, knowing it made me look older. If lip gloss and eyeliner could help my confidence, I would use it, thanks very much. This was the most out of my depth I had ever been in my life, and I was guessing it was going to get deeper.

He leaned across the table. "So tell me, what name would you have chosen at such short notice?"

"Sage," I said without hesitation. "It's my mother's maiden name, and I love it. But anyhow, you need to answer my questions, not the other way around. Name, please."

"My name *is* Levi," he insisted, "but, ever since I was a baby my mom called me Chris, which is my middle name. I think it was because it was my father's name, and he left us when I was only three months old, and rather than get bitter, my mom just always dreamed that he would return one day. She used to make up stories about him; that he was at war, involved in espionage and all sorts of other fantasies. I don't think she ever got over him. My dad named me Levi, but mom said it just made her think of blue jeans, so she never used it."

"Where is your mom now?" I questioned, being drawn into his story in spite of myself.

"She's dead," came the tight-lipped reply, "and no, I don't want to talk about it."

It didn't take much to figure out that was all I was going to get, so I moved on. "Why the name changing though? *Am* I entering a world of espionage?"

He grinned, and his eyes crinkled at the corners (not that I noticed of course). "You're going to hate me for this, Jazz – I mean Sage – but I can't really give you too much information. Suffice to say that you should be on your guard, and trust no-one – and at this stage, I guess that includes me."

I thought of my conversation with Elle, glad now that I hadn't told the complete truth about what I was doing, or put her in a dangerous position. Now I was being silly; I don't even know what the dangers are! I'd always thought that it was stupid to worry about anything going wrong until it actually did. It's like worrying about a shark attack when you're swimming in the ocean. Why worry? If a shark is going to attack, you're pretty much toast anyway, so may as well enjoy the water while you can and go into survival mode only if or when a shark ever does come calling. I would use this logic on the Grey Phantom too, guessing I would find out if he were a shark or not soon enough.

I tossed my hair and scrutinized Levi's face to see if he was playing games again. Mistake. One look into those eyes, and the circuit was connected, the electricity flowed, and the current was getting stronger each time, and harder to break. Jeff arriving with huge plates of food was the only thing that saved me; his arms lowering the plates in front of us cut the supply line. I could feel my cheeks reddening, so I put my elbows on the table and cupped my cheeks in my hands, closing my eyes.

Levi did the same, only interwove his fingers, and began, "For what we are about to receive, may the Lord make us truly thankful. Amen."

"Amen," I muttered. "Saying grace? Where did that come from?"

He shrugged. "It's become a habit, sort of like a reminder that we are all part of a bigger picture, and understand so little of what it looks like. I think that's the way God intends it to be – sort of mysterious and intriguing at the same time – am I right?"

His smile was devastating. I looked down at my food. I was thankful for it, that's for sure. As for the bigger picture, he was right. I just needed to relax and go with the flow. After all, how bad could it get?

This time it was Levi's turn to interrupt our 'date'. Half way through his huge plate of hamburger, fries and coleslaw his phone rang and he mouthed 'sorry' at me as took the call. I listened to the one sided conversation for clues.

"Yes.

No, no that will be fine. I can't believe he thinks that's ok…ha ha!

Yep, fill it up – you've got my fuel card…

Just check with Jarven, he'll know what to do…

OK…OK…Yep, you too…bye."

I aimlessly ate, not really tasting anything. It was a typical pit-stop meal, safe and familiar, as long as you added every available condiment for flavor. I was stirring a chip in a figure of eight through a dollop of ketchup wondering who Jarven was, when Levi playfully grabbed my arm and guided the soggy red chip into his mouth.

"Yu-uck!" I squealed. "That's so something my brothers would do. Disgusting!" I pushed my half empty plate across the table. "You may as well finish them off – I'm done. Any news on the bike? And by the way, does it have a name? Our cars always do."

Levi looked lightheartedly at me, with two fries hanging like fangs out of his mouth. "Iffs clld v moffntr..."

"Whaaaat? Speaka da Eengleesh pleez," I protested.

"It's called Miss Motion," he repeated, having devoured the fries in a single gulp. "I bought it with the money my mom left me. It reminds me of her; we were always in a state of perpetual motion, but it wasn't often happy. I guess I combined the constant motion with *The Terminator* movie, and came up with The Motionator, now shortened to Miss Motion."

His eyes held a distant memory, and I could tell that the thought of it was ricocheting fear, anger, and distress around his mind – a seemingly common theme whenever family came into the picture. I involuntarily shivered, wondering what sort of childhood cognizance could evoke such strong emotions.

Before I could read anything further, his demeanor changed, and he was once again flippant. "As for news on the bike, it is all good. Miss Motion, as we shall now refer to her, has been found intact, and she's on her way back to us as we speak. She should be here just after seven tonight."

"How on earth...?" One look at his face told me I wasn't going to get any more details than that. A veil had fallen over his eyes, and I let the matter drop, and checked my watch instead. It was 4.30pm – two and a half hours to go.

Levi abruptly decided to go and help the evening crew set up. They were obviously amateurs, and could do with a hand. I certainly wasn't about to argue with him, and I needed some head space anyway. This was an adventure, and it was about time I let go of the reins and allowed fate to complete the story, however it may end.

The bar was beginning to come to life, people stopping in for happy hour drinks and social networking, older teenagers trying, like me, to blend in and look at home. The noise levels were slowly rising, and I was not going to get any thinking done here. Levi was busy laughing and rearranging technical equipment, and Jeff had just brought over a guitar for him to check out and tune – I wouldn't be missed. Scrawling a quick explanation on a serviette, I hauled my bag over my back and slipped quietly out, breathing, with relief, the fresh highway air. It was surprisingly light outside after the dim interior of the café, and a high wind was stirring the clouds into weird shapes. The car park was filling up, and I made my way through the collection of vehicles towards the grassy verge, thinking I might just stare at the sky.

As I passed an old beat-up blue ford Ute, the passenger door unexpectedly swung open and then shut right in front of me. Skidding to a halt on the loose gravel, I glanced into the window, only to find my eyes traveling down over the empty seat to a little blond-headed boy crouched on the floor, peeking through a long fringe up towards me. I knocked on the window and waved. He was so small, maybe only five or six, thin with enormous brown eyes set into a finely sculptured face. He continued to peer up at me, but didn't move a muscle. I glanced around the car park, expecting to see his mother approaching the car, having picked up some supplies for the evening meal or something, but there was no one in sight. Dilemma. It wasn't as if I could open the car door and see if he was OK – he might freak out. I figured it was best to just proceed to the grass bank and keep one eye on the car just in case. I waved bye-bye, like my mom used to do in kindergarten days, smiled and continued my journey across the car park. I chose a spot where I could easily view the blue ford, and settled myself down to watch the clouds and ...What was I going to do? Think? Not likely, I thought ruefully. I was all out of brain space; better just to let my mind settle, day dream the clouds into weird and wonderful creatures and let time slip by. And slip by it did.

When my eyes opened again, the dusk light was settling over everything, and crepuscular rays were shooting the last of the sunshine every which way. I jumped up, slightly disoriented and stumbled across the car park, sure I was actually going to wake up properly any minute and find out everything, including Levi, was just a dream. I looked up just as I was passing the blue ford, and there was the boy again, sitting up this time, chomping his way through a big bag of potato crisps. This I couldn't believe – it must be a dream – surely no one would leave a small child locked in a car for this length of time, would they? I mean, he looked OK, but anything could happen and no one would know! I needed to find his parents, or tell the café owner or something. Running through the front doors, I looked around wildly, hoping something would make sense. The bar was definitely in full swing by now with happy patrons, and I despaired of finding any responsible grown-ups – or finding Levi for that matter.

I didn't have to. Before I could decide which way to turn he was by my side.

"I was keeping an eye on you through the front window. You've been motionless for about an hour and a half. Lot's to think about, eh?"

"Umm, yeah ... kind of." He was guiding me by the elbow back to the booth we had sat in earlier, which now had a "Reserved" sign on it. A fresh juice was waiting for me and I gulped it down gratefully.

"Miss Motion is nearly here, so I've asked to bring song time forward, so we can get on the road. You OK with that?" He looked at me curiously, probably because I kept glancing over his shoulder, trying to spot the blue Ute. Aahh, there it was – and there was the boy, jumping up and down on the back seat. It was the movement that had caught my eye.

"Levi! Quick! Look!" I blurted out, pointing in the general direction of the car in question. "See? Not the white one, the blue one! See the boy?" Levi nodded. "Well he's been in there the whole time I was outside. I'm really worried; no one has checked on him, and it's been hours. We need to do something!"

Levi's eyes narrowed, and not taking his eyes off the bouncing boy, he scowled deeply. "Leave it to me," he said, and still frowning made his way up to the bar, whispered something to the manager and swiftly made his way over to the stage. The manager followed, picked up the mike and began.

"Ahem ... attention everyone. You know this is Karaoke Night, and tonight we have a very special guest, but before I introduce him, would the ... ahem ... owner of the blue ford Ute parked outside please come and see me? That's the owner or driver of the blue ford Ute. Thank you, thank you. And now …"

Before he could say anything else, a voice from the bar hollered "If you're wantin' to ask about the lad, he's fine, jest fine. Bin sittin' in that there wagon couple of nights a week ever since I can remember. Mainly over Charlotte way, not here usually, but can't bring him in, can't leave him at home. What's a lonely father to do? He's got food! He's got water, leave him be, I say! He'll be asleep soon enough!"

There were enough liquefied people there to yell out support for him, and as I watched Levi I saw his jaw stiffen and his back go rigid. He whispered something to the manager again, who nervously started talking once more.

"Ahh, yes, well, come see me, sir, soon as you can, and ahh ... before we hear from our special guest, we have a volunteer to start off our tribute to karaoke style. So put your hands together for S.J! Sage Jules, ladies and gentlemen, Sage Jules!' I looked around for the mystery volunteer before it sunk in: my pseudonym!! I was gob smacked! Me? Sing in public? What was he thinking? Was Levi playing games again? Then it sunk in. This must be a diversion. Levi had disappeared, and I dithered whether to trust him or make a run for it, but before my brain could make an informed decision, I found my feet were already leading me through the crowds and up onto the stage. Yep, back in that dream again. I checked the song Levi had bought up on the monitor for me, and was relieved to see I knew it well enough to at least attempt singing. It was a James Taylor classic – one I had been humming earlier in the day, and as the intro started, I could feel the good-time vibes spilling out over the crowd, relaxing the mood. I could do this.

I didn't have to worry at all, the crowd were swaying to the beat and joining in the words; hey! This might even be fun, if I wasn't anxiously looking around for Levi every few words. Halfway through the third verse I saw him at the back, the young boy in his arms, clinging on for dear life. I emphasized the next line, hoping he would get the hint:

And hey babe the sky's on fire, I'm dyin'...

He didn't seem to catch my drift, and so I played along, deciding to finish the song in style. After all, I might never get another chance. I belted out the chorus, not that you could hear me now above the tavern choir. Aha! Here were a couple more lines I could emphasize for Levi's attention:

"Dark and silent late last night
I think I might have heard the highway calling..."

As I finished up, Levi finally moved, pushing his way through the crowds still clutching the little boy tightly. He stood behind the microphone and waited until people realized what his bundle was, and hushed each other up. I looked over at the father, his head was down on the bar, his hand tightly around a bottle of beer; he had no idea of what was unfolding.

Levi spoke: "See this boy in my arms? His name is Adam."

At that the father's head jerked up and with his slowed reflexes raised his hand. "Hey, that's ma boy y' got there. You leave him be now y' hear!' And his head slumped over the bar again, too drunk to really care. The manager had sent two burly men to stand either side of him.

Levi continued: "Now Adam has told me he's scared, not of being in here right now, but scared of being out there in the dark all by himself." Adam's hands tightened their grip around Levi's neck, and his head stayed firmly implanted into Levi's chest. Turning sideways, Levi pointed to the scar at the side of his face, and as the light caught it, it appeared as a silver streak. "See this scar? I've had this since I was about Adam's age. Want to know how I got it? Anyone? Do you want to know?" I could hear the fury in Levi's voice, and so could a few others, some muttering inconclusively. "Well, whether you like it or not, I'm about to tell you. I was locked in a car once, outside a similar place to this, waiting for my neglectful mother to return. I was as terrified as Adam is; sure that something would come out of the dark and get me." He leaned down and whispered in Adam's ear, and then mine. I nodded and together we prized Adams grip from Levi's neck and transferred it to mine. I took him over to the manager, who led me to a staff room out the back, where we could still hear through adjoining interior window, but could close the door and pull down the shutters. Food was laid out and I sat with Adam on my knee, gently soothing him, and explaining that everything was going to be OK. I could hear Levi continuing, like a preacher on a mission.

"One night, people, someone did come – and it wasn't my mother. I cowered in the back seat as the window smashed and glass rained down on my back. Whimpering and petrified, unable to help myself, I gave my presence away. A rough hand reached down and grabbed me, pulling me over the seat and out the front window, throwing me roughly onto the ground. As my head came through the window, the side of my face was dragged over the jagged glass, and I was cut, deeply. The assaulter laughed cruelly and kicked me aside, joking, 'born a bastard; a bastard he will always be.' I heard him still laughing as he drove off. This was just after dark. My mother didn't reappear until around 2am, and wandered through the car park, too drunk to even realize her car had been stolen, and when she finally did, she wasn't in any state to track down the little boy she had left in the back seat, so she took the easy way out and tried to kill herself. It was the taxi driver dropping someone else off in the area that found me, semi-conscious, barely breathing, and colder than ice. Then he found my mother, collapsed in a heap beside a bottle of pills, and took us both to the hospital."

The crowd was deathly silent, all the fun and jokes sucked out of the atmosphere, which was growing heavier by the minute.

"Want to hear more?" His voice was hollow, unemotional. "Maybe not. The party's over, folks – for me anyway. And for Adam and for Adam's father. You know I read somewhere that evil only exists when good people do nothing. Well to hell with evil!"

And he walked off the stage, past Jeff who was standing there with his mouth wide open, past the recalcitrant father, who had fallen into a complete drunken stupor, and into the staff room where we sat in stunned silence.

"Time to go," Levi ordered. I was up in a trice with Adam and meekly followed Levi to the back entrance, where a black leather-clad biker stood beside a beautiful sight: Miss Motion, all bells and whistles intact.

Levi raced forward and swept the biker, who was now bare headed, up into a giant hug and swung around. I saw blonde hair flying everywhere and put two and two together. Bailey. I suddenly felt grumpy and tired, and Adam seemed very heavy.

"Oh." Bailey sounded put out as well, as Levi lowered her to the ground. "What's she doing here?"

"Getting me into trouble," Levi said ruefully, "just like she's meant to I guess."

Bailey didn't look pleased, and pulled Levi off to one side saying, "Who's the boy? What's going on? What do you need me to do? I can take her home if you like."

Levi laughed. "You should know by now that I'm always up for trouble, and I'm not going to dump trouble and run away. However, as for the boy – Adam – there is something you can do ...Did Jarven follow you?"

And that was all I heard before they moved out of earshot. Adam had gone to sleep on my shoulder, and I sat on the back stairs feeling weary, but still protective of this defenseless little soul. I imagined what it must have been like for Levi at the same age and I shuddered, starkly realizing how sheltered my own happy childhood had been. I had never really thought about children being treated so badly. I felt tears rise in my eyes, and moved to brush them away, not that there was anyone nearby to see them. To hold them in I tipped my head back and gazed at the sky. It was clear and glittery and the liquid in my eyes magnified the stars like crystals. It was so beautiful.

"Glamour girl..." a dark throaty voice growled in my ear

and I felt something sharp at the base of my throat. I involuntarily stiffened and started to scream, but a sweaty, beery hand covered my mouth and smothered anything more than a tiny squeak. The whispered voice, sounding off balance and crude continued. "Think you can go around stealing folk's kids eh? Think you can mess with the big J Man? Well, now you know different. You're gonna find out how different."

The smell of his breath made it to my nose and it reminded me of decaying fish mixed with bad body odor. The back of my mouth went dry and I began to perspire. I thought wildly of struggling, but didn't want to wake Adam and have him see his father like this – although I was guessing he had seen similar scenes in his short little life. The Foul Man, as I mentally had been referring to him all night, shoved his knee into my back and jerked me to my feet.

"Time to go, little lady." He tried to purr, but it sounded more like a mangled motor mower. I felt hysterical laughter rising in my throat. Levi was probably just around the corner, yet I couldn't raise the alarm. This was just too comical for words. Perhaps it was time to wake little Adam up after all.

I actually didn't mean to pinch him hard at all, but after years of fighting off big brothers, or annoying them when I was bored, I was better at it than I knew. Adam leapt in my arms and let out an almighty scream "Aaaarrrggghh!" and a number of things happened very quickly. The Foul Man clumsily launched his hand from my mouth to Adam's while trying to coordinate slashing my throat with the broken piece of glass in his other hand. Not a chance! I was wild now – and I kneed, kicked and shoved, yelling as loud as I could. Levi appeared beside me at lightning speed and threw a punch that would have made my brothers proud. The Foul Man staggered backwards, feinted left then struck out with his right fist, catching Levi in the region of his kidney. It was all a blur after that, as a wiry looking man stepped into the fray and finished the Foul Man off with a few well aimed hits. It was the sound effects that made the biggest impression on me – grunts, snorts, gasps, thwacks and scuffles, then silence, interspersed with heavy breathing. And of course

Adams' howling, which jerked me back to reality. Levi gently removed him from my arms and passed him to Bailey. Without hesitating, he turned straight back towards me, yelling over his shoulder "Thanks Jarven thanks Bailey! You know what to do now! Like we discussed – hurry!"

In one swift moment he lifted me into his arms, threw me on Miss Motion and straddled the bike behind me this time, tucking my hands underneath his on the handle bars.

"My bag..." I murmured feeling more dazed now than I did when facing The Foul Man.

"In the carrier on the back of the bike," he said soothingly. And then I heard no more, apart from the billowing banshee of triumph, as we roared off into the darkness of night.

5. CHARLOTTE

LEVI DROVE LIKE A MANIAC, BUT I HAD TO confess that even with all my insides upside down after The Foul Man episode, I reveled in being on the front of the bike even more than the back. I could see the road rushing up to meet me through the beam of the headlight and not much else, unless of course I looked up at the stars, which is not easy while wearing a helmet. Through my palms I could feel the throb of the engine, while Levi's steady hands kept mine warm as he steered the bike through the black countryside. The ordeal of the last couple of hours dropped by the wayside as I felt the euphoria of speed settle over us. After a couple of hours Levi gently guided Miss Motion off the highway down an exit to a well-signposted rest area. The silence of the night was extreme after the throaty rumble of the Triumph, and my ears rang with percussion sounds until they adjusted to the quiet darkness. We sat without moving for a few moments to recalibrate, then Levi carefully removed my helmet, and then his own. I shivered in spite of myself, part from cold, part from the unknown. He immediately pulled me back against him, unzipped his jacket and wrapped his arms and his jacket as far over me as he could manage.

"You OK?" he half whispered. "That was quite a scene

back there. I felt so primal when I came around the corner and saw that glass at your throat! I should have seen it coming. I was just so concerned for Adam – getting him away from his father. Better not to have a father at all than have one like that!" It was a voice full of bitterness and anger.

I murmured something inconsequential back, knowing that he just needed to vent; an exercise I was very familiar with. Besides, I had not yet let myself evaluate the happenings of the past few hours. It was probably the most interesting thing that had happened to me in my short life, even if it was disturbing, and I needed to be alone to evaluate my reactions, both immediate and delayed. Anyway, I was still not sure if I might not go into shock at any moment, and didn't want to give myself away. Levi continued, his warm breath sweet on my cold face.

"Sorry about the speed demon in me; I just had to cut loose, you know? I hope I didn't freak you out or anything."

"The whole night's been freaky – but I understand the whole speed thing, it actually helps with the adrenalin I think." I managed to say shakily. Where are we, anyway?"

"About sixty miles outside Charlotte. I should have driven you straight home, but I…I …You don't mind, do you?"

I shrugged. "I'm in way over my head. But strangely, I'm ok with that. We could just sleep under the stars and decide in the morning."

What was I saying?!

I liked the way he didn't fuss, didn't tell me to phone my parents or try to be like my brothers and order me around. Cocking his head to the side, the Grey Phantom just shrugged back.

"I'm game if you are." It was a new feeling to be treated like my own person, almost like an adult. We stood weighing each other up, and I felt like this was almost some sort of test – a test for some reason that I did not want to fail.

"I'll get a fire going," I stated firmly, and smiled at him cheekily. "And you get to sing – seeing as you got off scott-free back at the diner. I'm expecting big things, you know."

""'No way! I bags making the fire – then you get to sing

again and I get a good laugh!"

"Hey, watch it buddy. Didn't you see me take it to the Foul Man?" I feigned a Bruce Lee kick in his direction, unable to stop a giggle from escaping. Levi responded with his best Jackie Chan impersonation, and soon the giggles regressed to hard out laughter as the stress, tiredness and strangeness of the day finally caught up with us. Man! It felt good to laugh this hard.

Eventually the laughter subsided to the odd hiccup as we scrounged for some old newspaper in the rest area rubbish bin, and grabbed a few rocks that were conveniently lying around. It looked like this wasn't the first time a fire had been lit here. Levi arranged the rocks by the untidy row of low trees shielding the rest area from the highway. Now, wood. Better not use the picnic table, I thought with regret. Walking back up towards the highway, I suddenly remembered seeing a group of small hoardings lining the side of the road as we drove in, advertising something-or-rather. Sure enough, there they were! I waited until the headlights in the distance had zoomed by, and then tugged at one of the signs. It came away pretty easily, and very soon I had a stack of four. I dragged them slowly back down the gravel byway, realizing I was no longer cold. Damn – matches! I didn't have any, so I hoped Levi did. I smashed the signs by leaning them against the rocks and jumping on them, and arranged the fire just the way Dad had always taught me. He always said it would come in handy when he took me to New Zealand one day and we caught fish and cooked them on the beach. "Damn!" I said out loud again, just to emphasize the annoyance at having no matches.

"Damn what?' came that rugged voice from somewhere nearby. "Need help?"

"Yeah, come and breathe some flames for me, would you? I need some hot air!"

"Not scared I might just blow smoke?" Levi retorted. "But if you're looking for one of these ..." He tossed over a cigarette lighter, which landed in my lap.

I looked up at him curiously, realizing again how little I knew of him. "You smoke?" I asked him incredulously.

"Not since I got out of jail." He threw back at me and in the darkness I couldn't tell if he was joking or not.

Bending down I coaxed the small flame to catch the dry paper, and within seconds there was a strong orange glow, which I shoved into my roughly formed pit. As the fire took hold, I kept loading on bits of the broken signs until I was satisfied it wasn't going to go out. Levi had found a couple of larger dead branches, and we put those aside to use later. Getting my bag from off the bike, I put on all the layers of clothing I could find, and then texted Elle to let her know I was OK, sparing the details.

Desperately trying to appear busy, I kept arranging the fire and the wood, not wanting to think about the fact that we were alone again, miles from anywhere familiar, on a journey that was growing as strange as the sky was dark. Dark, yes. The light of the fire encircled us, and everything outside the glowing orb seemed blacker than black. Levi threw across a blanket he had retrieved from the bike and I gratefully wrapped it around me. He came and sat close, presumably for warmth, and together we watched the fire, each lost in our own thoughts. It's a funny thing when all activity ceases, all distractions dissipate; you are suddenly confronted with only what is directly in front of you – in this case the fire ... and Levi. The fire I could handle; Levi I wasn't so sure about. I wondered what he was thinking and how his mind worked. I'm sure he was referring to me when he talked to Bailey about "trouble." Was that what I was – trouble?

His shoulder was warm, and I leaned against him, closing my eyes, not caring. Maybe I was overworking things. I was just so tired now, wishing I was all cozy in my bed. My head dropped further as my body relaxed and finally slipped onto Levi's chest. I was half aware of him moving around to accommodate me, and felt his arm around my shoulders, cradling me in front of him, his back to a tree. It felt nice, and I kept my eyes shut with sleep nearly upon me. He began talking gently, rhythmically, and I gave him a drowsy smile.

"I have no family, Jazz. I am alone in the world, unless you count Bailey, and the band, but I like it like that." His voice hardened slightly. "No one can hurt me anymore. When I'm on stage it's like being on an island where no one can reach you or touch you. Jarven, the Framer who trained me, said the day for me to actually be a Carrier was coming, but I thought the time had passed and I had missed out, but he was right. I saw the mark on your wrist and I knew! No matter how many walls I had built up, nothing could protect me from the onslaught from that point forward. So, Jasmine Blade," his voice dropped to a whisper, "I will lower my guard in order to proceed with the task, but I will not become vulnerable, I will not let you in." The music of his words was so low now I nearly had to stop breathing to hear them. "But first I need to wake the Reader up, and this may be the last chance I get."

I didn't know whether I was dreaming or not and his words didn't seem to make any sense, but I felt the shadow of his face inch its way towards me and his warm lips hesitantly find mine. The pressure was firm, and I felt my mouth yield under his, the meeting of our lips even more intense than the linking of our eyes had been, if that were possible. I could sense a searing heat as if I was being branded, not by a red hot iron, but by an emotionally charged liquid wax. When it felt as if I could bear the heat no longer and would have to cry out, it ended as suddenly as it had begun. I could feel Levi shaking, and I involuntarily opened my eyes. His head was leaned back against the tree, and he was looking up through the branches of new leaves to the stars beyond. I pretended to stay asleep, not knowing what to think, or if I even wanted to. I guess some things should be felt, not thought.

It was the birds that woke me very early, just as dawn was breaking. Levi was asleep behind me, his head propped against a tree root, having slipped to a more horizontal position during the night. The first thing I did was touch my lips; they felt unusually warm. Had it been a dream? I ran my tongue over them, and they began to tingle. Strange. Very carefully I slid out of Levi's loose embrace and tucked the blanket up around him. He didn't look that different from Adam when he was sleeping; boyish and vulnerable, not so much of a man after all. I blushed.

I needed to run. Sipping some water from the bottle

attached to the side of Miss Motion I slipped on my shoes and set out towards the highway, enjoying the steady movement of my body. What was it that was different this morning? I felt so alive, so awake, so ... so ... in focus! It was as if my awareness of all things had intensified one hundred fold. Perhaps it was sleeping out in the fresh air, or perhaps it was ... I shook my head and looked at the sky in wonderment instead. The sun was just flirting with the horizon, fluttering lashes of blushed pink and orange amongst the lilac and blue left behind by the shadow of night as it tried to rush its way to the other side of the globe. The colors were so intense, I marveled, and viewing them through the framework of giant trees still in early bud provided a stark contrast that was breathtaking.

I had found a well-beaten track through the woods, and ran for a steady twenty minutes until I came to a cliff made of huge weathered granite, and I reached out and touched the rock, wanting to feel its solid sleeping bones; to connect with this vast and silent mammoth of nature. I pressed my lips to the cold stone, hoping to quell the heat that seemed to be consuming them, before turning back, each step still recharging rather than depleting my energy levels. The only distraction was this tingling warmth in my lips. It appeared to be intensifying rather than dissipating, and I was very aware of the heat, using my tongue to moisten them every few minutes with the hope of cooling them down.

By the time I arrived back Levi was up and had cleared the remains of the campfire, obviously keen to get going. As I ran over he swung around, staring at me in that intense way of his, so I ducked behind a tree to stretch out my leg muscles and give myself time to gain some composure.

"You run." It was a statement, not a question, so I didn't answer. "How often?" he finished.

I came out from behind the tree, using the sleeve of my sweatshirt to wipe the sweat from my face and wondering if my lips were bright red, they were so hot.

"Every day or two, usually with Chad. I'm not fast; I just like the feeling it gives me, like I've achieved something – and it gives me time to think. Unfortunately, it also means I need a shower!"

"Yup, that and breakfast – coffee especially! Hop on; I think I know just the place."

His mood was unreadable, and he kept looking at me like I was going to morph any minute. Maybe my lips were changing color, I anxiously thought, but he didn't say anything else, so I swung myself over the back of Miss Motion, being careful to leave a space between us. I could hold onto the sides this time, and it seemed Levi agreed, since before my feet had completely left the ground the bike revved to life, and the sudden forward lunge caught me holding on for dear life. Maybe he really did need that caffeine fix.

We made it to the outskirts of Charlotte relatively unscathed and in good time, although my hair was sticking to my scalp and that un-showered feeling had overpowered my morning energy levels. Levi pulled off the road and down a long driveway that was lined with budding old oak trees, perfect for climbing. A stately house greeted us as we slowed to a halt, and I jumped off the bike in relief, my body telling me that the hours spent on it had started to take their toll.

I looked at Levi questioningly, and he explained. "I stay here sometimes with the band. It's kinda like a student hostel, and they also operate a café downstairs during the day. It's the only place I've found around here that knows how to make a decent coffee. The owners are Australian, so maybe that has something to do with it."

An hour later I think we were both feeling much more ourselves, having washed away the smell of the road and changed into clean, dry clothes. I always felt happy when I pulled on my favorite jeans, and I almost felt ready to face Levi and the rest of the world again. I peered at my tingling lips in the mirror, examining them carefully for any sign of change. They certainly didn't need any extra color, but they were a bit dry, and was I imagining it? A bit plumper maybe, as if I had jabbed them with a shot of collagen. Not possible, I told myself as I rubbed some lip gloss in to soften them up and ran my fingers through my hair one last time. It felt so good to be helmet-less!

Levi hadn't bothered to dry his hair, and dark, wet tendrils were dripping onto his cotton shirt. He looked like the rock star again, nonchalant and aloof –reeking of indie coolness. How did he do that, I wondered? It wasn't like his clothes were anything special, it was more the way he wore them, I decided. He turned around as I walked over and suddenly something inside me felt reckless. With a toss of my hair I looked straight into his eyes, determined not to feel anything.

"Eggs," I said. "Sunnyside up, bacon, toast, yogurt and fruit. Oh and gallons of water. That's me decided; how about you?" I didn't wait for an answer. Somehow I had to tear my eyes away before my knees gave way – thankfully I managed to flick them towards a group of dandelion heads down on the grassy lawn. Seconds later I held one in front of me and wondered at the awesomeness of nature, gently blowing to release the seeds on their solitary journey of faith. Watching as the air currents lifted them away I felt again that sharp focus of my mind, similar to when I had watched the bubbles just days ago in my back yard. I had a nagging feeling that science and nature were talking to me – if only I could hear.

"Jazz!" That increasingly familiar voice broke my reverie, and with a wistful look at the minute parachuting pods, I headed back up to the veranda, stopping only to pluck another dandelion head on my way. I handed it to Levi saying "Make a wish." He laughed. I protested. "What? That's what you do ... blow the fairy parachutes and send a wish on its way to the fairies."

"Guess I missed that when I was a kid."

"Now close your eyes and wish hard ... but don't tell me, or it won't come true," I ordered.

"If only the boys could see me now," he muttered, but obediently closed his eyes and gently blew.

"What did you wish for?" I eagerly asked.

"Is that a trick question?"

"Ohhh ... I know you're not supposed to tell, but I can't help it. I always want to know."

He looked at me quizzically. "If I said I wished for great

coffee, would that satisfy your curiosity?"

I grinned "Maybe – or maybe not!"

And like magic, the coffee and food arrived. Levi had ordered me coffee as well, and the aroma was so tantalizing I decided to give it a go. Nothing ventured, nothing gained. It was smooth and rich and tasted dangerous; no wonder Levi liked it.

It wasn't until Levi was on his second order of coffee that we faced up to the day in front of us. My goal was to make it to the international airport, not that I had told him that, but I had no idea as to his agenda, other than procuring a package for me from somewhere.

Levi took off to pay the bill, refusing to take the cash I put on the table, much to my chagrin although I knew I would need every cent for the journey ahead. As I stood to go, I spotted the perfect oak to climb, and leaving a note on a serviette saying "up a tree," I sauntered off towards it, my eyes searching for the best route up. It was actually quite tricky, but I reveled in the challenge, finding the best branch to clamber onto and survey the surrounding neighborhood. Ahhh! Bliss! I had bought my phone with me, and although the battery was alarmingly low when I turned it on, I managed to send a quick message to Elle before it cut out, letting her know I would phone her when I reached the airport.

"Great place to talk," Levi's voice wafted up from below, and within seconds he was beside me, all of a sudden making the tree seem much smaller and less majestic. I shuffled over on the branch, and we sat with our legs swinging, looking out towards the bustling metropolis of Charlotte, the sun sending ripples of light through the forming leaves.

"I haven't got long today," continued Levi. "I have to be back in Beaufort by 3pm. We have a band meeting before we head out on tour, so we need to get going. But there are three things I needed to give you on this trip, and here is the second." I didn't ask what the first one was, but my tingling lips kept reminding me. I didn't know whether to ask about it or not; maybe he had assumed I was asleep, and that's why he was ignoring it, but if he wasn't acknowledging it, I certainly wasn't going to!

He dug into the pocket of his jeans and pulled out a silver ring, quite wide, and exquisitely engraved. Before easing it onto my middle finger he gently pressed the ring to his lips...

"Late birthday present?" I quipped attempting to lighten the mood.

"If you like, but it would belong to you even if it wasn't your birthday." He held out his hand and I noticed a similar ring on his middle finger, slightly chunkier, and with fewer markings. "Yours is the ring of a Reader, mine is that of a Carrier. Look at the markings and tell me what you see."

I held my hand up to my face and peered closely at the engravings. I saw now that there was a pattern emerging, and that between the patterns there were very fine lines, almost like those in a cobweb, linking tiny indentations together. I explained to Levi what I saw, and he nodded as if in confirmation.

"Only the eyes of a Reader or Carrier can see those lines; they are indiscernible to the average eye. Never take it off, Jazz, or if you have to, wear it around your neck on this chain." And he leaned forward and clasped a fine silver chain around my neck, gently lifting my hair out of the way. Why was it that I trembled? Every time Levi used the word "Reader" it was said in reverence, creating an atmosphere that was charged with vision and purpose, and this morning I sensed a growing intensity within me to discover what it was to be a Reader. It still seemed so mystical, so abstract, and it was harder to stay patiently waiting for the big revelation – if there was one coming at all.

"Thank you. I will wear it, although it still seems hard, not really knowing what this is all about. I'm only your average girl trying to fit all the pieces of life together, but there is something about when you say "Reader" that sounds familiar, almost like I should understand. It's most frustrating."

"Jazz, if you're average then I'm a joke. From the first time I saw you I knew there was something bigger than the both of us unfolding. You know that song I sang when you were on stage at the school? Well, we had been playing that for weeks, but the lyrics just hadn't clicked. When you were washed up on the stage, they came to me in an instant. This game we're about to enter is like a fast wine, Jasmine Blade, heady and unpredictable, that is why you are the Reader and I am the Carrier. Be patient. The third gift I have for you will help immensely."

"Well what are we waiting for?" I said playfully, making a fake shove at him, as if to push him off the branch. He pretended to lose his balance, but then righted himself and simply jumped like a giant cat to the grass, some ten feet below, smirking up at me.

"Jump!" he ordered, and out of surprise I actually did, exceedingly grateful that he easily caught me. Before releasing me he whispered, "See, you're learning to trust me; it's not that hard, is it?" I laughed, hoping to hide the fact that I might trust him, but I wasn't sure if I could trust myself.

Time moved very quickly after that. Within the next half an hour Levi was guiding me into a huge multi-leveled book store, the biggest I had ever been into in my life. There were search computers everywhere, sofas for reading on, a café, play area, and whole floors dedicated to different genres of literature. There was no time to look around however, as Levi had me by the elbow and was rushing me to the elevator at the rear of the store, pushing the button for the basement. We hurried through a maze of corridors until we came to a small counter, sign posted "Special Orders." Levi rang the bell, and we waited until an untidy middle-aged lady came to the counter, wearily asking us for an order number.

"LCM3692." Levi rattled off, showing his most devastating smile. "Please."

"One moment," came the unimpressed voice again, as she bent down to search in the recess under the counter. You could just see a graying bun on top of her head with about a million hair clips sticking out, and I stifled a chuckle, nudging Levi in the ribs. He elbowed me back and I lost my balance, hitting the counter quite heavily. The bun disappeared and we heard a bash from under the bench then, "Shhhhiii...ver me timbers!!'"Her beady eyes reappeared, flashing like an angry toucan. "Patience is a virtue, didn't your mothers teach you that?" she squawked, and I had to bite my tongue and walk around the corner; Levi shook his head in mock disappointment. I missed the arrival of the parcel and any exchange of money as I couldn't trust myself not to burst into uncontrollable laughter. Once we were back in the lift I began to chuckle in earnest, until I was nearly doubled over. Levi's impersonation of a parrot in a death throe didn't help either and by the time we reached the ground floor I was wiping tears from my eyes. It felt good to lighten up a little and relax. Still looking amused, Levi handed me the package.

"I've just got to check out a couple of magazines and see the manager and give him some promotional stuff, but after that we need to get going. Meet me by the front entrance in five – but leave the package intact until you get home and have time to go through it properly." He winked, touched my lips with the ring on his hand, and walked off, leaving me to regain my composure.

There was nothing I wanted to look at, so I wandered over to the front entrance to wait in the sun. The bookstore was busy, and the high glass foyer was filled with light. Across the road I could see a row of buses, with people rushing on and off. Right at the back I noticed a bus that said "Airport Shuttle" on the back, and on impulse I raced out the entrance, across the road, and hopped on board. I hadn't been looking for an escape route, but it had found me. Maybe it was easier than explaining to Levi what I was actually doing here. After all, there was no way he would let me jump on an airplane to New Zealand, no way at all. I felt guilt rising up inside me as I saw Levi at the front entrance of the bookstore, looking around for me, and I slid down in my seat so he wouldn't see me. I would send him a text; he would understand. After all, the note from my grandparents had said to tell no one. Shouldn't I trust them? Damn! My battery was flat. It would have to wait until I was at the airport. Damn again!

My face felt hot, my lips even hotter. Was I doing the right thing? He had been so good to me, bringing me all this way, never asking too many questions. All of a sudden I thought of all sorts of things I wanted him to know about me, and all kinds of questions I wanted to ask him. My gaze fell on the package, and it was addressed to Levi Gibson. Gibson! I hadn't even known his last name! It also had his address and cell phone number, and I ran my fingers across the words, as if to bring him closer.

9401 Ocean Drive East
Emerald Isle

Did I really want to go it alone? Maybe Levi would be on my side and take me to the airport if I asked him? I sneaked a glance out the window to see if he was still there. It wasn't too late to hop off – or was it? Where was the book store? Dismayed, I realized the bus had been moving during my reverie of the last few minutes, and I was well on my way to Charlotte International Airport. Alone.

6. NIGHT FLIGHT

ALL THROUGH THE BUS TRIP MY INSIDES WERE churning. What had I done? What was I thinking? I felt like I had abandoned Levi, abused his friendship, his trust. Me, the reliable, predictable Jasmine had acted irrationally and now had no idea what the consequences would be. In my defense, it wasn't as if I had planned to ditch Levi; it had just been a momentary slip in common sense, a nonsensical lack of trust, a spontaneous decision to jump ship (or bike in this case), but is that how he would see it? I sighed heavily. It was too late for regrets, the die was cast and there was little I could do to rectify the situation. As soon as the bus pulled into the airport I was out the doors and into the terminal, wildly searching for a mobile recharge station. Once located I fumbled the cord out of my bag, plugged it in and impatiently waited for the screen to light up, desperately trying to think of a message that would convey how I felt. All I could come up with was:

Sorry, Levi – had 2 do this on my own – going to visit relatives. Don't tell anyone plz – I'll explain when I get back. Thx for the ride. Love Jazz.

I wondered if I would get a message back. I wasn't going to hold my breath and wait though, and I resolutely put my phone away, along with the sweet memory of being with Levi, and moved onto the next thing on my list: the locker.

Finding locker B24861 was not difficult, but choosing to open it was more so. Anyone might have thought I was opening Pandora's Box, my nervousness was so evident. Have you ever had your mind tell you one thing, and your heart tell you another? My head was pounding "don't do it, don't do it, it's all a big joke," while my heart was saying "go for it, go for it, go for it."

If Levi had texted me back my heart may have led me in another direction, but he didn't and I'm guessing the hurt in my heart was stronger than my head. This was no time for logic, so I turned the lock.

There was a neatly wrapped package inside with my name on it, much like the one with Levi's name on it. I sat nearby and carefully opened one end, pulling out a mobile phone and three envelopes. One was addressed to my parents, but wasn't sealed. The next was addressed to me. The third revealed a huge wad of cash. I didn't want to pull it out and count it as there were way too many people around, but I presumed it was enough to get me where I was supposed to go.

The letter to my parents was brief and to the point, letting them know of my decision to visit my grandparents in New Zealand and assuring them of my well-being and safety. The first half was written by my grandmother, Arabella, and then there was a large gap for me to fill in anything further. I didn't know what to say, so I shoved it in my pocket to finish later.

I opened the letter to myself, but there was nothing personal, only extra information consisting of a bank account number in New Zealand, the address of the house I was to make my way to on arrival, and a car rental company voucher.

What next? I trembled. Flights. Was I really going to do this? I made my way to the rest rooms and stood in front of the mirrors, splashing cold water onto my face. Looking objectively at myself, I thought I saw a new wildness in my eyes, and my lips were definitely bigger. Pressing them together I was aware that the tingling I had been ignoring was stronger, and I dabbed more water on them, hoping to cool them down. Better keep ignoring them, I decided ruefully.

The next flight to Los Angeles International Airport was via Houston, Texas, and it was due to depart at 1.15pm. I might just be able to make it, and the lady at the ticket counter assured me there was a connecting flight available in LA to get me to New Zealand. The time constraints helped me make my decision. If I didn't act, then I would be stuck waiting, and waiting for what? For Levi to come and rescue me? As if. It was now or never, and as I stewed over my options, curiosity got the better of me, so, throwing caution to the wind, I walked purposefully up to the ticket counter, acting decisively rather than deliberating any longer.

The flight to Los Angeles was uneventful. I posted the letter to my parents in Houston, writing a long garbled dialogue about Destiny and me and why I was acting so differently from the last seventeen years, hoping, just hoping that they might understand. I shuddered to think how much trouble I must be in. I was certainly gaining a list of people who were disappointed and angry with me: my parents, probably my brothers, Levi, and now Elle as well. When I phoned her to fill her in on my adventures and dropped the bomb shell that I was flying to the other side of the world on a whim, she really went to town. Apparently my parents were suspicious and had been hassling her, and when she heard I had no intention of coming back any time soon, the frustration in her voice was evident.

"But this summer, Jazz, we had so much planned! New Zealand? Did I hear you right? What are you thinking? Plus, you promised to come to my dad's beach house with Matt, Sam, and I for at least a week and I can't exactly go without you, and all my other friends have disappeared for the summer. You can't do this to me!" she wailed, and I held the phone out from my ear feeling guiltier than ever. No one had ever told me that freedom carried such burdens.

It seemed that everyone wanted a piece of me, and I was getting a bit sick of it, so I interrupted saying, "Elle! Listen! I have to do this. Wouldn't you if you were in my shoes? I'm sorry I've let you down, but I am not changing my mind. Who knows, my grandparents might hate me and I'll be home in a week or so, but if not – well I *am* sorry, and that's about all I can say."

She went quiet then and her voice came down the line tightly. "Right then, *friend*, I'm guessing this is goodbye. I was going to tell you all about me and Matt, but you're obviously far too preoccupied with *yourself*!" There was a slam in my ear, and then silence. I leaned against the cool phone booth wall and wondered if it was worth it. I couldn't remember the last time I had let someone down, and now I'd managed it twice in the same day! I fiercely shoved both packages to the bottom of my bag, thinking they could rot there for all I cared right now. So much for being footloose and fancy free.

I arrived in Los Angeles at 5.30pm and booked a ticket to Auckland, New Zealand that left at 11.45pm. That was good; I could sleep all night on the plane and arrive in the morning. Sitting in the departure lounge feeling very alone and very sad I followed my grandparents' instructions and texted them the flight number and arrival time. I spoke to no-one, other than placing my order at the fast-food counter. If Levi were here this would be fun, I couldn't help thinking. The overwhelming silence of my cell phone reminded me that I really had shafted him big time. I twisted the ring off my finger and attached it to the chain around my neck, not wanting any visual reminder of the trust I had broken. I picked up my phone to check the screen – and froze! Of course, I had only plugged it in to send that text to Levi; I hadn't charged it, so it was still as flat as a pancake! The table I was sitting at was by the wall, and I scanned along it for sign of a power point. I spotted one and shifted further down to another seat and plugged in, anxiously waiting for the screen to light up. Drumming my fingers on the table, the familiar Buzz Lightyear signal seemed to take ages to finally sound, and when it did, I jumped nervously. Four new messages: three from my mom and the last from West Carteret High reminding me to return my remaining text books before the end of the week. Fat chance! I slumped in the seat, dejected and more alone than ever; obviously moral support was not on the itinerary for this trip. I hadn't even had a confirmation back from my grandparents on the phone they had left me to let me know they got my message and would be there to meet me.

How sad was that! Sniffing a few times, I felt the sting of tears behind my eyelids as I listened to the messages from my mom, her voice sounding a little worried.

"It's so unlike you not to call or text, Jazzy. Do let us know if there's anything we can do. You know we do need to talk about the other night. You can't stay at Elle's forever you know, but we do love you dear. Just don't do anything rash or foolish please."

At this point the tears fell out of my eyes and plopped into my half-eaten hamburger. Having ditched my friends I was around 2500 miles from home all by myself, and possibly on a wild goose chase. Did that count as rash and foolish? I sent a quick text that probably didn't console her much, but what else could I do?

Once on the flight I asked for a pillow, blanket, and eye mask and focused on one thing only: sleep. Unfortunately it was a full flight, and due to my rather long legs, the bulbous man next to me, who alternatively fidgeted and snored, and my lips that were now throbbing, sleep was the one thing that evaded me. Having a window seat was my only relief, and I tucked up as compactly as I could manage to wait out the long night. I thought about Levi's package in my bag and contemplated opening it, but decided not to, partly because I knew I needed privacy to read it, and partly because I felt like a sour puss, sorry for myself and the situation I had gotten into. There was no sense of noble reverence, even when I whispered to myself, "Come on, you're a *Reader* – a *Reader*," I just felt silly. What was the purpose of a Reader anyway? I still had no idea. I must have drifted off at some point, because when I switched positions I could have sworn Levi was leaning over me, tucking the blanket in around my chin, and I smiled contentedly, picturing his eyes staring deep into mine, willing me onwards.

7. HISTORY

TRAVELING TO NEW ZEALAND IS A BIT LIKE TAKING a long walk down to the very bottom of the garden – it seems a hassle to find the time and make the effort, but once there you suddenly find you believe in fairies again, and the old childhood magic begins to take hold.

Wrapped in a blanket, I was sitting on a windswept beach at the base of Kauri Mountain towards the northern end of the North Island, staring out to sea in contemplative solitude. I had been in New Zealand for two days now, but had slept the first full day and night so I wasn't really counting it. It had taken two hours of waiting at the airport and finally rechecking my instructions to realize that no one was going to meet me, and two headaches later I had managed to hire a car, purchase a road map and drive on the wrong side of the road for what seemed like an eternity to the address my grandparents had given me. The house was at the end of a long treacherous gravel road, but it was definitely the same as in the photograph I had been sent, and something stirred inside as I came around the last corner and realized I had been here before: it was the house from my memory, and it clutched at my heart like high voltage power lines. Flashback images flooded my mind with vivid colors, shapes, and scents of this strangely familiar place.

A mild winter chill had its grip on the land, and although everything was green, it still looked asleep. There were no close neighbors; the house was the original farm cottage for the surrounding land, but what must once have been fields were now interspersed with regenerating native bush. For a pioneer farm shack it had been positioned well, facing north east out over the sand dunes to the sea beyond, and the views from the deck were magnificent. Unlocking the stiff wooden door I was relieved to see that the welcome was not as cold as I had feared. Someone had stocked the fridge and pantry with fresh produce and the hot water, electricity, and heating were all functioning. Pity I couldn't say the same for myself. I managed the ten steps or so to the main bedroom and collapsed on the bed, worn out from the emotional assault of the past few days. It was a full twenty-four hours before I surfaced, and my first inclination was to step into the wide open coastal space and let the clean, green, kiwi magic begin to do its work.

After forty minutes or so I jerkily stumbled back to the house. It was colder than I had first thought, and one blanket was just not enough to shield the biting wind. Slowly defrosting, I boiled the jug to make a hot drink and raided the fridge, finding a punnet of kiwifruit, some blueberry whipped yogurt and a couple of croissants, which I put in the oven to heat. Moving into the lounge I spotted an open fire place and a stack of freshly cut wood. My eyes lit up for the first time since I had woken. How I loved an open fire – although it was still too painful to think of the last fire I had sat beside just nights ago on the opposite side of the globe, with Levi. Weird.

I busied myself with setting and lighting the fire and preparing my breakfast/brunch/lunch (my time clock was still all over the place), not wanting to give my mind any room to step back into the past. The warmth and glow soon provided heat to both my body and my soul, and for the first time I was glad I had been brave enough to come. Looking with interest around the room, I realized it had been furnished intentionally. It had a kind of retro 1950s feel, but was surprisingly fashionable. "Kiwiana" knick-knacks were everywhere, and some of them brought an unexpected smile to my face – like the over-sized red, yellow, and black striped wooden bee on the shelf above the fire. It was mounted on wheels, and when pulled along the wings turned around and it made a buzzing sound. There were old fashioned glass milk bottles filled with shells from the beach, a driftwood mobile hanging from the low ceiling, a cowhide ottoman and some nostalgic New Zealand landscape paintings on the walls that looked like originals. All in all, nothing belonged together, but everything fitted just right to the naked eye, and I spent the next hour examining the treasures on the walls and the shelves in each room of the cottage, realizing with each new find that a part of me belonged here also.

I wondered what I was supposed to be doing, other than waiting; I was glad my grandparents had given me some space to settle in and gain my equilibrium. The last thing I wanted was to meet them while in a state of emotional decline. The short note I had found on the bedside table when I first woke simply said *Dear Jasmine, settle in, enjoy and relax; allow yourself the luxury of solitude. We will join you in three days' time xx A & A*. Was I supposed to call them Alistaire and Arabella rather than Grandma and Grandpa? I hadn't thought of that – after all, the last time I had seen them I couldn't even talk!

Stoking the fire I glanced out the window, realizing that the dark shadows in the water were actually surfers. The waves were about four feet high and it was obvious that this end of Ocean Beach was used by surfers with local knowledge who must have beach access through the farm at some point. I watched as a rider caught a wave nicely into the shore, dancing with each turn of the wild water, making it look so easy. Chad had tried to teach me to surf once. I was pretty average, but seeing the water so close made me want to give it another go. I suddenly missed Chad dreadfully; he would have all the right jokes to keep me from diving into a sea of seriousness, and the right music to mix with my moods. Music! That was what was lacking! I located the stereo and CDs, and pulled out the first one that came to hand: The Doors – wow – classic rock. I found the track "Riders on the

Storm," and sat watching the surfers until all but one had left. The rain, which had been threatening all day, finally came and as it lashed the dunes and the deck I sat, occasionally getting up to stoke the fire, re-enforcing the shelter my hideaway provided. If only my heart could be protected in the same way. It still felt battered, bruised, and guilty. Every now and then I stood, pressing my lips against the cool glass, still with a heightened awareness of them, although the tingling and heat had subsided.

Finally, when I had to acknowledge the nagging voice in the back of my mind, I dug Levi's package out of my bag and carefully placed it on the ottoman in front of me. Flashbacks came thick and fast as I remembered laughing at the lady in the bookstore, and Levi's playful wink and his ring brushing my lips as he handed me the package. I bet he wished he'd never trusted me with it now. I gently eased my fingernail under the tape until it broke away, opening one side at a time until all that remained was to pull back the paper and reveal the contents. I took a deep breath, and repeated the grace Levi had said when we ate at the Pit Stop: "For what I am about to receive, may the Lord make me truly thankful." I didn't know if I was ready to receive, but it seemed appropriate; although it wasn't food for my body, perhaps it would provide food for my soul – even if I felt a bit silly doing it.

There were three items in the package (why is it that things usually come in threes?). The first was a cardboard storage tube; the second two were hardcover books, one small and slim, and the second old and heavy, much like a Readers Digest annual. I chose to open the tube first; it had an air of mystery about it, and the markings on it appeared to be Middle Eastern, perhaps Arabic if the stamps were anything to go by. Popping the end, I eased out the scrolls gently. They were not ancient, but crisp and freshly etched on heavy white paper and the quality of the calligraphy was exceptional. The scent of exotic spices accompanied them and I couldn't help but feel my anticipation mounting. I unrolled the first sheet, and was disappointed. The letters were so closely formed that I couldn't make sense of them; in fact the whole page was bursting with letters and words, with scarcely a white space to be seen. It didn't help that it was in Arabic. I set it aside and turned to the second papyrus, which was so exquisite it took my breath away. In larger, beautifully formed script it simply said "***Welcome Reader,***" and was framed by the white expanse of paper surrounding it. The words further down the page jumped out at me, as if they had been waiting for the longest time to be read:

'Even before there were words, there were feelings. And before feelings there exists a cavernous space, as yet untapped. There is nothing inside or outside of space that does not speak to us – if we listen, if we look. Consider the ways of the ant.'

The simplicity of the words struck me, and I set them aside to think on at a later time.

The third sheet was rolled tighter than the other two and was held fast by a wax seal in the shape of a heart. Should I break it? I wondered whose hand had put the seal in place, and whether they knew whose hand would open it. The day light was receding, and I rose to turn on the lights and bring in some more firewood from outside the back door. It might be a long night. Sitting again, I held the scroll up to my warm lips to soften the wax, and was then able to prize it open, keeping the seal intact. The lettering again was flowing and poetic, and it was entitled:

Precepts of a Reader:

1. A true Reader understands that blank spaces are crucial, and has the ability to discern knowledge in the spaces between words, formulas, calculations, and spheres, spaces that lie unseen and undiscovered by all others.
2. A Reader has the responsibility to decipher the unseen code and convert the knowledge into a practical application.
3. A Reader must commit to utilizing their discovery for the betterment of human kind in both a local and global context.
4. A Reader must protect the sanctity and secrecy of the Reader's

heritage, and be willing to make whatever sacrifice is required to fulfill their given destiny.
5. A Reader shall commit the first four precepts to memory and then destroy this scroll, thereby protecting the code of Readers from those that seek to destroy it.

Underneath was written my name and a short message:

"Jasmine Blade: your journey into space is destined by Esmovoir."

Set by edict of the Council of CFR (Carriers, Framers, and Readers).

The word Esmovoir caught my eye. What was that? I had taken a semester of French at school, and it did sound kind of familiar, but I just couldn't place it. I read over the precepts again, this time absorbing them on more than just a superficial level. *"Blank spaces are crucial..."* – well, I agreed with that. I picked up the first scroll, which was jammed with words and letters – no blank spaces in sight. Perhaps it was included as an object lesson? Spaces were the same in science. I knew that every time scientists have discovered what they have thought to be the smallest particle of matter, more information has been discovered in seemingly empty space, providing further knowledge and insight into things previously thought of as miraculous. I thought of my research into the properties of bubbles, and how there seemed to be a space between the physical manifestation of a sphere and its correlation with emotive thought.

Esmovoir! That was it! *"To move the feelings, to set into motion the primary emotions."* Was this my task – to create a vehicle to capture and move emotions? But that was what I had been mulling over the past couple of years; dreaming in fact, of being able to store emotions in bubbles, rather than bottling them inside! Why did this Council of Readers and whatever's want me to do this too? Was this finally my Destiny, my purpose? And even if I did crack some scientific code, how could I use it for the betterment of humankind?

I abstractly rose to my feet and paced the lounge and the kitchen, automatically cleaning up, organizing my world, creating the space for a long evening of introspection. I never made it to bed that night, but the wing-back chair beside the fire place provided adequate comfort for the two or so hours I did doze. Memorizing the precepts proved no problem after my years of focused study, and I had burnt the scroll well before the middle of the night. Waking early the next morning I felt ready to face whatever the day might bring – including my grandparents. They had texted to say they would arrive after lunch, which would give me time to hit the beach for a run and a swim. I was churning between feeling confident and then confused as to my new calling as a Reader, and the number of unanswered questions was mounting by the minute.

The large annual had proved to be a handmade scrapbook, providing historic documentation of Readers from the past, and I was surprised to find myself in good company. Several of my science heroes were identified in the book, as well as artists, writers and inventors whose achievements I had thought were attributable to genius, talent, and overcoming adversity. Not so. Each of these persons had been destined to be Readers before they had succeeded in their chosen field, and each had written in their own hand testifying to their calling and reiterating their commitment to improving life on planet earth. The early Readers were predominately from places in North Africa and the Middle East, slowly spreading to Europe and America – although most seemed to have led nomadic global lives as they pursued their quest as Readers. Some succeeded, some failed, and some were cut down during or after their mission by Jaggers, and their Carriers or Framers had to finish the log book entries on their behalf.

I had to check the compact booklet to understand what a Jagger, a Framer, and a Carrier were. It was entitled "Readers Dictionary," and included lots of regular dictionary entries, with those pertaining to my new found destiny hidden in between. My brow wrinkled as I concentrated on making sense of it all, I thought I might end up with permanent furrows.

A Framer was defined as *Friend: "One who imparts the framework of the quest to the Reader and directs them to the Carrier."*

A Carrier was summarized as *Friend: "One who awakens the Reader; antidote in time of greatest need."*

A Jagger was the last definition I looked up, and it was described as *Foe: "One who seeks to sabotage the Reader and twist the advancement of knowledge for evil rather than for good."* I shivered.

Information overload! I needed to clear my head again, and looking out the window the sight of the sun rising over the outlying islands gave me all the impetus I required. Grabbing a towel and changing into my bikini and running gear I set out for the beach, jogging through the dunes to the wide open spaces. The beach curved like a crescent moon for a distance I estimated to be around six miles, although the sparkle of the sun on the incoming tide could be deceiving me. I would need to run quite a distance to be brave enough to face the chill of the winter sea, and the clouds were already dressing the sky warmly, as if to warn me to do the same. The sand down by the water's edge was firm and easy to run on, and I reveled in my long strides, soaking in the fresh air and the wild beauty that surrounded me. It would be nice to have someone to share it with, I mused, my mind immediately turning to Levi, and I crossly shook my head. I had purposefully not recharged my phone since I had got here with the hope of exorcising the hold he seemed to have on me, but it obviously wasn't working too well. I consciously shifted gear, both physically and mentally, and decided to run up to the soft sand and the dunes to give my legs a real work-out. I stumbled rather than ran up the first dune, but running down the other side was a blast. "I'm a Reader!" I yelled to the wind and the sky and my momentum carried me over each undulation until my legs and my lungs were burning.

I stopped on top of the tallest dune yet, and surveyed my surroundings. The ocean was to one side, and was beginning to look very inviting. To the other side was mound upon mound of tussock dune, leading up to a series of Pohutukawa trees and a rough broken line of farm fencing. At the bottom of the dune I was standing on, I spied a funny white mound, and raced down the side to take a closer look, screeching to a sudden halt when I got close enough to realize what it was: a woolly white sheep. It was just lying there like it was asleep, but I was guessing it was much more than asleep – it was dead, very dead. I stood looking at it curiously; it seemed so bizarre in such a beautiful place to have such a stark example of lifelessness, and the more I looked, the more surreal it seemed. Just as I was about to turn my back and break the somber mood that had caught me unawares, I had a sudden flash of focus, and in an instant could see exactly how that sheep could be brought back to life – not a thought of the miraculous, but an instantaneous equation of the scientific explanation for reviving a lifeless animal – and as quick as it came, it was gone. I was left with an impression that I had witnessed something great, even if I could no longer remember it. The words on the second scroll came to mind, which I had also committed to memory: *'Even before there were words, there were feelings. And before feelings there exists a cavernous space, as yet untapped. There is nothing inside or outside of space that does not speak to us – if we listen, if we look. Consider the ways of the ant.'*

I ran back to where I had dumped my towel, looking down at each grain of sand with a new focus as if I were using a microscope to view it. Sparkling like hidden treasure, I knew that there were even spaces between the tiny particles I was running on, just waiting for a Reader to un-package their secrets. Turning to the sea, I stripped off my t-shirt and shorts and sprinted at top speed towards the waves. This was going to be one short swim! A lone surfer out the back of the break caught my eye just before I dived, and I briefly wondered if he was the same one as yesterday, before the water slammed into me like a washing machine on a cold rinse and spin cycle. It was not as freezing as I had thought it might be, and I felt an intense pleasure at the salty feel on my face and the powerful surge of liquid energy all around me. It was funny how, since Levi had … kissed me … it was as if everything I stopped and properly looked at or chose to engage with would suddenly have a heightened clarity, as if pre-kiss my focus was fuzzy, and post-kiss the lens through which I viewed objects and experiences had been cleaned and adjusted, creating a surreal indefinable something.

I swam out through the breakers, being careful to dive underneath them as they broke so as to avoid their full force and thereby conserve my energy. The deeper I went the colder it got, and I began to wish I had a wet suit on like the lucky surfer I had seen. Turning reluctantly for shore, I decided to swim right up the estuary that fed into the sea to avoid the cold biting wind, rather than walk up the beach to my towel. Kicking on my back I enjoyed the sensation of floating and the white torrent my legs were stirring up as they propelled me through the water. Realizing that I was now in the shallows I gave one last thrust to turn myself over, when I felt an unexpected spasm of excruciating pain rush up my left leg. Hauling my body onto the sand, I saw a flutter along the top of the water, and two huge flat wings just above the surface: stingray! I looked down and as the blood gushed out I again experienced that weird clarity of mind, summarizing to myself exactly what had happened. Stingrays sit in the shallow water during the winter, trying to soak up any heat they can; obviously I had kicked it with my foot, and in reaction it had raised its barbed tail and spiked me in the ankle.

That was my last coherent thought as I struggled to my feet, my head spinning. I tried to get my body to respond to my brain and run back to the house, but instead I found myself swaying from loss of balance, and collapsed to the sand in agony. I think I cried out, but there was no one to hear me.

The next thing I was aware of was being shaken vigorously, and I opened my eyes directly into a worried set of deep brown eyes and heard a calm voice saying over and over, "Can you hear me, mate, can you hear me?"

My lips moved, but no sound came out, and I was scooped up into unfamiliar arms. The stranger's voice decided: "We need hot water. I'll take you to the house on the dunes. Hold tight if you can." Waves of pain were coming thick and fast, so without thinking I dug my fingernails deeply into the solid flesh and I heard the voice say, "Give me a break! I said hold tight, not claw me to death!"

I had left the house unlocked, and in record time we were

inside and I had been dumped unceremoniously on the bench, with my foot in the kitchen sink. Warm water gushed out over my leg, and I felt an immediate sense of relief that increased as the water heated. Soon the sink was full of what my glazed eyes told me was warm blood, but my brain argued was just bloody water. Over the next half hour the pain continued to spike and then decrease and whoever it was kept topping up the hot water until I wanted to remove my foot. The person disappeared for a while and came back with my towel, draping it around me and drying me off, then searched in the cupboards for a medicine box, muttering "Mate, must be some antibiotic cream here somewhere. Ooohh yum, choccy bikkies." I heard a ripping sound and some crunching before one was shoved in my mouth. "Bit of sugar will be good for you. Right, that must be a good forty-five minutes. Let's get you on the couch and take a proper look."

Lying on the couch I was finally able to stop the vertigo and focus my eyes. A head of blond curly hair was bent over my foot, examining my ankle and drying it with a clean towel.

"You're lucky," came the thick New Zealand accent, "no sign of any barb stuck in your leg, and it's a clean puncture wound. Looks like it just missed your artery." They almost sounded cheerful. "No need for a doctor, unless you start feeling sick or it starts swelling. I'll wrap it in a hot, wet tea towel with some ointment. There, that should do it. I take it you're staying here at Ali's house? Mind if I make us a drink?"

My mind had caught up with the present and gained control of the pain now, and I was able to clearly focus on the person standing in front of me. He looked a little taller than me, and probably a bit older, but it was hard to tell as he was still wearing his wet suit. His eyes were definitely brown and friendly, like a big puppy dog, and his blond hair was quite long, contrasting strongly against his olive skin. "Ummmm..." I vaguely replied, waving my hand at the kitchen.

By the time he reappeared with two steaming cups I had covered myself with the blanket from the night before, and shuffled to a sitting position, my leg stretched out along the couch still throbbing, but manageable. I gratefully took the drink.

"Thanks for the rescue," I said. "How did you know what to do? I saw the sting ray swim off, but the pain was so great I didn't stand a chance. If you hadn't been on the beach..."

He sat on the edge of the chair, grinning at me. "I heard your scream from the back of the surf! You dropped like a possum in the head lights, so I knew something was up, and," he shrugged, "the surf was getting pretty mushy anyways, so no worries." He looked at me with interest. "You're from America," he stated, like it was a different planet or something.

"Ah, yeah. I'm Jasmine, Jasmine Blade. I take it you know my grandparents?"

"Ali's a grandfather? Wow. He never told me. I surf with him sometimes, and Arabella, she cooks us a mean feed after, if they're staying out here." He glanced out the window. "Where are they now?"

"Coming this afternoon," I grimaced, remembering. "You haven't told me your name."

"Dan, Dan Picoult. Local surfer extraordinaire and Ocean Beach lifeguard. You were lucky. I've known your grandparents for years —everyone knows the Blades round here."

"Is that a good thing or a bad thing?" I wondered out loud.

"Depends who you ask. Me, I think they're awesome!" He flicked me that cheeky grin again, reminding me of my brothers. I really was more comfortable around boys than girls, I thought with a sigh.

"Well, Dan, the least I can do is offer you lunch – if it's lunch time yet – my time clock is still adjusting, sorry."

"Near enough," he responded cheerfully. "Might just go grab my stuff from the beach though. You'll be alright while I'm gone?" He didn't wait for a reply, obviously not too worried about my injuries.

"Some comfort," I muttered wryly.

I staggered to my feet, steadying myself against pieces of furniture and the wall until I made it to the bathroom. I needed to shower. Turning the water as hot as it would go I washed away the salt of the sea and lathered my hair until it felt clean and smooth. Balancing on one foot I hopped to the bedroom, wrapped in a towel, and tipped my bag on the bed, surveying the contents of my scant wardrobe. It was definitely time to do some washing, I thought ruefully, and probably go shopping. Grabbing my only clean t-shirt and not-so-clean track pants, I dressed quickly, lying on the bed, where possible, to reduce the woozy feeling that being upright gave me. I could hear Dan in the kitchen clanging and banging, making himself right at home, so I took the opportunity to put my washing on.

The machine was in the bathroom, and I leaned against the wall, turning my clothes in the right way and checking pockets. Reaching into my jeans, I pulled out half a packet of gum from of the front pocket, and a well-worn slip of paper from the back. I nearly screwed it up to put in the waste basket, but opened it up to quickly check, finding random handwriting, a bit like a shopping list and frowned. I didn't recognize the scrawl; it certainly wasn't mine. As I read down the list it gave a series of dates: June through August, each with a different town written beside it. Of course! The first day I met Levi! He had swapped it for the jasmine in my hair, and I had completely forgotten about it. This must be a list of tour dates and venues. What was the date today, I wondered, my heart quickening. My birthday had been on the 20th June – how many days had passed since then? It was all such a blur and felt like a lifetime had passed since my party, but surely it couldn't be more than the 25th today. The first date on the list was Saturday 27th – this Saturday!

I reluctantly slipped the scrap of paper into the drawer beside the bed, wishing I had the time to check, and rejoined Dan in the kitchen. He looked half-pie decent now, and certainly older in his board shorts and quicksilver t-shirt. He looked at me sheepishly.

"I think I've burnt the cheese on toast, but I've opened the window."

I had to laugh; how hard could it be? Opening the oven I salvaged what was left, cutting off the black crusts and tossing them out the window to the birds.

Sitting at the table, we spent the first few minutes in

comparative silence, hungrier than we realized. Finally Dan looked up and asked, "So why come to New Zealand? Other than to see family of course."

I kept my head down, trying to think of an answer that made sense. "I want to see the world before I start college?" I said with a questioning tone.

"Hey, you're telling the story! Doesn't matter to me. I'm saving for my O.E. at the moment, working part-time at the timber mill and part-time for the surf lifesaving club."

"O.E.?'

"Short cut for 'Overseas Experience'." There was that grin again. "Lots of kiwi young people head overseas to see the world – usually to the U.K. though, or Aussie, but not so much to the U.S. of A. Me though; I'd like to go to the States. My old man rocked over there when I was just young, and ever since he's been arguing with my mom to let me join him."

"Where is he based? America is a big place, you know."

"Oh, he was in San Diego, but he recently went over to the east coast somewhere to help out a mate. He shapes surf boards for a living; pretty transient type." Dan sounded almost apologetic.

"What about your mom?" I asked.

"She's still back here – kiwi through and through. I stay with her over in Whangarei Heads. She was pretty cut up when Dad left, but she's all good now, found a new bloke and he's OK. Maybe they'll get married and then I'll feel free to take off, do my own thing." I leaned my head down against the table, feeling a loud pulse begin to pound in my temple. Dan looked at me sharply. "You feeling OK?"

"Just a bit woozy," I whispered. "Any pain killers in those first aid supplies you found?"

"I'll get you some, just a minute," he said, and he calmly picked me up like I was a small child and carried me through to the bedroom. He gently lowered me onto the bed, closed the blinds and ordered: "Stay put!"

I dizzily smiled. He sounded just like Levi when he said that. I picked up my ring from the bedside table, pressed it to my lips as a reminder, and then slipped it on my finger. The kiwi boy was back in a flash with a glass of water and two tablets, which he fed me like a baby, and then in that bossy voice proclaimed that I was to stay still, try to sleep, and he would wait for my grandparents to arrive, checking in on me every half hour or so to ensure I was doing OK.

I was too tired and achy to argue, and gratefully closed my eyes. I was asleep before he could even leave the room.

8. FAMILY

I have never been much of a dreamer, but this was so much more than pictures in my sleep. "Jazz?"

"Levi?"

There was nothing but sand below and sky above – a stark blue and yellow landscape. We stood staring at each other, waiting for something to happen, until I decided it was silly, and walked quickly up to him, pinching him hard on the arm.

"Ow!! What was that for?"

"You're not supposed to feel anything. This is a dream – go on, pinch me back. Ouch! Not that hard!"

We continued to stare, waiting for something else to happen. After all, dreams have a life of their own and don't need any help in becoming crazy. I tapped my toe impatiently.

"You asleep?" I said.

"Lay down for a bit of shut eye before band practice…I guess so."

I punched him this time. "Feels so real."

"Ow again! You really shouldn't…" and as he talked his body just faded away, in fact everything faded away and I dreamt no more.

I kept my eyes shut, hearing again the crash of the waves and slowly becoming aware that my ankle was throbbing. I tried to picture Levi in my mind, but he was gone, although I could hear a deep voice coming from the room next door. I strained my ears, and slowly the resonating sounds began to make sense. I recognized the voice as Dan's as he continued talking.

"I've been checking her every half hour or so. I'm pretty sure that there's no secondary infection or allergic reaction. Last time I went in she must have been dreaming as she kept calling out for someone named Levi. Is that her brother or something?" He sounded hopeful.

A voice I didn't recognize replied. "No – although she does have plenty of brothers. We really appreciate you helping her out, Dan. I was hoping to bump into you on the beach anyway as I wanted to introduce you to Jasmine myself and ask a favor – a big favor actually. Any chance you could stay with us for a few weeks? I won't give you all the details now, but Jasmine is here to learn and I think your input would really help."

Another voice joined in, female this time. "We would pay you of course, Dan, darling, and you know how much you enjoy my cooking!"

Dan laughed. "I'll need to check with my boss at the mill. He's usually pretty flexible, but I'm guessing I could still do my life guard duties?"

"Of course – goes without saying – a dangerous beach like this needs its lifeguards. As long as you don't mind spending time with our granddaughter?"

There was a long pause and I didn't hear the reply as they had moved into the kitchen. Bother! Bother, bother, bother! I didn't need a babysitter! I was just starting to enjoy being alone. Boys always get in the way, I sulked, wishing I was still asleep and hadn't heard anything. After a few minutes of near silence, I decided I may as well crash the party. Might hear something useful, and anyway, it was about time to meet the grandparents who had engineered this whole debacle.

Approaching the kitchen I felt very self-conscious. They were all still laughing and talking, and my partial entry went unnoticed. I politely cleared my throat. Before I could move fully into the kitchen I was swathed in voluminous clouds of purple and green floaty fabric, underneath which was a very petite woman, all animation and energy.

"Jasmine, darling, I should probably tell you off for being out of bed, but it is just so wonderful to see you! Let me get a good look at you. Oh Ali, she is so like her father; that thick, gorgeous dark hair; those green eyes. Why you're even more beautiful now than when you were two!" I was hugged repeatedly while Alistaire stood back looking amused waiting for his turn and Dan shuffled from foot to foot, as if caught in the wrong place at the wrong time. "Now," gushed Arabella, "you are to call us by our first names. We both like the informality and heavens; I'm only *just* old enough to be a grandmother. It's going to take a while to get used to. Alistaire! Give her a hug!"

Looking at me a little apologetically, Alistaire gruffly pulled me into a bear hug, reminding me so much of my dad. He whispered, "Welcome home, honey, we really hope it will feel like home to you. It's been a lifetime." I heard a huge sigh, as if there were regrets that could not be voiced, before I was dragged through to the lounge, with Arabella fussing over me, insisting I put my feet up while they all waited on me hand and foot.

"Sit down Gra- I mean Arabella. Dan will get us all drinks. He won't mind a bit, will you Dan?" I smiled sweetly at him, and I think he saw the challenge in my eyes because he left the room very quickly, nodding his head vigorously. Ha! He *should* be scared of me; I crowed in my head, I know how to make annoying boys go away!

The afternoon was spent with Arabella firing questions about family, school, and life in general, with me answering and Alistaire listening. Dan disappeared shortly after playing waiter, on the pretext of work and "making arrangements." Whatever! I thought, as I said goodbye, although I did have the grace to thank him again for coming to my rescue.

Arabella was a good cook. She had sent Alistaire and me to sit on the deck and watch the close of day, insisting that the kitchen should be hers alone. I liked this quietly confident man with his thick gray military-style hair and casual attire. He looked as if he would be comfortable whatever the environment or company he found himself in, as if he had seen enough of life not to be surprised by anything or anyone. And he was easy to talk to. I had discovered that his business was in textiles, exporting merino grade wool fabrics to fashion designers all around the world, as well as supplying the local market. He had been a sheep farmer when my father was a boy, right up in the high country of the South Island. He still owned the farm today, but it was all managed on his behalf. Arabella was far too extrovert for the isolation of farm life, and when my father was young they used to split their time between the farm and the bright tourist lights of Queenstown, known as the "Adventure Capital of the World."

"Arabella and your father used to do everything together," Alistaire reminisced. "My wife doesn't like sitting still; it seemed even before Nick was walking he was skiing, biking, and riding on jet boats. It would have been nice if he'd had a brother or sister to share the action, but it wasn't to be."

I knew my father was an only child; he had always told us how lonely his upbringing had been, despite having his mother's undivided attention. Maybe that was why he and Mom did the big family thing, having all of us. But I still couldn't understand why he was estranged from his parents – they seemed so nice to me.

It wasn't until after dinner that I had a chance to ask any real questions. Arabella had surpassed herself, serving up pure Angus Beef fillet steak: "You need an iron injection after losing all that blood," she advised me – not that I needed any encouragement as I loved a good steak. It was served on a bed of local kumara or sweet potato mash with Portobello mushrooms, steamed green beans and a tangy sweet mustard jus. And to finish, a creamy chocolate mousse, which Arabella had chilled in parfait glasses, making one extra to keep for Dan. I ate it slowly, savoring the velvety texture, content to listen as my grandmother began her side of the story. The fire and the candles had been lit, and in the soft flickering light Arabella looked younger and more vulnerable.

"When you were born, Jasmine, there was great excitement. You see, not only were you a blessed daughter after four sons, you were also born a *Reader*. How did we know this you ask? Well, your parents didn't, as they were not party to the world that your grandfather and I had become involved in. Alistair and I are both Framers, Jasmine dear. Do you know what a Framer, or for that matter, a Reader is?" she asked anxiously. I nodded, and she looked relieved. "So your parents did tell you," she said, her face optimistic as she glanced at Alistaire.

"Ah, not exactly," I rejoined hesitantly. "It was someone else, someone recently." I didn't want to say his name, not yet.

"Someone by the name of Levi?" Alistaire gently prodded. "Dan said you mentioned that name whilst you were sleeping."

"Ummm...yes. Do you know him?" (Did I sound too hopeful?)

Arabella interjected. "There are lots of flakes out there who think they know something about our world, but it's unlikely that whoever this Levi is knows anything much." I let it slide, not ready to divulge any information yet. Arabella continued. "It is only a Framer or a Carrier that can identify a Reader, and only by finding a mark you may not even realize you have. Stretch out your left hand, darling."

I extended my arm over the end of the sofa and she turned my palm to face upwards. Placing her thumb over the point where my wrist began, she pressed down firmly, holding still for about twenty seconds, all the while still talking.

"You can try it when you get home. None of your brothers carry this mark. We have a theory that often the youngest sibling is chosen to be a Reader, perhaps because 'Last Born' are known to be daring and explosive, the risk takers in life. In fact, *Time* magazine once referred to them as 'loose cannons.' There!' She removed her thumb, and within the imprint left I saw a silvery blue star, almost like someone had tattooed it onto my skin. I grabbed her thumb and turned it over, checking for any evidence of fresh ink. Nothing. Why had I never noticed it before? Is that how Levi knew I was a Reader? When he grabbed my wrists at school that day? I inwardly gasped as I made the connection, not sure why he didn't explain this himself.

"It will fade away in half an hour or so. No Reader has found the explanation for that yet," she exclaimed with some satisfaction. I rubbed the star, which, with every passing minute, was looking less like a star and more like a bruise. I couldn't feel any change, only see the evidence. Unlike my lips, I mused, which were still slightly tingling and definitely bigger. Not that I minded; I thought they were a vast improvement and I curled them into a smile to prove it. Thanks, Levi, I mentally noted.

"OK," I responded, "so I'm branded, but I still don't get the whole never-seeing-my-grandparents-til-I'm-eighteen bit. What happened next?'

Arabella and Alistaire looked tellingly at each other before Alistaire finally spoke.

"The strength of a Reader is most concentrated during the early years of life. If a Reader is identified before the age of five, which is not common, the understanding is that they are to be raised by Framers, thereby 'framing' the world view of the Reader and focusing their gift from day one. This understanding is as old as the tradition of Readers is. Remind me to tell you the foundational story of the Reader another time."

Arabella continued: "When we explained all this to your parents, they were horrified. The thought of giving you up, even if it were to your grandparents, shocked them. To your mother, particularly, family was everything." Alistaire had stood and was pacing in front of the fireplace, agitated, searching for the right words.

"You see, Jasmine, every Reader is unique and special, but your future lay in pioneering one of the last bastions known to mankind: the science behind emotion and feeling. He stopped and looked at me fiercely. "Do you see the magnitude of this? We could not, would not give you up without a fight. This was not just about your family – our family – but the global family we all belong to. We only wanted to ensure that you would be fully equipped for the journey ahead of you, if you chose to walk into destiny."

I was stunned. Playing with bubbles and feelings was one thing, but I had no warning of this. I saw immediately how the power of emotional science – if harnessed and focused – could be used for good, and more upsetting, for evil. Did I really want to pursue this? I thought again of the dead sheep in the sand dune and involuntarily shuddered.

Arabella's voice was still calm, but very tense. "The last day we saw you, you were two. We had all tried 'sharing' you; and Nick and Ashley had made every effort to accommodate us, but Ash was dreadfully homesick by then, what with five children under ten and so far from her home and family. Oh Ali, we *were* too hard on her! We were asking her to do what we weren't willing to do ourselves: give up our rights to family." A soft sob escaped her throat. Alistaire whispered over at me:

"So Nick dug his heels in. We were all on holiday here at the batch, and emotions were running high. When he said he was taking you all back to the States and to hell with New Zealand and to hell with Destiny, I saw red..." There was shame in Ali's face. "I was so intent on elevating my own position within the CFR delegation (that's the Council of Carriers, Framers, and Readers) that I no longer had my son's best interest at heart – or that of my granddaughter." I could barely hear him now, and I could see tears glistening in his eyes. "I had invited the Carrier who was assigned to your mission to meet you, and my reputation was on the line. I had made promises it seemed I wasn't going to be able to keep."

Arabella came to his rescue, having managed to subdue her sobs. "And so, in our anger and disappointment we cast off our own son, his wife, and his children – our own flesh and blood, bitterly vowing that we would not see them again unless our demands were agreed to and you stayed with us in New Zealand. And that was the end ... until today."

"You have no idea what this means to us, dear Jasmine," Alistaire was kneeling before me and Arabella was beside me on the couch, each reaching for my hands. "Having you here right now is more than we ever hoped; more than we deserve."

I let them take my hands, my mind racing. "All the times my dad has visited New Zealand have you seen him? Have you made amends?"

"Yes," Arabella smiled weakly. "About two years after you left your father visited, and we agreed that we would remain silent about your unique gifting until your eighteenth birthday, at which point we would have his blessing to offer you the opportunity to find out more. Until then, we were to remain at a distance, so as not to stir any latent Reader awareness in you without knowing."

Alistaire added, "Since then your father has visited, and our relationship has been restored – although I'm not sure how he will react to your decision."

I wondered that too. I had sent a short text letting them know I had arrived safely, and had received an equally short reply. Perhaps they were just giving me space.

"Let's ring them now," Arabella suggested. "North Carolina is sixteen hours behind New Zealand time, so if it's 10pm here, it'll be ... let's see ... 6am over there. How would that suit your folks, Jasmine?"

"They are both early birds, so it should be fine." And it was fine. I felt a sudden rush of home sickness spending half an hour on the phone first to Mom and then Dad. After they had received the letter I sent to them and the initial shock of my abrupt departure had worn off, they had understood my need to discover for myself the untold story.

Mom had assured me. "You know, Jasmine, that we just want the very best for you. If this is what you hunger for, then we will stand by you one hundred percent, even though my heart might be in my mouth. Are you sure you understand the full implications of being a Reader?"

"Not quite," I hesitated, "but there is something within me that rings true, as if my soul knows this is what I was born for, and it's no coincidence that I have already been researching along the same lines as the brief I have been given. It's almost like I am finally waking up from a long sleep."

Mom sighed. "I do love you, Jazz, and we all miss you terribly. Elle has been around three times, asking for any news and telling me to let you know she's sorry – whatever that means."

My heart lifted. "Tell her I'm sorry too, and that I'll write. I miss you all too; there's something about family that goes deeper than deep. Hey Mom?' I lowered my voice. "Thanks for keeping me, for holding onto me. I know being part of such a strong family will make me a better Reader, despite what Grandma and Grandpa say."

I could hear the emotion in Mom's words. "You kids are my life's work, my joy. I will always be here for you, but enjoy your time with your grandparents. For all the water under the bridge I know they have your best interests at heart, and have much wisdom to impart. Here's your father."

Dad's words surprised me. "I'm proud of you, Jazz, we both are. Despite our bias for the path of your future, we know that the time has come for you to choose, and that should be an informed choice. We will be your biggest cheer leaders, whatever life you decide to pursue. That's what family does. By the way, your brothers have left on their big band tour with Alien Potion – very exciting. The lead singer, Levi – the one who turned up at your party – left an envelope here for you and asked if I could forward it on. Do you want me to post it? I won't ask what it's about!"

I somehow managed to say "Yes please."

When I finally got to bed, I drowsily thought that if my life were a book, my family might have abandoned me at this point, creating lots of heartache and tension. I was one of the lucky ones, and if my life could serve to strengthen the values of family for others, then I was ready to commit. People whose stories were more like Levi's deserved better. As I slept I saw the desert again in my dreams, but it appeared only like an empty mirage to play with my subconscious mind.

9. SOUND WAVE

THE VERSATILITY OF THE WAVE HAS ALWAYS fascinated me: mechanical waves that require a physical medium to be seen, such as water, wind or wire; electromagnetic waves that invisibly deliver light and sound; matter waves that are produced by electrons and particles; and then the more metaphorical waves, such as a rush of feeling, a wave of opinion or of hot weather, a flutter of the hand in greeting or farewell. But the waves I like best are definitely those you find at a surf beach. Dan had become part of the furniture at the beach house and I grudgingly had to admit that he was good company. For the past week he had insisted I join him in the surf every morning, having sourced a spare wet suit for me and a board from the surf lifesaving club. He wouldn't listen to my protestations about being a beginner, and neither would Alistaire, who joined us on the first morning.

"It's all in the mind, Reader," Dan advocated, having been updated on my newfound status and enjoying being able to label me.

"Yeah right," I dryly quipped. "If that's the case I'll just head back to bed and practice behind the back of my eyelids."

"Not a chance," Alistaire was already walking towards the beach. "Us Blades are made of tougher stuff than that! Prove him wrong, Jazz."

I couldn't resist a challenge, and grabbed the long board, running past Dan and poking out my tongue. "See you in the whitewash, sucker."

Water was air to Dan. He lived and breathed the ocean like it was part of him, and watching him surf was poetry in motion. My participation, on the other hand, was more like a comedy act, and by the end of that first day I came back to the shore having swallowed more than my fair share of salt water, mainly from opening my mouth to laugh or object at the wrong moment.

Dan admirably suffered my short temper and frustration, and by the end of the week I was more competent, and started thinking that I might even take up surfing as a serious hobby. Alistaire and Arabella had given us all a few days' reprieve from whatever training they had in mind, espousing the value of relaxation and spending time without pressure, restoring and forming relationships, and it was working. Having the blessing of my parents, the forgiveness of Elle, realizing a package was on its way from Levi, and being surrounded by such natural beauty I felt more lighthearted than I had in years. The water and the waves were a tonic to me, and engendered such happy tiredness that each night I fell into deep, dreamless sleep.

Even Dan commented at the end of that first week together. We were playing a game of scrabble in the late afternoon (which I was winning).

"You've changed, Jazz. You were so tense when we first met."

I was indignant. "It might have had something to do with the fact that I'd just been mutilated by a sting ray!"

"Yeah, there was that, but you appeared to me like a tightly coiled spring, one that was ready to snap at any moment. And now, it's as though you have adjusted the tension and oiled the wire; the strength is still there, but it has more focus."

I thought about it for a moment. "I guess you could say that, like I have the focus needed to BEAT you in scrabble," I retorted, and promptly made a triple word score that equaled one hundred and ten points. "Game over, methinks!"

He scowled over at me, looking about half his age. "I've never liked scrabble anyway; it's a girls' game."

My observations of Dan were mixed. Most of the time he was just an annoying boy, putting his mouth into gear before his brain, and constantly competing with me, even for Ali and Arabella's attention. I was faintly amused that they humored him so much. It was almost as if they were reliving the early days of my father's youth through him. But every now and then Dan revealed a perceptiveness that was astonishing as it was unexpected, and these were the times I felt closest to him.

It's funny I mused, how enforced companionship forges unlikely friendships. It was easier to think now of my time with Levi and realize that although we were worlds apart – in distance and in status – when fate threw us together a strong bond had been formed. Every day I wondered where he was and what he was doing. Dan seemed to know that when I got that distant look in my eyes it was time to let me be, but he always appeared again before my introspection became too maudlin.

Before dinner I usually went for a run, even though the air was cold and the dark descended with alacrity, as if to hasten the land through winter as fast as possible. I used this time to think, particularly about *Esmovoir*, and how I might find the crucial connection within the gaps of my research. I knew that the frontal cortex of the brain is a key player in the cognitive regulation of emotion, and I focused my mind on recalling moments of intense emotion in my life, allowing them to build strength until I could feel physical symptoms of my emotional memories. Where did the manifestation of emotion display itself most strongly within my physical frame? How could I be sure I was accessing not only the long-term declarative memory from my brain, but also my emotional memory, the raw recollection that something significant happened before from my subconscious? Something Dan had said that morning stuck in my head, and I thought it through now. I had been explaining to him the two phases of emotional response: first we sense an emotion – fear, anger, joy, love, etc., and react instinctively with a physical manifestation such as goose bumps, tingling, heart palpitations, sweating, or tears, and immediately act to either defend ourselves by freezing or hitting, or outwardly express our joy by leaping, for example. This pathway speeds from our senses (sight, smell, taste, touch, and hearing) straight to our subconscious, which is the center for emotion in our brain. Only after these initial instinctive reactions do we put our conscious mind into gear to analyze our reaction and decide if it is rational or not. At the same time, but on a slower pathway, our eyes, ears, and other senses pass the sensory information to the sensory cortex that results in perception, and a more detailed appraisal occurs in our brain.

Dan had asked, "So, say for example that I'm tossed from my board by a big wave, thrust under the swell and am struggling to make it to the surface, my reaction is to kick and twist and turn to find the surface, feeling the fear rising in my throat and burning up the little oxygen I have left. What if the emotion comes in waves: first the will to survive, then a wave of hopelessness, then a surge of survival mentality? What's in between the waves?"

It was a good question. As I ran on, a theory began to take shape in the back of my mind. What if I could get a wave of feeling or emotion – or its physical presentation – to sync with a wave of matter? After all, some scientists believe that all particles have a wave-like nature. What reaction would occur? At the point of contact, would any information transfer take place? I felt the thrill of discovery just ahead on the horizon, and hoped my new-found focus would sustain its momentum. I ran faster than fast back to the house and on the pretense of showering and tiredness, locked myself up for the evening with a pen, paper, and the best my brain could offer.

I didn't sleep that night, feverishly making notes and scribbling equations, sparing only a moment to think jokingly that all I needed was the white hair to complete the crazy scientist image. Even before the sun made its grand entrance over the curve of the globe, I was standing in the whitewash, anxious to begin collecting samples to test my theory. Nature had conspired to help me in my experiment; the wind was offshore and the waves were near perfect: no breaks, just set after set of unbroken swells that rose like energy personified, curling their lips in disdain, then launching into a free fall releasing their limitless power and crashing challenge at the interface between sea and sand. I was the only being on the beach, and as I stepped over the line between wet and dry I felt myself move past the point of no return. Closing my eyes and clutching one of the bottles from my bubble set, I breathed in the salty air currents and forced myself to focus on the caress of the water embracing my legs.

Slowly inching deeper, I waited until I was nearly at waist height to open my eyes. A new set of waves was on its way to shore, and I knew it would be the last wave of the set that I should wait for. Wrestling with each wave that passed through me, I managed to keep my head above water, and positioned myself for the final wave, swimming a few strokes to meet it. It rose up before me like a sheet of green glass forged in the fire of the deep, and was so transparent I could see right through to the sunlight and sky behind. It hung suspended for the longest time, gathering every last drop of latent energy to emphasize its magnificence. Underneath me I felt its pull, and I allowed my feet to leave the comfort of mother earth, mesmerized and willing to sacrifice myself to the power of Neptune. As I was carried up the face of the wave, it was as if someone had attached a rocket to my back, and I felt an explosion of pleasure and ultimate freedom, as the green curtain swirled, tickled my face, and invited me in.

I focused on the emotion, and used that focus to increase the intense joy I was experiencing. Shivers ran down my spine, and at the precise moment the pleasure peaked, I broke through the very crest of the wave, my eyes pricking with tears of pure joy. The wave left me there, and treading water I took the glass bottle in my hand and captured the tears mixed with the salty wave off my face, still clinging to a remnant of euphoria and a now corked bottle that may or may not contain the message I was looking for.

Racing back to the house I was relieved to find it empty. A note on the bench informed me that Alistaire and Arabella had decided to take the rental car back to Auckland and would be gone for a couple of days; Dan was on duty at the surf club down the end of Ocean Beach for his three-day rotation, and he might just sleep in the club house rather than come back to the cottage in the evenings, but to let him know if I needed him. Need him? Ha! What I needed was peace and quiet, and that's exactly what they had unintentionally given me. I was familiar with the intense focus required to "ground" a theory, and wasted no time setting things up. The bubble kit that Harley and Fale had given me before I left had already come in handy and it was on the kitchen table, ready for action. I placed the bottle of salty tears to one side labeling it "Joy," and began to scribble furiously in the note book from Marcus.

Page after page, hour after hour, formulas drafted and crossed out, new drafts made, more coffee, another apple, until my eyes protested vigorously and my hand ached, but the cogs in my brain were still turning. Oh how weak is the flesh, was my last thought as I laid my head in my arms on the inviting table and surrendered to my body's plea for sleep.

My first thought, when I woke sometime late afternoon, was that a good old-fashioned brain workout takes as much out of you as a ten-mile run, if not more. I looked over my notes, relieved to see that they did make sense, and I wasn't just chasing the wind – hopefully.

Next on the list of priorities was a walk over the farm and I collected a variety of wild flowers and plants that might hold the key I was looking for. It seemed that spring was anxious to show her face – if the wild freesias had anything to say about it. Sticking them in a milk jug and giving them pride of place on the mantelpiece, the small cottage was soon filled with the fragrant, heady scent of the colorful blooms. The rest I dumped in the sink to deal with later. I knew I needed to let the chaos of all my equations and theories settle before I began to assemble any substance, and so I turned my mind to other things.

Finding my phone next to my Readers Ring in the bedside drawer, I decided to text Dan and ask him for dinner. He might be able to bring some supplies as well. I abstractly looked down as I pressed the "power on" button and slipped the Ring onto my finger. I hadn't worn it for the last week because I hadn't wanted to lose it in the surf. It looked beautiful, and I smiled, kissing it gently. My phone screen flashed an alert - bummer – there was no coverage. I set it back down and headed to the land line phone in the kitchen and found Dan's cell number on the fridge. Dan picked up. It was nice to hear another human voice after my solitary vigil.

"Hey, Jazz, what's up?"

"How did you know it was me?"

"Aha, caller ID, stupid. I've got Ali's number stored, so I guess you're the only one it could be with A and A being in the big smoke!"

I ignored him. "Thought you might like to come over for dinner tonight – not that there's much to cook – but you could pick up some supplies on your way."

"Why Jazz, are you asking me out? I hadn't thought of you that way, but now that you mention it..." I'm sure he knew I was blushing, even from the other end of the line. "Or maybe you just want a man slave, is that it? You just want to use me, I know!"

"I was..." I began sarcastically, before he interrupted.

"I would actually love to come. Mind if I bring a mate? And don't worry about food; I know where to get some freshly smoked kingfish and some hot chips, so there's dinner done. You just take care of dessert. Anything else you require, m'lady?"

I ignored his comments again and rattled off a list of food to get, adding in a big bar of chocolate I was sure I would need very soon if I had to put up with much more of Dan's banter.

It was obvious that the temperature was dropping, and for the first time I missed having any media contact with the outside world. I was sure temperatures were near freezing and a storm was closing in. Stoking the fire, I shivered and rechecked the wood box outside. Yes, it was full to overflowing. I dragged the wing-back chair closer to the flames and after grabbing a quilt from the bedroom, sat soaking up the warmth until Dan finally arrived. He let himself in and I was glad; there was no way I wanted to leave the heat of the lounge.

"Where's your friend?" I asked as he entered the lounge

alone.

"Ohhh, Jack – he's here – probably just not what you expected." I looked at him in bewilderment.

"Jack's a dog," he explained as if talking to a child, and I looked down at his feet, where the cutest little Labrador puppy was wagging its tail and looking at me with soulful brown eyes.

"He's gorgeous," I enthused, "Can I have a cuddle?"

"Why certainly darling," Dan joked. "I didn't know girls from America were so forward." I punched him in the arm and bent down for the dog, wrapping my arms around the wriggly package.

"And you're wearing my clothes too!" he protested.

"Beggars can't be choosers," I retorted. "My stuff is all in the wash. It's just an old shirt I found lying around," but all my focus stayed on the rich, chocolate-brown bundle of joy. "Where'd you get him?"

"A friend's bitch had a litter – pure bred – and I just couldn't resist. I mean, look at him! And Labs are just so faithful and friendly – a man needs a best friend." I had to laugh at that – trust Dan to have a puppy for a best friend.

"I'll put him in the laundry while we eat; there's an old cushion he can sit on."

"He's staying right here," I said hiding Jack inside my shirt. "You can't put him all alone in a cold room on a night like this! He's just a baby!"

Dan rolled his eyes, but didn't argue; he was learning, I thought to myself with a smile.

The smoked king fish was divine. We ate straight from the newspaper it was wrapped in, and the chips were served the same way, with lashings of thick chutney tomato sauce. The fish was freshly caught this morning, Dan informed me, smoked to his mate's secret recipe and glazed to perfection – all soy sauce and brown sugar, I was guessing.

Sitting by the fire, hearing the wind tormenting the skies outside, and the rain pouring down in protest, I was content with Jack on my lap sleeping, warm and snug. Dan chose some music.

"Not much from our era," he complained. "We'll have to

make do with granddaddy tunes – ancient Beatles records to be precise."

I hadn't noticed the record player on the corner shelf, and was stoked. The crackly old recordings suited the mood of the evening, and we sang along, giving the brewing storm a run for its money. As the evening got later we mellowed, and I was almost asleep when Dan broke the happy silence.

"You got a boyfriend back in the States, Jazz?"

I looked at him startled and was unsure what to say. "Umm ... no; never really made time for one, although I've got lots of boys as good friends." I thought fondly of Matt and Sam, wondering how they were, and then inadvertently my mind turned to Levi ... oops. I needed to refocus. "How about you?"

"No, no boyfriend. Always been a strictly girls kinda guy."

"Ha-ha, very funny. How many *girls* on the go right now?" I added some heavy sarcasm for good measure.

"Oh ... none really. Well, maybe one. Just watching and waiting really. No point in rushing these things."

"Yeah, I know what you're saying. I mean when do you know for sure if things are going somewhere?" I pondered out loud, thinking of Levi again. I didn't notice Dan's eyes fixed on my face.

"I guess it comes down to acting in faith in the end, and having the courage to jump in," he said as he rose to his feet and walked towards me, accidentally knocking the coffee table on his way past. The sudden movement made Jack jump in fright, waking from his doze in an untimely manner. He wriggled free and ran from the room yelping, straight out the back door, which must have unhinged in the high wind, running full tilt into the wet black weather.

"Jack!' We both yelled simultaneously, and raced out after him. A dark wee dog on a dark night – he could run anywhere! Dan went towards the beach and I circled the house, calling for him over and over: "Here, Jack; come on boy!"

Once I got around to where Dan's car was parked I stood still and tried to listen. It was difficult as the storm was mounting and between the surf, the wind, the rain, and the rustling of trees;

it was a very noisy party. I closed my eyes and focused, thinking that if I were a puppy, I would be whining by now – and sure enough, I could hear him! I knelt down, and there was a set of scared-looking eyes peering out at me from underneath the car. Gently murmuring to him, I got right down on the ground and carefully stretched out my arms, ensuring I made no sudden movements. I must have smelt good, because he leapt forward from under the car and buried his head into my shirt, which I wrapped around him and stood to hurry back inside. As I turned, I noticed a large package on the back seat of the car, and clearing the fog from the window, saw that it was addressed to me.

Dan came around the corner at that moment, starting to say, "He's not anywhere..." and then petered out as he realized I was holding a shivering bedraggled bundle of fur. "Where was he? Thank goodness! Quick, let's get inside before we drown out here."

I handed Jack to him, and half yelling over the storm said, "I noticed a package in your car – is that for me?"

"Oh, sorry – yeah. Ali asked me to clear their P.O. Box before they left. It arrived today. I forgot to bring it in as I was so distracted by the smell of hot chips. Help yourself, the car's unlocked."

I didn't need to be told twice, and in an instant had the package in my hot little hands (actually they were freezing) and was back in front of the fire. Dan had grabbed some towels from the hallway cupboard, and was furiously scrubbing Jack's tiny frame. I threw about three more logs on the fire, grabbed a towel and gave myself the same treatment.

"It's a big package" Dan offered.

"Yeah, I'm hoping it includes some of my clothes. I kinda left home in a hurry and didn't pack much. Do you mind if I open it in the bedroom?"

He shrugged. "Go ahead. I probably should get going anyway."

"You're welcome to stay. It's a shocking night to be out on the roads, and besides," I appealed to his love of water, "there might be some gnarly waves in the morning."

His eyes brightened. "You could be right there. Maybe I will stay, if you're sure you don't mind me 'n' Jack being here."

"I already said its sweet." My voice disappeared down the hallway to the bedroom. I was anxious to open my package. "Night Dan."

"Woof!" replied Dan – or Jack – I'm not sure which.

Once in the bedroom with the door finally shut, I ripped open the brown paper, tearing at the excess lengths of cello tape impatiently until they finally gave way. Everything had been neatly stacked inside a large plastic shopping bag, and I tipped the contents out onto the bed. Sure enough, Mom hadn't let me down, sending lots of clothes and one of Chad's old sweatshirts. She knows me too well, I thought happily. I quickly changed, pulling on Chad's sweatshirt and turning to the two envelopes remaining on the bed. One I knew must be from Levi; as the handwriting was the same as on the list I had found in my back pocket. I checked to make sure and then put it aside to open last.

The other envelope was stuffed with paper, and inside I was delighted to find letters from each of my brothers, as well as from Mom and Dad – and from Elle too! I read her one first:

Dear Jasmine,

I am so sorry I was so grumpy with you on the phone, I just over reacted. I was so disappointed you weren't going to be around this summer – and that you had left without including me in your plans. Hope you can forgive me. (I smiled – nothing to forgive, really, a friend is allowed to be disappointed when another friend lets her down like I did.)

...wanted to let you know that Matt and I am an item! But I'm not going to tell you all the juicy details till I see you again in person – so hurry back! Summer is just not the same without you,

Love, Elle

P.S. Keen to hear what you're up to if you get a chance to write??!!! Xox

My fingers were itching to write back already – her and Matt? What was she thinking?

The boys' letters were brief and full of facts, like:

Chad: *Went for a run today but just not the same without you.* (Oh, sweet!)

Marcus: *Hope the note book is coming in handy ... started doing press-ups every morning – up to fifty – beat that sis!* (Hmmm ... might be worth a crack!)

Fale: *Band stuff is crazy – Levi is awesome, he's really making things happen for us ... love you sis.* (No comment!)

Harley: *Have borrowed your CDs –hope you don't mind – using them on the bus between gigs across states. Levi says to tell you he hates the Croney Avidors!!* (Cringe – I thought I had hidden that!)

All in all I spent half an hour or so feeling like I was back in the lounge of the Pecan Tree Inn, soaking in family news like a sponge.

Mom and Dad just re-iterated what they had said on the phone, that when I was ready to return the beach house at Emerald Isle was still available for me to use, should I want to. Wow. I really did have the world's greatest parents, and now I had at least a day's worth of letter writing to do!

I turned Levi's letter over and over in my hands before opening the envelope, wondering what it was that I wanted to hear. That he forgave me for taking off like that? That he missed me and when would I be back? I sighed. It was what I *didn't* want to hear that made me stall. What if he was angry and hurt and never wanted to see me again? What if he said he regretted ever meeting me?

Bah! Either way, I needed to know, and with one final sigh I slid my finger under the fold to release the flap.

Hey, Reader:

Had a weird dream I met you in the desert. You pinched and punched me. Felt so real. Go figure?!

Let me know what you think of my new song.

Over and out

Levi

I shook my head, gasping in disbelief; the words of the song not even registering. I was still stuck on the first part; the desert; the pinch; the punch…how?? What the…??? What had he said in the oh-so-real-dream? That he was napping before band practice? My head kept shaking from side to side, the scientist in me trying to figure it out.

That night I was determined to dream of him, and I turned up Alien Potion loud on my iPod in the hope that it might encourage my subconscious mind. But try as I might, sleep evaded me. I just couldn't get my brain to relax as it spun like a record on a DJ Table, round and around and around. Finally in the pre-dawn fuzz I gave up pretending and got into my running gear. If I couldn't sleep it off, I would run it out. Something would shift, I was sure of it.

10. TESTING THE THEORY

JACK WAS CHEWING ON A CUSHION WHEN I CAME OUT, while Dan lay prone on a rug in front of the dying fire. Stoking the embers and throwing some smaller logs on to reignite the flames, I kicked Dan at the same time.

"Time to play daddy," I said grumpily, dumping Jack on his chest, "and you might want to find something to clean up the mess your cute little puppy has made before Arabella gets back tomorrow!"

Dan sat up, groaning when he saw the little piles of smelly mess Jack had made during the night. "Wanna go for a surf?" He still sounded half asleep.

"Uh-uh," I hesitated. "The surf looks a bit rugged for me. I might go for a quick run though – that's if I can fight my way through the wind and rain."

Dan rose and peered out the foggy window. "Errgh. Waves look pretty messy too. Mess here, mess there, mess everywhere." He sounded grumpily disappointed. "Might head back to the club and check out the waves at the other end of the beach – you never know. Won't make it back tonight, but see you tomorrow?""

I didn't reply, and was out the door before I had time to change my mind, deciding to run in bare feet. Running in the rain was both painful and exhilarating, suiting my confused mind perfectly. Although the wind made my face and legs sting, I reveled in the wildness of the wet and cold, slowly feeling my senses come alive, running nearly to the other end of the beach and back, each step intensifying a strange new joy, which I could only assume was a natural "runner's high." As soon as I returned, and before my euphoric state diminished, I took the small bottle labeled "Joy" and with a cotton bud swabbed my heavy perspiration until I had squeezed three or four drops down inside the glass.

I would need to be at my best today, as I put together the first trial mix of "Emospheres,", as I had decided to call my bubble mixture. Armed with a hot cup of coffee, I pulled out all my supplies onto the bench again, and set to work, trusting in gut instinct, my previous research into bubbles, and my newfound focus to guide the way.

I wanted "Emospheres" to convert raw emotional energy into emotional electricity, and then send it out in waves of bubbles. I was working on the "keep it simple, stupid" premise and had before me only a few ingredients.

Firstly, a layer of traditional bubble mixture from the make-your-own-bubbles-kit.

Secondly, my vials of newfound Joy – tears and sweat, two physical manifestations I had experienced during a state of heightened emotion: swimming, or more to the point, freedom in the waves, and running, both things I am passionate about.

Next was alcohol – the base solvent for many formulas. Any would do; I found a bottle of vodka in the cupboard above the fridge.

Finally, a selection of the different wild flowers and herb-like weeds I had collected the previous day. I laid them all out, methodically inhaling from each, then chopping and grinding with a makeshift mortar and pestle, peering at the texture, oil, and scent from each in turn, before carefully selecting the most promising.

After an hour of trial and error, I slumped over the dining table in despair, having not found a plant with all the attributes I was looking for. Actually, come to think of it, I didn't really know what I was looking for; it was as if some silent force was willing me towards an herbal formula, and that elusive "whatever" was sitting between the spaces in my mind, refusing to budge. What could possibly trigger my emotional DNA to transform into active Emospheres? Closing my eyes, I rested my head on the table, tiredness finally overtaking me. Twisting the silver Reader Ring on my finger, tears wet my eyes. *This was ridiculous – the whole thing was stupid. This was the real world, not some la-la fairy-tale land where the impossible happened at the shake of a magic wand. Who was I fooling? Maybe, just maybe…*

I squinted my eyes in the bright light, faintly aware that the soles of my feet were burning. Stripping off my sweatshirt I threw it on the sand, quickly hopping on top. Sand? Wait a minute! Looking around wildly, my eyes took in the same blue sky, the same endless yellow sea…and Levi.

"So it wasn't a dream," he said.

"What is it then? Time travel?"

"Look at your ring. It's glowing." He took a step towards me, hand stretched out, his ring emanating an iridescent white light. "Jarven told me about this – I just laughed at him." He laughed now, pinching me lightly.

"Jarven?" I knew I sounded stupid, even to myself.

"My Framer. He's been training me over the past year. He's of Middle Eastern descent, so knows lots of stuff about this whole Reader/Carrier thing." He patted the sand beside him, and I obediently sat.

"So who knows how long we'll both be asleep for," Levi continued, "so fill me in – what's up down under?"

I decided to put the whole dream/reality thing aside and just go with it – after all, my heart was leaping about like a crazy thing just sitting next to Levi. If this was a dream, I was determined to make it a real good one. Staring at my glowing ring, I told him of my travels, only looking over to see his reaction as I explained my quick departure back in Charlotte. He just rolled his eyes, so I pinched him. It was nice to joke about it and to feel like I didn't have to explain anything.

"But I'm stumped. I have the Emosphere formula on the tip of my tongue, the edge of my brain; but I can't seem to capture it. It's driving me crazy…"

Looking down, my hand was fading in and out of focus; the desert was slipping away beneath my feet. Levi pointed at my ring, and I awoke with his parting words in my head: "It acts like a map...you just have to learn to..."

Then nothing.

I thought as hard as I possibly could, Levi's words still ringing in my head. Still with my lids shut, I got up and began to wander around the house, and then outside, hoping that something might generate an idea. Stumbling over an old wheelbarrow, my eyes flew open. I was not far from the front of the house, where a few broken boards allowed glimpses under the elevated veranda, inviting me to explore. The long grass was wet, but at least it had stopped raining. Everything looked as if it had been bathed in liquid sunshine, and to prove it the sun had finally broken through the heavy clouds and was making rainbows to show off Mother Nature's handiwork.

Although there were plenty of gaps and ragged timber holes, underneath the veranda was surprisingly dry. The cavity was longer than I had thought, and as my eyes adjusted to the gloomy space, I felt an overwhelming sense of déjà vu. I had been here before, hadn't I? Sitting on the dry fine sand, I suddenly saw the fuzzy picture my brain had stored for years revive in Technicolor and fast forward focus. Memories surged through me, creating an almost physical response. I was two and a half; I was under here. It was so cool and breezy, and I was so hot, but then I heard them all fighting. I didn't understand, and it upset me. I wanted to get away, run away from it, and I had dug my hands into the sand but a hidden nail had scratched me, deeply, blood dripping onto the sand, fast, scaring me. I had screamed, and Mom had found me; Mom had found me.

I was trembling as I remembered, feeling the fear through the emotions of a two-year-old. They were strange feelings, perplexing emotions. I had thought I was escaping from having to take a nap, but after scratching my hand it was as if sleep descended, dragging me down, making me sluggish. Was I only just waking up – after sixteen years? Staring at the sand in confusion, I crawled further in, trying to make sense of what made no sense at all. Ducking down to avoid a timber joist, a gentle scent wafted towards my nose, and lowering my sightline I could just make out the beginning of a twisting vine with tiny leaves and dormant buds. And the smell – it was like a paradox – sour yet sweet, intense yet fragile, a mysterious fragrant melting pot. Reaching out to pick a handful of leaves and buds, I noticed my Reader's Ring pulsating on my finger, burning hot and glowing. A curl of excitement and certainty grew in the pit of my stomach. This was it; I just knew it.

Back in the kitchen I examined the ring closely and read my mistake – sand was required to create the space for change and to act as an abrasive mixing agent.

Acting purely intuitively I combined the mysterious plant discovered under the deck (ground to a liquid), sand, alcohol and emotional indicators. Leaving the cottage, I located the old stile out the back of the house, and followed the decrepit fence line as far up along the cliff line as I could go. Looking back along the beach, I was surprised at how high I had climbed. No wonder I was puffing. The vista spread out before me echoed the magic of this place back to my eyes; the long curve of the coastline languorous against the vermilion green of the farmland and native bush. A long white cloud lay along the distant horizon, and I was reminded of the Maori name for New Zealand: "Aotearoa," meaning the Land of the Long White Cloud.

The early evening was still, and conditions to test my bubble mix or "Emospheres" were perfect. I stood for a moment, feeling like I was balancing at the end of a high diving board, hovering between the hold gravity had on me and a free fall descent into the unknown. Everyone at some stage in their life wishes the world was at peace, and potentially I held in my hand the early engineering for such a dream to become reality. Gosh, if I have found a way to spread joy like an electromagnetic wave, why not peace? Why not love? Why not hope? Excitement curled again, stronger, in the pit of my stomach.

Taking the first bottle I positioned myself downwind so

that when I blew the bubbles they would float back towards me. I grabbed my notebook and pencil from the bottom of the container to record any observations. Easing the rubber stopper from the bottle, I raised the built-in bubble wand to my lips and gently blew. The moment of truth was at hand. The bubbles were small, and their surface shined like oil on water. Hovering in front of me, they danced in the light breeze, teasing me. Impatiently I walked into them, feeling tiny pops as they exploded on my face ... and then nothing. Waiting a full fifteen minutes before trialing the second bottle, I wrote a description of the bubbles and the outcome, ignoring my disappointment. The second bottle produced the same results ... zilch ... and my disappointment became harder to hide. Waiting a further fifteen minutes, I took bottle number three, feeling like I was holding my reputation in my hands. Lucky I was alone, I guess. Blowing gently ... ping! On my face ... nothing. I waited ... anything? No. Now I was angry! I was so sure! What was I missing? Furiously I shook the bottle and yelled at it childishly, "Work! Work why don't you! Work! Arrgghh!!"

"What? No one ever taught you to blow bubbles?" My focus had been entirely on my failing experiment, and I had not seen Dan slip up behind me. Whirling around I angrily retorted, "Of course I know how to blow bubbles! Watch me!" Blowing into the freshly dipped bubble wand, we watched as the bubbles rose above our heads then slowly descended. Hundreds of tiny spheres – many more than last time – were popping as they landed on our heads and faces. It was crazy, like standing inside a bottle of fizzy drink. Without warning, we both began to laugh; every nerve ending tingled and I felt a wave of euphoria rising up and over us. Dan began swooping like a sea gull and whooping in glee, whilst I found myself running on the spot, giggling and squealing with delight. It was as if we were living in a *Sponge Bob Square Pants* episode, nothing was too silly and life was simply for living, no more and no less. I experienced wave after wave of joy, each wave bringing intense laughter soaked madness like never before, ribs aching and face wet with happy tears. The whole world was funny and every moment was deliciously blissful.

Giddy, I launched myself down the nearest grassy bank and straight into the huge flax bushes. Dan saw this as a new game, and 'flax jumping' became a work of art as we dived, tumbled, bombed and flew into bush after bush until I nearly wet my pants from laughing too hard. It seemed that everything we did was a game and everything was fun.

I wished it would go on forever, but as the effects slowly wore off we sat, not caring that it was almost dark and our butts were soaked in the early evening dew, contemplating what had just happened. I smiled a slow triumphant smile, one that belonged to an explorer who has just conquered the seemingly impossible, and turned to Dan who was staring at me with a bemused expression.

"What just happened?" he asked with only a hint of suspicion.

"I really can't tell you," I admitted, "except I think we might have just experienced Emospherica." My eyebrows knitted together, and I muttered to myself, "Was it because I shook the bottle? Did it stir up the particles and that motion then creates waves?"

"Huh?" said Dan. "This is an experiment to do with being a Reader?"

"Something like that, so thanks for being my guinea pig!"

"You experimented on me without my written consent?" He gasped in mock horror.

"Hang on a minute! I was happily experimenting on myself until you rudely interrupted, so don't complain! Now tell me, what did it feel like for you?"

He waited a minute before answering. "I just felt … happy. I came up the hill grumpy and annoyed that I had to chase you all the way up here to let you know that Ali and Arabella are going to be home later tonight, and ask if you needed anything specific from the shops, and then you blew the bubbles and I forgot all of that, forgot my tiredness, and felt all of a sudden like I could change the world, like I wanted to fly, like life is worth living. I can still feel it now; it's just gently fading."

I was scribbling furiously as he talked, and demanded, "Is that all?"

"Yeah, that's about it…other than it being like a belly aching bliss! Now take my hand as we head back to the house. Don't want you falling, and I know this hill backwards, even in the dark. Ooh!" he exclaimed as he took my hand, "the joy just spiked again."

I looked at him quizzically, searching for any sarcasm, but his eyes were just dancing with a remnant of joy. His hand was warm against my cold skin, and I was grateful for the connection. Even though the joy still lingered, I was not much of a fan of the dark.

11. IN TRAINING

THE GLOW FROM THE COTTAGE APPEARED AS A light in the darkness, warm and inviting, letting us know that Alistaire and Arabella must already be home. I felt eagerness at seeing them again, anxious to share my discovery and begin my training in earnest. There was so much I needed to know if I was to be a Reader. As we paused outside the door to wipe our shoes on the mat, Dan turned to me, still holding my hand.

"Jazz, I was wondering if..."

"Jasmine dear! Dan darling!" The door flung open and there stood Arabella, as exuberant and colorful as ever. I was guessing that she would light up any room she graced with her presence, and felt a faint rush of pride that we were related. I dropped Dan's hand and held out my arms.

"Dear Granny," I teased, "may I call you that just this once? I so missed you both. We both have, haven't we Dan?" I turned back towards him, and he was standing on the door step as if chagrined at being interrupted, but quickly transformed his expression into a rueful smile.

"That we have, Arabella, especially *your* cooking. If you're going to teach Jazz anything, I think it should involve cuisine lessons."

"My chocolate pudding is first class," I retorted

indignantly, stepping past him into the house then through to the lounge. Ali had already lit the fire and was playing some old-school jazz music, creating an upbeat ambience. The soft candlelight danced around the room, adding to the happy feel.

"Sit, sit!" encouraged Arabella. "We picked up some Thai takeaways, so dinner is served!"

Sitting casually in the living room and treating our taste buds, Arabella updated us on their trip to Auckland, interrupted occasionally by Ali.

"It's so nice to be in the wide open spaces again; the traffic and noise of Auckland drives one to despair, doesn't it Ali?"

Ali smiled. "That's priceless, coming from you honey, who always likes to be where the action is."

"But Ali," Arabella sounded surprised, "the action is right here with Jasmine. There is nowhere else I would rather be – except perhaps Milan or Paris," she chuckled a deep throaty chuckle, and we all found ourselves joining in. I wondered if the Emospheres were still wearing off.

"Anyway," Arabella continued, "after dropping the rental car off, we checked in on a couple of designers who we supply our merino wool to, and were shown their latest offerings, and I must say I was impressed! What they can do with our wool is astonishing. Preparation for fashion week is underway, and they're busily assembling their collections for next winter, in order to meet the northern hemisphere buyers. They offered me some samples, so I chose a couple with you in mind Jasmine. Hope you like them."

I did like them. The first was a gun-metal gray hooded mini dress, with a stenciled koru design offset to the right, and it reminded me of the earrings Dad had given me.

"You can wear it as a dress on its own, or over jeans as a long sweater," Arabella explained.

"It's so soft and light. Thank you," I said delightedly.

"And warm," added Ali. "The qualities of Merino wool just about border on the miraculous," he enthused. "Merino are a mountain sheep breed, and the wool fiber we produce from them breathes and regulates temperature, allowing moisture to escape. It is as fine and soft as cashmere; it won't itch you, and it won't shrink; plus it is very easy care and extremely durable."

The second item was a bulky winter jacket, which was lined with merino that had been woven into large black and blue checks, the exterior being black Gor-Tex with a tailored finish. It was so stylish I almost hesitated to try it on.

"It's OK," laughed Arabella. "In New Zealand the checks are associated with the woolly jackets farmers often wear. This is a modern take on an old theme – still rugged, but very fashionable!"

"And warm!" Ali repeated.

"I love it," I announced, leaning over to give them both a kiss.

There was one other small package Arabella handed to me. "This isn't just made from our wool, but is the result of a new venture with a friends' company, who is seeking to address the problem of wild possums in New Zealand."

"What are possums?" I queried.

Dan jumped in. "They're small furry marsupials – a bit like little hairy-tailed foxes, and are veracious eaters of our native flora and fauna. The Department of Conservation would love to eradicate them. Poisoning and trapping are the most common methods. They are a real pest; I hate them. They reckon there are around seventy million of them in New Zealand now, and they are a real threat to the kiwi, amongst other birds."

Ali continued: "This friend of ours, Gerard, has a huge native bush block not far from our farm in Southland, and he has been paying trappers per kilogram for the possum fur. Together we have developed a merino/possum/silk blend, which is being trialed in products like you are holding now."

I had removed the tissue paper, and underneath were some gorgeous green socks – or so I thought at first. "There are no feet in them,' I exclaimed, looking puzzled.

"That's because they're not socks for your feet, but for your hands. Look, you stick your thumbs through these holes at one end, and they sit on your hands and arms like the long end of a jersey, and your fingers are then free to move around." Arabella sounded quite enamored by them. I wasn't so sure.

"The possum fur is very soft," I started, "and the knitting is so fine. I love the texture and cable pattern, but I'm not sure how they'll stay on," I finished dubiously.

"But they're warm!" ended Ali and Dan together, and we all laughed again.

"Now," said Arabella as she opened a box of gourmet chocolates, "what has been happening here?"

Dan and I looked at one another, not sure where to start.

"We went surfing," Dan began.

"Dan got a puppy called Jack," I added.

Silence.

"That's nice Dan. Chocolate? Where is he?" Arabella seemed more interested in the chocolates – a woman after my own heart, I thought, taking one.

"Oh – I left him with my mate who owns the bitch. He's getting all the pups vaccinated tomorrow. And yes, Jack is chocolate."

Arabella looked up puzzled. "Huh? I meant would you like a chocolate ... to eat."

We all laughed again as Dan explained Jack's breed was Labrador and the color was known as "chocolate."

I had been waiting all night for the right words to explain my scientific success, but they weren't coming, so I finally blurted it out, half a chocolate still in my mouth.

"Emospheres!"

"I beg your pardon?" Ali responded politely.

"Ummm ... I think I've done it." I was mumbling, unsure of what to say next.

"Done what?" Arabella looked worried.

"You know, become a proper Reader; discovered the formula for emotional electricity, you know, 'Esmovoir' and all that ..." I petered out, as both Ali and Arabella were looking at me with shocked expressions. The room went very quiet.

"How do you know about the code word?" Ali half whispered.

"The code word?" Now I was puzzled.

"Esmovoir. That's what you said, wasn't it? You can't have heard it from us; we've been so careful ..."

"Oh," I breathed out, suddenly understanding the confusion. I hadn't told them about Levi and the package he had given me. I quickly showed them the ring and explained to them my journey with Levi up to Charlotte, leaving out bits here and there as I thought might be prudent, finishing at the point we had collected the parcel and then how I had given him the slip. Ali and Arabella looked slightly impressed at that. I could feel Dan's eyes on me, scrutinizing my face.

"Levi – that's the name you called out in your sleep the day I found you," he stated flatly.

I blushed. "Did I? Well, we had just traversed half a state together on a motorbike. I guess I was reliving the discomfort in my dreams."

He didn't look convinced. Arabella still looked worried. "But we don't know this Levi character. How do we know he's not a fake, that he didn't steal a real Carrier's identity? Jaggers sometimes do that. They are the ultimate deceivers."

I remembered reading about Jaggers in the dictionary. Weren't they the enemy of the Reader, determined to steal whatever discovery the Reader intended for good and use it for evil? Not Levi, surely.

"The only way we'd know for sure is if he kissed you on the lips," Ali mused, looking at me surreptitiously. Dan leaned forward to hear my answer.

"Why's that?" I innocently questioned, trying to sound nonchalant, but refusing to look Ali in the eye.

"Because the kiss of a Carrier to a Reader is the seal of the quest from the Council of CFR and it is always accompanied by a burning sensation for both Reader and Carrier, like the seal of hot wax on paper. The Carrier represents the wax, a symbol of secrecy, strength, and service, while the Reader is like the paper: the receiver, the blank canvas, where a fresh chapter of knowledge is recorded and sometimes even results in global deliverance. The kiss represents the fusing of Carrier and Reader, which are then forever bonded. It cannot be counterfeited, nor can it be imitated; and it will only happen the once. Perhaps the seal could possibly be broken by a Jagger with great evil powers, but that has never happened before – to my knowledge."

As he was talking, I was intensely aware of my lips, and it took all my self-control not to raise my hands and touch them. I was sure they must be pulsating, and their plumpness obvious to all, but some inner sense cautioned me from giving the truth just yet.

"Wow!" I tried to sound believable. "Guess that's the beginning of my training. Anyone for coffee?" And I walked through to the kitchen, only shaking on the inside, I hoped.

As I prepared the coffee, I tried to order my thoughts. Levi knew what he was doing! He knew he had to kiss me – that's why he said he would proceed with the task, and that I needed to trust him. I tried to ignore the part of me that was feeling maudlin over the fact that he kissed me because he had to, not because he wanted to; I had no time for boys anyway. Everything inside was all jumbled up, and although the tray of drinks I was carrying back to the lounge looked perfect, I couldn't think straight about anything else, so I decided avoidance would be the best option until I had time to order my thoughts.

"So how much do you know?" Ali restarted the conversation. I pulled out the two books that had been in the parcel from Levi, and showed them. "Well," Arabella said slowly. "This speeds up the training process. This Levi person either knows people in high places, or is an excellent thief. This information is privileged, and only available on special request. Have you read it all?"

"No, I was hoping to be able to go through it with you. I don't want to misinterpret what I read, and I want to be able to ask questions. I have had a quick flick, but that's all."

"Good. Good girl. We'll start tomorrow morning." Ali sounded decisive. "As for your discovery, now that we've cleared up the confusion, please fill us in. This could speed up time frames again."

I showed them my notes, and the small bottle labeled #3,

explaining that I had not expected to confirm my theory so quickly, but also shared how I had been working on such a possibility for months, both as part of a research study at school, and in my own time.

"I have always loved bubbles, their fragile membrane and delicate beauty, and they seemed symbolic to me of how tenuous our emotions are, and how we trap them inside of ourselves. I wanted to burst the bubbles, and instead of finding nothing, store within them an emotional energy that can transfer as electricity to others. I started with joy, because I think it has more purity than happiness. It is less selfish, less self-serving, and more altruistic."

"Have you trialed it?" Arabella asked curiously. Dan and I looked at each other, smiling at the not so distant memories.

"Dan helped me out," I couldn't help giggling, "He made a great sea-gull."

"Don't you mean guinea pig?" Dan questioned.

"No, you looked like a sea gull swooping and diving once the Emospheres hit you. It was so funny!"

"You can talk!" Dan retorted. "You acted like Tigger on steroids, bouncing up and down."

"We need a proper test," Ali mused, "a test all of us can observe to corroborate your results. You do realize, Jazz, that this must be kept top secret. You too Dan – NO ONE must know; not your mates, not your mom, not Levi." He looked over at me sternly. "If your findings are accurate, everything must speed up – your training, your mission – everything. You need to be prepared Jazz. I had thought we would have so much more time than this. Off to bed now; we start at first light. Dan, we won't require you until early evening – perhaps dinner time – does that fit in with your schedule?"

"Yep, I'm off duty for three days now, so it's all good." He hesitated. "By the way, I have an idea of where Jazz could test her bubbles. Our Northland Premier Rugby Team – which I play for," he glanced over at me to gage my reaction, "is playing in town next Saturday. Lately there have been some problems with fighting both on and off the field. If you guys came and watched, Jazz could use her bubbles to change the mood of the crowd if it gets ugly, and even the players, if they're close enough."

Ali looked thoughtful. "I suppose it's worth a go. It's going to be important to observe the results in crowds, to ascertain how powerful these Emospheres – is that what you call them? – are. You get us some tickets, Dan, and we'll be there."

I listened with interest. I had heard about rugby; Dad was always trying to get us interested. It was a crazy game, sort of similar to American football, but they play with no padding or helmets. It was nuts! Other than that, it was a mystery to me. I mentally noted to ask Dan to explain the rules to me before we went.

We all drifted off to bed, me thanking Ali and Arabella for their kind gifts again (it was going to take a bit of getting used to, this being spoiled by grandparents). Arabella patted my cheek and her eyes misted over.

"There is nothing we wouldn't do for you; you know that, don't you? Not just as your Framers, but as family. You are the most precious thing in our lives now."

"I know you are there for me, and I am glad that I came. Goodnight dear Arabella." Her cheek was soft as silk as I bent to kiss it, and she smelled like the early morning dew.

I found it difficult to sleep, my mind turning over and over, wondering who to trust, who to keep in the dark, and who to tell what to. Logically, my first loyalty should be to family, but I hadn't seen my grandparents in years, and I couldn't ask my Dad to verify everything they were telling me. Dan was part of the equation, but I still had no idea why Ali and Arabella wanted him around, other than to watch out for me. As for Levi, how could I not tell him? I pounded my pillow in frustration, realizing that although I felt excitement and a thrill at discovering Emospheres, life was likely now to be fraught with uncomfortable decision making. I needed to have a clear, firm direction, and stick by it.

The night ground on, black and murky like stale coffee, and my head pounded in overtired dismay. In an effort to quiet my mind, I listened intently to the sound of the waves. In the aftermath of the huge storm the world seemed at peace, all worn out from the effort and energy expended. A bit like me really. My eyes closed as I felt the first stage of sleep quietly slip up on me, and I relaxed into the floating sensation it bought to my busy brain.

CHHHAACHKKK! I instinctively sat bolt upright, knowing I had just heard the most terrible and frightening sound of my life. My heart beat like it wanted to fly out of my body, and a metallic taste swam around my mouth – so much saliva! I fumbled in the dark for one of the small glass bottles beside my bed and spat into it. I felt much better, but I must have been dreaming. I lay back against the pillows, willing my heart to slow. I would think of something happy ... I know, I would imagine I was on the back of Levi's motorbike.

WCHHHAUCKK! There it was again, sounding like a cat either possessed or high on meth. My mouth was utterly dry now, not a drop of moisture, and I almost gagged. I thought New Zealand had no dangerous animals, not even snakes! This was right outside my window. I yelled silently, absolutely petrified. My mind was telling me to go investigate, but my body was frozen in place, unable to move. I tried to raise the alarm, but only a croak escaped. Lying still with my heart thumping I could hear rustling in the bush outside, and wait! Was that a shadow? It looked like a huge catlike shape – maybe a wild cat? That's not so scary. THUMP! Now it was on the window ledge, I was sure of it. Had I latched the window? I desperately tried to remember, but was still unable to move and starting to feel sweat form all over my body. Could I get any more scared?

Watching the window, I was sure it was slowly opening, but my vision kept going in and out of focus. I squeezed my eyes shut, willing the fear to go away, when the noise came again, but this time louder and closer. I forced my eyes open, and found myself staring into a pair of evil, glowing red eyes, just meters away. In that instant I found my voice, screamed at the top of my lungs, and jumped out of bed to run from the room, but before I could reach the door I felt sharp stabbing pricks behind my legs and a solid mass pushing me forwards. The demon-like creature clawed its way up my back, and I fought in a frenzy of self-preservation, writhing and twisting to try and release its grip on me. The door to my room flung open, and Ali raced in swinging a pillow wildly, closely followed by Dan, who wrenched the animal from my back and ran from the house. We heard a whack! And then silence. My eyes were wild, and still feeling panic rising in my throat, I pushed Ali off as he tried to hug me, disoriented and unsure if the danger was over or not. Arabella arrived then, with a bowl of hot water and a towel, and with gentle shushing noises, she guided me back to the bed, helping me to lie on my stomach.

"It was a possum, dear, that's all. I know they sound like a chicken stuck in a blender, but they're usually quite harmless."

"Harmless?" I managed to squeak. "It's cut me to shreds, I'm sure. Ow! Ouch!" I moaned as Arabella pulled up my sweatshirt to assess the damage to my back.

Dan came back to the bedroom, panting slightly, and pronounced emphatically: "Dealt to the ugly critter. It's as dead as a door nail. Heck – are you alright, Jazz?"

"Do I look alright?" I snapped, looking at him murderously.

"The thing is; the possum probably thought you were a tree and went to run up you. Their eyesight is not very good and apparently they can mistake anything tall for an escape route."

"Small consolation," I spit back, the pain from the scratches was pure agony. "Now why don't you make like a tree and leave!"

"Jasmine Blade!" Arabella said in a shocked tone. "Dan has just rescued you – for the second time! The least you could say is thank you. Pain gives you no excuse to be rude!"

"It's alright, A," Dan replied. "I know she doesn't mean it. Better ask her when she had her last shots though; possums can be carriers of tetanus and tuberculosis." And with that he left the room.

I did feel kind of bad, but I was sick of being rescued – first the Foul Man at the Pit Stop, then the sting ray and now a possum. What was with my luck lately? I blinked back the tears; I missed home like crazy; it was so safe, so familiar, not like the territory I had entered into now, which was hazardous and unknown. Would life ever be the same again?

"Come on honey," murmured Ali, "it's a trip to A&E for you."

"What's A&E?" I muttered back, feeling chagrined.

"Accident and Emergency Department," he responded soothingly. "Let's get her into the car 'Bella. Can you walk at all, Jazz?"

I managed the walk out to the car and fell across the back seat, not wanting to rest my back against the leather. The pain in my heart was greater than the physical pain, and I wallowed in it, feeling utterly miserable.

Ali drove, and Arabella sat in the front beside him, slightly twisted around to keep an eye on me. She chatted about inconsequential stuff and nonsense, probably thinking it would keep my mind off the pain. But she didn't know the pain I was feeling, and I didn't even properly understand it myself. It was as if all the changes, all the drama, all the strange new people and places in my life, were all crushing down on me, creating desolation. Is this what independence feels like, I wondered?

As I lay there, caught up in my introspection, Arabella swiveled in her seat and waved something in front of my face.

"Your bottle of bubbles, sweetie. Might come in handy right now, do you think?"

I almost reluctantly grasped it, not sure I wanted a way out from the self-pity I was wallowing in, but I didn't want to let Arabella down. Blowing gently, I felt a foreign rush from deep within, a spark of joy I didn't know I had. Opening my eyes, I felt my lips unconsciously curve into a smile. Looking up I saw hundreds of tiny bubbles fizzing and popping, making their way over the front seat, Arabella stirring the spheres around the small space, making sure some hit Ali, a twinkle in her eye. After a few moments, Ali burst into song, lots of songs.

As I listened and almost joined in, I thought of all the wonder in my life: my awesome, loyal, and fun-filled family; my friends; new adventures; new people and places to love. All that I had seen as a negative just a few minutes ago suddenly became joyful opportunities to live, really live! And finding my Destiny – priceless! It might be tough living it, but boy was it going to be worth it.

It turned out that the scratches were just that: surface scratches, thanks to the thickness of Chad's sweatshirt and Dan's quick hands. The tetanus shot was essential, and the doctor praised Ali and Arabella on the quick action they had taken. I think he was a bit bemused by our happy personae after what should have been a traumatic and harrowing experience, but perhaps he was also relieved to meet a few optimistic patients. *The front line of medical practice must be a glum place to work*, I pondered as a nurse cleaned and covered my battle scars – *dealing with germs, maladies, and distressed people. Sickness and injury have a lot to answer for. Maybe Emospheres can have a medical application*, I thought; *prescribing joy in the midst of suffering – imagine the possibilities.*

We sang the whole way home in the car, and even though the Emosphere electricity was slowly wearing off, the placebo effect kicked in, and the journey seemed like minutes. Arabella insisted I took the sleeping tablets prescribed, and they worked too well. *No night visit to the desert for Jasmine Blade* I remember thinking with regret before deep dreamless sleep descended.

The following morning Dan had left the house before I got up, and I didn't get the chance to offer the apology I needed to make. When Arabella kindly bought me breakfast in bed, we had a granny/granddaughter chat, and I discovered that although she was all effervescence on the outside, there was a wealth of wisdom she had to share from inside her heart. She tactfully pointed out that the pile of apple cores I had distractedly placed on the window sill would have attracted the possum to my room, and I slunk down in the bed, feeling dreadful.

"Dan's set a possum trap outside your window before he left this morning, so there shouldn't be any more late night visitors." I think Arabella was trying to cheer me up, but it just made me feel worse. Why did Dan have to be so jolly nice all the time?

Ali obviously felt that the best cure for possum scratches was to distract me with work. Well, it wasn't really "work," more like a history lesson as to how the whole Reader thing came to exist. He sat on my bed, Arabella having insisted that I stay put, and to begin with, told me a story that went something like this:

"Once upon a time there was a little boy called Tarjeen, who lived in a place called Alehsa Oasis, when there were known to be lions in Arabia. The ancient palaces in Mesopotamia and the Fertile Crescent oasis paid tribute to the lion with many statues showing their strength and glory. The oasis was fertile and green, right in the middle of Saudi Arabia, with figs, apples, granade, and orange trees in abundance. One day Tarjeen was sent by the Chief to take a message to a neighboring village that a hungry and ferocious lion was roaming nearby. To get to the village, he had to cross a wide river, and rather than cross at the closest point and get wet, he went to where the villagers had placed stepping stones, and jumped across the river from rock to rock. Next, he had to traverse the briar patch, which had long sharp thorns. He did not want to get scratched by a thorn, so he balanced on top of the old fence posts that ran through the midst of the briars. Finally, he had to make it over the swamp forest, and he swung from vine to vine because he did not want to get stuck in the mud. It was two full hours before he arrived, only to find that one of the village children had been killed by the claws and teeth of the terrible lion.

Tarjeen felt dreadful! If only he could stop the lion, which he tracked in the direction of his own village. As he sprinted back towards the swamp forest, he frantically tried to think of a way he could stop the lion. He was so intent on running that he did not look where he was going, and ran straight into a British Army Captain, who had also heard about the lion and its marauding ways. This was divine intervention, thought Tarjeen; two heads are better than one! As they ran towards the swamp, Tarjeen got ready to swing from vine to vine. The Officer turned to him and said 'Don't waste your time, sonny boy! It will be much quicker to run straight through – I may not have a gun with me, but nature can provide us with all the weapons we require; we just have to search for them in the spaces that no one else bothers to look.' Tarjeen followed behind in the Officer's footsteps, which had sunk deep into the mud. As they came to the far edge of the swamp, the Officer smeared the mud all over his body, and grabbed a handful of mud, which he put in his pocket. He indicated for Tarjeen to do the same.

Next was the brutal briar patch, with its spiky thorns that tore at your flesh. The Officer didn't even hesitate, but ran straight through. Tarjeen paused for a moment, but as he heard no screams of pain, he proceeded into the briar patch to find that the coating of mud on his body protected him from the sharp spikes. They made very quick time through the briar patch, and before they went on, the Officer uprooted a medium-sized thorn bush, being careful to grip it right by the roots. He winked at Tarjeen, and the little boy wondered what the strange white man was thinking.

Keeping up the fast pace until they reached the river, Tarjeen stopped to recover his breath, but the Officer had rushed straight into the water, and carefully positioned the briar bush on the first stepping stone, betting on the fact that the lion, just like humans, would take the path of least resistance to reach the village, the scent of those yummy little children driving him on. He helped Tarjeen into the nearest thicket, and then climbed a little way up the tallest tree to spot the lion's approach. As soon as the lion came into sight, he jumped down and flung the mud from his pocket into the lion's eyes, and Tarjeen did the same. The lion could not see properly, and jumped forward into the river to wash the mud away, landing on the first stepping stone. The briar bush tangled into his mane and he roared in frustration and pain. Before he could free himself from the brambles, the Officer dived into the river, grabbed a stone from the river bed and bashed the lion's skull, knocking it into the river and downstream to the waterfall, never to be seen or heard again.

Tarjeen stared at the Officer with an open mouth, and then bowed down before him saying, 'Oh wise master, teach me your ways.'

The Officer replied, 'Have you ever been to the Wadi Rum and set your eyes upon The Seven Pillars of Wisdom?'

'No master,' replied Tarjeen, 'what is this Seven Pillars of Wisdom?'

'It is a wonder of nature, a rock formation that the great Lawrence of Arabia so named, and I am on a pilgrimage to seek not only the seven pillars of wisdom, but the truth that lies between.'

'May I join you on your quest, oh one-who-defeats-lions-with-wisdom?' Tarjeen asked humbly.

The Officer paused, looking grave. 'If you come with me, little one, your life will be changed forever, and you may never return to your village. I will wait for one hour on the path to Wadi Rum. If you are there, you are there; if not, life go well for you and farewell.'

Tarjeen ran and said goodbye to his mother and father, brothers and sisters, and the village Chief, saying, 'I will go with the one who outsmarted the king of all beasts, and I shall become wise – that is my Destiny!'

His family and village, who did not understand, but humored the little boy's imagination, said good bye, not realizing it would be the last time they would ever see Tarjeen again.

As the Officer and Tarjeen began their long walk, Tarjeen asked, 'Master, how did you know to defeat the lion?'

Smiling down at the little boy, he answered, 'People pass over the tools that are right in front of them. They fail to see the answers that lie in the spaces between objects in nature. I simply choose to live in those spaces, and I will continue to seek the knowledge that exists there, no matter how small or seemingly impossible it is to find.'"

"Wow." I looked over at Ali, unsure what to say. "So that Officer was the founder of the Order of Readers?"

"Ah..." replied Ali, "wrong. The Officer – no one ever found out what his name was – became known as the first Modern Framer, and Tarjeen was the first Modern Reader. The order is built upon the Seven Pillars of Wisdom, which originate in the Book of Proverbs in the Bible: Proverbs 9:1, to be exact. We will be teaching these to you, and they are to become the basis for all your decisions and actions from this time forth. The word "seven" in Hebrew is "shevah," which comes from the root word "savah," meaning to be full or satisfied. And because it means full and satisfied, it is, therefore, the number that symbolizes perfection."

"But what about the first Carrier? Who was that? Because isn't the Carrier the one who awakens the Reader? That's what the scroll I opened told me."

"You are very right, Jazz, and that part of the story is to come later. Right now comes lunch!"

I was surprised, lunch time already? "Didn't we just finish breakfast?"

"Time flies when you're having fun," Ali replied with a flourish. "Let's move this party to the kitchen."

In the kitchen Arabella had been at it again, and the most

delicious smell of fresh baking was wafting down the hallway as we opened the bedroom door. What was that smell? It wasn't even vaguely familiar, but it certainly was heavenly. I asked Arabella what it was as we entered the kitchen to the sight of a table groaning from the weight of the food laid out on it.

"It's feijoa, my dear. I'm guessing you don't find them too often in North Carolina? Here, take a look at one and tell me what you think." She threw one across at me and I held it up to my nose to breath in the scent. It resembled a cross between an elongated lime and a kiwi fruit, deep green in color. My nose expected a green sort of smell, but instead it provided a tropical mélange that evoked guava, strawberry, pineapple, and violet notes. "Yummy," I responded with a smile.

The feijoa shortcake was served on luscious green plates, with lashings of freshly whipped cream. I really felt I had died and gone to heaven, and was probably gaining pounds by the minute, but what the heck – it was worth it. I could run it off later anyway, and a little comfort eating to ease the discomfort from the possum scratches on my back was warranted, I figured.

We stayed at the dining table after lunch, as the afternoon sun was warm and friendly. Once the dishes were done and everything wiped down and put away, Ali continued with the lesson. As we dried the crockery, Arabella had asked me lots of questions about Levi, and I had realized how little I knew about him. It was obvious that she was less than impressed with his pedigree, and was concerned that I had spent so much time alone with him.

"Do your parents know he took you to Charlotte?"

"Ah, not exactly, but they do know Levi because of his association with Fale and Harley. It was a bit hard, Arabella, trying to find a way to get to the airport without raising any suspicions."

Arabella sighed. "I know; it's just that I worry about you. You need someone around to take care of you, and it's going to become even more crucial now you're in the Code of Readers."

"We'll discuss that later," chipped in Ali. "Now, let's get on with it; time is precious." Arabella bought over three steaming mugs and we sat, waiting for Ali to begin. "Now let's start with the Seven Pillars of Wisdom that the Officer based the Code of Readers on."

"Are they similar to the Precepts of a Reader?" I interjected, "because I know them off by heart."

"Um … no, Jazz, they are not. I am presuming the Precepts were included in the package from Levi?"

"Yes. It said to destroy them after committing them to memory, which I did. How do the Seven Pillars differ?"

"Well the Precepts are a summary of the Seven Pillars represented by the four jewels of a Reader: Space, Sagacity, Service, and Sanctity. If you notice in the ring Levi gave you, there are four tiny indentations. This is where each jewel is placed once the Council of CFR determines you have displayed the characteristics of each jewel adequately. The Seven Pillars, on the other hand, may equally be referred to as the Seven Foundation Stones, as they are the bedrock upon which all Readers, Carriers, and Framers must build. The Precepts simply reflect the heart of the Pillars." He cleared his throat as if preparing for a great speech, and continued: "Pillar One: Prudence. Prudence is a rather old fashioned word that personifies self-restraint and sound judgment, or shrewdness, if you like. A Reader needs to gain knowledge, which in turn enables them to discriminate between truth and error, becoming 'as wise as a serpent and as harmless as a dove.' They cannot afford to be naive. This shrewdness also assists them to find what is hidden in the spaces assigned to them – in your case *'esmovoir'*.

"Pillar Two: Knowledge and Discretion. The knowledge to aim for is simply knowing what is right, and then having the discretion to action it. The Hebrew word for discretion is 'mezimmah,' which roughly translates as 'the power to form plans.' A Reader who can reason and plan their actions towards their future direction will quickly achieve their quest because they are sagacious. In other words they show sound judgment and keen perception; they will not be tricked or fooled by Jaggers.

"Pillar Three: Fear of God. Fear, in this instance, means service to a higher calling and turning from evil – hating evil with a vengeance. Do you have any faith in God, Jasmine?" Ali paused to ask.

I looked at him thoughtfully. "These last few months it has seemed as if I have been guided towards my Destiny, and Levi said grace when we were at the Pit Stop. I have been using it ever since: 'for what we are about to receive, may the Lord make us truly thankful' – yes, I do believe I have a faith, or at least a seed of faith. Mom and Dad used to take us to church when we visited Mom's parents, and I definitely hate wrong doing and injustice. When I found that little boy all alone in the car, I was so angry and so sad at the same time."

"Good," he responded, "continue to explore that seed. Now an acronym for the seven pillars, which will help you remember them is: 'Please Keep Framers Code Secret UP.' Your job as you go for a run tonight is to figure out the remaining pillars, beginning with C, S, U, and P. Now, can you repeat the first three to me?"

I closed my eyes to focus. "Prudence, Knowledge and Discernment, and ... err … Fear of God. But do I possess any of these pillars?"

Ali smiled over at me. "I think you have the seeds of each of them in your heart, but it is up for you to find the source to water them, and before long, as you journey on in your quest, they will begin to grow."

I didn't go for a run that night, only a walk, as my back and legs felt slightly stiff, and the scratches were pulling at the edges. Unnecessary pain was not on my agenda. Dan accompanied me, which gave me a chance to apologize without any interruptions, although he wouldn't really let me when I tried.

"Sheesh, Jazz, you were totally out of it; I don't blame you for snapping at me."

"But I am sorry," I persisted, "and I need to thank you for rescuing me – again."

"Yeah; guess it's becoming a bit of a habit." He grinned as he picked up a small stone and skimmed it across the steady water. I pushed him, and he feigned a stumble, laughing at me.

Stopping to pick up a couple of cool shells, I abstractly

asked him about the rules of rugby. "I don't want to seem like a total moron when we're at the game, and Dad's never really told us anything other than that it is known as the national sport of New Zealand, and that the kiwi team 'The All Blacks' are considered the best in the world."

It was the right question to ask, and for the next half an hour I didn't have to say anything at all, as Dan waxed lyrical about the wonders of rugby, the intricacies of the rules, the position he played and what to watch out for during a game. All I could remember afterwards was that he wore a jersey with the number 15 on it, which meant he played full back, and that the aim of the game was to get the ball over the opposition's try line, which gave your team five points. Other than that, it sounded like one big bun fight full of running, tackling, and something called "scrums." But I did end up with a lovely collection of shells. One in particular, a perfect pink Paua or abalone, nestled nicely in the palm of my hand and shone with unusual hues of shimmering pink, cream, and a hint of blue.

"...and so," Dan seemed to be finishing up, "Northland is about fifth on the Points Table, which is really good for us, so Saturday's game against Auckland is very important. It's a must win."

I tried to look as if I understood, and nodded intelligently. "So it's really quite similar to football then," I stated.

He groaned in exasperation. "Jazz, I've just been telling you how different it is from the football you play in America. Weren't you listening at all?"

"Of course I was. The balls are both oval, aren't they? And you play on a grassy rectangular-shaped field? It's a whole lot of boys and testosterone chasing each other? Sounds very similar if you ask me." I glanced over at him, an impish twinkle in my eye, and began sprinting the final one hundred yards to the house. Dan overtook me in the first ten.

"Ouch! Ouch, ouch, ouch!" I yelled, having momentarily forgotten about my war wounds. I had also forgotten that I was supposed to figure out the last four pillars of wisdom, so I had an extra-long shower before dinner and pondered under the comfort of the soothing warm water. But Ali had different plans for the evening, and spent the night in cahoots with Arabella until around 9.30pm, when they joined Dan and me in the lounge, looking very serious.

Arabella perched on the edge of the wing-back chair and looked over at me with sad eyes. I had my nose in one of three little booklets Alistaire had given me on each of the first three pillars, and was revising each of them in turn, when I looked up to find them both staring at me.

"What?' I pronounced, wondering if I had done something wrong.

Arabella sighed. "Sit up, darling. It's the CFR Council; they've asked to meet with you. In ten days."

I quickly made myself vertical and asked with interest, "Meet me here?"

"No," Ali pursed his lips, "back in the U.S., which leaves us only just over a week to complete your orientation as a Reader. It's expecting too much."

"They don't know that you've deciphered Esmovoir yet," continued Arabella. "I think they want to have more input into your training, and have you in a place where they can monitor your progress."

"That Vander is far too preoccupied with control and dictatorial edicts," Ali grumbled. "He doesn't want to move into the twenty-first century and recognize that a global village is at our fingertips and distance is immaterial. In fact, it could almost be to our advantage."

Arabella patted his hand. "We've been over this, Ali, and there's nothing we can do." She turned to face me, and looked from me to Dan and back again. "We have decided to send you to Emerald Isle," she transferred her gaze to Dan again, "to visit your father, Dan, and we want to ask you to accompany Jazz, as her bodyguard." We both looked at Arabella in stunned silence, letting the information sink in before the questions poured out in rushing torrents.

"Why Dan's father?" (Me)

"You want me to go?" (Dan)
"A bodyguard?" (Me)
"When do we go?"(Dan)
"Who is Vander?"(Me)
"A bodyguard?" (Me again)
"Why my dad?" (Dan)

"Whoah! Steady on! One at a time." Ali settled himself more comfortably and crossed his lean legs in their tan drill trousers before replying.

"Arabella and I have known your dad, Neville, for years, Dan. In fact, you may not know this, but he is a Carrier himself." Dan started to say something but then stopped himself as Ali raised a finger and continued, looking over at me. "Neville was the Carrier who visited you on that day back when you were two years old, Jazz; as a representative of the CFR. It is he who was assigned to your quest, and has carried a gift for you all these years. I'm sure that if he were still here in New Zealand, the CFR would not be so intent on dragging you back across the globe, but Vander feels that Neville's location at present is more important than yours, Jasmine, so the decision has been made."

"But who is this Vander? And why is Neville's location important?" I interjected, ignoring Ali's hand gesturing me to wait.

Dan joined in. "My dad's involved in all this crazy sci-fi stuff? But he's so ... so..."

"Exactly," smiled Arabella. "That's why he's so good at what he does. He has carried another Reader in the past, and is very well prepared to receive Jasmine – with the added bonus of seeing his son again. Plus it gives a great cover for you, Jazz, visiting your boyfriend's father."

"My what?" I spluttered, almost falling off the couch.

"Your boyfriend." Arabella said with a cheerful matter-of-factness. "You never know when a Jagger is on the prowl, and we can't afford to take any chances, especially now you have the power to create Emospheres."

Dan had a silly grin on his face and I glared at him.

"Don't you dare agree, Dan. This is a dumb idea!"

"Actually, Jazz," he began, straightening up in his chair and adopting an adult voice, "the idea does have merit you know. It means I can stick close by you and no one will get suspicious, and Dad," he slumped a bit, "will have to behave himself around you." I raised my eyebrows at that. "He's a bit of an extroverted ladies' man," he added apologetically.

"Oh, great," I exclaimed, jumping to my feet and pacing the small square of carpet between us. "So I'm supposed to just take all of this lying down?"

"Ah, you're standing, Jazz." Dan's timing was way out.

"I should have a say in all of this!" I vented. "After all, I am the Reader here, not you. I do not want to stay with Dan's loose cannon father; nor do I want to play silly games!"

Ali crossed his arms as well as his legs. "But you do want to return to America the week after next?"

I wheeled around and glared at Ali now, feeling furious. "Yes, of course I do; it is my home, after all."

Ali's voice was quiet. "Well, that's the conditions then, it's this way or no way."

"But I thought the CFR wanted to meet with me? What would you say to them?"

"Oh probably that you're just not up to it, that you're a bit frail."

"Me? Frail?" The speed of my pace had increased. "I'm not frail, and I will be ready!"

"Even if it means dealing with gnarly Neville and a fake boyfriend?" Arabella pressed me.

I stuck my chin out. "I'm up for it if you are," I said, looking at Dan with a challenge in my eye, "on one condition."

"What's that?" Ali and Arabella asked in unison.

"That I get to stay at the beach house my mom inherited from her parents. It's somewhere near Emerald Isle. And that Chad, my brother, stays with me rather than Dan. Chad works in the area, so that shouldn't be a problem. Besides," I added with heavy sarcasm, "we wouldn't want anyone to think we were behaving improperly now, would we Dan darling?"

Ali stared at me thoughtfully. "I think we could make that work," he replied slowly. "Now sit down, Jazz, you're making us all feel tired – unless of course you're offering to get drinks?"

"Drinks it is." I huffed loudly, and without waiting for a reply I raced to the kitchen, unable to stop my heart from beating "Levi! Levi! Levi!"

Levi's name must have continued to pound in my brain, because as I slept I found myself in the desert once again. Levi sat in the shade of a boulder and I sank down beside him to escape the suns heat.

"It worked! You were right! The ring showed me the missing element of the equation and I tested the bubbles and joy just exploded when I blew them – it was amazing; so powerful; crazy…" I babbled on and on, caught up in the excitement of sharing, but when I turned to smile at him, he was fading from sight.

"No, don't wake up! Not yet! So much more to tell you…" I heard myself saying as I woke feeling frustrated. I hadn't even let him say a word - when will I learn to shut-up??? We really need to coordinate the time difference in our sleep patterns…

12. TESTING

I RAN AND RAN THE NEXT MORNING, TRYING TO PUT as much space between my mind and the alternate reality from the previous night. As I settled into a steady pace, I felt the familiar sense of well-being that came from a healthy habit, and my thoughts turned in a more constructive direction. A week was not long, and I wanted to be as prepared as possible before I came face to face with the CFR. I spent some more time pondering on what the last four pillars of wisdom might be, knowing that Ali would be asking me on my return.

I also wanted to produce a second vial of joy Emospheres to test their validity on a second sample, and then begin creating mixes for other emotions. The thought had occurred to me when I was clearing up my room after the possum incident, and found the specimen of saliva I had spit during my episode of fear. Combining this with a sliver of fabric from the sweaty sheets, I was hoping to use these physical manifestations from my night of terror to create Emospheres that would imitate my fear. It could be a useful weapon in the midst of a battle against a Jagger, I mused. Not that I had any idea what such a battle would look like! Today I also needed to collect some more buds and leaves from the strange plant I had found under the deck. Perhaps I would try to make oil from them to transport back to the States. I would need it to create a range of Emospheres. I wondered what it was called. It kind of smelt like jasmine, but its leaves were a strange red underneath, and the buds dark purple. I would name it 'Destiny', I decided as I shook my head and adjusted my pace, 'the Destiny of Jasmine Blade'. Turning up my iPod for the long run home I repeated it over and over: The Destiny of Jasmine Blade, the Destiny of Jasmine Blade, almost like I could speak it into being. If I was on the cusp of discovering my life purpose, there was no way I would let it slip away.

As I suspected, Ali did want to get down to business immediately. Arabella and Dan had disappeared into town to book air flights and make other arrangements. Dan would be late home as he had a tough schedule of rugby trainings this week.

"So, Jazz," Ali began, barely giving me a chance to finish my warm down stretches, "any ideas on those four remaining pillars of wisdom?"

"Well, I think the fourth pillar might have something to do with maybe getting advice or support; maybe Community? Fifth pillar: I have no idea really, possibly Secrecy? Sixth pillar: that could be Understanding. We need to understand why we are doing what we're doing. And the seventh I thought could be either Protection or Patience." I was still a little out of breath, and my answers were interspersed with pauses as I gulped down mouthfuls of fresh air. Ali handed me a glass of cold water, which I drank gratefully before adding, "Am I close?"

"Not too bad at all; definitely warm, but could be hotter. Join me in the lounge as soon as you can."

The rest of the day was like a speed course in wisdom, if that's possible. "You were on the right track with Pillar Four when you mentioned getting advice. Pillar Four is C for 'Counsel' – meaning not only to offer wise advice to those around you, but to seek guidance and wise counsel from others that you trust, such as your Framers and Carrier. It is a foolish Reader that walks only in her own judgment."

"But you and Arabella won't be there when I return to the States."

"We're only a phone call away," Ali reassured me.

"What about Dan," I continued. "Do I trust him? Ask for his advice?"

"Dan will be as faithful as that Labrador pup of his; we Framers have a great sense in character judgment, and Dan is completely trustworthy according to us, but, as the Reader, it will be up to you to discern for yourself and determine what and how much you tell him or ask for his opinion."

I nodded, sensing the wisdom in this. After all, wasn't I already using discretion in terms of how much I revealed? I still had told no one about Levi's kiss, and intended to keep it that way until I knew the time was right. Right now I aimed to do all the listening, rather than the talking, and discern from the knowledge and counsel I gathered who to place my full trust in.

"Pillar Five!" Ali's sergeant major tone ended my reverie and bought my wandering mind back to the lesson at hand.

"Err ... 'S'... ummm ... no idea, really, other than 'Secrecy'," I admitted.

"No!' Barked Ali. "The 'S' stands for 'Sound Wisdom,' which is the outworking of Pillars One through Four. A Reader needs to exercise wisdom in their day-to-day living, not just to become wise, but to *do* wisdom – turn it into a verb – practice using sound judgment on a daily basis," he slapped my hand away from Arabella's chocolate box, "including wise eating!"

I screwed up my nose ruefully and sighed. "Nothing like starting straight away."

"That's my girl," Ali rejoined, throwing me an apple from the bowl beside him. "You were spot on with the Sixth Pillar though: 'U' for 'Understanding.' A Reader needs to 'stand under' the pillars of wisdom, truly understanding them, their instruction and application. Seek not to just *know* what is good and evil, but to *understand* why it is so. This way the pillars will protect and shield you because you are not just familiar with them in theory, but in reality. Knowing and understanding are two very different things – can you see that Jazz?"

I frowned. "Yes, I think so. It's like Emospheres: I can know all the theory of the principals of science involved, but it's not until I actually understand the mechanism of emotion that I can create the vital link to make them work. It's like thinking with both the head and the heart – is that right?"

"Yes, yes!" Ali enthused. "Spot on! The head is technical and *knows* truth and goodness, but it is the heart that *understands* the vitality of truth and the gravity of the battle between good and evil. The head will think, but the heart will discern. The two exercised together are a powerful force, which brings us to the final Pillar: 'P' for 'Power.' Power is both the simplest and most profound of all the pillars, and needs no explanation." I looked puzzled. "Go on," urged Ali, "see if you can figure it out."

We sat in silence for a few minutes, before my head and my heart synced, and I knew the answer: "It's because if you gain the wisdom of the first six pillars, the power of the seventh comes naturally: you are strong and fortified with wisdom."

"Bingo!" cried Ali. "The seventh is the pillar that many seek but few attain. Most try to shortcut their way to power, but there isn't a shortcut. Wisdom is a path that has no deviations from truth, and the end does not justify the means."

And so we spent the rest of the day discussing truth and wisdom and other esoteric subject matter. I found it stimulated my brain, and I wondered about the culture we were creating in the Western world – one of shallow pursuits and selfish causes; but I couldn't bring myself to look closely at my own life. Was I selfish? Was I shallow? These questions I set aside to ponder; right now I let myself soak in the noble offerings before me, hoping some small token might take root and grow.

Exercising the brain while engaging the heart is a wearying pursuit, and I slept long and hard in preparation for the following day. Each night I spent at least a few moments with Levi in the desert, updating him as fast as I could, but there was never enough time before one of us would begin to fade out of the picture. It seemed to be a series of frustrating and unfinished dreams.

In contrast to the nights, every day that week was the same: early morning run, Ali and/or Arabella waiting by the door, lessons in the lounge, absorbing information, asking questions, debating, and reasoning. By Thursday I felt I was gorged on the diet of a Reader, and was ready for some time out. Dan suggested he take me to town with him to pick up the airline tickets and choose some gifts to take over for our families at the same time. Arabella chipped in to say it would be a great chance for Dan and me to hang out properly, and nudged Ali in the ribs when he started protesting.

And so off we went for a couple of hours: me feeling like a silly schoolgirl who has finally been granted a pass from the boarding hostel to visit the local town; Dan happy to play tour guide and chauffeur. I had dressed up for the occasion, wearing my new merino dress. Arabella had a spare pair of tights, and I borrowed her long sheepskin boots to make up for the shortness of the dress.

Dan whistled appreciatively, commenting: "She does scrub up nicely for a first date. Looking good, Jazz, looking good!"

"Nice to see you out of your board shorts, too. I thought they were a permanent fixture!" I joked in reply, slightly embarrassed and wondering if I should have stuck to the jeans option. Once in the car I turned the radio up loud, and it felt nice to be in touch with the outside world again.

Whangarei is New Zealand's warmest and northernmost city, and is nestled amongst one hundred or so superb beaches and some very romantic countryside. With a population of over forty thousand, it is big enough boast some good shopping, art galleries, and cafés, and, Dan elaborated, I had the added bonus of visiting with a local who knew all the best places to go.

I hadn't spent any of the birthday money I had bought with me, and my fingers were itching to begin. When it came to shopping, perhaps I was shallow; I didn't hanker to go to the mall back home, but when given the opportunity I loved to spend. In the end I found something for everyone, except Levi. I picked out some gorgeous Paua earrings for Elle, and asked the jeweler for some black twine to thread through the shell I had found on the beach. Tying it around my neck then and there, it nestled in the hollow of my throat, and I felt like I never wanted to take it off.

Even Dan commented. "Wow! That is an awesome Paua, Jazz – just a baby one, but perfect – you were lucky to find it." He cocked his head to one side and looked at me speculatively. "It suits your beauty, you know – sort of wild and free."

I blushed in response. "Wild and crazy, don't you mean?" I turned away and brushed off the compliment with a toss of my hair. "Anyhow, have you found anything for your dad yet?"

Dan leaned against the wall of the shop and his eyes were sad. "I don't think Dad would want anything that reminded him of New Zealand. When he left he said he never wanted to return; that New Zealand was a pimple on the world's bottom, actually." He smiled briefly. "Or something like that."

I was horrified. I could never imagine turning my back on my birth place. "Maybe you could get him a bar of soap?"

"Why?"

"So he can use it to wash his mouth out," I replied caustically.

"Ah – he's not that bad," Dan protested. "He was just bitter at the time he left – about all sorts of things."

"What about some favorite candy or something; it might sweeten him up." I was starting to make up my mind that I wouldn't like Neville very much.

"Candy?" Dan questioned. "Oh, you mean *lollies*. Not a bad idea actually; he does have a sweet tooth. Come on; time to educate you with a trip to the local dairy."

So Dan took me to candy heaven, a shop called a "dairy" that sold everything you could imagine, but seemed to specialize in "lollies" or "sweets" as they call them in New Zealand. You could select your own mixtures including jelly jet planes, tiny "milk bottles," spearmint leaves, tingles, jubes, Jaffa's (orange candy-covered chocolate balls), jelly snakes, and sour squirms, just to name a few. Sound judgment went out the window, and we both came out with a big bag each, full to the brim of sugary delights. We walked and ate our way down to the Whangarei waterfront, where the myriad of boats moored for the winter made a colorful sight. It didn't feel particularly cold – kiwis didn't refer to Whangarei as the "winterless north" for nothing.

There were a few small stalls set up along the pier, and I slowed to take a look, whilst Dan walked down the wharf to see if the determined fishermen were getting any bites. An elderly Maori woman sat on a small stool beside a display of jewelry, and I couldn't help but stare at the elegant spiral tattoo chiseled into her chin. Not wanting to appear rude, I politely asked the significance of the tattoo.

"This is my Moko; it tells the story of my lineage, my heritage, which is rich and varied and so I wear it with pride. You are interested in a carving?"

I tore my eyes from the story of her face and looked down at the display board, which was covered in necklace pendants made from whale bone and a rich dull green stone, also known as jade, *Pounamu*, or just greenstone, the old lady explained. My eye was drawn to one in particular, a smooth, milky white pendant with soft flowing lines. It felt warm and silky to touch, yet the finish was like polished glass, and in my hand it felt as if it were an extension of my body.

"Wise choice," stated the wizened old woman. "It is a piece of Maori art that stylizes the '*Pitau*,' which is symbolic of unity. The shape is representative of the '*Patu*,' a Maori weapon signifying strength."

It was not cheap, but in my mind I could picture it around Levi's neck, and knew without a doubt that he would love it. Plus, the symbol of unity seemed fitting, and I liked the black flax woven adjustable cord – simple and understated.

A tiny pair of crinkly eyes looked into mine as I took the small package and paid the money. "Be blessed, my child," came the ancient voice, "be at peace with yourself, your creator, and your Destiny. Give this to the one who completes you. It is written in the stars. Read them and see."

I nodded my head, and for a moment our eyes spoke to one another wordlessly, one culture to another, two souls connecting on a level that can only be described as spiritual. I heard Dan call me, saying it was time to move on, and with one last smile and nod of my head the old woman and I parted ways, but, I thought to myself, her face and words will always remain with me, drawing me further into my Destiny.

We drove back to Kauri Mountain laughing and joking, sharing stories of high school pranks and childhood memories, until Dan leaned over and turned up the radio.

"Wait! I love this song!" he said.

Here we go again, I thought. I would recognize that voice anywhere, and as we drove along the unsealed roads back to the beach house, the gravel tone that defined Levi blared out over the airwaves, with Dan singing along at the top of his lungs, "First time I saw you, I swear I knew you..."

I closed my eyes and he was there; I opened them and he was gone, so I kept them open, staring at the lush countryside without seeing and trying not to feel whatever it was I was feeling. As the song drew to a close Dan turned the radio down.

"They are so awesome. Top of the charts this week, climbing the ladder of success faster than you can say Dan is the Man. Ever heard of them – Alien Potion?"

"Umm … yeah ... I have ... heard of them. Never thought I'd hear them down-under though."

"That guy can really sing. Wonder if he writes the songs too?" Dan mused, partly to himself. I declined to answer, not wanting to give anything away. I guessed Dan would find out soon enough. Alien Potion! The tour must really be big time for them to be getting international airplay. I wondered what I would find on my return. Would Levi even want to be my Carrier anymore?

Later the next morning I pressed Ali for the rest of the story about Tarjeen, and how he became the first in the order of Readers.

"Recite to me the Seven Pillars of Wisdom, and it shall be." I smiled at Ali's melodramatic act, but rattled them off, having spent so much time during my runs going over them in my head, that I could recite them backwards if he wanted. "Very good. Now where were we in the story? Let me think ..."

"The Officer and Tarjeen were setting out on the road to Wadi Rum, to visit the Seven Pillars of Wisdom," I prompted, as I curled up on the sofa, clutching a retro cushion made from an old woolen blanket, wrapping my arms around it for warmth and comfort. Ali leaned back in the old wingback chair and placing his feet up on the ottoman began to tell the tale, leading me into a distant and foreign world.

'Now from the Oasis Al-Ahsa, which is sixty kilometers inland from the Persian Gulf in the region of Qatar, it is nine-hundred miles to Afqaba in Jordan, where the Wadi Rum and the Seven Pillars are located. The journey was long and arduous, and Tarjeen learned many lessons in the six weeks it took to get there. The Officer taught him the significance of the Seven Pillars of Wisdom, and told him great tales of Lawrence of Arabia and his pursuits in the desert. Tarjeen asked questions incessantly and soaked up the answers like a thirsty sponge. He particularly loved to hear stories of the lands beyond Arabia, and even beyond Jordan, far away across distant seas. During those six weeks Tajeen became strong and resourceful, finding water where it appeared there was none and hunting even the smallest prey for food. And so it was that they taught each other: the Officer instructing in the way of the heart and the mind, Tarjeen teaching skills of survival and physical prowess.

There are many legends that remain from that historic journey, which in time will be told to you; but for now you only need know that they arrived at Wadi Rum on the back of all their adventures, strong and in unity with one another. One man from the Western world, one boy from the East – a strength of unity compounded by their distinctive world views and the high esteem in which they now held each other.

As they stood before those mighty pillars of rock, silently contemplating the awesome stature and presence of nature, a figure emerged from between the first two pillars. Standing like a rock himself, he bellowed: 'Are you one who comes to seek wisdom?'

The Officer nudged Tarjeen, indicating he should step forward and respond, whispering from behind what he should say:

'I am here to understand the wisdom of the Seven Pillars and to receive the gift that comes to those that search for wisdom.'

The figure fell to his knees and began to sob. Tarjeen and the Officer raced over, fearing for the man's sanity. He looked up at them with a tear-streaked face.

'For fifteen years I have waited to hear those words,' he said, 'and

this morning I told myself "one more day, one more day of waiting and then I shall return to my Master with the sad news – the stars were wrong – there is to be no New Order of Readers." And today you have come!'

He jumped up now, and began dancing around in jubilation 'Halleluiah! Halleluiah!' The loud cries of joy echoed off the pillars and it seemed as if a whole choir was shouting along with him. By this time it was getting dark, so the Officer and Tarjeen quietly went about preparing a fire to sit by. The crazy man insisted he provide the food, and disappeared behind a series of smaller rocks, reappearing soon after with dates, figs, and dried meat. As they ate, the stars came out and the man, named Tamul, revealed his master's wishes.

'I am a servant of the great House of Al-Bashar. My Master is an inventor par-excellence and his dream is to build sun-powered cells in the Arabian Desert, turning the sands around us into a lush paradise. But, on receiving several death threats he visited this place on a spiritual pilgrimage nigh on fifteen years ago, and was led to discover a box that was buried at the foot of the Seven Pillars. In that box was the history of a secret order that had existed since the beginning of time. And that night, the very stars we see above us now displayed a message saying that seventy new stars would be born, and each would take an invention that my master could only dream of inventing, and thus if his life was cut short, there were others who would continue his genius.'

The servant Tamul paused and dramatically scooped up a handful of sand, letting it sift between his fingers. 'From the iron in this very sand, Al-Bashar forged seventy rings and left them for seventy days on a solar sheet, moving them each day between the Pillars of Wisdom. Infusing each ring with the power of the sun and the power of his mind, he then wrote the precepts for those who were chosen by the stars to receive the rings to read – thereby calling them "Readers." The rings were then scattered throughout the globe that no race may claim superior knowledge over others, and Destiny was left to distribute them, according to the will of God. Once destined, each Reader will subconsciously explore the spaces between the sun, the stars, and Al-Sabah's stored energy to discover the quest assigned to each of them. You are, I believe, to be the first Reader, and your acceptance will bring about a new order, a new Council of Carriers, Framers, and Readers. I therefore offer you this ring and this scroll. May God bless you in your every endeavor for truth.'

He then turned to the Officer and continued. 'You have given the

Reader the framework he needs to keep the Seven Pillars of Wisdom, and therefore you shall be known as the first Framer, according to ancient tradition. And I have fulfilled my master's wishes, and passed on the gift to the Reader, therefore I am the first Carrier.' He paused again for effect. 'We three, then, begin this new tradition, one where the world will see that which is considered magic become science; that which is miraculous become fact; that which is eternal truth become reality. Amen.'

Ali stopped talking and we sat quietly, as I was trying to take it all in. Tarjeen was so vivid in my mind and I wondered what it was he had read, what space he had discovered. I had so many questions again. If there were only to be seventy Readers, how many had been already? How were Carriers and Framers chosen? Was my ring one of the rings Tamul was talking about? What had happened to the House of Al-Bashar?

Arabella interrupted my reverie with the arrival of lunch, and as we ate I pressed both her and Ali for the answers to my questions.

"Tarjeen kept working in the desert, with help from the House of Al-Bashar. He was fascinated with sand, the spaces between the particles and the effects of the sunlight on them. Unfortunately, Tamul's Master was tragically killed in a 'car accident' in the United States. There are many of us who believe it was no accident, but the work of Jaggers. The House of Al-Bashar lives on and is very rich and powerful – they still support the work of the CFR around the world."

I shuddered. "So what was Tarjeen's quest? And did he succeed?" I pushed on with my questions, taking a handful of grapes.

Arabella continued. "As Tarjeen stood between the pillars of Wisdom one day during a sandstorm, he observed the sand particles dancing in the air, twinkling like little lights, and in the spaces he saw electrical charges. His quest was to harness the electrical energy of the sand, which was extremely important for military application during the Second World War. The full implications of his discoveries have never been released, due to the impact they would have on the international oil economy."

"So, if Tarjeen was the first Reader, what number am I?"

"You, dear Jasmine," Arabella replied over the top of her teacup, "you are the seventieth; the last."

I must have looked shocked, because Ali reached out and took my hand. "Nothing to worry about, dear. The stars are still in control under the hand of the Almighty."

I gingerly smiled back at him. "And my ring, then, it's the real deal?"

"That it is; that it is." I looked down at it, warm and smooth on my finger. It seemed to suddenly take on a new glow. "Levi," I said absently. "Levi had a ring too. Where do Carriers' rings come from?"

Arabella and Ali looked at each other. "I've never heard of a Carrier's ring before," Ali said slowly. "Are you sure?"

"Um ... well, he definitely wore a ring; I'm not sure how similar it was. Anyway, how are Carriers and Framers chosen?" I pushed my plate away, no longer hungry.

Ali took another bite of his apple. "Each Framer and Carrier over the years has been guided to an apprentice to train up in the precepts – information, other than the original scroll, which is copied and given, is passed on by oral tradition – stories and instructions that must be memorized. They may choose to train more than one Carrier or Framer, which ensures a network of support for the Reader and also provides protection from Jaggers, helping keep the whereabouts of a Reader under wraps."

I looked over at them both, dubiously. "These Jaggers then, how worried do I need to be about them?"

"Not at all, not at all," Ali replied far too quickly, jumping up to clear the table.

"You have the truth on your side," Arabella gently added. "Stick to the precepts, and the power you require to overcome any Jagger will be there when you need it."

"Now," busied Ali from the kitchen, "are we all set for our Emosphere testing tomorrow? The game is at 5pm, so that gives you time to pack your things. I take it you have arranged to use your parent's batch? You fly out lunch time on Sunday, you know."

“All good to go,” I responded, folding my arms and wondering at Ali’s sudden and hurried clean up and semi-frantic actions. “I spoke to Mom and Dad the other night, and they’re going to meet us at the house. They’ll also send someone to pick us up from the airport.”

“Well then,” replied Ali, finally stopping to look at me, “we are on track.”

The rest of the day was a whirl of packing, cleaning, and revising all the information I had gathered to date: careful filing of all my notes and materials for Emospheres, and sending text messages out to family and friends from the top of the hill.

Lastly I packed the precious bottle of oil I had extracted from the ’Destiny’ vine under the verandah. Only a few drops seemed to be needed in each bubble mix so it should last a lifetime, but its value could not be underestimated. I wrapped it in bubble-paper, and added it to my hand luggage. I would tell no one – not anyone at all – about the plant. I was sure it had grown from the pool of my blood when I was two years old, and Destiny had nurtured it all these years for me to find – to stumble across it like that was no accident.

Dan was grumpy the morning of the big match, and I figured pre-game nerves were kicking in.

“Hey Dan,” I threw at him, “you heard about the rugby player who went to the doctor and said, ‘Hey Doctor, every morning when I get up and look in the mirror I feel like throwing up. What’s wrong with me?’ The doctor replied: “I don’t know, but your eyesight is perfect!” Ha-ha – you get it?”

He looked at me with murderous eyes. “Are you this annoying to your brothers?”

“Guess you’ll have to ask them when you meet them,” I teased.

“Guess I will. Now make yourself useful and fetch me some more toast, eh?”

“Toast it is, O Great-Strong-Rugby-Player! Don’t forget to wave to me during the game, ok?”

He rolled his eyes at me. “As if, Jazz. I will be totally focused on the game, alright, so don’t distract me!”

"Okey dokey, Danny," I replied meekly, laying it on as thick as I knew how.

"Right, you!" He grabbed me from behind and tickled me till I screamed for mercy, then left me in a giggling heap on the floor and walked out the door, laughing, his bad mood forgotten. Job done, I thought. Good luck Dan and the team!

The night was fairly mild and the sky was slowly darkening as we approached Okara Park, home of Northland Rugby, and anticipation hung heavily in the air. Vehicles were parking wherever they could find a spare space, pulling up on grass verges and empty commercial parking lots. It seemed like the whole town had come out of the woodwork, and we crawled along trying not to crash into any punters while keeping our eyes peeled for a park. Ali finally found one right beside a tow truck company, where a big rubbish skip sat in the driveway. He parked right in front of it commenting, "Well, they won't have to tow us far if they want access to their waste bin!"

It wasn't too far to walk to the stadium, and I was glad I had worn the black jacket Arabella had brought me as it shielded the cold wind and felt deliciously toasty. I had declined to wear the possum-fur gloves as my recent tangle with the marsupial was still too raw in my mind, but I lent them to Arabella, and I had to admit, they did look stylish. Shoving my hands deep into my jacket pockets, I curled my fingers around the vial of Emospheres, another thrill of anticipation rippling through me, and I wondered how the night would unfold.

After buying the obligatory hot chips we made our way to the seats Dan had reserved for us, which were right in the front row, looking out over the middle of the pitch. Many of the supporters were young, and we were soon surrounded by a hyped up bunch of students; the mood all around was light-hearted and bubbly. As the players ran onto the pitch, the crowd jumped to their feet, us included, and a cacophony of noise erupted around us: whistles, yells, screams, and jeers for the opposition. I leapt up on my seat, searching for Dan, but all the Northland players looked the same in their blue jerseys, so I jabbed Ali in the ribs, yelling at him to point out Dan. Ah – there he was! Ali explained that he stood at the back as a last defense, and had to be cool under pressure, catching the high ball and making quick decisions whether to kick or run the ball. "Full Back" – that made sense now.

There was energy on the field and energy in the stands. I could feel it flowing all around me, restless and charged with emotion as the whistle blew and Auckland took the kick off. The ball went up so high, suspended in mid-air, taking forever to come down. Dan was underneath the ball, lining it up, and took the catch safely. The crowd heaved a collective sigh. It was game on! Eying up the sideline, Dan kicked for territory, and the ball shot down the field and safely out of play. I watched as Auckland took the throw in, and cringed at the sound of the heavy tackles made as each team vied for possession of the ball.

In the end it was Auckland who scored first, taking advantage of a three-man overlap (so Ali informed me), and running the ball wide out to the wing. Ali was disgusted and groaned, "Soft try, ref, soft try. Check the offside rules!" The crowd confirmed it by booing and hissing. The try scorer did a victory dance that further antagonized everyone, and I clutched the bottle in my pocket, wondering if now would be a good time to release some Joy.

Arabella whispered across at me, "Not yet, not yet. This is nothing!"

By half time Auckland was up on the home team ten points to three and I still didn't understand the rules. Apparently, the Auckland back line was off side all the time and there were "hands in the rucks," but it was all gobbledy-gook to me.

Despite my lack of insight, I found I was enjoying the mayhem, yelling when everyone else yelled, and shouting at the top of my lungs whenever Dan got the ball. The lads sitting behind us were vocal as well, and obviously had friends in the team because they kept shouting at the players by name. They also had some mates up from Auckland, who were giving them a hard time for being behind on the score board, and a bit of friendly pushing and shoving ensued. The tables soon turned though, as Northland came back from the break with all cylinders firing, and a stunning run from Dan up the middle of the field set up the first Northland try of the game. "Poetry in motion," Ali stated, over and over. A kick between the goal posts after scoring a try was worth two extra points, and when the ball sailed over, the crowd went wild as Northland locked the score at ten all!

There was ten minutes to go in the game when crunch time came and push turned to shove. One of the Auckland players made a high tackle on Northland's number eight. Another player came in low and lifted him high in the air, then dumped him down on an awkward angle, partly on his shoulder. His neck twisted as it hit the ground. Swiftly, a Northland player rammed into the tackler, taking him down, and before the referee could make a move, players dived into the mêlée, with fists flying and boots kicking – right in front of where we were sitting.

"Now!" screamed Arabella and I fumbled in my pocket, aware that behind me things were also heating up. I could hear cursing and feel a prickle of fear creeping up the back of my neck. With shaking fingers I managed to release the cap and furiously blew into the bubble wand. Damn! Too hard! Again I blew, more gently this time, and we watched as the wind carried the bubbles down towards the players. By this time the ref was blowing his whistle repeatedly, and other players, including Dan, were coming in to pull apart the marauding mob. Without watching any longer, I turned and blew some more bubbles, sick of listening to the string of profanities from the supporters behind me. It was amazing how many small bubbles were created by one blow, and the life they took on was exciting to watch, fizzing and popping as they landed on unsuspecting folks, most of whom didn't even notice them because they were too busy cheering on the fight and booing the ref for breaking it up.

I felt a silliness rising up inside me, and looked back down at the field. The mood of the players had been transformed and they were helping each other up, shaking off the pain, and one by one breaking into smiles until even the referee was wearing a silly grin! He called a two-minute time out for each team to repair any damage and for the captains to talk to their teams, which was totally unnecessary by now, as each team looked as if they had already won the game. The lads behind us had broken out into song, screaming at the top of their voices and the entire crowd joined in! Ali had to explain that it was a classic kiwi song "Why Does Love Do This To Me" by a band called "The Dance Exponents" that had been adopted for use at rugby games; and yes, here it came, over the loud speaker system as well. A Mexican wave around the stadium was next, and the final minutes of the game were played to the rules, ending in a ten all score line and everyone feeling very happy, even if they weren't too sure why.

Ali looked over and raised his eyebrows at me. "Very impressive, Miss Jasmine. I wouldn't have believed it if I hadn't seen it with my own eyes. Amazing, wouldn't you agree 'Bella?"

Arabella smiled and threw her arms around me. "It was meant to be, and yes, powerful and amazing! Emospheres are going to change the world! Talk about crowd control!"

It started raining then, big heavy drops of water from the sky, and I raised my face to the heavens, giving a whoop of joy. Everyone around joined in and began dancing in the rain, which had now progressed from light to heavy in a matter of seconds. I laughed at the craziness of it all; laughed until tears were pouring down my face and my side was aching. Ali and Arabella caught the contagious sound and we all shrieked for the pleasure of it, although Ali's sounded more like a guffaw, which set us all off again every time we got the giggles under control. Dan jumped over the barrier and bounded over the seats, gathering me up in a big wet muddy bear hug, which made me laugh even more.

"It worked, it worked!" Dan half yelled, half whispered. "The boys didn't know what hit them, still don't. They've gone all soppy saying stuff like 'I love you man,' and 'oh I just love rugby, it's all about the game.' Usually that doesn't happen until later in the evening when they've had a few too many drinks!"

"But you didn't win," I hiccupped, trying not to let the giggles escape through my nose as a snort.

"But we didn't lose either," Dan grinned at me, pulling me into another hug and swinging me around. I couldn't help the snort escaping at that point, and Dan roared with laughter, until we had to collapse in the seats to give our aching bodies a rest.

And so we sat in the rain, soaking in the aftermath of Joy, and The Dance Exponents music began again as the last of the happy crowd dispersed.
As I listened to the lyrics I thought of Levi, but I was with Dan, so I shook off the melancholy that threatened to descend, and when he kissed me on the forehead I looked up at him and smiled, hoping the tears that were forming in my eyes just looked like raindrops to him. I had no time for love.

13. HOME SWEET HOME

IT WAS STILL RAINING WHEN WE WERE SITTING IN THE plane on the tarmac at Auckland International Airport, waiting for our flight to depart from the bottom of the garden back to the big old homestead called the United States. I had let Dan have the window seat, and now he was peering out towards the terminal, trying to spot Alistaire and Arabella, even though I had told him it would be unlikely. I glanced around the cabin and saw that the flight was full. Great – twelve hours of torture was about to begin, I thought glumly. As glamorous as air travel was advertised, the reality was far from the glossy brochures – unless of course you flew first class. Suddenly a very naughty idea occurred to me, and I unbuckled my seat belt and stood, indicating to Dan that I was going to the front of the cabin. He gave me the thumbs up, intent on getting his headphones to work. Approaching the flight attendant I smiled, ducked into the loo and scrambled in my backpack until I found what I needed. Slipping out, I pulled aside a corner of the curtain separating the food service area from the cabin, and discretely blew a series of small bubbles. Waiting for a couple of minutes, I poked my head through, and was greeted by a very happy looking steward.

"Hey there, pretty Miss, how may I serve you?" His grin seriously stretched from ear to ear, and I wondered if his mother used to give him oversized lollipops to suck on. His mouth really was enormous. Smiling endearingly, I leaned over and whispered in his ear, and he patted me on the shoulder saying, "I'll see what I can do. Just wait here, hey?"

I leaned back against the wall, crossing my fingers for luck, and waited.

His smile was even bigger on his return, if that were possible. "It's all arranged. I'll take you through then head back and inform your companion. Please, come with me. Isn't it just a gorgeous day for flying? I can't remember when I last felt so happy."

"Well you've made me pretty happy too, so thank you." I smiled generously again, and marveled at my cheeky cunning. Surely Readers are allowed some perks?

When Dan joined me in first class he looked thoroughly confused. "The steward said we had been upgraded. What's going on, Jazz? He seemed awfully happy, which makes me a little suspicious."

"Oh, you know, just a little bit of kiwi ingenuity. I may sound American, but I am half New Zealander, you know!" I hiccupped a tiny joy bubble, and giggled mischievously.

"OK, stop there. I'm not sure I want to know any more. But this first air flight is going to spoil me for life. How am I supposed to handle traveling on a budget after flying in luxury?" Dan was finding it difficult to take it all in. I eased back in my seat; put my feet up and my hands behind my head, wiggling around to experience the full comfort of the Lazy Boy chair.

"Well you can always head back to your old seat if you'd like," I teased, swinging my feet across onto his chair.

"No way," he replied, shoving my feet off and sitting down quickly. "I'm sure I'll cope!"

I closed my eyes and reflected on the past twenty-four hours. It had been hard saying goodbye to Ali and Arabella, but as they planned to visit as soon as they could, leaving them was a little easier than I had expected. Dan's goodbyes had been more difficult, as his rugby coach berated him for leaving before the end of the season saying, "You're throwing away a huge opportunity here, as well as letting the team down. Are you sure you've thought this through properly?"

Dan had replied, "There's more to life than rugby, coach, and I for one intend to live it."

"Harrumph!' The coach had responded. "You know many young lads would kill to be in your position?"

"Don't I know it," Dan smiled, leaving the coach wondering if they were talking about the same thing.

Saying farewell to his mother had been awkward too, since she had no idea that he was planning to go, and pressed him for reasons, anxious that he was moving too quickly. She had only been mollified when Dan asked her to look after Jack whilst he was gone, promising he would be back in the not too distant future to claim the puppy back. As she held the cute chocolate handful, her eyes had misted over, and she had kissed Dan, wished him well, and nodded resentfully at me, then asked us to close the door on the way out.

"She's not expert at goodbyes," Dan explained as we drove off. "I think she's scared I'll never come back, just like Dad. Leaving the puppy with her was the right thing; it'll help soften the blow, and Jack's just about as cute as I am!"

I pretended to stick my finger down my throat and gag, but it actually wasn't far from the truth. With his longish blonde hair and big brown eyes he did have a puppy dog look about him. I bet lots of girls had fallen hard and fast for his boyish charm, but when I closed my eyes it was a different face I saw, no matter how hard I tried not to. I still didn't want to confront whatever feelings I had for Levi. It was as if he were in a different world, a different league from me, and our time together had been a parallel universe, something that happens in movies and other people's lives, but not mine. His life was far too full-on to worry about being a Carrier for some freaky girl-Reader and her so called quest.

Dan shook me back to the present time, "Buckle up babe, we're about to take off!" I only ignored the "babe" reference because he looked so excited, and a person's first time flying experience deserves to be enjoyed without interruption. Rolling down the runway, the anticipation began to build, and I felt that familiar sensation of vague euphoria mixed with a heightened awareness of lift off, loving the odd sensation of becoming airborne and rocketing up into the heavens like an arrow shot at the moon. Before we had even leveled out properly, the attendants were offering exotic drinks and snacks. I chose the sushi and sparkling mineral water, and flicked through the selection of movies available. Dan had moved off to the bar and had lined up three different energy drinks, taste testing each in turn, while chomping on a bowl of nuts and discussing rugby scores with the purser. Wanting to leave the real world for the sublime and the ridiculous, I watched every episode of "Flight of the Conchords" back to back, chuckling and snorting at everything and putting it down to a slight dousing by the Joy Emosphere. Dan joined me towards the end, and having made the most of the in-flight food and beverages he was in a talkative mood.

"So, girlfriend, what's up?" he began, obviously forgetting that it didn't pay to enter conversational sword play with a girl trained by four older brothers.

"The sky is still up, this plane is still up, and my feet are up. Care to rub them?" I threw over the massage cream from the box of first-class goodies. "Can't call me girlfriend if you're not willing to wait on me hand and foot. Oh, and while you're at it would you, pretty please, ask the steward for another quilt and pillow? I'm a bit chilly."

"Listen here!" Dan sat himself down and leaned over, hissing at me. "You think I like this babysitting job any more than you like being sat on? I'm just following orders, and if I'm getting paid, then I'm damn sure I'll do an excellent job. So no more playing games! You're to act the girlfriend whether you like it or not!"

I batted my eyelids. "But I am, Dan; Dan, I am," and I slipped off my sneaker, wiggling my toes at him.

"Just ... just don't lay it on so thick, alright?" he growled, grabbing a dollop of minty cucumber cream from the jar and beginning to rub my bare foot.

I giggled, placed my other foot on his knee, and then frowned as a question formed in the back of my mind. "So why do I need a pseudo boyfriend-slash-bodyguard anyway? Humor me. It's not as if I'm going to run off anywhere you know. Aahhh, that's the spot; mmmm ... rub harder, these feet deserve it; they've done so much running lately." My foot looked tiny in his large hands, and I closed my eyes congratulating myself again on being so quick witted.

"Ouch!" I re-opened one eye and glared at him. "What was that for?"

"Just a little reminder not to get too comfortable, *babe*." His tone was a little sarcastic as he switched to the next foot. His voice lowered, as he became more serious.

"Ali told me he's worried that Vander, who is the chairman of the CFR, has been bought out by a Jagger of some importance, and he's concerned that Vander may double-cross you. He and Arabella want me to stick to you like glue and raise the alarm if I suspect anything. They've given me a direct-dial phone and everything. Me going everywhere with you will be more natural than Dad always accompanying you," Dan stated matter-of-factly.

"But what about Levi?" I blurted out, unable to help myself.

"Well, they're not sure of him either. They haven't been able to search his profile, so they are not that keen on you working with him. Anyhow, there won't be much need now that you'll be teamed up with my dad."

"*But*,' I emphasized, "It's my prerogative to decide that."

Dan shrugged. "Sure it is – just as long as I do my job I'm sure you can sort out all of that."

The steward arrived with my extra blanket and pillow, plus the added bonus of some cozy bed socks, which I got Dan to slip onto my now very soft feet. Dinner was served, which ended any intelligent conversation from Dan, and each new course that came out was greeted with a different exclamation of wonder as we took full advantage of our new-found status. Good food should always be followed by good sleep, and that's exactly what first class provided.

The stopovers in L.A. and Houston flashed by, and before I knew it we were walking down towards the terminal gates at Charlotte Douglas International Airport. Arabella had arranged one last connecting flight, which would land us at Craven County Regional Airport, just an hour from Beaufort. I was grateful we wouldn't have to drive the six hours along the road I had taken with Levi just over three weeks ago. Was that all it was? It seemed like a life time ago.

"Wow, it's warm." Dan had stripped down to his t shirt, and was fumbling around for his passport and boarding pass. We spent the two hours before the flight playing tourist, with Dan dragging me from duty free store to store gathering brochures and information on North Carolina, as well as buying a couple of ridiculously tacky t-shirts. I requested permission to shower and change to try and curtail his enthusiastic but stupid spending, and he decided to do the same.

The warm water was heavenly, and after hours of trekking across the globe (even if most of it had been first class) it felt good to freshen up. I kept my Paua shell around my neck, and tied my hair back, leaving a few strands out to soften the severity. Summer! It was nice to be heading back into sunshine.

The flight to Craven County was short and sweet, only marred by Dan grumbling at me as we lined up to board the plane: "You know you attract far too much attention wearing that skirt. Isn't it a bit short? I've seen five guys check out your legs already. We're not on a beach you know."

I snorted at that. "You're wearing board shorts for crying out loud! And, you're over reacting. Everyone looks at everyone in America, so you better get used to it. Look! See that counter attendant over there? She's checking you out right now. No! Don't turn around, she's still looking!" Dan was swinging his head every which way so I continued my defense. "Anyway, it's far too hot to wear jeans, and it's only my brothers' meeting us, so who cares?"

"Your brothers?" I had Dan's full attention now. "Which ones? I thought your parents were meeting us."

"They decided to head straight to the beach house to check everything's in order, so they'll wait for us there. Apparently they've been having some work done."

"So, which brothers?" Dan persisted, looking a bit worried. I had talked up my brothers quite a lot, over-emphasizing how protective they were of me, just to wind him up. I was a bit surprised Dan was taking me so seriously.

"Oh, the twins," I replied casually. "You know, I told you about them: Harley was the one who beat up that boy who kept throwing acorns at me when I walked to school, remember? And Fale, he pierced my ears for me. He's tough as nails; did all his own piercings too."

Dan was looking a little green. "Maybe we'll play it cool and tell them about the whole boyfriend thing when your parents are there as well."

"Sure," I smiled sweetly, "but being the first boyfriend, don't think dad will let you off the hook lightly." Twisting the knife had never been so much fun, I thought.

"If I'd known all of this I would have asked for more money."

"Ah, you get to see the world too, or part of it. Wasn't that what you always wanted?"

"I'm quickly changing my mind," he commented dryly as he picked up his bag and walked off.

The closer I got to home, the funnier I felt. To look at myself in the mirror I could see no obvious changes, but inside I knew I was not the same Jasmine that had run to an unknown destiny just under a month ago. Maybe wisdom was taking hold, but I sensed a new confidence, an increasing ability to be decisive and bold. Discovering Emospheres had done wonders for my belief in myself, and confirmed that I had been right all these years about a hidden Destiny and purpose. And now I knew what it was! Well, kind of knew. And meeting with the CFR in a few days would help with that I was sure. I felt a tingle in my tummy and my heart skipped a beat. Was I ready?

Coming into the arrivals lounge I scanned the atrium for a familiar face. Black t-shirt, black jeans – look for black, I told myself, remembering it was my brothers not my parents that would be waiting. Ah! There was Harley. Breaking into a run, I flung myself at him, wrapping my arms around his neck. Family felt so good!

"Harley! You made it! Thanks so much. Man I've missed you guys! Where's Fale? I so wanna hear everything that's gone down with the Cajun Braves. Aren't you practically local celebrities now or something?" Harley was laughing at my uncurbed enthusiasm.

"OK, alright sis, settle down, be cool. You're Dan I take it?" he asked, holding out his arm to shake Dan's hand. "Sup, man." I was still looking around for Fale. "He's not here," continued Harley. "Still asleep when I left; but I bought a friend along for the drive."

I had vaguely noticed a guy with a fedora hat pulled down low over his face skulking in the back ground, but airports were such busy places I had taken no notice.

"Oh," I said flatly, my face falling. I hardly wanted to share Harley with Dan, let alone some other dude.

"I think you guys have met before, anyway." Harley sounded monotone. "Hey Chris, come on over. Jazz is here."

As if he hadn't seen me arrive, I thought crossly, trying to remember which one was Chris. Better be polite, I told myself glumly, as he walked over and Harley introduced him to Dan.

"Hey, you look kinda familiar," Dan started.

"And you remember Jazz, Chris?" Harley finished.

If one word could describe my reaction in that moment it would have to be "undone." Completely and utterly, undone. "Chris" raised his head and as our eyes touched it was like history repeating itself. It had all seemed so easy in the desert – hardly real at all. But this was the last person I was expecting to see. On the outside my reactions seemed quite normal: I smiled, politely murmured, "Hi Chris, nice to see you;" but on the inside I felt a wild euphoria spreading through my veins, swirling around my limbs, rendering them useless should I try to walk. It was as if I had moved out of deep shadow into bright sunlight, and the energy from that sun was touching every nerve of my body, causing it to pulsate, the electric charges firing out between my eyes and his.

"Jasmine Blade," he began, causing me to grip the security rail that I was fortunate enough to be leaning against. "You're a wild one, you are; it's good to see you're still in one piece." I had flashbacks of driving along gravel roads at high speed.

"I've got it!" interrupted Dan, his voice excited and loud, "I would recognize that voice anywhere. You're the guy from Alien P..."

"Shhhh!" Harley clamped his hand across Dan's mouth. "Time to get out of here – now!"

Walking at high speed we raced to the nearest exit, but already a couple of teenage girls had retracted from the crowd and were in pursuit. "You go," urged Levi, "drive the car around quick as you can."

"You're far too nice to them," complained Harley.

I was still surprised that my legs were walking, but I guess my brain was clever enough to operate them on automatic pilot. As we ran to the car I glanced over my shoulder to see Levi having a photo with the two girls, an arm around each one. By the time we drove over, the two girls had swollen to six, but Levi expertly extracted himself and slid into the car before most of them even realized. Harley accelerated and we took off with Dan and Harley laughing in the front seat, and Levi looking totally unfazed. I had borrowed Harley's dark sunglasses and felt brave enough to look over his way, gesturing with my hands for an explanation.

"It's my stage name now," Levi explained. "I wanted to keep my identities separate."

I nodded woodenly, my body strangely uncooperative. Dragging my backpack onto my knees to cover my bare legs I wondered how I was going to stand the proximity without giving anything away. It seemed like every hormone in my body was screaming out to be released and I felt weirdly disconnected from the reality going on around me.

Dan was waxing lyrical about how big Alien Potion was in New Zealand, and were they thinking of doing an international tour. Levi didn't sound that interested, but replied that the band were focusing on developing more material and traveling around the U.S. first before considering a global tour. He passed the ball to Harley by commenting on the growing popularity of the Cajun Braves, and that started Harley off, filling in Dan on the local music scene.

I could feel Levi looking at me, but refused to turn my head towards him, staring down at my ring and twisting it on my finger. There was a sudden flash of white, and a small paper plane landed on my lap, on which was written in black pen: "it's not quite as hot as the desert here, but just about." A pen arrived in my lap next, and I wrote, "Meet you there tonight?" and fired it across the seat.

"Our eyes met and the smile on his face destroyed any composure I had regained.

When Harley asked me a question I could barely think straight, and had to ask him to repeat it. "How are our long lost grandparents? Is the beach house still standing?"

"Umm ... yeah ... house is way cool. Amazing view to the ocean; Alistaire and Arabella send their love. Dad is so like Ali, it was kinda nice."

"And Dan – you're here to catch up with your dad, is that right? Bit of a coincidence he's on the Emerald Isle, eh?" Harley was a good conversationalist and knew how to put people at ease.

"I haven't seen him for years, so it'll be a bit weird, but it's worked out well. Been wanting to come over for ages."

"What I really want to hear about though," Harley's voice got louder as he looked in the rear vision mirror at me, "is the big stingray rescue. According to Ali it sounds like Dan is the Man." I cringed and slunk down in my seat. "Got a good scar, Jazz?" Harley teased.

Dan cranked into the story, embellishing bits here and there, I thought. I glanced across at Levi to gage his reaction. Enigmatic as ever, he simply said in a low voice "Where's the scar?"

"On my ankle."

"Show me?"

As if mesmerized, I twisted my leg onto the seat between us, and there was the small silvery circle where the stingray had struck. Levi reached out a hand and gently ran his thumb over it, causing me to nearly pass out from the direct contact.

"Not much to show for such a wild story, Jazz."

"Oh you should see the stingray," I weakly quipped.

"That's only the start," Dan twisted to look back at Levi. "You should have seen her wrestle with a possum!"

"Whaaat!" exclaimed Harley. "Those wild animals in New Zealand gang up on you or something?"

I sighed. "Oh brother, it's good to be home!"

Dan told that story too, and what with Harley's quick wit and comedic tendencies, all the boys in the car were soon laughing. I wasn't sure if it was with me or at me. In the end I had to join in, realizing that although the experience had been petrifying at the time, the retelling did have a funny side.

"Bet you'll never leave apple cores lying around again." Harley was on a roll. "Mom'll be stoked! Speaking of whom, here we are now. Home sweet beach."

We pulled into the wide concrete driveway and there stood both Mom and Dad. Mom was waving frantically at me. Jumping out, I was smothered in hugs and kisses, and everyone was talking at once. Mom welcomed Dan with open arms, and Dad turned towards Levi.

"Hmmmph!" Was all he said, reminiscent of how he treated Chad, and I realized he must still be upset with Levi for the escapade on his motorbike. Levi stood his ground, saying nothing, but winking at me sheepishly. "I'll be off then, folks. See you later, Jazz." My parents studiously ignored him, although I could tell Mom was not comfortable doing so. Harley walked him over to his bike, while I had no choice but to grab my suitcase and head towards the front door.

As we followed Mom inside Dan scowled at me, whispering, "Levi? That's Levi? I thought his name was Chris? He's like a mega rock star. He can't be a Carrier! You should have told me!"

"It's not like I had much of a chance," I hissed back. "Get

over it."

The narrow front entrance and hallway led into a large open-plan living area, where it was obvious builders had been knocking out walls to achieve the spacious feel of the room. The floor to ceiling glass was dated, but afforded an uninterrupted view of the beach, and although we were standing inside, we may as well have been on the dunes. Mom had cleverly brought the sea shore inside by using soft wicker furniture and natural wall colors, complimented by the sea green cushions, mats, and old glass bottles. On the walls were some of the whale and dolphin photos Dad had taken over the years, enlarged to enormous sizes and printed in black and white onto huge canvases. The effect was understated and restful, and I immediately felt at home.

"Wow!" enthused Dan, "this is awesome Mrs. Blade. Are you an interior designer by any chance?"

"Thanks for the compliment, honey, but the only interiors I design for are right here," Mom replied patting her stomach. Dan looked confused. "I'm a chef, Dan," Mom had to explain.

"Oh!' Dan immediately brightened up. I glanced over to where Dad stood, hands jammed in pockets, staring out at the ocean.

"Excuse me Mom, Dan, I need to talk to Dad."

"That's fine dear, you go on. Dan is going to help me get dinner ready, aren't you Dan?"

Dan looked at me, then towards dad and sighed. "Of course I will, but Jazz and I have something to tell you at dinner time, don't we Jazz?" He went to nudge me with his elbow, but I had already walked away, and I pretended not to hear him.

I thought Dad needed another hug, so I gave him one, and he winked at me "Nice to have you back baby."

"Nice to be back, Dad – although New Zealand did get under my skin."

"That's my girl." He kissed me on the top of my head. "But you gave your Mom and me a real fright, Jazz. Fale & Harley have assured us Levi is a good guy, but you're my only daughter – I need to know for myself."

"Well that's not going to happen if you won't even talk to

him," I retorted. "He took good care of me on that trip, and I went of my own free will, and I'm eighteen now, and he may be around for a while, so you're gonna have to make an effort…for me, Daddy?" Using the 'daddy' weapon seemed a bit cheap, but it had never failed me before.

"He's becoming famous, Jazz, that's what worries me. People change with fame…I just don't know…" He sighed deeply. "I just can't come to terms with you growing up I guess. No boy would be good enough for you – and now there's two of 'em on my front door step!" He looked pointedly towards Dan. "What gives, Jazz?"

"It's complicated…" I began slowly, and Dad groaned.

"Well right now I have to get the barbecue sorted out, but I'll expect a full update at dinner time."

"Sure, Dad." I smiled again fondly at him. "Man, you look like granddad!"

"Oi you! Mind your manners!" And with that he playfully put me in a head lock and drop kicked me back towards the kitchen. "Now go help your Mom!" He ordered.

Dinner had the potential to be a very dismal affair now that Levi had gone, leaving me in a desultory mood, which I was having trouble shaking off. Without Levi around, gravity seemed awfully heavy and the atmosphere was dull and boring.

How is it that Moms seem to know the right time for a hug? Saying nothing, she glided from behind the island bench, holding out her arms, and I fell into them, soaking in the unconditional love they offered. After a few minutes she softly spoke.

"I'm sorry we appeared rude towards Levi, Jazzy, but your Father was very upset when he found out where you'd disappeared to and who you were with. But I'd be blind if I didn't see your connection with him. Listen to your heart, Jazzy; you'll know what to do."

"It's complicated," I replied woefully, repeating the same words I had to Dad just minutes earlier.

"And if it wasn't, you wouldn't be interested. Complicated is a challenge – a challenge I think you're up to, and you have family standing right behind you. Remember the saying 'to thine own self be true'? Well, now's the time to prove it. Levi and Dan are both a part of your world right now; whether they will be in the future only time will tell. As for now, you need to continue to be yourself, and complete this Destiny you have pursued. You owe yourself that at the very least. You're going to have to find a way to put this all aside until you have fulfilled whatever tasks you have been set. I really don't know much of what is going on, but enough to realize you will need all your wits about you if you want to succeed."

"I don't even really know what my task is yet. Ali and Arabella put me through a crash course on being a Reader, but I'm not meeting with the Council of Carriers, Framers, and Readers until the day after tomorrow, when hopefully I will be told something more. It's all so frustrating – and Ali insists that Dan masquerades as my 'boyfriend,' basically so he can protect me, but from what I don't know. Arrggh! And Levi is driving me crazy!"

"He is pretty cute," smiled Mom. "They both are." Her expression was stone-faced as she passed me the salad bowl to put on the table, and I rolled my eyes, having forgotten that the number one favorite pastime in my family is teasing.

"Who's cute? You talking about me again?" drifted a voice from down the hallway. I squealed loudly and ran from the room, nearly bowling Chad over as he approached the kitchen. Fale wasn't far behind, and I felt the mood in my heart lighten somewhat, thinking that brothers were much better than boyfriends anyway – they didn't mess with your emotions, and if they were annoying you could hit them real hard.

"Where's Marcus?" I asked hopefully, wondering if I might get lucky and have Dan receive the full force of the brotherhood.

"Oh – he's off on some wild business chase, dreaming about making squillions again. He's been great with sorting out all the band contracts and stuff – pretty impressive really." Fale sounded almost interested.

"Hey, new stretcher!" I admired the larger hole in Fale's

ear, knowing he would love showing it off, and he tickled my ear in return.

"You want one, sis? I can arrange it you know, while you're asleep even!"

"Ha-ha bro. Just remember I could also rearrange *your* piercings while you sleep!"

I hugged him again, and then Chad, who squeezed me back until I couldn't breathe, let alone talk, and carried me through into the kitchen, just as Mom was shouting "Time to eat!"

Dinner felt very familiar to me, but probably very strange for Dan, who wasn't used to such rambunctious and rowdy meal times. Everyone talked at once; whoever talked the loudest got heard, and we had each learned the survival skill of participating in more than one conversation at a time, just in case something was said that we wanted to challenge. Dan looked at me half way through the meal with "help" written on his eyeballs, so I took pity on him and jabbed Chad under the table, an age-old signal that meant "be polite to the visitor." Chad waved his fork at me, but picked up the cue and said as he finished his mouthful, "So Dan, I hear you're a surfer?"

"Uh, yeah. Been riding the waves for a few years down in New Zealand. Do you get any big waves around here?"

"Big waves! We're on the edge of the Atlantic my man! If you stick around for a while I can show you some unreal wave action." Chad always sounded enthusiastic when he was talking about waves. "What are you intending to do while you're here, other than surf?" Straight to the point, that was Chad.

"Well," replied Dan nervously, feeling six sets of eyes on him, "I wanna hang out with Jazz a bit, and then of course I might help my dad with his work. He shapes surfboards and stuff."

"No way!" Chad leaned forward over the table. "Who's your dad? Not Neville, is it?"

"You know him?" Dan leaned forward in response.

"Know him? I work for the man. He took over from Adam Sinclair, about two months ago, just as Adam decided to follow the pro circuit for a while with his son. Neville makes a pretty mean board. Man it's a small world!"

"I thought we only said that down under in New Zealand," Dan quipped, and we all laughed.

"Neville ..." Dad mused, "That name rings a bell. What's your last name, Dan?"

"Picoult."

"Picoult," Dad repeated thoughtfully. "Your father was an associate of my father Alistaire, is that right?"

"Yes sir," replied Dan. "They have stayed in contact over the years since my parents split and my dad moved over here. They have asked me to take Jazz to meet him, if that's OK with you."

"Oh, fine by me. Jazz is eighteen now; she can make up her own mind."

Dad smiled, but I didn't think the smile quite reached his eyes. For a while he looked distant, as if he were thinking about the past, letting the chatter wash over and around him, but I don't think anyone noticed apart from me – probably because I was feeling maudlin myself.

The rest of the meal passed swiftly after that. Dan relaxed and tentatively joined in the multiple conversations, and although he wasn't one of the family, he managed to hold his own. I still felt restless, and wished over and over that Levi had been able to stay. I was relieved when dinner finished and Harley offered to drop Dan at his dad's house before he and Fale went to band practice. Both Mom and Dad could see I was exhausted, and after I handed out the gifts I had bought they cleared up the kitchen and departed; leaving Chad and I to begin our summer stay by the beach. Chad had been living in it for a few weeks already, overseeing the renovations and bringing every decorating idea of Mom's to life. As I walked towards the sand-dunes before turning in for the night, I realized how thankful I was that it was Chad and not Dan staying with me. There was no need for niceties or worries over sharing the bathroom and I was too tired to discuss anything with Dan, although with the looks he threw me at various times during the night I knew there was plenty he wanted to talk about.

The view from the top was sublime, and I sat, staring at the ocean, grateful for the calmness it offered me. Today had been way too turbulent. It was a few minutes before I finally realized I was no longer alone – I guess some part of me had intuitively known he would be there.

I took a deep breath and spoke first, never taking my eyes off the Atlantic in case I lost my nerve.

"It's kinda like a desert."

My voice dropped to a whisper. "I didn't tell you, but I know about the kiss." I couldn't help the tears that rushed into my eyes, and I, wrapped my arms around my legs protectively. "Ali told me it bonds a Reader and Carrier together, but I didn't tell them you had, you know ..." I was barely audible now.

Levi dropped onto the sand beside me, his closeness making it even harder to think. I just wanted to lean against him, feel his arms around me and melt into his warmth, but I didn't. We both continued to look straight out to sea until Levi spoke again.

"Did your lips burn? I'm sorry, but I have to know.'" He almost sounded regretful.

"Yes." I paused. "Did yours?"

"Yes; yes they did." He turned to me now, and I reluctantly looked into his eyes, knowing I was about to completely lose any ability to think straight. "That's why I must continue as your Carrier. There's so much we need to talk about, so much I need to tell you. I know we met in the desert, but we didn't exactly have much time to really talk."

I was still lost in his eyes, my thoughts somewhere between how-deep-will-I-fall and I-never-want-this-time-to-end...

"Jazz?" He reached over and touched my lips, his fingers gentle. "Will I have to kiss you again to get any sense?"

I jerked away, the burning sensation in my lips flaring up again at the contact.

"Uh ... Esmovoir ... my quest ..."

"Right," Levi said. "To move the emotions. I was so stoked you made it happen so quickly, but you disappeared from the desert before I could tell you." He looked back out to sea, his face unreadable. I let out my breath, suddenly aware I had been holding it.

"I've figured it out, Levi. It's the most amazing crowd control I've ever seen." I smiled at him as he turned towards me, and he grinned back.

"I'm guessing you could control a huge crowd all on your own. Seriously Jazz, you have no idea of your power over men, do you? I saw the way Dan looked at you. He's fallen hard."

"Um, there's something I should tell you about Dan," I started, intent on being truthful.

"Let's not talk about him right now. I'm just gonna sit here basking in your beauty while you tell me all about your discoveries. Again."

His eye had a very naughty twinkle in it, so I pushed him off the top of the dune, managing to offset his balance and he tumbled down its face in a series of comical somersaults.

"I'm falling for you ..." he sang as he fell.

"You, Levi Gibson, are a big tease, and your Dan impersonations are not appreciated. Now, do you want to hear about how I can play your emotions, or would you prefer me to show you? Emospheres are powerful you know!"

"Emo what?" he had come to an abrupt stop at the bottom and was gazing back up at me, sand in his hair and over his face, and most of me just wanted to tumble after him and brush it off, running my fingers through his thick hair and over his shoulders, so I quickly averted my gaze and adopted a school teacher demeanor.

"Emospheres. Tiny spheres contained in a bubble formula that store emotion, and when released cause that particular emotion to manifest itself in whoever it touches. It is very powerful and potentially dangerous in the wrong hands."

He was crawling up the dune towards me, and I couldn't help but wonder if I was facing a much bigger danger than Emospheres. He stopped in front of me and lay on his stomach, his fists stacked underneath his chin, concentrating on what I was saying.

"So which emotions? Every emotion? And how does it work?"

I edged down the dune and lay beside him, finding it easier to look at the sand rather than into his eyes. I needed to focus. The sand was still warm from the heat of the day, and silky smooth against my skin. I wiggled down into it, relishing the glow of comfort it brought. We lay there for what seemed like hours, and I explained how I had started with Joy, the tests and trials and eventual success, the rugby game, and the collection of emotional formula I was beginning to assemble. Levi was a great listener, asking intelligent, probing questions, and respecting the fact that the exact mix needed to be kept secret. He took my hand and gently pressed his thumb into my wrist until the small star symbol appeared. I wondered if he could also feel how fast my heart was beating. Brushing the sand aside we both looked at the small star until it began to fade, and I continued with my story, explaining my hope for Emospheres to be used for medical purposes eventually, and my dreams to see a world at peace, if that were possible.

His voice was husky when he spoke. "Jazz, I'll carry you and your Emospheres wherever, you know that, don't you?"

My voice no more than a whisper. "I do know. I don't know how or where this quest will take us, but thank you for being ready – for not giving up on me. Oh! I nearly forgot – I got you a gift while I was away." I wiggled over onto my back and felt in the pocket of my skirt for the bone necklace, grateful that I had decided to keep it on me rather than in my bag. I passed it over to him and explained. "The Maori carving etched into the bone is representative of unity, and the long curved mallet shape is definitive of strength and power – the power of unity."

He sat up. I adjusted the slip knot system and lowered it over his head, tightening it until he indicated it was short enough. It glowed softly against his smooth skin, and I told him about the old lady, and how she had explained it became an extension of whoever wore it, and that the bone had come from a whale that had been washed up on a Northland beach, unable to be revived.

"Did you know my name, Levi, means 'united'?" His

voice had softened, and I could sense a wistful note, as if he was reliving an old memory. "Hopefully that will communicate to you better how right this is, how I will treasure it."

"I didn't know that, but maybe the old lady did; she was pretty mysterious."

I stood, brushing the sand from my legs, unaware that my silhouette was enhanced by the setting sun, and Levi's eyes were on me, deep and searching. Looking up and back towards the house, I saw Dan walking along the path, looking up to where we were hidden from view. "Damn it!" I softly swore under my breath. "I thought Dan had gone."

He was up the dune in a trice, casually commenting, "Left something behind, so thought I'd quickly check out the water, see if there are any good waves around here. Wow, pretty beautiful! Didn't expect that."

Levi smiled. "Yep, Emerald Isle has a reputation for beauty." His eyes were on me though, and I blushed.

Dan walked over to me and slung his arm around my shoulder. "By the way, Chris or Levi, whichever, has Jazz told you? We're sort of 'together', if you know what I mean. All that time on the beach in New Zealand, we got pretty close." He pulled me over towards him, and I stiffened in protest. Good one Dan! I thought angrily; great timing!

Levi had jumped up and was looking out to sea, saying disinterestedly, "That's nice, yeah, I think Jazz was about to tell me. Anyhow, I was just off, so I'll leave you to it. I'll umm ... I'll text you Jazz. Nice to meet you Dan."

Dan sized Levi up before responding. "Yeah – you too. I'm gonna introduce Jazz to my dad tomorrow. He's a Carrier too – you might know him. He's going to help Jazz with her quest." Levi looked over at me sharply, then back out to sea, missing the helpless look in my eyes. "His name's Neville Picoult," Dan continued, not waiting for a reply.

Levi shrugged that characteristic gesture of his, already heading down the sand dune. "It's a small world," he said, his voice fading slightly in the wind. "Give your father my regards."

I might have been mistaken, but I thought I sensed him

smile as he spoke, although his posture was stiff and jerky. We turned back towards the house. Dan's arm was still around my shoulder but I didn't care. Suddenly I didn't care about anything very much, and even though it was summer, the world seemed very empty and cold.

That night I met Levi in our desert, where he told me stories of past readers, stories his Framer Jarven had told him. Neither of us mentioned Dan. We sat, under desert stars this time, shivering in the cold night air, intensified by the closeness of our bodies and the dream-like chemistry swirling in-between the gaps in our conversation. By the time we began fading from the desert landscape the sun was just beginning to light the horizon. Sleep took me then, sleep in big armfuls…

14. THE OAK TREE

… UNTIL 8AM, WHEN CHAD CHEERFULLY JUMPED on me, holding one of his running shoes under my nose.

"Smell the scent of the street … the roads are calling you ... breathe the sweet sweat of a morning run ..."

I groaned and rolled over. It couldn't be morning already? He continued to taunt me with the shoe until I shot an arm out from under the covers, grabbed it and shoved it up into his face, then jumped from the bed, retrieved the other shoe and threw them both out the window. This led to a chase down the hallway and a five-minute wrestle for supremacy, after which I had to admit defeat. Some things never change, although Chad was impressed that I had held out for a full five minutes.

"Impressive, Jazz – that's up on the usual two minutes. You been working out in New Zealand?"

"Actually," I heaved myself up onto my elbows, "I've been surfing. Dan taught me; and Ali – he surfs as well."

"Ohh ..." Chad rolled his eyes dramatically. "My sister as a surfing buddy – just what I've always dreamed of." I punched him for that.

"Scared I might show you up, bro?"

"As if!"

We hit the road ten minutes later, with Chad choosing a

route that veered into a local park then circuited back, weaving up and down various paved running tracks, past some of the most magnificent oak trees I had ever seen. One in particular caught my eye; its symmetry was almost perfect, its branches low and weeping, just begging to be climbed. I made a mental note of its location and resolved to slip back later in the day to explore its majesty. I decided it would be a direct insult to the mighty oak to simply admire its beauty but refuse an invitation to sit awhile in its wise old branches.

Chad had to be at work by 10am, and after showers and breakfast there was little time to catch up properly, so we booked in another run for the following morning. I had reminded Chad that I would be out that night, as Dan's father was taking Dan and me to dinner. My stomach churned just at the thought of it. I really had no idea what to expect, and was nervous about any pressure to have Neville as my Carrier rather than Levi.

After Chad left I rang Elle, having promised to do so as soon as possible after my return. Hearing her voice was like drinking water after a day in the desert, and I stretched out on the couch to prepare for a lovely long conversation. But before she asked for too much information from my trip down under, I quickly interjected.

"So what is the low down with you and Matt? After all these years of liking him, don't tell me you finally asked him out!"

"Actually," Elle sounded slightly proud, "he asked me out – the night of your party. We went to the dance club with everyone after they left your place. Sam ditched us early, and Matt ended up walking me home. We sat outside my place on the steps till nearly dawn talking and something just changed." I could picture Elle on the other end of the phone, twirling her blonde hair around a finger, probably lying on her bed.

"What'd he say?" I found myself curious, wanting to hear every detail, as if it would make up for the uncertainty and void I felt within my own heart.

"He just said that when he's with me he doesn't want to be anywhere else, and that my mom makes the best fudge brownie he's ever tasted. You know Matt; he has to make a joke out of everything. So after we kissed …"

"You what?!" I yelled down the mouthpiece, enjoying tormenting her.

"We kissed, Jazz, heard of that? I took him inside and we ate brownie and ice cream for breakfast. It was very romantic until little bro came downstairs and started annoying us."

Elle kept talking, and I kept listening, every now and then making the right noises, but inside I felt churned up. There was something in Elle's story that struck a chord deep down; if only I would listen.

Then it was my turn to talk, and I filled her in on all the kiwi highlights, keeping my newfound role as a Reader unspoken. Anyway, she was more interested in the surfing, the puppy, and the rugby than anything else. Elle loved watching any sport that involved boys chasing round leather objects.

"How about Matt, Sam 'n' I bring over pizza tonight and meet Dan?" she enthused.

"Um ... sorry; have to have dinner with Dan's father tonight."

"Bother. Then we're busy the next few nights. But I could get tickets to Alien Potion for Saturday night. You said Dan is into them, and now's our last chance. I think they've only got two more state concerts before they gear up for their U.S. tour. It's in Charlotte this weekend."

"Yeah sure," I rejoined, forcing out a small laugh, not wanting to give any enthusiastic signals out. We hadn't even talked about Levi.

"You OK with going, seeing as ... you know ..." Elle hesitated.

"Know what?"

"Oh nothing ... only won't it be weird being in the audience when you know Levi? And seeing your brothers on stage?"

"Exactly why I want to go. Nothing like being an anonymous observer. It will give me heaps of ammunition to store up and let loose on Fale and Harley. Can you get the tickets, Elle, and I'll pay you back? It'll be fun to go all together."

Later, as I sat in the branches of the old oak tree I had seen on my run earlier that day, I wasn't so sure. Standing in a crowd with Dan and watching Levi at the same time might not be as much fun as I first thought. Now Dan had made a direct dig at Levi, going to the concert could just be throwing fuel on a fire. I swiveled around and stretched my legs out along the branch, lowering my body back down onto the sturdy bark and looking up between the myriad of leaves and branches above, admiring the cool dappled green cavern that sheltered me. The particular branch I lay on was nearly wide enough to accommodate two people, and although it hadn't been an easy climb, I had relished the challenge, thinking now how worth it the end location was. No one could see me from the ground, and even though the branch was sturdy, I could still feel the gentle sway of the tree rocking me as I began to contemplate the feelings I had been avoiding.

The bubble of green gave me space to allow the swirling emotions I had trapped deep within to emerge into my conscious mind. It was as if I finally felt safe enough to admit that Levi, that ragged, soulful musician, had made me feel things I had never felt before. Seeing him again had unequivocally confirmed this. It was a startling revelation, one which began as a whisper and increased to a shout, which then reverberated off the mossy green ceiling and echoed its truth within the core of my being. My heart was well and truly hijacked; even the scientist in me had to admit it. For a while my head and my heart swam in the intoxicating discovery, diving deep to dredge up the look in his eyes, the touch of his hand, the warmth of his lips and the sound of his voice. I allowed myself that much – to soak in the memories I had been storing up, reliving each one in all the glorious intensity I could summon.

After a time, I pulled myself back into the present, feeling the warm rumpled bark beneath my back and the feathery kiss of summer leaves on my arms. It was time to face the facts. I could not allow my new found focus to be distracted by my feelings for Levi. My life was now set on course as a Reader and any preoccupation might reduce my ability to think clearly and act wisely. I thought about the Pillars of Wisdom I had studied, and how I wanted to outwork them in my life; about the advice my Mom had given me last night; about my conversation with Levi in the desert – yes. If we were to work together as Reader and Carrier I needed to find a way to purge myself of the out of control dizziness he had brought into my life. But how?

I sat up, thinking hard, and swung my legs in time to an imaginary beat. Looking down at the Reader's ring on my finger, I was reminded of the four jewels I needed to earn: Space, Sagacity, Service, and Sanctity.

Space: Emospheres – what if I captured this love I felt in an Emospheric formula? Would that suck it from my system, and could I then bottle it to be reopened at a later date, when the time was right, when I knew how Levi felt?

Sagacity: I needed to plan a right direction to move in, one that was the best for me, for Levi, for my destiny as a Reader.

Service: my first priority is to undertake my quest from the CFR to contribute to the betterment of life on earth.

Sanctity: A Reader must be willing to make whatever sacrifice is required to fulfill their given destiny.

Wow. Plan A: Bottle love. Hide it away. Pursue Destiny unfettered.

Alternative (Plan B): Become a crumpled romantic mess.

Hmm ... Plan A it was then. Closing my eyes, the movement of the branch rocked me and I could almost feel the life blood of the tree flow into my veins, strengthening my resolve. Trees, I mused, feeling more meditative by the minute, are a gift to humankind providing a solid, unchanging absolute; standing independently and digging their roots deep to establish a near immovable presence, always there through seasons, over years, silently growing, offering shelter and shade, and a place to simply BE.

As the day drew to a close I regretfully slid my way back down to earth and whispered my goodbyes, promising to return soon. Glancing at my watch I gasped in horror: 5pm! What time was Dan coming – was it five?

Obviously it was five. I arrived at the beach house

panting, with hair flying everywhere only to find Dan pacing back and forth outside the front door. Oops. Sneaking down the side of the house I retrieved the key from under the deck and quietly let myself in the back door. Racing down the hallway I took a deep breath, ran my fingers through my tangled hair and opened the door, plastering the sweetest smile I could muster on my face. I didn't even have to lie.

"Oh, you are here! Good. I was worried." he looked a bit sheepish.

"Worried? About what?" I stood tall and imperious.

"Oh nothing. You know, after blowing off Levi last night, I thought ..." he hesitated and I jumped in.

"Well, you didn't need to think at all, did you? Now, help yourself from the fridge while I get dressed. Casual or formal? What time are we due at your dad's?"

"Umm ... 6.30. Sort of casual party dress, if you know what I mean. We're heading out to a restaurant, but Dad says it's a fun sort of place. Oh I don't know Jazz, just wear whatever!"

It didn't take long to decide what to wear. My eighteenth birthday dress was hanging in the closet, freshly dry-cleaned. Slipping it on, I looked at my reflection without paying any particular attention. I felt free, knowing my meditative afternoon had been worthwhile, and my decision sound. Now, all I needed were samples of the emotional triggers. What would they be for love? I watched myself blush at the thought, and felt my pulse begin to accelerate. One physical symptom must be in the blood, I thought excitedly, but what is the other one?

"Jazz?" Dan's shout broke through my thoughts, and I jumped, startled out of my reverie.

"Coming!"

"Gosh!" Dan exclaimed as I raced down the hallway towards him, still slipping the back of my sandal on. "You look as if you've run straight out of the sea – like a ... like a sea nymph or something." His mouth hung open.

"And you," I retorted, "look like a stunned mullet. Am I overdressed or something?"

"No, no, not at all," he spluttered. "It's just different

seeing you on your side of the world all dressed up." He cocked his head to one side. "It suits you."

"Thanks. You, on the other hand, are a fish out of water. Hasn't anyone ever told you not to wear a green tie with a blue shirt?"

He ruefully pulled a second tie out of his pocket saying defensively, "I did bring another option just in case ..."

I nodded. "Very wise. You've just got time to change it. Let me help – I tie them for my brothers all the time."

He loosened off the knot at his throat and drew the green tie over his head. I stood waiting with the second choice: a taupe and blue narrow tie, which really did work much better with what he was wearing. I slung it around his neck and moved closer to begin the knot, my brow furrowing as I concentrated. Dan lifted his hand and ran his finger over my forehead.

"Jazz ..." he whispered softly, "don't I stand any chance? We're so good together ..." He leaned into me until his eyes were inches from mine, breaking my focus on the tie.

I almost laughed, part from nervousness at being in such close proximity, and partly because his puppy dog eyes really did look so sad.

"We are good together, Dan; good friends. You must know by now I need to focus on succeeding as a Reader and that means no distractions – none whatsoever – understand?" I spoke gently, realizing suddenly how important Dan was as a friend, and how much I didn't want to lose him.

He let me finish knotting the tie before he spoke again, sighing, "I guess you're right, but I had to let you know, I had to ask. Maybe one day?" His eyes were almost pleading, and my resolve softened.

"Stranger things have happened, Dan, but don't hold your breath, OK? Now let's go play-act for your dad!"

He smiled at that, and hooked his arm through mine. "Lights, camera, action!"

Dan's father was the spitting image of Dan (or vice-versa). It was uncanny. He didn't even really look much older than his son in the soft lights of the restaurant. I was slightly unnerved by the similarity, but found him impossible not to like. Nev – as he had asked me to call him – looked like he had stepped straight from a promo advert for the state of California: blond shaggy hair (no bald patches visible – how old was he?), tanned skin and a lithe, fit frame. He wasn't as tall as Dan, but exuded energy from every pore, making it seem like he took up more room than he actually did. He seemed to be moving constantly, and just being near him was like taking a party pill. You could easily imagine him shouting out "Party on Me!" and immediately generating a crowd and an atmosphere. The restaurant we were at was the only one in Emerald Isle that opened right onto the beach. The tables spilled out onto a patio, which trespassed onto the beach with a volleyball net set up where people were still playing under floodlights. Inside was a large dance floor, twinkling with lights and music that made your feet want to tap and your body want to move. I had heard of "Elation Station," as the restaurant was aptly named, but had never been, and now I already wanted to come back.

"Cheers!" Nev raised his glass, and Dan and I did the same. I looked dubiously at the cocktail Nev had ordered us all, but didn't want to be rude, so after the clink of our glasses I took a small sip – delicious!

"A fruity concoction, with only a hint of alcohol," Nev assured me. He was also easy to talk to, and before I knew it we were all laughing as Dan retold tales of how we met in New Zealand, me throwing in the odd protest and Nev finishing if off with a hilarious quip or a story of his own. It was as if we were old friends rather than new acquaintances, shooting the breeze, enjoying fine food and wine, and catching up on old times. I was finding it hard to believe this was the same man Dan had described to me back in New Zealand. He really knew how to make everyone feel special, as if they were the most important person on the face of the earth – from the sweet doe-eyed waitress, to the elderly bar man – even me. I decided Dan must be bitter about his dad leaving his mom so suddenly or something. Nev listened avidly as the conversation turned more to my quest as a Reader, hardly interrupting as I explained how my journey to New Zealand had changed the course of my life forever.

"And now Destiny has brought us together!" Nev exclaimed as I finished up, "that's something to celebrate! The Reader and the Carrier united, ready to fight the dark forces of evil!" He ran his fingers through his hair excitedly and continued, leaning forward, and half whispering to me. "Twelve midday tomorrow, by the fountain of light, just ten minutes from here, we meet the CFR. Big day for you, eh Jazz? They've some pretty influential people, you know, but you'll be fine. You are pretty composed for one so young." I met his gaze directly, and wondered if he thought I wasn't up to the task. Dan had excused himself and headed to the restrooms, and Nev leaned even closer towards my ear. "I'm glad you have my Dan to look out for you. He's a special kid, that one, so ... nice."

I drew back a little and tossed my head. "I'm actually not that bad at looking out for myself, you know." I retorted more sharply than I intended.

"Oh – don't get me wrong, love – I think you are more than capable of looking after number one. It's just that I'm sure your confidence in Dan is not unfounded, and he practically worships the ground you walk on." Nev winked at me, and I couldn't help but smile.

"I wouldn't say that, but he has been good to me," I admitted.

"That's my boy; I knew it! By the way, anyone informed you about the 'Carrier Kiss'?" His expression was nonchalant, but I could tell he was observing my reaction carefully.

"Umm ... Ali did mention something about it, but given our age gap, and ... Dan ..." I swallowed uncomfortably, "I wasn't sure what the case might be."

Nev grinned widely. "Don't know what they told you dear, but pressing lips can hardly be seen as ... inappropriate. You up for it? May as well get it over with and seal the deal."

I wasn't sure if I wanted to "seal the deal," but I could hardly kick up a stink. Before I had an opportunity to discuss it further, Neville leaned over the table and briefly joined his lips to mine in a very business-like way.

"There, that wasn't so bad, was it? As for the gift I have kept hold of for you for the last seventeen years or so, here it is."

I felt a little sick in the stomach as I anxiously waited for any lip tingling to begin, but my optimism slowly grew as my lips stayed under control. There was no sign whatsoever of any funny business. Nev handed me a small black velvet bag and I smiled hesitantly at him, tipping the bag gently into the palm of my hand revealing a silver locket on a delicate chain, with engravings not dissimilar to my ring. Opening the locket carefully, nestled inside in tiny writing were the Seven Pillars of Wisdom in beautiful calligraphy. Looking up at Nev, my eyes glistened a little, realizing this gift had been set aside for me since my birth.

"It's perfect, Nev. I have already memorized them, but having them close to my heart will be an awesome reminder."

He looked slightly uncomfortable, as if awkward with any display of emotion. "Chosen by the CFR, sent from Saudi Arabia. All I've done is kept it safe for you."

"Well ... thanks, Neville. I appreciate it. Look, here comes Dan, he can do up the clasp for me." I was relieved that our time alone was nearly over, Neville was a mixed bag and I still did not quite know what he would pull out next.

We both watched Dan weave his way back towards us, slightly overawed by the venue, and still not used to everyone looking at everyone else.

"Maybe the dance floor will loosen him up," Nev suggested, and I nodded my head in agreement. As I got up to approach Dan, Nev lightly grabbed my arm. "Before the meeting tomorrow, Jazz, it would be great if you could update me on your progress with your, you know, task as a Reader. It is crucial that we work together on this."

I was immediately on guard. Should a Reader have two Carriers? This was the moment I had been dreading. Emospheres were still such a personal discovery, I wasn't sure I was ready to tell someone I just met, even if he was nice. I hadn't even told my parents or brothers yet!

"Sure, Nev," I replied as smoothly as I could, "but I'm

also working with Levi Gibson. I understand you know him?"

"Know of him," Nev replied, his unlined face looking as relaxed as ever. "I had presumed with his newfound success he would be too busy to take up any Carrier duties, but I may be mistaken. I'm happy to just help where I can, Jazz. Just let me know what I can do. It's not easy starting out as a Reader – trust me, I've carried others before."

"Yeah, well, thanks, Nev. I'm sure there's a lot you can teach me, and you're right; this is a completely new game to me!"

He grinned, and it was like looking at Dan as he joked, "Game of life, my dear, and the winner takes all."

Dan had almost reached the table and before I could say anything he jerked his head towards the dance floor saying loudly, "You keen Jazz? The music's not bad and there are enough people on the dance floor to cover any bad dance moves you might pull."

"Boy you are cheeky! As if! Bring it on, buster. Can you just do up this chain for me first? It's Neville's Carrier gift to me; isn't it gorgeous?"

"Almost as gorgeous as you," he whispered daringly into my ear as he fixed the clasp around my neck. I turned and looked at him sternly, swiftly grabbing his hand and dragging him towards the thrumming dance floor, thinking some exercise might take his mind off me. Ahh! An oldie but a goodie: Black Eyed Peas "Tonight's Gonna be a Good Night" began as we got there, and the entire floor shook as everyone jumped up and down to the beat in unison.

It was a good night! Dan wasn't a bad dancer for a rugby player, and after a couple of songs Nev joined us, with people making room for him like an old friend. Some did know him, and soon we had formed a circle, folks showing off their moves in the middle, with much encouragement from the ring of spectators. Nev surfed an imaginary wave, Dan did the robot and I strung some moves together from the fusion dance lessons I had taken over the years. The floor was crammed by now, and as both Dan and Nev had plenty of girls vying for their attention, I slipped off the dance floor after a while and headed for the beach. Just in time. As I exited the building, Alien Potion blared from the speakers and I sped up, past the tables and over to where the beach volleyball had been. The sky was well and truly dark now, and my eyes slowly adjusted, drinking in the sight and sound of the ocean. I kicked off my sandals and nestled my toes into the warm sand. A few meters away a guy and girl were locked in an embrace, kissing passionately. Not wanting to intrude, I took a few steps backwards towards the sound of Levi blaring through the outdoor sound system, when suddenly it dawned on me: the fusion of lips, reciprocal transferal of passion, the layers of skin and the space between each one, mixed with saliva. I raced back to our table, grabbed a serviette from under my glass and a pen from my bag and began scribbling furiously the Emospheric formula – not the base formula, but the additives required to capture love. I was more than sure I had it right. In that moment of epiphany I saw it clearly and had to get it all down before it disappeared. My cheeks flushed as I wrote. All my concentration focused on the task, and I jumped as Nev and Dan collapsed into their chairs. I hadn't even seen them approach.

"What'cha writing Jazz? List of song requests for the DJ?'" Dan jested.

"Something like that," I mumbled, stuffing the pen and serviette into my hand bag, desperately hoping I had everything I needed.

Nev observed from across the table, as he poured each of us a large glass of water. "Comes with the territory of being a Reader, I'm guessing," he commented sympathetically. "Inspiration can hit at the oddest of times. Now, dessert anyone?"

I am never one to say no to dessert, and we finished the evening on a sugar high mixed with plenty more dancing and laughing, Dan finally dropping me home around 1am. As we pulled up in the driveway I leaned over and gave him a quick hug and a peck on the cheek, hopping out of the car before he could start talking. I knew I had to get inside and begin my formula. My brain was buzzing and sleep was not going to be an option, especially if I was to meet Levi in the desert again.

"See you tomorrow, Danny," I sang over my shoulder before I opened the front door and disappeared inside. Tiptoeing to my room, I gathered everything I needed and headed back to the kitchen, laying out my notes, bottles, and finally rummaging in the en suite to the main bedroom, wondering if Mom had left a supply of Dad's diabetic kit here, thinking that I might just get lucky.

Feeling very cathartic, I lay prone on the living room rug, plugged in my iPod and scrolled to Alien Potion. I let Levi wash over me, and the memories in my mind began to flow like a motion picture through my heart and into my blood stream ... at school, feeling rough denim against me; the soft oak scent that clung to his shirt; the gray of his eyes and the sweetness when I saw into his soul; his nearness on the motorbike; the stories we shared; the night we kissed; my burning lips ... More and more scenes and conversations slipped quickly in and out of my mind's eye, and a slow ache began in my limbs, a throbbing, sweet pain that beat through my veins in time to the music in my ears until I felt I could bear no more. My lips burned and it was as if the love I felt within wanted to burst out and I knew then it was time.

Rising from the floor I moved in two states of being: firstly, the wild Jasmine, pulsating with a deep earth-shattering love, and secondly Jazz the scientist, observing my actions and calculating the results. Dad's thumb-prick kit was waiting, and it took just one quick puncture, and droplets of blood dripped into the small bottle, each red splash purging a memory from my mind. The pain was sweet and sad, and I was glad a few drops would suffice.

I added a small sample of saliva and skin cells from my lips, and a measure of vodka and Emosphere Oil. The formula was almost complete. Labeling the bottle "Love," I willed myself to think no more, and only embrace sleep as fast as I was able.

I did dream of the desert that night, but it must have been just that: a dream, because Levi was nowhere in sight.

15. COUNCIL OF CARRIERS, FRAMERS & READERS

BOOF! MY BODY BOUNCED AT LEAST A FEW INCHES off the bed, which was more than enough to wake my brain from its slumber, even if my physical being had no intention of responding. I lay like a large sea slug, unmoving, my mind assuring me that the Chad-like bug bear on my bed would disappear if only I kept still and ignored the pokes and prods in my back. But when the tickling began, all hell broke loose. Sheets and pillows flew everywhere and I fought like a wild cat. The cacophony that erupted would have been enough to scare the neighbor's two doors down!

"Mercy, mercy," I moaned in between gasps and hiccupped laughter, and Chad finally released me, retreating to the chair on the far side of the room, out of my reach. I was too exhausted from the late night and the tickle attack to contemplate revenge at that moment anyway. I lay like a slug again though, just to annoy him. Finally I spoke, but the sound was muffled by my pillow. "I'll come IF you get me a glass of orange juice and IF we can run along the beach."

"Your wish is my command, O Sister-Who-Stays-Out-Well-Past-Her-Bedtime. It's great to have you back though. I've missed having someone to torment – and my running buddy.

How was your big night out, anyway? Hang on; hold that thought. One OJ coming up."

He was back in a trice with the OJ, and the chance to fall back asleep was denied me as he demanded to hear all about meeting Nev. I summed up the night pretty quickly, glossing over most things. I wanted to know what Chad thought of Neville.

Chad looked thoughtful when I asked him. "He's great to work with, that's for sure; always upbeat and happy – almost too happy if you ask me. Kinda gets annoying after a while. He comes and goes a lot from the shop, but he's been nothing but good to me so I'm not complaining." He started rummaging in my wardrobe for my running gear. "How's it going with Dan? You two an item yet?"

I removed the t-shirt he threw at me from off my face to reply. "We are *pretending* to be an item. He's just a friend."

Chad turned and stared at me in surprise. "Pretending? Since when do you play games, Jazz? What's really going down? Mom and Dad said that Grandma and Grandpa had provided a spontaneous birthday gift for you to travel to visit them in New Zealand, but I didn't really believe them. Figured you would tell me when you were good and ready."

I sat up, hugging my arms around my knees, and the stories of my adventures over the past month came flooding out, starting at the point Levi picked me up on his motorbike, all our crazy experiences on the road, how I ran away and followed the instructions from Ali and Arabella. "So it was kind of a spontaneous birthday surprise, I guess." And then I filled him in on my calling as to be a Reader, the Pillars of Wisdom, the mark on my wrist and the ring Levi had given me. "I hope it doesn't sound too mumbo jumbo," my voice sounded anxious. "I'm still getting to grips with it myself. And now Ali and Arabella have asked that Dan masquerade as my 'boyfriend' to 'protect' me, and arranged for Nev to be my Carrier, when Levi has been doing that role very well to date."

My face flushed as I thought how very well Levi had kissed me all those long nights ago. Darn it, I laid down those feelings last night, but perhaps bottling them only stored a little of them rather than remove them altogether. Stupid me.

Chad was still staring at me, and all of a sudden it was as if the lights went on. "Oh!" he exclaimed, "I get it."

"Get what? Me being a Reader?"

"That part I don't have a problem understanding. I've always thought you were born for something more than the average girl – after all, you're my sister. No, I've just clicked – you like Levi, don't you?" My face was on fire now, and I shrugged helplessly at him.

"Now there's someone I would approve for you, and I'd trust you to him far more than to Neville, that is for sure."

"You approve? Not that there's anything to approve of," I added hastily. "Anyway, Levi thinks Dan is my boyfriend, and I guess it doesn't matter, as I need to focus on meeting the CFR today, and then on the quest they'll give me – no distractions."

My eyes wandered over to where the bottle of First Love Emospheres sat on my dresser beside the crumpled serviette with my notes on from the night before, waiting to be completed. Chad waved his arms at me and threw over shorts and a bikini onto the bed ordering, "Enough for now, I need time to think about all of this, but I want to trial these Emospheres later. Now, get dressed and let's run!"

"You expect me to wear this?" I argued, holding up the string bikini he had bought me for a joke last summer.

"First swimsuit I could find," he replied cheerfully. "You might hurt my feelings if you don't. Anyway, it's just us, not a beach party!"

It was 8.30am by this time, but beach goers were still pretty thin on the ground – mainly mothers with young children, and a few locals. The pristine white sandy shores contrasted stunningly with the blue of the Atlantic Ocean, and I wished I had brought my sunglasses. Originally intended to be developed as a huge ocean resort, Emerald Isle had been sold by the Fort family to a developer in the 1950s, who divided it into 1100-foot residential and commercial blocks. When the bridge connecting the Isle to the mainland was constructed in 1971, it became a popular holiday destination, and anyone who lives along the coast of North Carolina knows why: its natural beauty is hard to beat. The lush nearby forests and the blue green of the ocean makes it look like a gem in the middle of the sea, hence the name "Emerald Isle." From Mom and Dad's beach house, it was about eight miles east along the sand till you reached Indian Beach, and twelve miles to the westerly reaches of the Isle with white sand forever in each direction.

Chad set a fast pace, choosing to go west so the sun was on our backs and telling me he wanted to work up a good sweat before diving into the sea on our return. It felt good to focus only on running, and I pushed myself to stay alongside my brother. He took pride in staying in shape, and his physique was a good mix of lean muscle mass and toned definition. He always told me that if you keep fit, everything in life seems easier: work (because your brain is awake); sleep (because you actually need it); sport (because you can focus more on fun and skills rather than gasping for air and trying to keep up); and, of course, eating – you can eat plenty, and Chad loves to eat!

He had pulled ahead slightly as my thoughts had been distracted thinking about all of this, and I watched as he slipped his cell phone out of his pocket, dialed, and then after a few moments was obviously talking to someone. I wondered who could be important enough to distract him while running, so I put on a sudden spurt and with a huge effort, managed to close the twenty-meter gap that had opened up between us, just as his phone went back in his pocket.

"Who d'ya call?" I managed to pant out.

"What was that?" Chad replied easily.

"I ... said ... who ... were ... you ... calling?"

"Ha-ha," laughed Chad, "I heard you the first time. I'm just enjoying your misery!"

"You are pure evil, you know ... that ... Chad Blade?"

He charitably slowed down for a second or two. "See that gray house up over there? The two-story one with the big deck over the dunes?" I nodded. "Well, that's Levi's house. I rang to see if he wanted to join us for a swim; we've just about run three miles you know."

He sped up, but I was too quick. I grabbed his t-shirt and pulled us both up short, demanding, "You did what?" And then, "What did he say?" My heart was already accelerated from the running, now it couldn't beat any faster if it tried.

"There's your answer." Chad started running again and pointed to a figure standing on the deck of the gray house, looking down towards us. How dare my heart jump again? I looked at the sand speeding beneath my feet and suddenly keeping up with Chad wasn't a problem. "We've met for a few runs and swims since you've been gone. He keeps himself in pretty good knick for a musician. This beach is perfect for him 'cause it mainly houses older folks who have no clue how famous he is becoming, or empty holiday homes. Hey Levi! Bring some extra towels, would ya?"

"Don't you DARE say anything," I hissed violently at Chad, and he looked at me with a hurt expression.

"As if, sis, as if!"

Levi disappeared for a few moments, and then reappeared, bounding down the stairs in easy leaps. The sight of him coming towards us made me weak at the knees, and I bent over, placing my hands on my legs, pretending to stretch. I still had time to notice the way seeing his bare chest made me feel, and I felt the blood rush to my head. Rats, time to straighten up.

"Hey Levi," I said weakly, trying to get a grip on myself.

"Jazz, Chad," he nodded, tossing a towel at each of us. "Race you to the water? Last one in gets dunked!"

He dropped his towel and belted off towards the water with Chad in hot pursuit, as all he had to do was slip off his t-shirt and runners. No socks, I noticed – unfair!

By the time I removed my shorts, t-shirt, shoes, and socks, the boys were well out past the breakers, so I didn't bother hurrying. The further away they were the better, I figured, cursing Chad for hassling me to wear the total joke yellow polka dot bikini. It was really teeny, and I felt terribly exposed. I contemplated wearing my t-shirt into the water, but thought crossly as I tossed my hair, "just pretend he's another brother – they've seen me in a bikini often enough!" And with that I ran into the water and dived under the first wave I could, anxious to cover myself with the wild water. I swam out to join them, the salty waves both cleansing and exhilarating and I smiled as I surfaced from the last wave of the set; my eyes closed to maximize the enjoyment. In that brief moment I felt two sets of hands on my head, pushing me under again. So the fun and games had begun! I should have expected it with Chad. Down I went, so far down with the momentum that I managed to twist my body and grab a handful of sand before I shot to the surface. I fired the sand at the back of their retreating heads. Disappearing under again, I popped up in a different location, just in case. I couldn't see either of them, and treading water I nervously waited, knowing they couldn't stay under forever. I scanned the water around me, looking for bubbles.

"Pigs and barnacles!" I yelled as I felt two hands firmly clasp my hips and thrust me into the air.

"Catch, Levi!" Chad shouted, and before I could blink I found myself flying through mid-air, landing up close and personal with the object of my desire, the same desire I had tried to purge myself of the night before.

Warm strong hands gripped my waist, skin against skin, and my green eyes were level with beautiful gray ones; I was mesmerized for a second before we went under, Levi jerking away from me as we sunk. My eyes flew open, and through the clear water I could see him staring back at me and wondered what he was thinking.

He shot to the top before me, and I stayed down cross legged near the bottom, wishing like I did as a little girl that I could become a mermaid and never have to surface. But as my lungs began to burn I made the ascent, bursting into the sunlight with a shocked gasp.

"Ha-ha! You ok?" Chad asked.

"Fine." My reply was short and non-committal, as I floated on my back staring at the blue sky with my head swimming.

"So where's your boyfriend?" Levi broke the silence. Chad guffawed loudly.

"Jazz doesn't know the meaning of the word boyfriend, my man, but if you're talking 'bout Dan the kiwi man, he's coming to get her around 11.30 – is that right Jazz?"

I glared at him as I swiveled upright again, treading water. Levi was looking at me, the question still in his eyes.

"I was trying to tell you the other night," I said, my eyes moving between Levi's eyes and his lips as I struggled to recover some composure. "Dan is ... oh, never mind! We're meeting the CFR today with his dad, Neville. I presume you're coming as well? Twelve midday? By the fountain?" I looked at him, my eyes pleading.

"You sure you want me there?"

"Of course I do – you know that. You're my Carrier."

He shrugged. "Well, I'll be there then. I said I would stand by you." His voice sounded stiff, and he turned to swim to shore, beating Chad and I back easily.

He used the time to re-gather the towels, and as I walked through the breakers, he held one out for me to step into, his eyes hidden behind the fluffy white sheet. I clutched my arms over my chest, and hurried into its soft folds, glad for the comfort and the cover-up.

Chad had stayed in the water, body surfing the shallow waves, and so with the towel firmly wrapped under my armpits and up around my body, I sat on the warm sand, retrieving my t-shirt and hastily pulling it over my head. Levi sat straight down on the sand, hands clasped loosely around his knees, and we both watched Chad for a few minutes in silence, before I spoke.

"You weren't there last night." I felt rather than saw him smile wryly.

"Musician's hours. Stayed up all night song writing. Bailey's onto me to finish songs for the album…I felt inspired, so…"

I didn't reply; my eyes glued on Chad. Levi turned to face me.

"So are you going to work with Neville?" I was thankful for the change of topic.

"He seems nice enough, and he has lots of experience,

but ..."

"But what?" Levi prompted.

"But I'm just not sure. I want to meet with the CFR today before making any decision. After all, I don't even know what the quest is yet, do you?" I was curious to find out if he knew anything.

"I have my theories ... and suspicions." He sounded strained.

"Like what? My grandparents warned me that they suspect Vander, the Chairman, of having disloyalties to the CFR."

"I was going to warn you of the same. We need to be cautious; try to pick up any clues. He's very crafty and many members of the CFR would like to see him gone. It's just a sensitive situation; any sign of dissension in the camp and respected statesmen and institutions will no longer want to work with Readers. There is a long tradition of the CFR – Readers particularly – helping government agencies like the FBI, United Nations, etc. It's a long story, but basically it all comes down to one Reader decades ago whose quest merged with espionage and surveillance advancements. The CFR approached authorities both in the Middle East and America to trial the equipment, and it was so successful they asked to be kept informed in the future. The CFR have Councils in strategic locations around the world: Saudi, where it all began, Israel, Poland, Cuba, and now Beijing, as well as here in America."

"Wow. I had no idea it was all so huge. Aren't I the last Reader though?" I half asked, half stated.

"Who told you that?"

"My grandparents."

"Mmmm. I guess that's partly true. But a lot has been stirring, and more facts uncovered in Saudi Arabia since then." His voice petered out before he continued. "But that's not important today. What is important," and now he turned to face me fully, "is that you listen, observe and learn. Look for my signals and we'll compare notes later. That OK with you?"

"Sure." I would agree to anything he said once I made contact with those eyes, but I couldn't resist, and gave him the full force of my gaze. "But, Levi, how do you know so much about all of this? You're not that much older than me, are you?"

"I'm older than you'll ever know," he murmured enigmatically. "The Framer I trained with, Jarven, he has been around the CFR forever; he told me that one day I'll have to take you to meet him – perhaps – if you behave …" His eyes twinkled now, lifting the somber tone of our conversation.

I was on automatic pilot, caught in the deep blue-gray sweetness of those eyes, the eyes that looked into my very soul, so open. It took a huge effort to finally look away, and it felt like our eyes had conversed for hours, not seconds. How is it that meeting eyes with most people can hold no agenda and no hidden messages, while meeting the gaze of a particular set of eyes can start a silent conversation that picks up where it left off each time you meet them? I was just hoping it wasn't a one-sided conversation.

Chad was coming up the beach now, and although I was feeling a little light-headed I stood, the sun warm on my arms and legs, restoring some normality.

"We're coming to your concert on Saturday night, so here's hoping you're on form." I casually commented to Levi as I threw a towel hard at Chad's head.

"You are?" I think he sounded pleased.

"Yep, my friend from high school, Elle, got us the tickets. There's a group of us coming. I even got you a ticket, Chad, just in case."

Chad was toweling himself off, and shook his wet hair at me, but I jumped back, half anticipating it. "I'm already there, sis – stage hand request from Fale and Harley."

"I can get your friend a refund for that ticket," Levi interrupted. "Could have got you them for free if you'd asked you know."

"Oh ... yeah ... I guess. Didn't want to bother you." I stuttered, feeling a bit stupid.

Levi winked at me, and I couldn't help but smile. "How about backstage passes instead – any help?"

"Gratefully received," I grinned wider. "Elle will be

stoked! As long as you know Dan's coming too."

"Kinda figured that," Levi replied easily, his expression unreadable. "Just leave Neville behind, eh?"

"Done deal!"

"Time to shoot through, Jazz. Good to see ya Levi – thanks for the towels." Chad was slipping on his shoes, and I hurriedly did the same, brushing as much of the sand off my feet as I could. I pulled my shorts on before I handed the towel back to Levi, glad to be clothed again.

"See ya at twelve?"

"You can bet on it." He touched my lips with his ring, and a strange feeling of déjà vu rushed through me as I remembered the last time he did that – in the bookstore, just before I ran away. I nearly didn't start running.

It was 10.30 by the time we arrived back at the house, hot and sweaty again. Straight in and out of the shower, I threw on a simple cotton floral dress that floated. It was a favorite because it made me feel like I belonged in a French market place. The blues and greens swirled over the crisp white, reminiscent of summer day in the country. Sunglasses. Did I look like a mysterious individual? Grown up? I tossed my hair, noticing it had grown longer again and was nearly down to my waist now. It was time for a chop, but other than that I felt curiously ready, as if I had assumed a character and it was time to move out in front of the cameras and record a scene.

Chad approved. "Very nice, very nice, even if you are my sister. By the way, did I tell you about the look on Levi's face when you stripped down to that bikini and ran into the water? Priceless!"

I blushed. Again. "Yes, Chad, you did tell me," I sighed. "Three times now. All I can say is that you'd better watch your back bro after that throwing-me-in-the-water stunt."

"Awww, come on, Jazz, anyone could see the sparks flying between the two of you. The electricity generated could power a small country, I reckon!"

"But he's got Bailey," I said in a small voice.

"Bailey? Oh ... her ... well ... I can only call it like I see it.

You should talk to him."

"Like I said, Chad; *no* complications right now. I need all the focus I can get. Anyhow, he could always talk to me if he were keen. I'm a bit old fashioned like that." I sounded sarcastic, but before we could get into an argument about gender stereotypes, a knock at the door sounded.

It was Dan and Nev. What was the time? I glanced at my watch as I opened the door to them. "Hi guys, you're early! It's not even quite eleven yet. Come in, come in." I smiled, trying to look confident and assured, removing the sunglasses I had forgotten were still on my face.

"We actually don't have time to come in," Nev sounded apologetic. "The CRF office rang to say they need to bring the meeting forward an hour, and could we make it by 11.We've raced over here as quick as we could."

"Did you not get my text?" Dan added.

"We've been for a run and a swim, and my phone battery is dead as usual, sorry." I indicated behind me to where Chad was leaning against the wall listening. "But I am ready to go, so that's a relief. I'll meet you in the car." Turning to Chad as I shut the door on them I pleaded, "Would you text Levi and let him know the meeting time is now? He's supposed to be joining us there."

"Where?" Chad questioned.

"He knows where; just let him know I'm on my way, and to get there ASAP. You've got his number. Thanks, Chad … later. Love you bro."

"Back at ya."

Man, I thought as I ran down to the waiting car, brothers might have been a pain when I was little, but boy are they worth their weight in gold now! No – let me rephrase that – Chad is still a pain, but I guess now I can see the gold. No pain, no gain! I am going to think up a dastardly revenge to exact on him later.

Dan looked different today I thought as I hopped into the car; older somehow. He was wearing dark denim jeans with a slim fit black t-shirt and his blond hair was hidden under a Carolina Panthers black baseball cap. He'd only been here five minutes, and he already owned more sport merchandise than me! Nev, on the other hand, still looked pretty young. They could have been brothers rather than father and son. Nev was wearing t-shirt and jeans as well, although the jeans were scruffier, the t-shirt white, and he wore a tan blazer over the top in Miami Vice style. He was straight away down to business, the second he pulled out of the driveway. This was another side of Nev, brusque, efficient and intent on gathering facts.

"So," he began, making me think of a CIA interrogation scene, "Esmovoir; to move the emotions. How would a Reader achieve that, Jazz? Any ideas yet?"

I shot a mutinous glance back at Dan, who had given up his place in the front seat for me, warning him not to give anything away – that is, if he hadn't already. I had forgotten how much he knew, and wondered where his loyalties truly lay. I replied carefully.

"Well, I have been working on a formula – that may or may not work – taking the physical manifestations of emotional responses and attempting to morph them into a more concentrated form." Dan rolled his eyes at me.

"Good, good," Nev encouraged. "Any success?"

"As a matter of fact, yes. I think I'm pretty close now." It was just a couple of small white lies, but it meant I hadn't given too much away.

"So do you need any special equipment, anything I can get for you?"

"No thanks, I'm pretty well organized, actually. It comes from years of being a lab geek at high school."

Nev gave a short laugh. "So how much longer do you think you'll need? And what emotion in particular are you trying to emulate?" He used a whole lot of gestures as he talked, his hands hardly on the wheel, almost as if he wanted to disguise the probing nature of his questioning. I stayed as polite as I could, but it was hard not to become irritated. Nev was assuming too much if he thought that one fun night out was enough to buy my trust and friendship, even if he was Dan's father.

"Ahh ... all the positive ones, really; love at the moment."

Dan leaned forward in his seat. "Really? So you can use it

to make someone fall in love with you?" He didn't even sound skeptical.

"Umm … no, not really. More just to create an atmosphere of love around people. What they might do with that love is another matter altogether."

"Oh." Now he sounded deflated. "Have you trialed it yet? I could help you." He was hopeful again.

"No, I haven't, and yes I suppose you could, but I haven't decided when, and it's not ready yet." I really wished no-one knew what I was doing. It would feel a lot safer, that's for sure. To change the subject, I asked Nev if he knew the people we were about to meet. We were almost there by the looks of things; I could see a huge spume of water from the fountain appearing over the top of the cars parked up ahead.

"We'll be parking in a minute or two, so listen hard," Nev began, his eyes scanning for an available car park. "The Chairman first: Vander Bustle has held the chair for seven years now, and is very well respected. He used to be with the FBI and coordinated the relay of information between the FBI and CFR. After he was granted extended service leave, he got more and more involved with advising the CFR and was eventually asked by the Council to mediate in a dispute between the then current chairman and two committee members. To cut a long story short, the debacle ended with the chairman resigning and the position being offered to Vander in recognition of his diplomacy and negotiating skills. He still has very powerful connections.

"Next is Melinda Cole, the Preparatory Operations Director. Mel is an international scout, coordinating with CFR council's world-wide, touting strategic leaders and global organizations for decompositional societal trends and then rats out deficiencies in cultural, political, and business arenas that could benefit from CFR input and assistance. It always is and always has been far too much work for one person, but Mel is the one to make things happen. She creates miracles from mysteries.

"Then there's Blair Cummings. He's supposedly Vander's 2IC, but he's more bodyguard than brains I think. He's very fast at actioning instructions, as long as you only give him one at a time. But, as he has acted in many high profile movies over the years – you may even recognize his face – he has a huge network of power brokers in the entertainment industry, who, without wanting to sound crass, keep the bank rolling, if you get my drift."

By this time we were sitting motionless, Nev having squeezed the car into an impossible-looking space parallel to the curb and just opposite the fountain. It was dead on eleven. I looked around for Levi, at the same time realizing it would be futile to think he had managed to arrive here before us.

"That's about all we've got time for, guys. It's time to rock and roll." Nev might not look old, I thought to myself, but he sure sounds it. He continued. "At least there'll be three of them and three of us – all even stevens – not that you have anything at all to be worried about," he added hastily as I raised an eyebrow at him.

"Actually, there'll be four of us." It was Nev's turn to raise an eyebrow. "I invited Levi to join us." I looked at each of them in turn, inviting a response.

Dan continued to look out the window having chosen not to be a part of this conversation from the beginning.

Nev's face was non-committal as he replied, "Better not keep him waiting then, or the Council for that matter. Let's go team!"

Stepping from the car I was hit by a wave of heat from the strengthening summer sun, and I drew energy from it, raising my face to drink in the sunshine. Nev was already walking across the road, and Dan tugged at my arm.

"C'mon Jazz. Hopefully there'll be time for a bit of sun worship later."

I grinned at him suddenly. "It's a far cry from winter in New Zealand, eh?"

He smiled back. "Loving it."

We crossed the street half way and into the middle of the huge round-a-bout where the fountain sat like the centerpiece on a cake. The white marble pool curved gently round, echoing the form of the traffic island. There was a wide, green, grass band on the outer edge, then a shallow pool that reflected the blue of the sky, and a magnificent fountain statue shaped like a dandelion, which threw water ten feet into the air with a pressure that turned the pristine liquid white and frothy before it fell into the waiting pool. I just wanted to dive in, or at least take off my shoes and paddle.

There were few people standing or sitting around, but most were rushing through, using the traffic island as a shortcut to somewhere else. None of those nearby even remotely looked like Levi, but I reminded myself he would probably come slightly disguised to avoid attracting attention, so I took my time looking, just in case. At seven minutes past eleven a huge limo drove slowly by, its tinted windows looking mysterious and important.

"Weird place to choose to meet, really," I commented abstractly to whoever was listening as I watched the stretch limo roll by. Perhaps Levi was in it. Nah, I thought, it's far too pretentious for him – or maybe not, as I remembered his flash motorbike, Miss Motion. Now that was a good memory!

"Or maybe not so weird," Nev's voice broke through my flashbacks of roaring along the night roads. "Follow me."

He walked to the edge of the roundabout where the limo was still crawling along like an over-sized ant, and tapped three times on the rear window. The tinted glass lowered a fraction in response and Nev whispered an unintelligible word. In a flash, the car stopped, the door was opened and Nev thrust Dan and me inside, and followed closely behind. It all happened so quickly I was caught by surprise, and as my eyes blinked to adjust to the dim interior light, I realized the limo was moving, and the fountain was disappearing from view.

"Hang on a minute," I protested, "we're still waiting for someone to arrive."

The man sitting on the far opposite side to me said smoothly, "If you're talking about Levi Gibson, he won't be joining us today; said to pass on his apologies."

"But," I persisted, "I'm sure he's coming."

The man, who I presumed must be Vander, smiled a tight, hard smile. "Yes, well, that's number three on the agenda. But shall we introduce ourselves first?"

I slumped back in the seat, realizing there was nothing I could do. Levi would probably think I had run away again, unless Vander was telling the truth. I needed to refocus, fast. Crossing my legs and straightening up, I looked the man straight in the eye.

"My name is Jasmine Blade, verified Reader, here to meet the CFR as per their instruction. Beside me is Dan Picoult, accompanying me at the request of my Framers, Ali and Alistaire Blade. I assume you are already acquainted with Neville." I indicated to the far end of the seat where Neville sat, looking relaxed and supportive. "And you?" I questioned, continuing to meet Vander's gaze, not yet ready to take my eyes away and measure the other occupants of the vehicle. I sized him up as he spoke.

"Ahem, nice to meet you, Jasmine; likewise Dan," he nodded at Neville and continued. "I am Vander Bustle, Chairperson of the CFR. Next to me are Melinda Cole, Director of Preparatory Operations, and then Blair Cummings, Deference and Defense Coordinator."

I nodded and murmured hello to each in turn. Vander was not a large man. Actually, he was skinny beyond belief and it was hard to tell how tall he was sitting down, but I guessed not much taller than me. His face had a marooned look about it, like he had spent too much time alone on a desert island and was uncomfortable around people. He stuck a finger in his collar to loosen it, as if proving my point. With very little hair it was probably his eyes that made the biggest impact: they were a piercing blue, stabbing, and direct. Other than that, it would be very easy to lose him in a crowd; his nondescript persona totally underwhelming on first impression.

Melinda, on the other hand, looked gorgeous and fun – and daring. She wore a fairly conservative skirt and jacket suit combination in a pale gray, but underneath was an electric blue blouse, with a canary yellow scarf. Very high heels and a bolt of blue dye through her very black hair gave her an avant-garde appearance, which either drew or repelled you, depending on your ability to keep an open mind. I could swear she winked at me.

Blair, on the other hand, was slightly scary, and I noticed Dan sizing him up from the outset. Your typical commando marine officer, he had short spiky blonde hair, a square jaw and bulging muscles. His eyes were like the slots of a coin-operated gaming machine, and he sat as if he were actually crouched waiting to pounce, rather than lounging in the back of a luxury car. My eyes quickly skipped over to Vander as he continued talking.

"Now, Jasmine, do you mind holding out your left arm?" He blinked almost apologetically. "We do need to check for the star; organizational procedure and all that."

As I did so I asked, "And what identification verification may I see of yours?" I fluttered my eyelashes apologetically back. "You'll appreciate this is all new to me and checking the authenticity of the CFR has been somewhat ... *difficult*." I emphasized it for effect.

"No problem, no problem at all. Melinda will provide documentation for you to check whilst Blair gets the drinks." He turned and smiled thinly at his colleagues, at the same time angling my wrist towards them so they could view the blue star that had appeared there. They both nodded, and then smiled at me, the early tension subsiding a little. It was almost as though this was some sort of test that I needed to pass. Everyone sat quietly and observed while Vander put me through my paces.

As Blair laid out the refreshments on the table between us, Vander checked my knowledge on the Code of Readers and the Pillars of Wisdom, plus my general knowledge as to the dynasty of Readers who had gone before. Satisfied with my answers, he finally took a small sip of orange juice and sat back in his seat.

We must have been driving for nearly forty-five minutes now, and I still had no idea where we were going. Fortunately, Dan decided to ask.

"Ummm, it'd be great to know where we are going and how long we'll be gone." His accent sounded very kiwi, more foreign than usual.

Melinda replied, and her voice was husky and almost

musical – quite deep for a woman, in fact. "Fair question, Dan. I apologize for not informing you sooner. We have no destination for this meeting; our offices are in Raleigh, which as you know is three hours away, and rather than waste your time or ours, this seemed an easy solution. We have other things to attend to on the Coast anyway. An acquaintance of Blair's has provided the limo for our use as a mobile meeting room for times such as this. Our driver will keep to the main highways in order to minimize disruption and the agenda will take an hour or two to get through, after which we will return you to the pick-up point."

Dan both nodded and shook his head at the same time, as if to say, "These Americans are crazy!"

I finished looking over the official documentation, and seeing nothing untoward about it, I checked with Vander. "May I keep a hold of this?"

"Certainly," he replied pleasantly, taking another small sip of juice and wiping his mouth delicately with the corner of a napkin.

Neville stirred impatiently in his seat. "No sense in prolonging this meeting more than we have to. Shall we proceed?"" He was directing the question at Vander, but it was Melinda who answered. Her voice was just as deep as before but slightly harder.

"Indeed, Neville. I have the agenda right here. Let's see ... first up is Remuneration. Second, Quest Précis, and third, Carrier Delegation. Shouldn't take long then."

She smiled at me, looking much younger than the thirty-five years I guessed her to be. Smoothing her skirt, she placed a slim, blue folder on her lap; reaching inside she handed me an envelope, saying, "You may open this now or leave it until later – your choice. Inside you will find a bank deposit slip, which, when you take it to the bank, they will issue you with the account cash card and a secondary credit card. Both have an upper limit, which I am sure you will find more than generous. The bank manager, Mr. Symes, will require your signature, photo I.D., and will set your security pin number. Every purchase you make may be traced, with a discretionary slush fund up to five thousand dollars permissible per month."

I couldn't help myself, I had to interrupt. "Melinda – hang on a minute – you mean I get paid for this? I thought this was all about personal Destiny, altruism, and philanthropic pursuit?" I must have looked flabbergasted, because Melinda chuckled; Vander snorted, and even Blair's mouth slightly twitched.

"The idea has always been that a Reader commits to their given Destiny and quest with no expectation of any reward – financial or otherwise. However, the House of Al-Bashar set aside funds from the very beginning in a 'Readers Trust,' with very specific directions as to how they were to be distributed and managed: the greater the quest, the greater the risk; therefore the greater the reward." She frowned at me, her face suddenly looking older. "It's no walk in the park you know. The expectation and pressure on a Reader to discover and develop the tools required to succeed at their given quest – in your case Esmovoir – are immense and unforgiving. The Destiny you carry will impact on us all, and potentially the world. The weight on your young shoulders will increase and may crush you if you fail. You do understand all of this?"

It was my turn to frown. "Yes, of course I understand. But these new experiences have unlocked a part of me that never seemed to fit and the peace from that balances the potential risk. The greatest tragedy would be if I didn't try. In my book, that would be the only evidence of failure." I lifted my chin as I spoke. "I am compelled to do this. It's as if a force greater than me is opening the way, and I am simply the sojourner who has chosen the path less traveled."

Vander interjected. "Very eloquent, my dear. So, tell us about your journey, Jasmine, your progress with Esmovoir. Neville has intimated that you have made headway, so let us put philosophy aside for now, and hear of your discoveries of how to 'move the emotions'." His voice was smooth and gentle, slightly mesmerizing, and I found myself eager to oblige.

Faultlessly and seamlessly, I explained the haunting ache I had carried for a lifetime; how it had shaped and moved me towards my Destiny and how the stars had aligned to carry me to

New Zealand and back again. I could feel inside me the emotions I bottled being shaken, the cap loosened, and I knew it was only a matter of time before the intensity within could no longer be restrained. But restraint was paramount, and as I told the story of creating Emospheres I pictured Tarjeen jumping across the stepping stones in the river, and told only what was absolutely necessary to communicate the potential that Emospheres might have. The big picture of my journey I painted in vivid imagery; the detail I withheld, knowing that to be wise I should exercise restraint so that the power of my newfound knowledge might not be lost. If body language was anything to go by, Vander was shouting with excitement. He was leaning forward in his seat, with eyes crackling and knees shaking in uncontrollable muscle spasms. It was like feeding the seals at the zoo: I threw the tidbits carefully, and watched for his response, remembering Levi's cautionary words. If he were a trustworthy friend, I needed him close. If he were an enemy, even closer.

"Perfect!" Vander cried as I wound up my journey thus far. "Perfect! Those Emospheres sound quite the thing. Time to reveal Jasmine's quest, wouldn't you agree Melinda? Blair?"

The others nodded in unison, and it was my time to lean forward in my seat. Finally there would be some purpose to all of this! In the back of my mind somewhere I realized it was not money that drove me, nor success: it was purpose – the knowledge that my life, my discoveries, my actions mattered – that pursuit of truth and goodness were worthwhile. That was enough. Surprise washed over me, followed by a wave of contentment. I was ready.

Vander began.

"I presume you recall the early days of President Obama's campaign trail?"

I nodded. "I went and heard him speak; my whole family did." Vander raised his eyebrows in interest. "We were staying at my maternal grandparents' place in Charlotte," I explained, "and they were huge Obama fans. When Grandpa heard he was speaking at Rock Hill, he urged us to go with them. It was at Northwestern High school, three months before the final democratic elections. It reminded me of being in a Black church congregation; there was such hope, such passion. Obama preached up a storm. I don't remember much of what he said, but I certainly came away thinking he could achieve the impossible." I shook myself back to the present. "What of it?"

"Well," Vander was choosing his words carefully, "there was a White minority at that meeting who were none too happy with Obama, and they are even less happy with him now. Melinda has been following their activities and infiltrated their ranks. Angry with the Obama administration, it is their intention to begin a series of protests that follow the campaign trail Obama originally made, coinciding with events at each location. They have gathered a core of around three-hundred White neo-Nazi extremists who aim to incite crowd hysteria, and once a riot is underway they intend to target as many Blacks as possible, beating them senseless. We've even heard they intend to stamp every forehead they can with the words "black plague." They simply don't care about the repercussions anymore; they just want their view point to be heard. They say they are sick of being discriminated against, just for wanting to protect the rights of Whites. Crazy, I know."

Melinda continued. "It's scary, though. The people involved would strike you as quite average, not your classic KKK-style personalities. Anyhow, I have put together an overview with all the information and background you will need – a bit of light bed time reading," she tried to joke, but it fell flat.

Vander took over. "The crux of your initial assignment, however, is centered on an event at the North Carolina State Fair Grounds in ten days' time. Alien Potion, whom you will be familiar with, is performing there on the Saturday night. It not only happens to be a venue from the original campaign trail, but Melinda has heard rumors that Obama's daughters will be attending, as they are huge fans of the band. White supremacist leaders see it as an opportunity to use shock tactics to push home their point, but we don't think the girls are in any actual danger. Your task, therefore, is to utilize these Emospheres to alter the mood of the crowd. As the rabble incites the masses, you need to read the atmosphere and release the correct emotional weaponry at the right time and location."

I shook my head in disbelief. "I find it hard to believe the problem is as big as you say. I know there was some discontent in the South at having a Black president, but I thought judgment by skin color died out years ago!"

Dan was equally incredulous. "Most of my mates back in New Zealand are brown-skinned Polynesian and Maori. If I showed a hint of racism they'd probably strap me to the side of a wild pig and throw me in a mud hole!"

Vander smiled a tight-lipped smile and directed his piercing eyes at me, ignoring Dan's outburst. "Do you understand the missive? It is important that you realize this is an opportunity to demonstrate the power of these 'Emospheres.' It is not the fulfillment of your quest, rather the opening phase. *If*, and it is a big *if*, crowd responses can be manipulated by Emospheres, then the FBI and high government officials will want to talk with regard to their potential on the world stage, particularly in countries of high military conflict. The UN might even step up. You are playing a game with huge stakes. There is a lot to be won, but even more to be lost."

I had already contemplated the gravity of my invention: the potential for Emospheres to become a new form of weaponry, and understood that once the CFR saw the power that came with manipulating emotions, I could well be thrust into a world of international intrigue.

"I am completely aware of the need to demonstrate Emospheres, and the potential for ... other applications," I replied, thinking of the experiment we had conducted at the rugby game. This shouldn't be too different.

"Good. Then we may proceed to our final agenda item: Carrier Delegation." He paused, shifted in his seat and looked out the window as he spoke. "The CFR have," he paused again, "appointed Neville as your official Carrier. Levi Gibson ..." I waited for the blow I knew was coming, "has been removed from your quest. He is deemed to be no longer available to fulfill the role of Carrier, particularly as at the event in question he will be on stage performing. Do you understand?"

His head whipped around and his eyes were like acid on me, as if to challenge me to argue.

I didn't disappoint him. "Surely it is my decision to make as a Reader?"

"Up until a certain point, yes. However, if the Council feel there is a conflict of interest, they have the power to step in and intervene."

I swallowed my disappointment. "My Framers never made me aware of this rule. Neville, what do you know?"

He spoke gently, as if to a child. "Vander is right; if Levi wasn't pursuing fame it might be different. But any distraction from the quest can be fatal."

"Well I disagree," I voiced strongly. "He will be in the best position on the day to identify any insurgents, and I know he wants to help."

Vander looked at me pityingly. "He wants to help himself, my dear, to whatever takes his fancy. His ego has clouded his abilities as a Carrier, and nothing can change that. This is not negotiable: an edict from the CFR is final."

Melinda shifted uncomfortably, but I appealed to her anyway. "Melinda, have you met Levi? Are you in agreement over this? Does he even know?"

"It has been decided." Her voice was soft and husky. "A message has been sent to him. It was best he wasn't here today. Levi has always been ... different. Maybe in time things will change."

She looked over at me, a sad, pleading expression in her eyes. Dan patted my knee but I ignored him, folding my arms and staring out the window, bottling up my feelings. I would give nothing else away today.

"So be it," I heard my voice say, hollow and strange; empty.

Within moments the driver pulled over, opened the door and we were standing again by the fountain in the strong daylight, but even the power of the sun wasn't going to give me back my strength at this moment. I clutched the folder containing my future to my chest and under my breath said goodbye to Act One. Time for Act Two to take center stage. I turned to Nev and smiled.

16. LOVE IS IN THE AIR

IF LIFE HAS THE ABILITY TO KICK YOU IN THE GUTS and then kick you again while you're down, that was the life I lived over the next few days.

After putting on an "I'm OK" act for Neville and Dan all the way home, I was exhausted. I had forgotten that Chad was hosting some Californian surfing buddies over the next two nights, and when we arrived, the beach house was well on its way to becoming party central. Yelling over the loud music, Chad invited Neville and Dan to come hang out and talk waves (Dan's eyes lit up), and I was able to excuse myself, pleading the need for a "Nana nap" without anyone taking too much notice. Once safely shut in my bedroom, I set aside my exhaustion and turned to my anger. How dare the CFR decide that Levi could not be my Carrier! Why on earth did Vander think Neville was more suitable? Should I just have told them that it was too late? That Levi and I had already sealed the partnership with a kiss?

I punched my pillow in silent rage, trying to make sense out of it all. I needed to talk to Levi face to face and explain why we weren't at the fountain this afternoon and perhaps see if there was any way to reverse the CFR decision.

Without thinking, I jumped out my window and snuck down the side of the house, over the fence and through the neighbor's property to the beach. The sand felt hot between my toes and I set off towards Levi's house at a fast pace, letting the sights and sounds of the ocean restore my equilibrium and soothe my troubled mind. What doesn't kill me only makes me stronger, I determined as I walked. Jasmine isn't a wild flower for nothing: tenacious and tough, growing in the most unlikely places. By the time I reached Levi's I had walked and talked my anger into some semblance of order and it was simmering gently, hopefully cooking up a plan rather than hissing and spitting out of control. But I wasn't quite ready to face Levi – unsure if my anger might not turn into tears when I saw him. Approaching from the beach, I hesitated, and instead of climbing the stairs up to the veranda, I ducked underneath and sat in the shade of the deck to catch my breath and my self-control. Damn! I should have bought my phone. I could have texted him to meet me. Lying back with my arms crossed behind my head I watched the sun twinkle between the wooden boards above, the cool shade sending a shiver through me after the heat of the beach, and I hoped it would chill my anger as efficiently as it did my body. The dark shadows reminded me of being under the house back in New Zealand, and I thought about the oil I had extracted from the strange plant I had found there and brought back with me to use for other Emospheres. Would it work with Love? A sudden creak from the wooden planks startled me, and I sat up, listening intently. It was Levi's voice I heard first.

"There's the beginning of a cool breeze out here, so it shouldn't be too hot. Please, take a seat Vander."

I stiffened in surprise. Vander? What was he doing here?

"Thank you, Levi, and for the drink also. It's been a long day."

"You know you didn't have to come all the way out here to tell me; it's not like I'm offended or anything." Levi sounded slightly amused, I thought.

"Well, the CFR know how long you have been waiting to perform as a Carrier, and seeing as Jasmine is so … striking, and by the looks of things a powerhouse of emotion, we wondered if you'd be able to resist." Vander just sounded smarmy.

Levi laughed an easy, long laugh. "Oh come on now, Vander! Jasmine is just a kid! And I have my hands full what with Bailey and band stuff. She might be pretty, and I'm sure she's got what it takes to be a top notch Reader – but you're right. Neville's obviously the right man for the job."

"Ah – you're so like your father was, if you don't mind me saying – straight to the point. But you don't think she has a certain ..." he paused "*je ne sais quoi*?"

"I can assure you," Levi's voice said confidently, "her power has no hold on me at all; Neville will be good for her; maybe teach her to focus. She will need good friends, though, and I'll be remembering that. Don't think I'm going to completely disappear from the scene."

Vander laughed nervously, replying "Of course not, the CFR values team work, especially when we're dealing with someone so young and inexperienced. So what we agreed upon inside stands?"

"Yep. No worries there. I will let you know what I discover."

During the short silence that followed I realized I was clenching fistfuls of sand and every muscle in my body was tense. If I had thought my anger before was extreme, now it was off the Richter scale; explosive rage pumped into my nervous system till I was shaking uncontrollably. How dare he? How ... how ... how dare he? And I had stuck up for him, even defended him in front of Vander this afternoon. If I'd known how he felt I wouldn't have bothered. What a low-life – a mud-sucking slimy two-faced jerk. I reeled off all the worst words of the English language in my mind to stop myself from marching up there and punching his arrogant face. I needed to listen – if I could hear over the blood boiling in my veins.

I stiffened as the veranda creaked loudly and I heard Vander say, "Well, thanks again for your understanding and support. We do need to stick together if the Readership is to survive. I can't tempt you to join us for dinner as I mentioned earlier? Melinda is dying to catch up with you."

"I would love to see Melinda; however, with the current

concert schedule I'm booked with rehearsals every night. In fact I'm running late already. Here, let me take that; but another time soon …" and his voice faded as they disappeared back inside the house.

I ran blindly, tears stung my face and my hair was whipping in the rising wind. I could feel rain coming. If only I could run away from the rage and the pain; bury it here on the beach as if it never existed; leave it for someone else to find and deal with so I could move on with my life. I was alone again, flying solo, no one to trust, no one to confide in. I thought about phoning Ali and Arabella, but then remembered that they were supporting Neville's bid to Carry me. Perhaps Levi was just bluffing with Vander, playing games – but why at my expense? Why refer to me as just a kid around him? Was I? It just hurt too much, even if it was an attempt to mislead Vander. Surely it was better to confront and be truthful? That was the way I had been raised. No. Levi was out of the equation; totally out. Knowing his comments about me, I never wanted to face him again.

I couldn't outrun my rage, but after an hour it settled to a simmer, and pity began to creep closer, looking to shower me in sorrow. Making my way home, I knew I needed to keep busy, and what better way than to mix Emospheres? I had been itching for days to complete the Love and Fear formulas, and the methodical process might soothe my angry nerves. I was relieved to hear loud, wild music booming from inside, as Chad and his friends chilled out in the final heavy heat of the day.

Climbing back in through my bedroom window I grabbed the small bottle labeled "First Love" from the drawer in my dresser and looked for the serviette with my notes from the other night. Hmmm. That's funny, I thought. I'm sure I remember seeing it here. Maybe it fell behind the dresser. No, it wasn't there. I tossed my hair impatiently. Never mind, it's not like I really needed to check. Taking everything to the bathroom, I locked the door and swiftly combined the ingredients. This time was different from the first experiment back in New Zealand; I worked with a surety, a confidence, like that of an experienced chef assembling their signature dish. There was no doubt in my mind that this would work, and in ten short minutes I held the small glass bottle up to the mirror, giving it a few good shakes. To anyone else it would simply appear as pretty pink bubble mix, no hint of the powerful Emosphere of Love it packed in a single burst. Slipping the bottle into my pocket I tidied the mess, cleaned up myself, and ignoring the angry flush that still stained my cheeks I made my way to the lounge. What I saw upon entering made me wish I'd stayed in my bedroom with the big bar of chocolate Mom had left for me.

Under the soothing notes of Jack Johnson and smothered in the late afternoon sun sat Chad and Bailey, blonde heads close together, deep in a conversation I couldn't quite hear. They didn't even notice me appear. I looked around, poised for flight, but Levi was nowhere to be seen. I relaxed slightly. Chad's mates, Sedge and Will, were with Dan competing for attention out on the deck, surrounded by a small cluster of girls, some of whom I recognized as Fale and Harleys "groupies." A few other randoms were out by the BBQ evidently sizzling sausages, but where was Neville? My eyes darted back to Chad and Bailey still engrossed in each other. Bah! What was going on? Why was *she* here? A voice at my shoulder made me jump. So Neville was still here.

"Feeling better? I did check on you once – not that you were actually *there* to check!"

"Yeah. I needed to clear my head, so I headed out for a bit of a walk, but I'm all good now." I hoped my tone didn't sound too false.

"I figured that," Neville said sympathetically. "The meeting this morning was pretty full on. I'm not quite sure myself why they're cutting Levi out of the picture completely; his involvement could still be of use. Maybe I can convince the Council ..."

"I wouldn't bother, Nev," I interrupted, turning to face him and not wanting to see Bailey with my brother any longer. "I've thought about it and Levi really doesn't have the time to commit; whereas you and I can work out a strategy for the concert and plan for any unforeseen circumstances – and we have

Dan to help out. You know what they say: 'too many cooks spoil the broth.' It's not about personal preferences, it's about what's best for the big picture, what's best for the mission, .and in this case we need to put as much time and effort in to that as we can, which is something that Levi can't afford."

I was so convincing I almost believed it myself, if it wasn't for the dull ache within reminding me of the huge wound I now carried.

Neville leaned against the wall with his arms folded and nodded eagerly. "You're right, Jazz. Sheesh! Methinks you are wise beyond your years. We need to focus on proving to the CFR that your Emospheres are as powerful and useful as you say they are. Talking of which, I would love to see a demonstration some time. When you're ready of course," he added hastily.

Huh! At least someone round here thought I wasn't a kid, and that I did have a brain, I mused sourly.

"I think we could arrange that." I smiled with a hint of mischievousness, and pointed to Chad. "See my brother over there? Well, he hasn't had a girlfriend in three years – hardly even dated. And see the blonde girl he's talking to?" Neville nodded. "That's Bailey. I know for a fact that she's Levi's girlfriend, or at least they're very close," I amended slightly, not completely sure myself.

"So?" Nev prompted me, and I shook off the melancholy that seemed to descend anytime I mentioned Levi's name.

I pulled the glass bottle of Emospheres from my pocket and waggled it in front of Nev's face. "*So*, no time like the present."

We were standing just where the hallway opened into the living area, and Chad was sitting with his back to us on the sofa nearest the hallway. Bailey was next to him, and could have seen us if she'd looked over, but she was far too busy focusing on what she was telling Chad. Waiting until I was sure no one was looking, I gave one last hard shake, surreptitiously removed the stopper from the bottle and gently blew. A cascade of tiny pink spheres erupted from the wand and danced towards the back of Chad's head. As they dropped, Bailey noticed and gasped delightedly, raising her voice.

"Look, Chad," she began to giggle, "Bubbles! Hundreds of tiny pink bubbles! They're beautiful!" And she reached out a hand to touch them.

Pop! The bubbles began to fizz and splutter over them both as Chad turned around with a very suspicious look on his face. "Jazz," he started saying, "those better not be what I think they ..." His voice petered off as Bailey's hand pulled his head back towards her.

"Oh Chad," she cooed, tears glistening in her eyes, "I just have this overwhelming sensation all of a sudden, it's like ... it's like ..."

Chad finished off her sentence. "It's like love is in the air!"

"Exactly!" And she threw her arms around him. Chad was not shy in reciprocating and a dreamy look entered his eyes.

"Wow!" Nev whistled long and low. You weren't joking, were you? That's potent stuff. I can feel the wave of love emanating from the couch all the way over here. It makes you want to ... hug someone!" Before I could react he swept me into a big bear hug, lifting me off the ground and swinging me around. "And now I'm going to hug my son!" And with that he released me, careering out to the veranda, startling Dan with his enthusiastic public display of affection.

I watched, amused, knowing Dan would be slightly embarrassed. I saw enough of him in New Zealand to know that kiwi blokes liked to err on the side of subtle when it came to showing emotion. A big part of me wanted to go and hug Dan myself, and I felt tears pricking my own eyes. He had become important to me over the last few weeks; a friend for life.

Caught up in my reverie, the sudden touch of cool hands covering my eyes put me off balance and I stumbled forward. "What on earth...?" I instinctively reached up to remove the hands from my face.

"Uh uh!" Came a deep familiar voice, and I twisted sharply to break the hold and see if my guess was right.

"Matt!" I spun right around and shared the love that was

welling up within, taking Matt completely by surprise.

"Whoa, girl! I know it's been a while, but you don't have to break my bones."

I ignored his comment, smiling up with a soporific expression until my eyes caught a glimpse of someone else over his shoulder. "Elle!" I shrieked, and she joined in the hug, laughing at my over-enthusiastic greeting. I looked from one to the other; my voice sounding like a love struck Amy Winehouse. "You guys ... man is it good to see you. Can you feel the love, or do we need some more?"

Elle looked at me suspiciously. "Have you been given illegal substances, Jazz? Or drunk something you shouldn't?" I had already dipped the bubble wand and was blowing softly, watching the effortless delicate embodiments of my Love float above us, suspended like twinkling stars, then falling, shooting, and releasing their hidden treasure trove of Agape, the highest and purest form of love in action.

Chad had made his way to the stereo and selected a play list from my iPod – a collection of love songs I had built up over the years. The softly crooning tones of Owl City swirled around the room and Chad's arms wrapped around Bailey as they began to slow dance. Matt and Elle went to join them as the Love-infused air wove its magic, while I decided that everyone else deserved a taste too, and I continued to blow bubbles at strategic points of the living areas – even releasing some out on the deck.

The evening took on an ethereal quality of its own after that, as all other feelings and emotions people might have had were overtaken by the overwhelming atmosphere that the Love Emospheres created wherever they landed. A strangely beautiful mood descended on everyone and I realized that something unique was happening here. This was no physical, sexual love, or a love driven by lust and selfish desires, but an all-encompassing love, selfless and graceful, encouraging a sacrificial willingness to embrace the intrinsic value of love in its highest form. One of the surfer dudes, Sedge, had grabbed a scrap of paper and pen and was scribbling furiously, and when I peeked over his shoulder it looked like a poem of sorts. Will was slow dancing with one of the girls; another guy was lighting all the candles he could find, both inside and out in the garden; yet another couple of Chad's mates had organized a huge pizza delivery, telling everyone it was their treat – no contribution required. I sat down, amazed at how everyone was speaking love in their own language – either with physical affection, written or spoken words, helping others, or showing generosity. Love, I thought, has so many ways to show it and we each communicate it so differently. It was fascinating to watch.

And that was when Dan found me, curled up on the couch, my arms wrapped around my knees, silently observing the effects of Emospherica, wide-eyed with wonder. Pulling me up on the dance floor he directed my arms around his neck and we joined the other swaying couples, the music soft and intimate.

"So this is what your love feels like," Dan's voice was hushed. "I had wondered if I would ever know."

"It's so surreal," I breathed back; "I can't believe how powerful the formula is. It's like the spheres are charged with emotional electricity where the voltage increases with each application, as if like they are recharging and reproducing upon impact. I wonder how long the effects will last."

"Dan to Jazz; come in Jazz." Dan's hand was waving back and forwards in front of my face, and I laughed; still sounding melancholic, but it was a laugh at least.

"Sorry Dan, I do tend to get very introspective when I'm evaluating results. It's my passion you see, and you're forgetting this is a science experiment after all!"

"Mmmm. But I've hardly seen you since we've arrived. And I'm supposed to file an update with Ali and Arabella tomorrow. What am I supposed to say?' I noticed his arms were now clasped around my waist, pulling me in towards him and I vaguely thought there was something wrong with this, but the spell had spilt over everyone – including me – and I was held by its power.

"You have seen me,'" I protested, "every day."

"But not by yourself. There are always others around." He was almost grumbling.

"We're not in the back blocks of New Zealand now," I reminded him. "I have places to be, people to meet.'"

"I know that, it's just I miss you, Jazz."

"I miss you too." I realized as I said it that it was true. Dan, unlike Levi, was simple, uncomplicated, a known quantity: a safe bet.

"Just tell Ali and Arabella the truth – that we're making progress, there's been no threats on my life yet – ha-ha – and update them on the fact I'm going to be working with Neville, 'D' Day being Saturday week. There! Not so difficult, eh? Speaking of Nev, where is he?"

Dropping my arms I went to look for him, with Dan following behind. Parting company at the kitchen, Dan headed outside to check there, whilst I searched the house; not that I had to look far. Nev was seated on the floor between the kitchen island bench and the fridge, clutching a bottle of strong smelling spirits. I slid down the face of the cupboards and sat next to him.

"Nev, what's up?" I asked gently. "You're not ... crying are you?"

"I'm sorry, Jazz," he half spoke, half sobbed. "It's just that when love comes to town I get depressed remembering my ex, and how I ditched her, and that I never got to see my son grow up, and I feel so (hic) ... bad inside." He leaned his head on my shoulder "And that makes me want liquid comfort. I'm sorry; you're a great girl, Jazz, you really are." I awkwardly patted his head, not sure what to think. "And those Emospheres are so amazing. Can I just look at them for a minute?"

I couldn't see the harm with that, and I handed him the bottle. He seemed more overcome with emotion than drunk, and I figured that maybe it would help him refocus his thoughts. He held the bottle reverently for a few moments, and then put his hand on the lid asking, "May I?"

I shrugged. "Yeah sure – but no blowing bubbles. There's enough love in this place to sink a ship!"

He deftly removed the stopper and held it up to his nose inhaling deeply. "Mmmm ... smells like roses."

Dan's head popped over the top of the bench. "What

smells like roses?" Nev looked up with a start, and before I could react, the bottle slipped through his fingers and smashed on the cold hard tiles, the pink liquid oozing over the floor between us.

"Oops." Nev whispered the understatement of the night.

I just sighed. Love is slow to anger, I thought ruefully as I used the brush and shovel from under the sink to sweep up the worst of the mess. I had focused enough on my anger today; I was sick of it. Dan had already rinsed a cloth, which I then used to mop up the remainder of the spill, and we all watched as the last pinky water washed away down the plug hole. I sighed again, thinking of the effort that had gone into making it, but I guess it was a good representation of my day: love shattered, broken.

"Take him home, would you? I think he needs to sleep it off." Dan nodded.

"Will do," he said, slipping Ned's arm around his shoulder, "but I'll be back in the morning for a surf. You could join us." His eyes looked determined.

I sighed once more, and walked them both to the front door. Next, I located Matt and Elle, thinking how weird it was to see them so wrapped up in each other.

"I gotta get to bed you guys – I'm totally whacked – but you're welcome to crash here and we can catch up in the morning."

"Love to," they both replied simultaneously, taking a break from hugging each other to hug me instead.

Lastly, I walked past Chad and Bailey, who were snuggled up and deep in conversation again, so I didn't interrupt – didn't want to anyway.

Collecting my cell phone from the hall table where I had left it to charge earlier in the day, I headed to the bedroom, too tired now to even contemplate cleaning my teeth. They could wait till the morning, and so could my phone. Slipping between the cool sheets I looked at my Reader's Ring, staring sadly at its simple beauty for what seemed like ages, before resolutely removing it and burying it at the bottom of the dresser beside my bed. Finally, I sent up a prayer for a quick trip to oblivion, which was answered; no desert, no Levi, and no answers.

17. LIVE & LET LIVE

I WOKE WITH SHEETS TANGLED AROUND ME AND breath that smelt like stale pizza from the night before – eew! The house was deathly quiet as I plodded to the bathroom and took care of my fuzzy-feeling teeth, taking a large glass of water back to bed with me. Turning on my phone in the gloomy pre-dawn light, the screen flashed brightly causing my eyes to blink rapidly. After a few moments it began bleeping, and I looked down again. There were three new messages on my voice mail; all from Levi's number. My anger had morphed into despair during the night, and the only solution I could think of was to put my head under the pillow and cry until sleep rescued me again.

It was 10.30 before I resurfaced, and the house still sounded quiet. I could hear the clock ticking like a time bomb from the far end of the hallway and I counted each second, not wanting to get up, but not wanting to stay in my bed either. A loud knock on the front door made me lose my place, and I sat up crossly, hoping someone else would answer it.

Another series of knocks began before I finally heard Chad mumbling loudly, "Coming, I'm coming!" After a few minutes Chad appeared in my doorway. "It's Levi – he wants to see you. I told him it wasn't a good idea this early in the morning, as you're not a pretty sight usually, but he's insisting." He laughed at his own joke, and I poked my tongue out.

"I don't want to see him. I might hurt him, I'm so mad. Or I'll cry. I'm not sure which is worse. Can you tell him … tell him … oh, I don't know! Tell him anything!"

Chad looked at me curiously. "Okaaay. Something's up. Want me to give him the big brother treatment? It'll cost you."

"Please do. Fine." I curled up under the covers, blotting out the word from view and intending to keep it that way for as long as I possibly could.

The next few days were a series of blots, me doing my best to wipe Levi from my life, refusing to return his calls or messages or wear my ring and with every advance he made I became more obstinate. Emotions should be bottled, I told myself fiercely; it's much safer for everyone that way – saves a lot of pain and heartache.

Keeping busy, I helped Chad entertain his friends, pacified Dan by joining him for a surf, researched the venue for the forthcoming concert, and discussed with Neville potential strategies to achieve the best outcomes on the day. Elle and Matt hadn't ended up staying on the Tuesday night, but had left a note saying they would pick up Dan and me for the concert on Saturday. I argued with Dan that we should skip the concert, but he was adamant.

"It's a great opportunity to suss out Alien Potion's performance and get some clues as to the timing of the gig. They'll probably perform the same sets the following week, so you'll know the program. It's all part of being prepared."

Nev agreed. "He's right, Jazz. It won't be the waste of time you think. Use it as a research opportunity: crowd dynamics, potential trouble spots, and techniques to move through the masses quickly – it's all gotta help. I would come, but I'm expected at a surfing tournament this weekend in Surf City. I'm judging, so don't want to let the organizers down."

I took my eyes off myself for a minute and realized that letting people down is not nice. I needed to snap out of this melancholy and engage with them: Dan, Elle, Matt, and my brothers. I hadn't seen Fale and Harley perform in ages.

And so Wednesday passed by, Thursday and Friday came and went. The only highlight was dinner with Mom and Dad on Friday evening. For once the whole family would be there. Marcus had arrived back in town, Fale and Harley had a rehearsal-free night and best of all, Mom was cooking. Chad and I collected everything she requested from the grocery store after he finished work on the Friday afternoon. Dan was driving Neville up to the surf carnival to check out some more of the coast, but would be back in time for the concert on Saturday, so I didn't have to worry about entertaining either of them. I could be selfish when it came to sharing family. When I picked up Chad from the surf shop Dan reminded him to keep an eye on me, just in case. Not that he needed to worry so much, there was no sign of any Jagger threat thus far; it had almost become a bit of a joke, with Chad and Dan flanking me whenever we left the house, acting like commando freaks or as if they were celebrity body guards. That was until I pointed out they were drawing a little too much attention our way, and they toned it down a notch or two.

It was the first opportunity I had to ask Chad about his evening with Bailey; he hadn't bought it up and my curiosity was itching to be scratched.

"So," I began nonchalantly, "made any new friends lately?"

He snorted. "You're about as subtle as a beet stain on a white shirt, Jazz. Why not just ask me straight up?"

"Alright then. You do know that Bailey and Levi are an item, so what gives?"

"Aha ... there's where you don't know it all, sis. Levi is a free agent. Bailey acts as a red herring, so she tells me. If you must know, she's known Levi for most of his life, although she didn't tell me exactly how. Anyway, her status with Levi is purely platonic. She's his agent, personal assistant, band manager, and, when she has to be, his pseudo girlfriend – a cover act for all those loopy groupies and media mongrels out there."

I nodded. I had seen her in action at the school concert first hand. I could laugh now, but at the time she really freaked me out.

Chad laughed at my story. "She's very protective of Levi – practically worships the ground he walks on."

"You still haven't answered me properly. What's going on between you and Bailey? You didn't even need the love Emosphere the other night to get cozy."

"That is for me to know and you to find out," he teased, "but we are catching up after the concert in the weekend. She's ... she's ... my type, I guess." He sounded surprised himself. "As for you ... you wanna talk about things?"

I shook my head firmly and clamped my mouth shut, and we traveled back to the beach house in silence.

Mom made a beautiful roast lamb for dinner with all the trimmings, and it tasted even better in the company of family. I marveled again at how lucky I was, how rich I felt. The CFR coinage seemed irrelevant in contrast to this, a family feast, a feast of family, where you loved each other at face value, no frills, no fakes, and a fail-safe net if you fell.

Towards the end of the meal, as conversations died down and we lingered at the table, enjoying the soft ambient candle light and satiated appetites, Dad called everyone to attention.

"Ahem, everyone, I haven't given Jazz any warning of this, but I think it's time that she filled us all in on her adventures of late, and the future path she has chosen. My premonition is that she will need family to stand by her in the next while, and that's only going to happen," he turned and looked at me, "if we all know what's going on. '*One for all and all for one,*' eh Jazz?" He smiled crookedly at me, and I recognized the line from one of our favorite movies, *The Three Musketeers*, which we had watched over and over when I was younger.

I smiled weakly as the family waited for me to speak, each with their own questions as to my recent disappearance and uncharacteristic behavior. I began hesitantly, searching for the right words to communicate the way in which my Destiny was unfolding, but as I saw acceptance and even admiration in their eyes I found my stride, and the fantastical story of my journey to becoming a Reader flowed – the highs, the lows, the precepts, the discovery of Emospheres, and the quest ahead of me. By the end I felt vulnerable and exposed, as if the seal I had so faithfully preserved over the years to shield the essence of Jasmine had been peeled gently away, and I was unsure if the fragility of that essence could withstand the scrutiny and freedom it was now suffering.

In the silence we sat, as each member of my family absorbed the sudden and profound realization that their sister, their daughter, had stumbled across a formula that could move the emotions. Not just the emotions of one, but the emotions of many. The enormity fell upon me again and I faced them despairingly.

"One for all…?" I whispered.

And slowly each of them whispered back, "And all for one."

It was a solemn moment, almost religious in its intensity, with the bond of family never stronger. Like Dad had said about any bullies we encountered at school: "You mess with one Blade, you better be prepared to mess with them all!"

We agreed to meet later in the week to discuss how best they could each support me on my first day of Emosphere testing, and I stressed the importance of secrecy – even suggesting Dan and Nev shouldn't know of anything we planned.

"I'm just not convinced of whom I can trust yet," I said as my eyes were pleading, "but I know I can trust you. Guess I'm asking for you to be my back-up crew."

"We're all in." Marcus spoke on behalf of everyone.

But Chad added on the end, "You know I'm in Jazz, but you gotta talk to Levi, OK?"

Mom added her two cents worth. "From what you've told us tonight, his loyalty looks questionable, but haven't I always told you to listen to your heart, to give others the chance to defend themselves?"

Fale chipped in too. "My money's with Levi. He's the man."

Dad looked unconvinced, but added "I'm sure Jazz will do the right thing, but as for now, I'm thinking the right thing is dessert! Am I right?"

When we saw what Mom had made for dessert, we were all definitely in agreement.

Saturday couldn't have been bluer if it tried. The heavens reminded me of rolled out Play-doh, fresh from the pottle, no blemishes or color confusion, just wonderful thick new blue – the bluest blue that invites you to dive in, coaxing your soul in its blueness. It was a pity I still felt a tinge of blue hanging over me. Not the sky blue, playful and free, but the be-devilled blue of the brokenhearted. I just couldn't seem to shake it off. Logically I knew what my family had said was right: I needed to give Levi a chance to explain. Perhaps it was my pride that wasn't letting me and withdrawing was my only form of self-preservation, ensuring that if Levi's words were true, he could not hurt me any further.

After returning from my morning run under the swimming pool sky, I took a long hot bath, soaking in the water scented with Jasmine oil for nearly an hour, performing every beauty ritual I could think of. If only I felt as beautiful on the inside; if only there were lotions and potions to soothe an aching heart. For what is beauty that is only skin deep? I contemplated the answer to that, and concluded that it soon fades like wild jasmine in the spring time, leaving the landscape barren and empty. The only way to fill my heart again, I decided as I sunk under the water and watched the air bubbles escape from my nose and mouth, was to focus not on myself, but on others. Today I would have an outward focus, finding within my heart remnants of happiness to share. Didn't Mom always say the best thing to have in your wardrobe is a big smile and a kind heart? And if worse came to worse, I could always use a bit of artificial stimulation in the form of an Emosphere bubble or two to get me going.

I prepared my mind also, focusing on the Precepts of a Reader and the Pillars of Wisdom. Wasn't the fifth Pillar Counsel? And wasn't that what my family had given me the night before? I knew I could trust them, so maybe I was one step closer to approaching Levi … just maybe. And what about the sixth Pillar: Understanding. I remembered the words Ali had said: *"The head is technical and knows truth and goodness, but it is the heart that understands the vitality of truth and the gravity of the battle between good and evil. The head will think, but the heart will discern; the two exercised together are a powerful force."* The only way I would find the truth was if I confronted Levi. The battle ahead would need my heart and my head to be in unison, not torn between fiction and fact, as they were at the moment.

As I finally dressed, both my physical and spiritual being was calm and relaxed, and my skin soft and silky. I wore jeans, knowing that although the sun was hot now, the night would cool things off pretty quickly. Throwing on a black summer singlet, I tied my Paua shell around my throat and studied the result in the mirror. I looked too young, I thought. My eyes were too big and my hair too wild, but I didn't feel like taming it today; it could fall where it pleased. At least my skin had darkened in the summer sun, I evaluated critically, and its olive tone looked healthy and smooth. Grabbing some cash and my cell phone, I smiled at my reflection, practicing happiness, and then slipped my Reader's Ring back on my finger. It was time to front up.

When I got to the porch Dan was walking up the concrete path, brimming with enthusiasm. *Time to think of others,* I reminded myself and smiled back at him, jumping up as I saw Elle's car coming along the road.

"Let's go, kiwi boy. Got your ear plugs?" I punched him lightly on the shoulder as I skipped past.

"Will I need them?" he replied anxiously, so I took full advantage of him.

"State regulations: won't let you into a rock concert without them." He looked over at me warily, undecided whether to believe me or not. "Deafness in young people is a big problem in America," I added innocently. "I for one have signed the petition to ban iPod headphones. Haven't you?" The expression in his eyes broke my resolve to keep a straight face, and my composure collapsed into giggles. "You should see your face – priceless – you've been punked, Danny boy." It was his turn to punch me in the arm, and not so gently. "Ow! You gotta admit, though – that was a good one."

He opened the car door and bowed as I got in. "O Great Wise Swami, lead on," he said, pulling a credible Indian accent and slamming the door behind him. Everyone was in high spirits, Matt and Elle in the front, Sam on one side of me in the back and Dan on the other. Introducing Dan properly to all of them was fun, and we were soon comparing life in America to life in New Zealand, all loudly proclaiming to be experts in cross-cultural communication.

"You kiwis are weird," began Sam. "You put minced beef in a pie and eat it for lunch!'"

"No, you're the crazy ones. You guys put pumpkin in a pie – a sweet pie – now that's just yuck!" Dan shot back.

"Aren't there, like, millions more sheep in New Zealand than people?" It was Matt's turn to act informed.

"Um ... you'd be right there. The ratio is about one to ten in favor of the sheep! We call them land-lice back home."

Matt and Sam thought that was hilarious and the jibes continued in good jest all the way to the venue, with the hours flying by. Inevitably, the conversation veered onto food again. Dan raved about hokey pokey ice cream, roast kumara and other sweet delights from kiwi land until we were all groaning and complaining of rumbling tummies.

"Food is first on my agenda after that long drive," Elle said firmly, putting on the handbrake and her lip gloss at the same time.

The Time Warner Cable Music Pavilion was located at Walnut Creek, an outdoor amphitheater in Raleigh, about three hours from the Emerald Isle. I had only been there once before, to a Kelly Clarkson concert a few years back. Marcus had been so into American Idol when he was seventeen, and reckoned he had picked Kelly to win right from the start; so when she shot to fame in the following years, he offered to take me to hear her live in 2006. Actually, all five of us had gone together – one of the few times we could all agree on a choice of music. After all, we had watched the TV series together, and happy memories add to the feel-good factor you get from pop music. The pavilion was accessed via a long driveway, and the amphitheater was not visible until you turned the final corner, and then it's like a sweeping first shot of an epic 3-D movie that hits you between the eyes and thrusts you into another world of sublime sound.

Once we walked from the car park and entered the arena gates I offered to stand in the food queue whilst the others visited the restrooms and the merchandise store. It was 5pm by now, and the crowds were beginning to swell; a buzz of anticipation grew in the air. Fale and Harley's band, The Cajun Braves, were due on stage in about half an hour, with the main act scheduled for 7pm. Despite all my attempts at being mature and wise in considering approaching Levi after the concert (I was sure Chad would help me out in locating him), I could feel a curdling in the pit of my stomach at the very thought of seeing him, let alone talking with him.

Prolonged silence does funny things to friendships, I mused as I waited to be served. Some you can ignore for months, even years, and then pick up where you left off at the drop of a hat; while other friendships are high maintenance, requiring constant communication otherwise one or the other is left feeling alienated and hurt. Then there are those friendships where you have to choose whether the fear of rejection outweighs the fear of silence and if you can summon the wherewithal to silence your nerves and break the silence – my current dilemma. Armed with two bags of burgers and fries and one takeaway tray of cokes I had the culminating realization that I didn't want to be silent anymore; I wanted to take risks, to be somewhere other than in a vacuum, untouchable and inward looking. The tightly curled ball in my midriff grew larger as I dared myself to break the silence tonight.

We positioned ourselves a little more than twenty meters from the main stage, which Elle adamantly said was close enough to the front. Any closer and the risk of being crunched by hard-core mosh-pit lovers and head bangers was outside her comfort level and I had to agree.

"Elle and Jazz are allergic to moshing – 'specially you Jazz, aren't you J?" Sam smirked, obviously remembering the trick they had pulled on me back at the high school concert.

I tossed my hair. "Only mosh-pits you're in, Samslamdunkinman," I said, using an old grade school nickname I knew he hated. Ahh … it was good to be back with friends!

"Shh! They're coming on stage!" Elle's voice was anything but quiet as she stood on tiptoes and peered through the myriad of heads to see who she could identify. "Look!" she squeaked, "there's Harley ... ohh ... he looks hot!"

"I'll tell him you said that!" I threatened, but Elle had gone to fan-land and couldn't care less. As the drummer began a huge solo to welcome the band on stage, the crowd roared and I turned to Dan, pointing to my ears and mouthing "wish you had ear plugs now?"

He grinned, and before I could react swiftly lifted me into the air and onto his shoulders. Now I could see everything! Letting out a fearful wolf whistle, I cheered my brothers on, and the throb of the bass and drums began its magic.

They have gotten good, I thought with surprise. I could actually understand some of the words. Looking down I got the feeling Dan might like to cut loose, so I tapped him on the head and slid down his back, with my feet landing safely on terra firma.

"Go!" I waved and shouted at him, and like dogs let off the leash at the beach Sam, Matt, and Dan were sucked into the vortex of insane dancing, while Elle and I were content to just watch and laugh.

Harley really knew how to work the crowd, and by the end of their forty minute set the excitement was nearly at fever pitch. I turned around to view the stands, and the sheer number of people was overwhelming! There must have been fifteen thousand and rising – and all here to see Alien Potion in concert! I shook my head in disbelief. It seemed surreal this meteoric rise to fame. I saw Levi's face on a black t-shirt worn by a young girl behind me, the Alien Potion logo printed cleverly on the cap he was wearing in the photo. I stared at it, until the girl noticed my intent gaze and raised her arm giving the "rock on" hand gesture and saying, "Chris is the man! Alien Potion is sick!"

I feebly imitated the gesture back and quickly turned away, remembering that Levi used Chris as his stage name and wondering what I had been thinking over the past few days, ignoring the calls and visits of someone so famous. He probably didn't even want to talk to me anymore, I had been so rude.

Resolutely trying to stay in the zone of putting others first, rather than feeling sorry for myself, I intimated to Elle that I would go and buy some water for the boys. Weaving in and out of the crowds was good practice, and I found that because I was reasonably tall and not too big, I could easily slip into gaps, creating minimal fuss. Within minutes I had five bottles of water and was working my way back, when a hush fell over the amphitheater, followed by a lout unified roar. Craning my neck, I glimpsed Levi moving into center stage, looking every inch the rock star. Something in my knees gave way, and I leaned into the stranger beside me for support as a crippling sensation began stealing my legs away. The bottled water I was clenching prevented me from using my arms to steady myself.

"Sorry, sorry," I gasped, willing my legs to work as the stranger looked at me like I was an idiot and pushed me upright again.

"Get a life, babe," he said, his voice sounding distant due to the pounding in my ears. "I'm not your leaning post, even if you are cute as hell. Hey, need a helping hand?" As he spoke his hand swung around and smacked my bottom firmly. It was all the incentive my legs needed, and I took off like I was an elite athlete, racing through the throng of people until I found the others. Dan, Matt, and Sam had emerged as if straight from a sauna, but I hardly noticed. My focus was on the sound that filled my ears, fast and furious, rich and raw: the voice of Levi Chris Gibson in full throttle.

For the next hour we jumped, swayed, held our cell phones high, and waved our arms, singing along, feeling the power and thrust of our generation, speaking the full measure of freedom that rock music transmits. I turned Dan down when he offered his shoulders to me again. What if Levi saw me?

Towards the end Elle begged me to accompany her to the ladies, and I did so, having managed to separate the "Chris" on the stage from the Levi I knew. Disassociation enabled my legs to work and my heart to beat normally, rather than at the speed usually reserved for roller coaster rides.

As we weaved our way back I tripped, falling into Elle's back and nearly causing her to fall as well. "Damn! Shoelace issues. I'll catch you up, Elle. Find the others and make some noise so I can find you."

A slower acoustic melody was dancing over the airwaves, enticing listeners to really listen, and I was grateful. It would give me the time I needed to tie my shoe without getting totally munted by the sea of feet around me. As I straightened, Levi's voice rang out again, this time speaking rather than singing.

"Raleigh! How we doing? Are the heavens dressed sky high in diamonds tonight or what?" The crowd roared and faces looked to the heavens to check out the stars. Levi continued. "Hey! Can you help me out tonight? I need to ask a big favor." His voice grazed into the audience loud and clear. "Yell if you'll help me!" The reply was deafening. "I need you to be real quiet like mice for a minute ..." he paused, letting his words sink in. "You see, I have an important phone call to make; I'm trying to find someone, and I think they might be here, hiding in the crowd. They're a VIP, if you know what I mean. Are you with me?" Everyone roared again. "So, I got my mobile phone here, and I'm gonna call their number. Stay very quiet ... shhh ... it's ringing, it's ringing ... shhhh." All the rest of the band put a finger to their lips. I stood wondering why a VIP would stand with the masses. Surely they'd be in the cordoned off premium seats? Maybe they were trying to see what it was like for the common people at a concert? It just didn't make sense.

Brrriiiing! Brriiinng! I felt a vibration in my back pocket, and goose bumps all over my body. *He wouldn't dare!* Pulling my phone out with hands that were acting like balls of butter, I felt eyes all around me zero in on my phone. A hot blush formed on my cheeks. Where was the damn off button when I needed it? Where was it?

I fumbled in the low light until a voice belonging to one set of eyes barked, "Here, give it to me. Oh it's *you* again!" It was the guy I had leaned on earlier, and he grabbed the phone out of my non-responsive hands, answering it with a swagger in his tone. "Hey, that Chris? You looking for a chick with long dark hair, sweet lips and big green eyes? She wasn't that keen on answering you know, so I'm helping her out! Man I love your band, wicked riffs and awesome songs, can you play Fast Wine again? Or maybe Potion Playground?"

Levi interrupted, yelling to the crowd, "Looks like we have a winner!" Then to the guy with my phone, "Sounds like you found her – thanks, man – does she have a bit of a wild look in her eyes? Looks a bit stubborn?"

"Totally, bro. She's got wild cat written all over her. Man, she's pretty mad I think."

"Can you do something for me? Um, sorry, didn't catch your name."

"Uh Davin, I'm Davin, big fan, man, *big* fan." I rolled my eyes, wondering whether to run, but Davin still had my phone held tightly to his ear, and I wasn't leaving without it.

"Well, Davin, I'll tell you what. We'll play Potion Playground, *if* you'll help me out. Deal? In fact I need all of you out there to lend a helping hand! Now, don't let her run, Davin, pick her up – can you do that?"

Davin had grabbed my arm by this stage, as had a friend of his to the left. Escape was not an option – at least I would get a chance to hit him, I raged.

Levi continued "Great, now, send her to me – AIRMAIL!"

The crowd began caterwauling and whistling, with Levi having successfully worked them into a frenzy. Was this even safe I thought? I knew his ego was big, but this big? Davin had planted his arms around me, shoved my phone back in my pocket, and as the thrumming sounds of the most hard core of Alien Potion's songs belted out and the fans began to jump in unison, him and another nearby set of arms thrust me up into the brave night sky and heaved me towards the front, the cameras searching for me in the crowd, and once finding me, transmitting my humiliating ride onto the big screen for everyone to enjoy. My head was whirling as my body buffeted its way to the stage with a thousand hands assisting my flight. Was this a dream? Would I wake up and find myself still back in exams at high school? It might even be preferable to this! Thoughts raced through my head one after the other, faster and faster until all I could see, all I could hear, all I could feel was a blur of movement, sound and heat – a pulsating energy burning me up. I didn't only want to see Levi now, I wanted to face plant him. I could feel my fists clenching and unclenching, itching with anticipation. He wanted a public spectacle did he? I'd give him a public spectacle alright, and more. Coming to an abrupt halt at the security barrier, I was manhandled onto the stage by two burly crowd control officers, and looked around dazedly, still suffering from delayed vertigo; plus the lights were so bright. Was that a spotlight coming towards me? I shielded my eyes in disbelief; his cheekiness knew no bounds, and then he had the gall to interrupt the song.

"Thank you Davin," he shouted. "C'mon everybody; put your hands together for Davin!" Cue the crowd go wild, I thought cynically, fueling my antipathy as Levi walked towards me with that rock star swagger and stage adrenalin more than evident; confident and provocative. His guitar was slung casually over his shoulder, his hair damp and messy, and eyes like deep pools of liquid blue topaz, flashing with cheeky excitement. Don't look into his eyes, my brain told me, don't look into his eyes, but I stared all the same, mesmerized at his approach; in awe of his stage presence and the hypnological quality of being right here, right now. I must have shivered, because he immediately removed the loose, long sleeved white shirt he was wearing, revealing strong arms framed by an electric blue singlet, wrapping the soft cotton around my shoulders.

"Everyone, meet Sage. Sage, meet everyone!" he said into the microphone. A huge cheer erupted, but it sounded so different from up here, almost how I imagined earth sounded to God from way up in heaven. He leaned urgently towards me and whispered as I pulled the shirt around me, conscious of my simple attire and scruffy hair, and willing to use anything to cover myself up and disappear into the white backdrop behind us.

"Please, Jazz, I know this was diabolical and underhand

and you probably want to punch me, but I couldn't think of any other way to get through to you, to see you. Work with me on this? Please?"

I shut my eyes to block out the power of his gaze, and whispered "Water ... water please?" He indicated over my shoulder, and a stagehand threw over a plastic bottle. I took it from him gratefully, opening my eyes and stepping right up to him until the only thing between us was his guitar. I murmured softly, "Thank you *Chris*." I fluttered my eyes and tossed my hair to distract him and with my other hand lifted the bottle past my lips, over his head and squeezed as hard as I could. The camera for the big screen caught it all beautifully, water pouring down Levi's shocked face and saturating his singlet, and we stared at each other for a split second, wondering what reaction each of us would choose, with the crowd roaring its pleasure and support. And then in an identical motion we grinned, the fever of the night catching hold, and I could feel the air around me thick with the essence of Levi, vital and driven. Our eyes were locked and unmoving as the stage crew replaced the cordless mike behind his ear, shaking their heads at me crossly, but I didn't care – and neither did Levi who had already started strumming.

As soon as his microphone was fixed, he spoke to the waiting audience and to me at the same time. "I guess I deserved that, eh? Maybe I can win her over with a new song I wrote over the last day or two. I think it belongs to Sage, so listen up Raleigh – the VIP town of North Carolina! Yeah!"

J is for Jasmine and oh she's fine
I looked into her eyes and I saw sublime
And so I'm calling now J oh J it's ok.
My heart here is soft as clay and its calling you out to play
Listen to me say it then weigh it and display it
Damn your misconceptions and forget your minds deflections
It's time now J oh J
To say...
All the people here gonna shout for you
Hands in the air will carry you through

And we'll find over time
That our eyes held the answer
No lies and no baggage
Said the singer to the dancer
It's ok J oh J its ok…

The sound was adventurous and bold, a play on words and a punt with music, and you couldn't help but want to join in. It was inclusive as if the song may have been written by Levi, but was already owned by the fans.

I smiled as I climbed into bed early the next morning. It was the smile of one who has been over saturated in joy and is leaking happy thoughts. I hugged myself as I curled under the sheets with Levi's shirt still around me, scented with the honeyed sweat of a rock star and the mysterious smell of man. I remembered how he looked at me as the concert ended, not into my eyes, but down at my lips, as if he wanted to kiss me right then and there, and I had watched his mouth as it curved into the sweetest smile, full of hope and promise. And that had been our only communication for a while as the stage crew began the pack down, with Levi and the rest of the band helping – a buzz of camaraderie and excess energy crowding the stage. I knew best to stay out of the way and for the most part was perched on one of the large speakers, taking it all in. Every now and again Levi would introduce me to another band member and they would say, "Oh, so you're Fale 'n Harley's little sis," or "no wonder Levi's song writing is on fire at the moment," and I would blush or laugh, depending on the comment.

Soon enough Chad, Fale, and Harley reappeared, having tracked down Dan, Elle, Matt, and Sam, and the night transitioned from post-gig to party.

Once the main band instruments were safely packed down and locked away, everyone other than the hard-core stage guys (under Bailey's management) made their way to one of the many function rooms, where girlfriends, family members, and the odd lucky fan were gearing up to celebrate a successful concert.

Even Marcus was there, talking up the CD sales for the Cajun Braves, reckoning they must have sold over five hundred CDs before Alien Potion took to the stage.

I rolled over blissfully in bed, remembering how Levi had located me after he had done the rounds thanking everyone and stroking the media egos. I had been catching up with Elle and the three boys, who fired question after question at me, with Sam cracking up over how Levi had copied their crowd surfing prank. Dan had just glared at me, obviously annoyed that I had deserted him and not taken my reconnaissance trip to plan for the following week seriously.

"Jazz," he had complained, "we need to report back to Neville with some intelligent ideas, and how can I protect you if you keep disappearing on me?" Right about then I couldn't really care less, and I had told him so.

"Chillax, Dan, have some fun. It might be the last fun you'll get for a while. You're at a backstage band party, revel in it!" And then I felt a warm hand slip into mine, and when Dan turned to get another drink from the roving drinks waiter, I was pulled away into the crowd and over to the corner of the bar, where the music was loud but the crowd was fewer.

Every word of the conversation we had was fresh in my memory as I got up and opened the bedroom window allowing the sound of the ocean into the room, and I relived it moment by moment. Levi had leaned over and handed me a drink, brushing aside my hair and whispering in my ear.

"What's gone wrong? Why wouldn't you return my calls, or see me? Why didn't you meet me in the desert?" The rich warmth of his breath sent a shiver down my spine and I was suddenly glad it was noisy. I took a mouthful of icy water and it was my turn to whisper. I bit my lip as I tried to explain, not even sure if I knew why I had ignored him anymore.

"I … I overheard you talking with Vander. I was underneath the veranda." It hurt to remember, but would his reply hurt even more?

This time his mouth grazed my lobe as he answered. "Well that explains a lot. No wonder you were mad." I felt him bite his lip as he paused. "It wasn't like what it sounded. I'm gutted Vander has cut me out, but I couldn't let him know that. I had to make him think you were just a kid, and that he would be able to control you…am I making any sense?" His breath was as melodic as his music, almost like a drug, and I was finding it hard to concentrate, let alone answer him. He took a deep breath in, his nose buried in my hair. "You really are Jasmine, right to the core," he murmured. "I did what I thought I had to; I tried to phone you straight after Vander left, but I didn't want to leave you a message, I knew we needed to speak in person. But then when I did come over you refused to see me – and I had no idea why! It's been driving me crazy, Jazz. I mean what was a guy to do?"

"Hmmfff," I huffed finally finding my voice. "That was some stunt you pulled tonight – extreme to the max! You so are a dangerous mix, Levi Gibson." Even saying his name gave me goose-bumps.

"It's Vander that's dangerous, J, fully dangerous. I don't want him anywhere near you. When I was told not to attend the meeting, I knew I had to meet with Vander, stay on his good side so he wouldn't be tempted to cut me out of the picture altogether. He asked me for information about my Father and Mother too; don't know why…it was weird. Wanted me to inform him if I learned anything new…" I noticed he didn't pull away after he finished speaking.

My heart skipped a beat. *Dangerous? You may well be more dangerous than Vander will ever be.* As if he had heard my thoughts he jumped off the stool and put a hand either side of the bar, trapping me on my seat. Slowly, surely he leaned in, his eyes boring into mine, that strange connection between us almost visible in its intensity.

"Forgive me." He almost begged, humbly and with a searching sorrow that I could not ignore. I stared back, knowing I was taking a risk, but although I still had many questions, I needed to exercise faith. "Forgive me for hurting you?" He leaned even closer. Could I make that leap of faith? He suddenly stepped back, snapping the tension that had been building between us, running his hand through his hair as if unsure of himself and gave a short laugh. "Sorry, Jazz. It's a musician's temperament – intense at times. I don't mean to put any pressure on you to accept my apology."

I breathed in the empty air and missed him. This see-saw of intimacy then withdrawal was driving me nuts. Standing, I took his hand and it was my turn to lead, weaving through the boxes of stacked glasses and the back entrance to where the stars were waiting. They stretched across the heavens like a school of flickering bait fish, silver and breathtaking in their midnight blue sea, and we watched, as if waiting for a sign.

"Did you know," I whispered reverently, "that my Destiny as a Reader was written in the stars? Do you believe in predestination? That some things were just meant to be from the beginning of time?" I turned towards him, struck to the core by the effect just looking at him had on me. "I want to do this right," I continued fiercely. "This whole Reader thing, I want to make a difference, to care about something that is bigger than my own small world. Remember the little boy we found in the car park? Adam? Sometimes I wonder about him, where he is, if he feels loved, if anyone cares – and I pray that God will make me someone who cares and someone who acts; you know what I mean?"

"Action may not always bring happiness, but there is no happiness without action." Levi shrugged at me as I looked at him questioningly. "Benjamin Disraeli said it and I know exactly what you mean. Shall we visit Adam tomorrow?"

I stared at him astounded. "You know where he is?"

"I guess I do," he said, his expression slightly smug.

"I have so many questions. There is so much I don't know about you – like who is your father? And why are you the only Carrier with a ring? And Adam? Getting Miss Motion back when she was stolen?" My voice petered out, wondering if I was being too nosy.

"Tomorrow I will answer all your questions, I promise.

No secrets. There's lots I have been waiting to tell you, Jazz." he paused; reaching out he gently placed his hands on my hips, and stepped towards me.

"In fact there's something you should know right now." He hesitantly bent his head right down beside my ear and with a husky, heartfelt voice whispered words I suddenly knew I had been waiting to hear since the day I met him. "I think I'm falling for you Jasmine Sage Blade."

My knees wobbled and as I turned my head in the direction of the spell he had cast. I felt his lips feathery on the side of my face, tracing an agonizingly slow but steady trail towards my mouth. My arms had somehow tangled themselves around his neck in an attempt to regain my balance and he drew a ragged intake of air as our bodies touched and he sensed my response. There was nothing I wanted more in that moment than to kiss and be kissed.

The physical sensation as our lips finally met was as spiritual as the first time, and I felt his body shake as violently as mine. The burning had returned to my mouth and I parted my lips, shocked at the surge of electricity.

Suddenly a blinding flash burned into my eyelids, and I felt rather than saw Levi push me away from him and down to the ground, throwing an old cardboard box from the stack outside the kitchen over the top of me. I lay dazed, wondering if we'd been struck by lightning, then I realized the flashes were continuing. They must be cameras. What the …!? I felt pinching fingers pull me up with the box still in place, and rush me back inside before I had time to even react. I heard a door slam and a dead bolt lock into place as I flung off the box, ready to protest vehemently. There stood Bailey, hands on her hips looking every bit as angry as last time she dragged me away from Levi. To the left of her was Dan, eyeball to eyeball with Levi, fists clenched in tight balls, whispering furiously. He must have seen us. Before I could move towards them Chad appeared from nowhere and Bailey hissed at him.

"Get her home, would you? I need to do some damage control. If Dan hadn't come and got me …"

Chad laughed and Bailey glared at him, obviously not amused. He shrugged apologetically. "I told Levi – and you – that Jasmine invites trouble wherever she goes. She's a Blade, for crying out loud!"

"Well, it means days of creating inventive cover-ups and bribing photographers, which means no chance of a day at the beach with me tomorrow. Now do you think it's funny? Just go!"

And with me only just clicking that this had something to do with the world of fame and paparazzi, I let Chad lead me away, stunned by the mangled meeting and anxious to know exactly why Dan thought he could interfere. The last thing I remembered before sleep descended was the text I had got from Levi after I arrived home:

"Miss Motion 7am. Still falling ... L."

The stars in the desert sky were one thousand times brighter than at Walnut Creek, and we stood slightly apart, eyes locked. The mood was too intense for either of us to move; the only thing moving was our breath, an icy vapor rising between our frozen bodies. If anything, the space between us held an intensity neither of us was willing to breach, for fear of breaking the purity of our passion. So we stood, and we understood. This was real.

18. STILL FALLING

I PONDERED THE DESERT AS I DRESSED THE following morning; it was becoming harder to discern between reality and whatever-the-heck the desert world was. My tingling lips kept the hope alive that last night had really happened and that Destiny was working for me, not against me.

After leaving a note for Chad, I slipped quietly out the front door, feeling the first zing of anticipation at seeing Levi again. I could feel my heart thudding against my ribcage as if it wanted to escape my body and beat me to the front gate to meet him. Eager to be first, my feet fumbled, promptly tripping over a large cardboard box that had been left on the porch. Falling to my knees I clenched my teeth to keep from yelling out in pain, and used the box to help me to my feet. It was addressed to "Jasmine Blade" in bold black marker pen. Curiously I tugged at the tape and pulled the flaps of the box open, only to find another smaller box inside. This continued over and over until I noticed a foul smell beginning to permeate the air around me. The next box was labeled with the word "Destiny," sending a shiver of premonition down my spine. Hesitantly opening it, I jerked back in shock at the contents: a decaying fish skeleton, its remaining eye staring up at me accusingly. On the side of the box was scrawled a messy message: "Decomposition of a Reader" it yelled in black angry letters. I gasped sharply and slammed the box shut, picking it up and running to the green wheelie rubbish bin, hurling it to the bottom angrily. Glancing around, I saw no one and nothing suspicious. My mind raced furiously; who could have put it there? Who even knew I was a Reader? That should narrow the suspects down. Had I told anyone I shouldn't? What should I do about it? Anything? Nothing? I could hear the roar of Levi's bike approaching and tried to pull my thoughts together. I was not scared; I was angry. Levi looked angry too. Motioning for me to hurry, he held out the orange helmet to me and I jammed it on quickly, glad I had grabbed Chad's leather jacket on my way out.

"Paparazzi. They followed me last night – even Bailey couldn't shake them, and they camped out in a van at the end of my road. Can we access the beach down the side of the house?" Levi's voice sounded strained.

"Yes, but ..." before I could finish we were off, sand flying out from beneath the tires as Miss Motion reveled in being off road.

"Hold on!" Levi yelled.

I clutched Levi hard as we bounced over the dunes and down onto the early morning beach, scaring a few sea gulls before reaching the hard sand below high tide. I could have released my hold at that point, but instead I snuggled closer, wishing I had an excuse to stay like this forever. Levi took one hand from the handle bars and placed it over mine, guiding it into the pocket of his jacket for warmth, gently circling his thumb over my skin, exploring my fingers one by one, like he was communicating his pleasure at seeing me again and easing my mind at the same time. I thought it strange that such an ordinary part of my body, a limb used for carrying things, holding a pen, stirring a pot, tying shoe laces could suddenly feel like the center of my being; vital, powerful, special; and my fingers trembled in response.

When he withdrew his hand to steer the bike through a narrow beach access back to the main highway, the loss I felt shocked me. If anything, the power surge between us had intensified from the previous night. I felt like a new light had been switched on, the glow pulsating in each finger he had touched. As if in tune with my thoughts, Levi placed his other hand with mine, which had found its own way into his deep pockets, and he repeated the exploration until I was sure he must know my hands better than I did. His skin was smooth yet hard from years of guitar playing and his fingers supple and strong. Just as our eyes had spoken of their own accord from the first day we met, his touch now spoke to me, gentle and reassuring, searching for my trust, despite the bizarre start to our day.

We were heading on the highway towards Moorehead City and Beaufort, and I wondered for a moment if we were going to visit my parents. Thinking of home gave me a slight nostalgic twinge; so much had happened since I left just weeks ago. But we roared right past, and as we slowed to enter Down East, Levi recklessly weaved the bike through narrow streets and turned onto the wharf at the ferry docks. Aha! So we were heading out to sea!

Parking Miss Motion, Levi indicated to the end of the dock, where folks were lining up to board the "Inlet Jewel." Having locked the helmets up, he laced his fingers through mine, as if he had done it thousands of times before. Before I could ask any questions, I felt my arm yanked from its socket as the sound of a fog horn indicated the boat was about to depart.

Helter skelter, we made it to the ferry with seconds to spare. Panting with the sudden exertion, we stood side by side, not touching, but intensely aware of our proximity *(would it always be like this)?* I could feel the movement of water beneath my feet through the motion of the boat, and once the wharf and the people were little dots on the horizon and as the white sands and green marshes of Ocracoke Island approached I leaned forward and pointed out the Ocracoke Lighthouse to Levi, although I couldn't stop my fingers from trembling just a little. "I haven't been here since I was a child…"

His eyes were like molten blue glass, melting my insides. "Stuff the lighthouse…What's wrong, Jazz?" His voice was a mere whisper, grazing my ears, and they burned in response. With my voice no more than a whisper I told Levi of the box I had found that morning.

"Damn!" Levi said under his breath, a shadow crossing his face. "You know it's just scare tactics, don't you Jazz? At this stage, anyway." His expression darkened further, and he gripped the guard rail tightly. "Who knows about the Emospheres?"

"That's what I can't work out. The only people I have told are my grandparents in New Zealand, Dan and Nev, plus my family – and I trust them. I haven't told Elle, Matt, or Sam." I shook my head. "It's puzzling, to say the least. I know it's just a threat, but to see that word scrawled on the box ... well ..." I shivered, despite the warm sunshine.

"Does Vander know about Emospheres?"

I shuddered again. "Right – I forgot! I had to tell him and Melinda and the other guy ... what's his name ... Blair. You don't think ...?"

Levi's eyes looked as cold as the Atlantic now and he spoke looking distantly out to sea. "I wouldn't rule it out, not for one minute. Let me think on this for a day or two. We need a strategy."

As his eyes turned to mine they changed from icicles to a waterfall of emotion. There it was again, the vulnerable window display he usually kept so well hidden, a complex kaleidoscope from a past I could only guess at, given the little I knew.

There was sixteen miles of pristine beach on the island, so finding a remote spot to talk was not difficult. I purposely did not ask any questions as we sat side by side, much like our times in the desert, until Levi finally leaned back, clasped his knees and stared out to sea, softly beginning to speak.

"I said last night I would answer your questions, but after your awful morning, are you sure you want to hear?"

I wondered about asking what Dan had said to him the previous night, but hesitated, not wanting to interrupt the flow of his thoughts. "Yes, yes I do." I put my hand on his arm, urging him on. "I've texted Melinda to report the box I found, and she's said they'll look into it. There's not much more we can do right now, so distract me."

He smiled, and I could read in his eyes the type of distraction he would prefer. He sighed reluctantly, still staring at my mouth, but his voice drew me into the tale he began to weave.

"After the ... attack in the car park," he pointed to the scar on his face, "I was kept in hospital for a few days. I kept asking to see my mom, but she never came." His face twisted at the memory.

"Did she ... not survive?"

He burrowed a hand into the soft white sand, covering it completely. "Worse. I wish she had died then. Aside from the severe alcohol poisoning they had to pump her stomach – she had swallowed enough aspirin to kill the average woman. She left the hospital without me, leaving only a letter stating that although she loved me, she would never be a suitable mother, and it was better that I be placed with a new family. Then she just wrote '*Goodbye, Chris, be a good boy now*,' and that was it." His voice was the most broken I had ever heard it. "I was only seven, Jazz, seven. How could a mother do that? Why couldn't she change and stop drinking?" He sighed heavily. "Some questions we never find the answer to, no matter how hard we try or how much we want to know." The sand ran off the back of his hand as he lifted it up, like water off a duck's back. If only life was like that, I thought.

"So what did you do? What happened next?" I looked out over the sand and the sea, blinking back the tears that were threatening.

"I went through three foster homes before I was twelve, each one worse than the previous. I was no angel, believe me. It was as if the hard ball of hurt inside me just kept growing, and my only survival technique was to hurt those around me. If I couldn't have my mom, I didn't want anyone at all. Something snapped when I turned thirteen, and I ran away." He turned to face me and lowered his voice further, sounding sad and lonely. "I did many things I am very ashamed of, Jazz. If you want to walk away from me, I'd totally understand. I've always been trouble on two legs," he made a feeble attempt at a joke.

I punched his arm lightly. "Guess that's good then; Blades and trouble go together like peanut butter and jelly – just ask my brothers. I'm not going anywhere. One question though: once you mentioned jail? Were you joking?"

His head dropped, but his eyes stayed locked on mine. "I joined a street gang – that's where I met Bailey. She was a distant cousin of the gang leader, Evan, and he treated her dreadfully. I grew tough and strong, feeding on the hate and pain inside me, until nothing and no-one could hurt me. By the time I was nearly sixteen I had escaped from police custody twice, and was staring at a life of hiding from the authorities, sleeping by day and stealing by night. The only thing that haunted me was Bailey's eyes. I knew she wasn't strong like me; that she wouldn't survive. If she didn't actually die, she would soon be dead on the inside. I formulated a daring rescue plan, determined to do at least one good thing with my life. During a night robbery I slipped behind the 7-11 shop counter and rang the police, tipping them off. I knew that the cash was always strapped onto Bailey, so I stuck close, and as soon as the police got in the door I grabbed Bailey's hand and ran, leaving Evan to the police. They had wanted him for ages, but he was always too sly for them. Unfortunately I didn't count on them having the back entrance covered, and Bailey and I were apprehended.

"Because we were under sixteen years old we only had to go to juvenile court and were sent to a youth detention camp for six months, in the hope of being rehabilitated. Evan got three years in prison on various charges.

"I swore to Bailey that when we got out I would never let anyone hurt her again. She had become like a little sister to me. Although she seems old, her emotional age will always be that of a child – her childhood was much, much worse than mine."

He fell silent, reliving a past I couldn't even imagine as it was so far from my happy childhood. Family dysfunction in our house was defined by someone not replacing the toilet paper, or drinking all the milk in the fridge. I didn't know what to say, so I simply reached over, ran my hand down his arm and crooked my little finger through his.

"Something to eat?" I asked. Levi nodded, and we wandered back to the tiny fishing village where he guided us through the narrow streets until we came to a bright green door tucked in between a small pub and a second hand junk shop. Pausing before knocking, he hurriedly explained "I really wanted to introduce you to Jarven, but I'm not sure he'll be home – he's often out around the island at this time of day, but if he is here, we could take him to lunch with us?" It was more of a statement than a question, but I didn't mind. My curiosity about Levi and those who knew him best had not yet been satisfied, and a chance to find out more information was welcome.

The door looked and smelt like the sea on a stormy day, and the man that answered it even more so. Or perhaps more like a desert in a sandstorm, I couldn't quite decide, other than he appeared to welcome a cacophony of color and texture in both his appearance and his manner, a jumble that seemed to work in the strangest of ways. Glancing to the left and the right with quick jabbing movements, he gestured us inside before even greeting Levi. Once the door was closed (it was painted yellow on the inside), the man I presumed to be Jarven leaned against it and closed his eyes, saying at the same time "Levi, Levi, Levi. Every time I speak your name, I speak a promise. I just know it. It rolls off the tongue, don't you think? V is my favorite letter of the alphabet, because it must balance so very carefully on a fine point, neither wavering to the left or the right, but staying just so…" and after a few seconds pause for effect, he continued: "So! Welcome!" His eyes sprung open like spring loaded castanets, intent on snapping as much information as they could.

"Jazzmine," he stated rather than asked. Levi nodded and I started moving forward to shake his hand, but he had already reached forward to kiss me on both cheeks, firmly gripping my shoulders.

"Finally we meet! Jazzmine, such a potent name, wouldn't you agree?" Levi nodded again. Jarven glanced over and waved a hand at Levi, stating: "It is lunch time, no? Go, buy some bread and olives. Jazzmine and I will talk." Levi nodded once more. I had never seen him so lost for words – with a slightly rueful raised eyebrow he turned and headed out the door, leaving me to be ushered into what looked like a scene from Arabian Nights.

"Levi has spoken of me, yes?" Jarven said as he settled me

down in a pile of red and purple velvet cushions by a low slung table, offering me a goblet of ice cold water and gesturing towards the large platter of apricots on the table.

"Ahh, yes, yes he has, but…"

"But you expected someone older? Fatter?"

"Well…umm…I'm not sure…"

He said nothing then, just gazed at me with piercing black eyes for what seemed like minutes. The funny thing was that the longer he stared at me, the more comfortable I became, relaxing into the cushions and drinking in the exotic nature of the room.

Finally, when I had almost forgotten he was there, he spoke.

"Ask me your questions, Jazzmine. It is right. It is time."

"But I have so many! Like how do you know Levi? And where is his father? Is his mother still alive? And what is it with our rings and the desert? And why can't Levi be my Carrier? Can I trust Neville? And what about Vander? Adam? Where is he now? And who stole Miss Motion? And why is Levi so…so…so I don't know; so *enigmatic*?"

Jarven didn't move a muscle but continued to look at me, into me. He could not have been more than 45 or so, but everything about him seemed ancient, from his flowing black hair to his caftan style top and old black jeans.

"I will just talk, and you will listen. Yes?" I nodded obediently.

"A Carrier is chosen, much like a Reader. They carry a mark on their left shoulder; a small circle which represents completion, for it is the Carrier's role to not seek rest until the Reader's quest is completed.

"Along time ago I provided a physiotherapy service to the Juvenile Detention Halls, and it was there I discovered Levi. It was written in the stars that we were to meet – I had been waiting to find the boy who would become the Carrier I was destined to train." Jarven shut his eyes before continuing.

"He was rough in those days; bitter, with tense muscles and hard lines. He needed solace and a father figure, and that's what I offered him when I signed up to be his guardian under

State supervision. He would not come without the girl, so Bailey joined us…" He smiled with his eyes still closed. "They were a handful; both of them, in the early days. I taught Levi to play the guitar – he needed time to trust me, time to ask questions before being made aware of his calling as a Carrier. As his Framer I had to move gently, slowly…so the music became the movement of his soul and in between the notes much of the pain slipped quietly away. And those notes told his story." He started humming, first gently, and then growing in intensity. I gasped.

"That song? But that's a Britney classic!" Jarven raised one finger to his lips and continued.

"Let's say I know people who know people. It was not hard to sell the song to them on Levi's behalf. He didn't know at first; didn't recognize his gift. Me telling him did not work; he was enough like his Mother back then to need the whole world to validate him." He shrugged his shoulders offhandedly, whilst I shook my head in disbelief. He should be telling this story on Oprah, by the sounds of it. And I thought my journey had been odd. Jarven continued.

"There was one thing neither of us knew. Through the publishing of that song, family lawyers were able to track Levi down, because he had used the name 'Chris' as a pseudonym – the name his mother had referred to him in her will. Felicity Forrest was famous – and rich."

I gasped again. "You're kidding, right?" This story was getting harder to believe by the minute. "Felicity Forrest had a son? Everyone knew her as the freewheeling 70s babe who reinvented herself in the 80s by being seen with the right people and keeping the hippie chick look, bucking the trend towards shoulder pads and leg warmers. Excuse me, and I'm sorry, but *Levi's mother*? Some even say the girl in Forrest Gump was loosely based on her." I shook my head in disbelief.

"She had died of a drug overdose and left everything in her will to Levi, although it did say if they couldn't find him within the year following her death, to donate all the money to the hospital she abandoned him in. There were two days short of the deadline when they found us. The only name Levi knew his mother by was 'Felix', which she liked to be called even by him because it meant lucky and successful. He told me she used to pinch him when she'd been drinking and say '*fearless Felix, that's me – footloose and fancy free.*' Strange the things that he remembered, no? She performed under her maiden name, Felicity Forrest, which added to the difficulty in tracing Levi to her."

"The lawyers had to use photos of her and him together, taken when he was about five, before everything finally fell into place." Jarven stood, stretched and walked towards the door, still talking.

"That was when the boy started to become the man. He knew his past, he dealt with his pain and he dreamed his future. Even before Adam he had started a foundation for at-risk and abandoned kids with his new found wealth…Levi!" The yellow door gave way to a pair of arms wrapped around two very large paper bags.

"I got carried away, sorry Jarven. I know you live on the smell of an oily rag. Thought I should top you up. Jazz, you should see the size of the shrimp!"

A feast was soon laid out on the low table, and we sat at floor level, scoffing the fresh seafood, olives, bread and hummus. I had never tried so many new flavors in my life, so I relished the opportunity, listening as Levi and Jarven talked like family would – about the mundane, the everyday things of life. Levi's eyes still spoke to me though; I found my eyes drawn back to his as if they were magnetized, and each time the sensations that stirred in my body grew stronger, making my knees feel weak. Again and again Levi or I would look away abruptly, as if to regain a sense of normality before our eyes would again lock together.

"What is your organization called? The one for kids like Adam. Jarven was telling me about it." My question blurted out almost rudely, so intent was I on not falling headfirst into Levi's eyes.

"Swings and Roundabouts."

"Swings and Roundabouts?"

"It just came to me one night: life is all about swings and roundabouts – sometimes you're up, and sometimes you're down, or going in circles. Sometimes you just want to get off, and then it's too hard to climb back on again. The playground of life is filled with accidents – some happy and some sad – but to kids and adults alike, a swing is usually associated with being carefree and happy and that's how I want to see more kids that have had a rough start in life, like Adam.

"I like the name," I responded firmly. "It makes me feel happy already, the notion of being on a swing on a summer's day. Hey, you should write a song about it!"

"You are so right. I have been working on a fund-raising album, and one of the songs is titled "Swingsong." I'll play it to you later. As much as the album will hopefully raise money, it's making people aware of how gross life is for so many children." He shook his head and turned his gray eyes to me again, pools of hope and worry at the same time. "Am I growing up too fast? Sometimes I feel like I'm two hundred years old rather than twenty-one."

I smiled, feeling younger than my eighteen years next to his life experience. "Maybe a little, but I think I'm beginning to know what that feels like. I wonder if we're meant to ... grow up fast I mean. If growing up means caring for others, then we all should do it, but what about your dad? Did you ever find him? Jarven, well Jarven kind off filled me in on your mom and stuff." I tore my eyes away to check with Jarven for reassurance.

"It's ok, Jazzmine, Levi knows I would only tell you if I trusted you…which, by the way," he reached for Levi's face and turned it towards him, "I most definitely do." Levi grinned, suddenly looking shy and then looked back at me, shaking his head.

"My mom was always adamant that it was a man called Carson, and I have no reason to doubt her – not that I ever remember him well. He was friends with Vander and had fringe involvement with the CFR, 'till he disappeared completely. Vander says he doesn't know what happened to him, but I somehow doubt that." He shrugged. "I found a photo of my mom hugging some other strange-looking guy under palm trees in the desert, dated the year before I was born. I've been thinking about tracing him to see if he knows anything. So the short answer is no, no dad."

"So that's how you can afford Miss Motion," I mused out loud, jumping from topic to topic to put all the pieces together. "And when Miss Motion was stolen…?" He looked at me apologetically.

"It's the gang connections from my past. Every now and then Evan – that's the gang leader – gets his mates to give me a hard time – usually when they want something. I'm trying to work with them, collecting in more kids like Bailey and I, but they like to 'borrow' my stuff on occasion, especially my bike! As for the house, it was one of Mom's holiday homes. I have yet to check out the two others – one on the island of Bahrain and the other on the Riviera – been too busy here in the States."

He closed his eyes and I wondered what he was thinking, this remarkable young man who was so much more than a rock star with an ego. At twenty-one he had already lived more life than most people ever do.

"There. Now you know." He opened one eye. "Rich. Famous. Good looking. Have I missed anything Jarven?" So much for not having an ego! At that point Jarven leapt along the table and tackled Levi into the cushions, where they wrestled for some time, fabric and food flying in all directions before Jarven finally emerged the victor, Levi pinned half under the table, half by Jarven's elbows.

"Just missed mentioning that you're weak and puny, no? And that you walk in your sleep. And that you lose stuff all the time, yes? And that…"

"Arrrggh!" Levi yelled, attempting to free himself. I could never look at him the same again now he was just human, and I told him so before clearing the leftovers to the kitchen and leaving them to it.

As Levi placed my helmet on back at the ferry dock, he softly said, "Just two things left to show you, J, that ok?"

I nodded my head, not trusting myself to speak. I never wanted this day to end. After a quick phone call ahead to order takeaways, Levi drove through the back streets, pulling up outside a small but tidy looking cottage. Beckoning me to come, we followed the fence along the side boundary past the house. Leaning down to peer through a small knot hole, Levi pulled me down to look. There, swinging in the back yard with a huge smile on his face was Adam. I gasped softly, and we crept away. I couldn't wipe the smile off my face.

"Bailey arranges the adoptions – I'm not much good at stuff like that. It's a happy ending for Adam thanks to her. He likes to swing at sunset – he wrote us that in a thank you letter…it's just a small start, but a hopeful one."

"Another questioned answered – still lots more though…" my forehead crinkled in concentration. Before I could verbalize the next one, Levi threw me back on the bike with an exaggerated roll of his eyes.

It seemed like just seconds later that we zoomed into the garage at Levi's house, the door lowering behind us as if by magic. Levi laughed as he removed his helmet. "Hear that?" I cocked my head, trying to hear something. "Exactly! Nothing – nothing at all. No Bailey, no band, no busy-ness. Just us ... and yummy Chinese food." Opening the front door, a neat brown paper bag sat, softly steaming and smelling divine.

Levi drew me into his arms slowly, and bending to find my ear, he whispered, "Shall we make our way to the kitchen, or should we eat here? I'm awfully hungry again." I felt dizzy, and food was the last thing on my mind, but I managed to nod my head obediently. Chuckling at my inability to make a simple decision Levi looked at me speculatively. "I think you definitely need food – and I know I do – riding that motorbike always leaves me starving."

Levi had obviously not spent a penny on updating the decor of the house. It reeked of faded glamour, ostentatious and cheesy, almost kitsch in the worst sense of the word. I stifled a giggle.

"What?" Levi protested, "Can't a bloke express his own taste in home decorating?" He was walking so close behind me it was as if we were one person. "Purple is my favorite color, I'll have you know."

"It's ... it's ... very Felicity, if you don't mind me saying."

"Not at all, but it's all I have left of her, although I must say the band have bets placed on how much longer I can live with it!"

"Mmmm. Might have to join that syndicate." As Levi collected some plates and cutlery, I lit candles and we talked about how Levi had formed the band and what it meant for him to live his dreams, before conversation drifted to our relationship as Reader and Carrier, outlawed before it even became a reality.

"It's unfortunate," Levi started, "but I think we need to stay underground for a while, to avoid suspicion. If Vander gets even a whiff of us collaborating, he'll shut down and end the mission."

"But I'm sure he'll know about the concert last night. He must have his spies out if he's that concerned." I wrinkled my nose at the thought.

"Yes, but I think I can deal with that. I'll just tell him that we arranged it as a stunt ages ago and my ego wouldn't let me back out of it. He'll buy that." He frowned. "But you'll have to deal with Dan and Neville. Think you can do that?"

"I think so. I'll probably just say that we've called a truce, and agreed not to disagree, then I'll mix it all up with some confusing girl emotional stuff, and that should put them off from digging any deeper. *Then* I'll move straight on to discussing plans for the concert; *then* we can arrange a secret meeting at my parents to jack up an alternative action plan."

"Now we're cooking! But Jazz," Levi looked at me anxiously, "you need to remember that this is not a game. We are messing with some very dangerous people here, powerful and crafty. I am kinda worried you might become a pawn in their game. Unfortunately, I think you need to tell Dan about the box you found. He needs to do his job and watch you like a hawk. I only wish it could be me."

"Unfortunately? Why? I have hesitated to ask what Dan said to you last night – he looked so … so … angry."

Levi studied the last mouthful of rice on the end of his

fork before putting it down and leaning across the table.

"He told me a lot of things, most of which I am not going to repeat, but the gist is that I should not employ underhand tactics to get your attention, and that perhaps it was time I backed off."

I dropped my eyes to the table and dipped my finger into the left over sweet and sour sauce.

"I'll manage Dan," I said with more bravado than I felt, "if you promise not to take any notice of what he said to you."

"Easier said than done," he grimaced. "Do you think that your Emospheres are potent enough to disarm those Neo-Nazis? Which one will you use? It's gonna have to be pretty powerful. Two of my band members are Black. You remember meeting Jamal and Terrance?" He spoke over his shoulder as he led the way out towards the beach.

"Yeah, such cool guys. Jamal showed me how to do the sweep-drop after your concert - it was so funny! That break-dance sequence they did during the concert was awesome! I'll probably use ah ... the Love Emosphere rather than Joy – it's more powerful. Love conquers all, you know."

"So Deep Purple said in the 90s. You still haven't had a chance to show me these bubbles in action. I find it hard to imagine you can actually manipulate emotions with them. Sounds totally crazy. As for Jamal and Terrance, they know skin heads will be there with 'The Order,' an anti-government revolutionary group that has Nazi sympathies. Terrance wants to get up in their faces, which I've told them will only add to the heat." He ran his fingers through his hair, a signal that he was searching for clues and answers. I only wished it were my hands in his hair, I imagined the texture and feel, then shook my head impatiently. Was I really that Levi absorbed? I didn't bother answering my own question.

"Let's think on it and graft our ideas together when we meet at your parents'. Right now, there's something I want to show you." He too seemed distracted now. "Here, take my sweater, it's getting cooler." He wrapped it around my shoulders, pausing as his bare skin touched mine and we both shivered.

I was surprised to find that twilight had fallen; a faint purple hue on the horizon was the only sign that the sun had paid a visit. Again Levi clasped my hand into his and I followed. The scent of his sweatshirt was musky like the redwood timber we used for firewood in the winter – so damn good. I wanted to stumble, just to feel his arm around me, but he was moving too fast and I couldn't bring myself to fake it. Down the stairs and over the dunes we went, but he stopped so suddenly that I banged into him, and his arm curled around my shoulder, pulling me close to him.

He whispered, "Ten steps to the east." I took nearly two steps to each of his, but when he had counted ten under his breath he turned sharply towards the ocean, and then counted ten more. I stayed as close as I could, mystified by the wild goose chase we were on, and it was not till he fell to his knees, pulling me down with him that I realized what he had bought me to see.

"Turtle eggs!" I exclaimed. "You've found a turtle nesting site –wow! Dad would be so excited to see this. He's always wanted to film a documentary on the local turtle population; he refers to it as his 'rainy day project'."

"I wanted to show you first. They're due to hatch any day now. I've been keeping an eye on them – look! Is that shell cracked? And that one there – it's already open!" Levi's whispered voice sounded boyish as our excitement grew. All of a sudden it seemed like the nest was coming alive, eggs jumping like ping pong balls as tiny beaks and backs began to emerge.

"They're Loggerhead Turtles,' Levi continued in low tones, "I checked the internet, and they're the most common breed in North Carolina. I think Bailey rang the Sea Turtle Protection Volunteers, but no one's stopped by yet. Quick, we need to make sure their path to the ocean is clear. Help me dig a trench."

We dug quietly yet furiously for the next fifteen minutes to create a channel that would lead the baby turtles safely down to the water's edge.

"Hey – let's count them as they hatch! Let's see: one, two

...”

We gave up at eighty-four. I had to admire their focus. They had one goal and one goal only, even though the odds were just one to a thousand of actually surviving, not one of them gave up the journey.

Levi sat behind me pulling me close, and together we marveled at mother nature and her protégées, feeling so privileged to be able to observe such a mammoth feat by so tiny an amphibian.

“We need to be like that,” Levi murmured into my ear, the heat of his breath sweet on my face. “Look at them – they’re so determined! Only an inch long and facing huge danger: birds, crabs, humans, but they just keep going no matter the challenge ahead. I’m so stoked we got to see this. Jazz, the challenges in front of you, of us, are huge, and we need to be like the turtles. We can’t even consider the possibility of failure.” He reached forward and nudged a tiny turtle back into the center of the channel. “I’ve got your back, Jazz; I’ve got your back.” And with that he gathered me even closer and we sat silently until the show was over and every last hatchling had found its way to the water. Finally, he pulled me to my feet and walked me home under a blanket of stars where we shared our hearts, our hopes, and our dreams. If this was Destiny, then I was sold.

19. KISSED

THE HOUSE WAS SILENT AND ASLEEP IN THE dark night, and Levi insisted on checking for anything unusual before he left me safe and sound in the hallway, whispering permission for a kiss goodnight. The trauma of the early morning discovery had all but washed away from my memory after a day with Levi. I felt his hands cupping my head, tilting it back, and we drank each other in; I never wanted to forget how he looked tonight, how he gazed into me, rather than at me, his eyes dark blue and flashing in the husky light of the entrance way, a strong and tender air about him. For the first time I felt I was seeing him without any cool façade, stripped by his honest revelations, letting me in to read the boy, the man inside. I had once thought I glimpsed his soul through his eyes; now I saw his very being. Lowering his face towards me as my eyes closed, I felt his lips brush mine, soft as a feather, teasing me, letting me sense the nearness of his teeth, his tongue, his taste. Turning my head only meant that he found my ear, sliding his lips gently down to my lobe and nuzzling back along my jaw line to reclaim my lips. I had to remember to keep breathing. The scientist in me slipped away, leaving nothing but raw hungry emotion, and intuitively I knew just how to respond. When our lips finally parted we were both trembling, but it was Levi who stumbled backwards, needing to put space between us.

"Where'd you learn to kiss like that?" Levi's voice was unsteady and his wild eyes were on my lips, like he wanted more. I looked at the ground.

"You're my ... first, actually," I whispered, reaching out to run my finger teasingly across his lips, surprised at how I seemed to know just what to do next. I had never met a guy I wanted to kiss before. Having lots of brothers had kept me from thinking of boys as anything more than annoying – until now, that was. My lips were on fire, just like the first time, and I wondered if our bonds were only forged this strongly because we were Reader and Carrier. I waited for his verdict.

Suddenly, swiftly, he kissed me once again, bruising my lips in agonizing passion, whispering, "Don't go anywhere without Chad or Dan, preferably Chad. Promise me?" I nodded, dazed, and then he was gone.

I leaned against the wall, letting the day wash over me again and again, feeling the love building inside me, until it felt like a torrent raging, clamoring to be released. Swiftly I headed to the bathroom, locating the thumb-prick kit and vial, dripping drops of blood to make another bottle of Emospheres, and scraping skin cells from my lips, mixing it together with a little saliva. I would mix in the alcohol and oil tomorrow. Satisfied I had again captured the emotion of love, I crept to the bedroom, one step closer to Destiny – or so I thought.

Sitting on the chair at the end of my bed was Dan, arms and legs crossed, looking as grumpy as I'd ever seen him.

"You, Jasmine Blade, have some explaining to do, so talk fast, before I beat you to it. How the heck am I supposed to keep an eye on you if you keep disappearing on me? And explain the rubbish bin."

His eyes were ominous in their anger, and for once he seemed less like the kiwi boy I first met, and more like the hired bodyguard. I fell back to earth with a thump, and stood there, unsure where to start, what to tell. I closed my eyes and wrapped up the day, putting it in an imaginary drawer in my head and resolutely closing it tight to reopen another time, when I needed it most.

Opening my eyes again, I crossed the room, slipped off my shoes and jumped into bed. "I'm really, really tired Dan, couldn't we leave this till the morning? I'll fill in all the gaps then. The important thing is that I'm OK right? Haven't been injured, murdered, or abducted by aliens. I'm sorry you were worried, but didn't Chad give you my message?"

"He did, but when I found the dead fish in the rubbish bin, I naturally got concerned ... and no, we are having this conversation immediately. I've joined this household for good now, so you better start talking so we can both get some sleep."

I sighed. There was no escape from the Dan Man, so I might as well get it over with. I was probably too wired to sleep anyway. Arranging my pillows behind me and pulling my knees up under the blankets I asked: "So what do you want to know?"

"Where were you today?"

"Levi took me to see Adam, the boy we rescued from the car park. Remember, I told you about that?"

"Then why are you so late home?" His tone was sour.

"We walked home along the beach – and Dan, it was amazing – we found a turtle nest, and the eggs were hatching. We watched them for ages, and helped if they got stuck. We should search for more – its turtle season, you know."

He looked at me skeptically. "You expect me to believe that?"

"Joking, right?"" I protested. "Ask Chad. Emerald Isle is turtle country for sure."

"Alright then. But you and ... Levi," he choked the name out, "what gives? I'm guessing it's pointless for us in pretending to be a couple any more as we've hardly seen each other lately."

My expression softened. "I never was much good at acting I'm sorry. But if it helps the cause in any way – which I can't see how – I'll make an effort, OK? As for Levi ... that's between him and me," I replied stiffly. "But, Neville is still officially my Carrier, and I haven't done anything stupid. Levi and I have called a truce and agreed not to disagree. I had to do this on my own, Dan. I owed it to Levi, and myself. He is better as an ally than an enemy and I ... I do have feelings for him. We have shared so much ... and ..." I looked Dan in the eye and rushed out my words, "I feel twisted inside when I'm alienated from people I care about; it stops me from being able to think clearly, to follow the precepts of Readership. I had to sort things out, and if that took a whole day, so what. There's still time to plan. It's only Sunday night and the concert isn't until next Saturday; that's a whole week, and now I can give it my focus – utterly and completely." I kept my gaze on Dan until he looked away.

"Fair enough," He grudgingly responded, looking away to hide his hurt. "But you're not to disappear again, alright? I don't want Alistaire and Arabella arriving to find their granddaughter like the fish remains from the box. Any idea where that came from?"

"None at all." I shivered slightly, not wanting to think of it. "Ali and Arabella are visiting? Goody! When?"

"They arrive Friday – just in time for the big show down. They're keen to see the Emospheres in action again. But back to the threat; we have to take this seriously, Jazz. If it's not a warning from a Jagger, it could be a message from the Neo Nazi group, but how would they know about you? It just doesn't make sense. From what Ali told me of Jaggers, they usually operate underground and don't give any obvious signals of their presence until they strike. But until we know more, I'm not going anywhere, and Chad agrees. We're going to take turns sleeping either outside your window or door. Better to be safe than sorry." He glanced at my bedside table. "I see you've made some replacement Love mix?"

"It's not ready yet," I hastily replied, "but it will be ready in time, I can promise you that."

"Have you showed them to Levi yet? Used him as a guinea pig?"

"Uh ... no. But he would like to see Emospheres working. There just hasn't been a good time, and it's not as if he's been around much." I sounded defensive.

"I see." Dan sounded slightly smug.

"Now can I go to sleep?"

"Sure, but I'm not leaving." He motioned to a sleeping

bag stretched out on the floor.

I sighed. "If you must, but you'd better not snore."

"You already know I do."

"Good excuse to kick you then." My voice was fading.

"I dare you to." His was a whisper. "Jazz ...we are still friends, aren't we?"

"The best," I breathed as I grasped my ring and felt the desert beckoning.

There was no space between us in the desert that night. Our kiss began the minute we both arrived, and continued until we faded back to our beds. We kissed under the stars and icy air, through the purple light of dawn, into the intensity of the desert sun, as if there was no beginning or end, as if our lips had been starved; as if our hearts were in our mouths. Never had a kiss been more profound; never had our senses felt so alive.

20. TEAM WORK

AT BREAKFAST THE FOLLOWING MORNING EVEN CHAD was A bit huffy with me.

"Ah, more information next time, huh Jazz? I'm not your PA you know. My head hurts this morning from all the calls I had to ward off yesterday. It was just rude, running off like that. You can be so bloody minded sometimes, you know – it drives me nuts!"

I had the grace to look a little guilty – but only a little. I decided to ignore his complaints.

"Ah, sorry; who called?" I was on a post-kiss high and I wasn't going to let Chad rob me of that – no way. I filled my mouth with creamy yogurt and reveled in the smooth flavor and taste.

"Like Elle, Mom, Sam, Neville, and someone called Mel-something I didn't recognize." He jammed a huge spoon of corn flakes into his mouth, chewing rapidly before they went soggy. There's nothing worse than soggy cereal.

"Mel? Mel?" I mused, rolling the name over with my spoon and adding a huge dollop of Mom's preserved apricots to my bowl. "Not Melinda, was it?"

"Yeah, that sounds like it."

"Mmmm. Interesting."

Chad didn't even look up.

We both fell silent and I mulled it over in my mind. Why would Melinda be ringing me at home? Maybe she had found my mysterious admirer and traced where the dead fish had arrived from. I guess she is sort of in charge of making sure everything is still on track from a CFR perspective. I abstractly pulled the morning newspaper towards me, flicking through the pages as my mind whirred over the possibilities. A picture caught my eye showing President Obama and his two daughters, holding up tickets towards the camera. The caption read "*Alien Potion Concert attracts President's attention.*" Skimming the article, it appeared that the girls had made their father purchase tickets online to the concert this coming Saturday at the Dorton Arena in the North Carolina State Fair Grounds. Apparently they were huge fans... "*A capacity crowd is expected to attend, and both President Obama's daughters will be there, although their father will not be in attendance, due to more pressing matters of state.*" I stared out the window to the distant horizon, not seeing anything. Was the presidential secret service aware of the scheduled anti-Semitic protest? Was there anything in the paper about *that*?

I furiously scoured every page, my bowl of yogurt forgotten. Finally, under the Public Notices section I found a minuscule notice: "*Meeting of The Order and affiliated groups, Saturday 24th July 2009 5pm. Please meet outside the NCSFG or contact Nathan Skinman for more information.*" Blah, blah phone number etc. Not hungry anymore, I excused myself to shower and change. I was still in the clothes I wore to the island with Levi, and felt decidedly shabby. Dan passed me in the hallway, rubbing his eyes as he made his way to the kitchen.

"Good sleep?" I greeted him chirpily.

"Whatever." He yawned. "Meeting in the lounge at ten. Neville is coming and Chad will be there too. Don't be late, 'K?"

"Got it, boss," I replied, and I dug an elbow into his ribs for effect.

"Ouch! Leave me alone in my misery, eh?" Then I heard him saying to Chad once he reached the kitchen, "Boy, the house sure seems noisy now Jazz's back, don't ya reckon?"

"Welcome to my world," Chad responded, and I imagined him rolling his eyes in mock horror. Before shutting the door I yelled down the hall: "Oh and check out page two of the paper, Danny-boy," knowing full well there was an article and photos showing new turtle nests found along local beaches. I turned the shower knob to hot, a grin on my face.

On the dot of 10am we were all assembled in the lounge, each looking at the other for a starting point. Nev was relaxed as ever, his feet up on the coffee table, hands interlocked behind his head. I smiled tentatively at him, unsure of what he knew and where I stood with him, but he patted the couch next to him, inviting me to sit. As I did so he slung his arm around my shoulder and plonked a sloppy kiss on my cheek.

"Ah, so great to have my girl around again. It's been too long Jazz, and now it'll be all work and no play!" His eyes looked so pathetically sad, I had to laugh.

Patting him on the knee I said, "There, there, Nev; I'll make sure Dan gives us a break every half an hour or so to do something silly for a bit of light relief. We all know you're work-a-phobic."

"Never told me about the turtles, either, Nev," Dan grumbled at him.

"Give it up already, eh? Never thought you'd be interested in the mating habits of amphibian, that's all. I've already said sorry twice since I got here, jeez!" His tone was still light hearted, and Dan finally managed to pull off a smile in response. "That's more like it. Happy hormones will make your mind work better, and we need to brainstorm, so let's rock and roll!"

Nev really was too, too much, I thought, looking around and realizing that everyone was probably thinking the same thing.

"Right," he continued, oblivious to the thoughts of those around him. "Here's a plan of the seven thousand or so capacity Dorton Arena at the North Carolina State Fair Grounds showing the seating layout and all entrance and exit points." He thrust it down on the coffee table and moved his feet back to the floor, leaning over the page with a black marker pen. "I suggest that

Dan takes the northern exits here ... and here, and I'll do the southern doorways here ... and here. Chad, best you man the front gates. I've heard there's going to be protesters there, as well as those heading inside the venue."

"But that leaves Jazz on her own in the crowds," Dan objected. "She can't be left without some sort of immediate protection."

Nev looked at him like he was an idiot. "But she's the one with the weapon of mass destruction. I've felt those Emospheres; they're lethal. Once she blows those bubbles, there'll be no danger whatsoever. Everyone will be all lovey-dovey."

Dan interrupted suddenly. "Why can't we blow the bubbles out as well?" he sat up excitedly. "We could all carry them! That would lessen the risk to Jasmine considerably."

I shook my head. "Don't think that'll work. The premise is that the bubbles require my breath to activate the emotion – after all, they carry my emotional DNA, but we can try, I guess."

Nev intervened again, dismissing the idea. "Give it a whirl and see what happens, and then let us know. Anyway, I propose we all have binoculars to keep tabs on her. We could also ask Levi to do the same from the stage – if that's OK with you, Jazz," he added hastily, glancing in my general direction.

"Whatever," I shrugged, looking as casual as I could, although my heart skipped a beat. "But how will I know when and where to release the Emospheres? Surely The Order will spread their people throughout the crowds to be less conspicuous? You can't have a big group of skinheads in one place; that'd be far too obvious."

"True, true, but I have thought of that. I'm sending Dan to make inquiries about their air conditioning unit, and to track down where the vents are. I figure if you work around each of the vents, the Emospheres will spread much wider and have greater effect. After that, I'm sure we'll begin to see any trouble spots that haven't been reached. As for when to release them, I haven't figured that one out yet, but we're making progress, don't ya think?" He sat back on the couch, looking very pleased with himself.

"Can the CFR arrange for us to blend in with their regular security staff?" Chad said suddenly. "It would make us less conspicuous, and mean that we could quite legitimately confiscate any weapons or hate literature before the event even starts."

"That would be child's play for Melinda; good idea, Chad."

I looked at Neville contemplatively, feeling a bit confused. "If you think Emospheres are so powerful, why *does* anyone need to be on any exit points? And as my Carrier, what is *your* role? Surely you do something more special that stand at a door watching. Come to think of it, no one's ever really explained to me what a Carrier can do – so spill, Neville. I don't want to go into this totally blind. You might think there are no risks, but if my years in a science lab have taught me anything, it's that there's *always* a risk."

Neville managed to look semi-serious for a brief moment. "You're right, Jazz. The trouble is that although each Carrier is endowed with an "Antidote" that will assist a Reader at a time of greatest need; Carriers don't even know what that Antidote is themselves, or what form it might take. There have been stories of almost super-human skills and feats, flashes of brilliance that allow a quick getaway – even sacrificing themselves for their Reader – so I can't really help you there, I'm sorry." He shrugged his shoulders. "At least not until the Antidote is needed."

"Who determines that?" Dan asked quietly.

Nev shrugged again. "It's a mystery. Quite often no Antidote is needed, and the Carrier's role is very small. No one ever knows what that Antidote might have been. It's very frustrating for a Carrier, you know."

I folded my arms. "But you've Carried a Reader before me; Ali and Arabella told me so."

"So true, so true." He clutched his hands in front of him, shifting in his seat to buy time. "It was another reason I left New Zealand. There seemed no point hanging around; particularly when your family relocated to the States. I felt an obligation to at least be in the same country as you, given my edict from the CFR to be your Carrier when the time came. Plus the CFR said there was another posting if I wanted it. Unfortunately, that Reader's status turned out to be a hoax ... Long story," he added hastily as my eyebrows raised, "but I've been around long enough to know a few things, so don't be concerned now."

"I'm not concerned," I said severely, "I am just wondering why Ali thinks you're so experienced. You didn't ... mislead them now, did you Neville? That's totally against the Seven Pillars of Wisdom ethos."

"Well, come on Jazz, you know letter writing, phone calls and all that. People can read between the lines you know." He shrugged again. "What can I say? I'm a talker, that's what I do best."

"Well stop for a while, hey?" I said, feeling chagrined. "Let's take a break while each of us thinks this through. Chad how 'bout you and I make sandwiches?" I beckoned to Chad to follow me to the kitchen and as we prepared the food I appealed to him for help in a low voice. "This is frustrating. I feel like I'm just being put on show for the benefit of the CFR rather than actually achieving any specific result. What are they hoping for? Just to calm down a few anti-Semitic freaks? I'm more concerned about the president's daughters. How secure are they? I need to talk to Levi and the family." I looked at him pleadingly. "Plea-aase Chad? For me? Will you secretly arrange a time with Mom and Dad and Levi? And the bros?"

Chad sighed. "You so know I will, sis. But Bailey comes too, OK?"

"Sure, no worries there. But – change of subject – why do you think we need you stationed on the doors?"

Chad looked thoughtful as he carefully sliced tomato and cucumber and I stacked the bread with mayo and ham. "Maybe it's because we can't be sure whether all the infiltrators will be inside, or whether they'll slip in at various times during the dark cover of the concert. They would be less conspicuous that way. Remember the Dorton Arena is inside the State Fair Grounds, so they could be blending in all over the park, waiting for the right moment to stage their protest. They might even have a secret code alarm or something."

"So let me get this right. If you're all on the doors you can text me if you see trouble approaching – or leaving for that matter."

"Yeah. But beyond that, you've already been told that this is a chance for the powers that be to observe Emospheres in action. I wouldn't be surprised if the president's daughter's escort is an FBI rep, sent to get the low down."

I shivered, getting that I'm-in-a-spy-movie feeling. "Better not disappoint, then, eh?"

We wrapped things up pretty quickly after that, allocating tasks to everyone and agreeing to meet again the day of the concert, not that I was expecting to get much space from any of them over the next few days. Dan, Chad, and Neville were all upset about the fish-in-the-box threat, and much to my consternation drew up a roster to sleep one outside the front door and one outside my window every night, as well as a baby-sitting roster during the day. At least that's what it felt like.

The rest of the day was pretty laid back: phoning Elle for a nice uncomplicated girl catch-up, agreeing to go shopping later in the week. I felt like I had achieved enough to at least spend a little of my CFR allocated slush fund on some new clothes. I also phoned Levi to let him know about the newspaper article and Melinda's phone call, and how I hoped she had solved the mystery fish puzzle.

"Any chance we can meet?" I loved the sound of his voice on the phone – deep and mysterious with a hint of mischief – but meeting would be better. I sighed.

"Chad's going to organize a pow-wow with you and my folks to sort out that back-up plan for the concert, but I'm wondering if that's not the kind of meeting you're referring to?" *(Did I just say that out loud? Cheesy!)*

"Anything's better than nothing, but I would really like to see those Emospheres in action as well. Maybe we could sneak a few moments after the meeting with your parents?"

I held my breath. Genius – something to look forward to. I just had to convince Chad. "Levi," my voice sounded funny, "are we ... are we ... you know ..."

"Boyfriend and girlfriend?" He sounded amused.

"Um ... yeah."

"Undercover Couple, that's what I'd call us. But as soon as this is over – whatever 'this' is – I'll even wear a badge with your name on it up on stage. Might even write you another song – a *girlfriend* song." He still sounded amused.

"This is a new game for me," I blurted out, half cross and half embarrassed. "I don't know what the rules are."

"Well neither do I – so that puts us both on the same page I'm guessing, and I can live with that."

"I should chill, shouldn't I? It's Jazz the science nerd again, wanting everything neatly boxed up and labeled. I'm sorry."

"Hey", he softly rejoined, "just relax; I'm not going anywhere. It's a bit like we're living in two worlds at the moment… (his voice grew soft)…and I know which world I prefer. As for this world, I'm guessing you're feeling the pressure building for the 'performance' on Saturday – and believe me, I know what that feels like. You will be fine, Jazz, and I will be there for you, I promise. Nev might be your appointed Carrier, but we both know that I am the Carrier destined for you. Maybe I need to come over and kiss you again to remind you." A slight groan made its way down the phone line, and I knew he was remembering the endless kiss from the night before.

"Your turn to chill," I joked, trying my best to escape the vortex of feeling between us, "but thanks. Thanks for yesterday, for sharing Jarven with me, your story, Adam, your turtle surprise – and Miss Motion of course – and thanks for right now. I feel much ... more relaxed. See you soon?"

"Very soon," Levi threatened, his voice husky, and I blushed, grateful he couldn't see the color rising in my cheeks.

I took to cleaning after that: the floors, the bathroom, the washing; and as I ordered the world around me, I ordered my mind, going over potential scenarios on Saturday, mentally dividing the line between the two camps: Neville and Levi. It was Dan I didn't quite know what to do with. Even Levi had commented last night that we had to trust him, and I did. But family loyalties run deep; I knew that also. And it wasn't as if I had anything concrete against Neville – it was Vander my intuition told me to watch out for. He was a relatively unknown quantity – how much power did he really carry? And if he was on the dark side, what did he hope to gain from the test case scenario planned for Saturday? I continued to ponder as I jogged down to the shops (with Dan setting the pace) and returned with the alcohol I needed to replenish my Emosphere formula, Chad's friends having made short work of the limited supply at the beach house. Once home, I sat and made lists until I was satisfied over who to trust and who to play games with. That was until Dan switched off the T.V. and suggested going for a surf.

"It's pretty much perfect conditions out there; come on Jazz, it's been ages!"

"Yeah, like a few days; but yep, be good to get in the water again." I smiled over at him, grateful for the distraction the surf would provide. By the time we arrived back at the house, the afternoon had long since faded, and after an egg on toast I announced it was an early night for me. My body was exhausted after the rigorous workout the waves had provided (at least that was the excuse I was using).

"Hold on a minute, Jazz." Dan swallowed his last mouthful and stood up, "Uh, Nev will be around soon; he's taking the night shift outside your window. I'm heading up to Raleigh with your mate Sam to check out the venue and the Fair Grounds. There's a Sports Memorabilia Expo on as well, so we might hang out for a bit, stay the night, and drive back tomorrow."

"Sam's going with you?"

"Well,' joined in Chad, "you couldn't exactly expect him to go by himself, and we are committed to keeping two of us with you at all times, so I rang in Sam. I didn't tell him anything, don't worry," he added hastily before I could protest.

I was actually too tired to protest, waving bye-bye across the table and warning Chad to make sure Nev kept the noise down. I just hoped he didn't snore like Dan did. I removed both vials of blood I had stored in the fridge and took them to the bedroom, thinking I might assemble the Love Emosphere as my last task of the day, but after mixing one and returning it to the fridge, I grabbed an apple to munch on as I worked, then cleverly used the apple to knock the bottle of vodka off the window sill, where it tumbled down the dunes spilling its contents into the tussock ... damn! Well, it could stay like that till morning, I thought, climbing under the sheets. I just can't be bothered fetching it and now it means another visit to the shops tomorrow. Hang on; aren't I shopping with Elle I wondered, yawning? I can't remember whether that's tomorrow or the next day...

Thud!! "Whoa!"

I sat up in bed with a start. "Who's there?" I felt disoriented in the dark room, unsure of how long I had been asleep.

"It's OK, Jazz," came a whisper from the floor, "it's just me, Neville. I tripped over something on my way to the bathroom. It's only midnight – not that late. Didn't Dan tell you I would be sleeping outside your window tonight?"

"Grrrr!" I flung a pillow over my face as I lay back down. "You guys are taking this *way* too seriously, and why couldn't you just find a pee tree outside? We're not that precious about the garden you know. *Man*!"

"Yep, not that easy I'm afraid; I'll have to try and adjust nature's call and all that. Sorry Jazz, go back to sleep; I won't disturb you again, I promise."

"Hmmmfh," was my muffled response, and I waited till he was gone before removing the pillow, huffing over and over in the bed until I got comfortable again. The pillow had uncovered my ring, and I was tempted to put it on, but I knew Levi wouldn't be there. We had realized that our nights in the desert affected our sleep levels, and agreed to stay away for the next three nights. It was going to be harder than hard.

Tuesday was boring. I bought more vodka and made the second Love vial, but labeled it "First Love" in honor of Levi. Then I labeled just about everything else in the place, even my underwear drawer and bathroom cupboards, separating Chad, Dan, Nev and my personal items with name stickers on each. This place was getting annoyingly crowded. Dan returned from his trip happy, which further annoyed me. Unfortunately the Dorton Arena has no air conditioning, but big fans will be in place around the walls – not quite so convenient, but workable I think.

Wednesday was … well … not quite so boring. Shopping with Elle was good. It was so nice to hang with another girl rather than all those smelly boys, although Dan skulked in the background. I found a dress to wear to Mom's place tomorrow night: *the* dress. Elle is the best. It was hard not to tell her everything, but she guessed about Levi. We went totally all-out girly for three hours before I reached saturation point – my longest time yet! Poor Dan ... not! Then we went to a kick-boxing class at Elle's gym. Now that took my mind off things, plus I pretended one of the kick pads Dan held up was Vander and the other Darth Vader. Oh what fun that was! Dan thought I was ferocious. I went to sleep with Levi singing softly in my ear – thanks Apple iPod.

I must have put my ring on in my sleep. It was twilight, and I rushed into Levi's arms as if I were a woman dying of thirst in the desert – which I was. We stood as a single silhouette against a lavender sky and watched as the sunset painted an intense picture on the horizon. "I couldn't stay away," Levi whispered, gently caressing the nape of my neck with his tongue, starting a fire as passionate as the deepening red glow of the sky. I turned in his arms and drew his mouth to mine, letting my hands run through his hair, pulling him toward me fiercely. "Shut-up," was my eloquent reply.

On Thursday morning there was a letter addressed to me with funny white powder inside saying in cut-out letters (how old school is that?) *"Stop Reading ... forever."* It turned out to be nothing but icing sugar. Dan got out the gloves and mask, but before he could check, Nev came into the kitchen, licked his finger and stuck it in to the envelope saying, "Mmmm ... sherbet. We used to make it back in New Zealand and put it in an envelope with a straw. Did your Mom teach you how to make it, Dan?"

We didn't even bother telling him, just rolled our eyes and chucked it in the bin. The letter left my tummy a bit wobbly inside though. I know I should be trembling in my boots, but it just seems so odd to me – definitely not freaking me out, just causing me to be a little more cautious when I leave the house. Who is so hell-bent on trying to upset me? I wish I knew. There's been much discussion, but no leads. Talk about frustrating. The picture of last nights' sunset is playing over and over in my head, and I know I'm stronger than I once was. I haven't been mooching around today ... much. I spent some time reading over Wisdom Pillars and Precepts to fortify myself, a bit girly-swat, but Ali might give me a surprise test. That would be just like him.

Thursday afternoon came and I phoned Melinda from the CFR on her cell. She wants to meet. I arranged for her to visit tomorrow morning, but I just have to make sure Dan and Neville are out.

Finally! Thursday night came into view, and I showered and dressed at lightning speed, which was probably a knee-jerk reaction to the forthcoming visit to my parents' house. Growing up in a large family you learn to be terrified of:

(a) CWS: The water going cold before you rinse the shampoo out of your hair; (Cold Water Syndrome)

(b) FOMO: Fear Of Missing Out on any action happening downstairs (or the last of the breakfast cereal);

(c) BPB: Giving your brothers too much time to prank your bedroom. (Brothers Pranking Bedroom)

Fortunately, none of the above was a threat anymore, and before I knew it I was sitting on the edge of the bed twiddling my thumbs, waiting for Chad to finish getting ready. I smoothed my hands over my new dress. It was perfect. My dad loved seeing me in a dress rather than jeans; it made him remember that I was actually a young woman rather than the tomboy who used to join in the family wrestling nights with gusto. I was a little hesitant about the rich ruby red, but now that it was on it made me feel brave, like I was a strong woman ready to take on the challenges I faced. I wanted to stare danger in the face, not run from it. No Jagger threat was going to make me cower in the background. If a little red dress was the bolster I needed, then so be it. I was so ready to rumble.

21. MEETING OF THE MINDS

ARRIVING AT THE PECAN INN (ALIAS BLADE ABODE) at around 6pm, I had been alternating between senseless chatter and prolonged bouts of nervous silence on the way over, driving Chad half mad, and he almost pushed me out of the car before he had parked. Levi was already there; I could see him seated uncomfortably at the courtyard table with my dad, but the jacaranda tree partially blocked my view. Feeling suddenly shy, I slipped in the front door and went straight to the kitchen, where I knew Mom would be. After a lovely long hug she threw an apron over my head, and together we chopped, stirred, checked the oven, and chattered until dinner was ready.

"You look very happy, Jazz," she pointedly commented right at the outset. "Any chance Levi would have anything to do with that?"

I predictably blushed, and together we laughed. Mom touched the side of her nose and whispered, "Say no more, Jazzy, say no more, but for what it's worth, I approve, your Dad is coming around; and surprisingly enough, all your brothers are ok with it too."

I groaned. "They all know?"

Mom nodded. "What do you expect, after the stage debacle last Saturday night? They were all there you know."

"Well I hope you've told them *no* teasing. You know what they're like: merciless!"

"Just like you when Marcus brought his first girlfriend home for dinner? What comes round goes round. You're on your own, hon." But she did pat my shoulder in mock sympathy. Pah!

Levi stood up quite well to the jests, quips, and downright cheeky comments, but I was relieved when dinner was finished. The red dress must have made me stronger, but it was still Levi that kept me from going insane. Mom had seated him directly opposite me, and every time our eyes met, which was often, I felt a meteor shower begin in my brain, pelting every particle of my being with an intense awareness of his presence, and I missed a lot of the jibes aimed in my direction, so intent I became with catching his eye. It was like our own private game; my new favorite game.

I noticed Dad didn't come to the rescue from my brothers' onslaught, but rather took a perverse satisfaction in joining in, making every effort to make Levi feel as uncomfortable as possible. Levi simply played along, and as the charade continued I thought I saw dad's reaction change to one of grudging admiration.

Chad had not stayed, but left to collect Bailey from the airport. She was on her way back from tour promotion duties, so it was well after 8pm when we were all assembled in the lounge for some more serious conversation.

Fale and Harley just couldn't help themselves with one last dig, picking me up and surfing me over their heads into the lounge, re-enacting the scene at the concert, then dumping me on Levi's lap and laughing hilariously. Levi let me scramble off in a hurry, but kept one arm fixed around my waist, pulling me close next to him on the couch, making it clear that he didn't care – in fact he was joining in the laughter. I glared at him, then at each of my brothers in turn, who were rolling on the floor at this point.

"I didn't exactly have much choice in the matter, you know; but," I stuck my chin in the air, "I actually like crowd surfing, it's ... its very retro. So thanks, Levi." I turned my face back towards him and poked out my tongue, then smiled sweetly.

"And you can all remember the family rule: *'what comes round goes round,'* so you better watch your backs, boys!"

"Oooohh!" Fale wailed. "So scared, sis. Haven't you forgotten Dad's other rule? *'It starts off in fun, and ends up in tears with someone crying ...'*"

"AND IT'S NEVER ME!" Dad boomed out the last words, reducing us all to giggling again, just as Chad and Bailey came in the door.

"What did we miss?" Chad began.

"Certainly not you holding hands with Bailey," Harley crowed, and Chad groaned.

"I thought you would have used up all the teasing on Jazz by now; give it a rest Harley."

Bailey had on her "*I couldn't give a fig you cretins*" look, which I now guessed was her shell of protection, built up by years of having to fend for herself.

Mom took over at that point, ordering Chad to bring another chair through from the dining room and Marcus to get the dinner she had set aside for them both. Patting the chair next to her, she invited Bailey to sit, pouring her a soft drink from the tray on the table, and then looked over at me to start the proceedings.

"Now, then, we all know why we're here, to provide some back-up for Jazz at the concert this weekend as she tests those Emo-thingies, so let's get down to business."

When Mom mentioned business, the fun was definitely over, and I for one was relieved. I sat forward, aware of Levi's hand on my back, burning a hole in my dress. Think, Jazz, think! I bought myself some time by explaining the arrangements made with Neville and Dan, with Chad contributing between mouthfuls. I also told of the second threat I had received.

Marcus interrupted to say, "Jazz ... it could have been anthrax or anything. Such a risk even opening it! It's time to do some research to determine patterns with these threats or other examples of similar cases of harassment. I know someone who might be able to help with this – confidentially, of course – let me look into it."

I looked over at him gratefully. Trust Marcus to "know" someone. And he'd probably come up with the goods.

Taking a deep breath and glancing at Levi for some moral support, I began to share my intuition as a Reader; it was not as if I had any clear direction when I arrived earlier this evening, but as I looked around it was as if all the pieces to finish the puzzle were in the room. I just had to decide where to place them on Saturday's board. Focusing on the emotional threads I felt running through my mind, I dug deeper, searching for the gaps, uncovering a hidden web of knowledge and using it instinctively to communicate my ideas and suddenly-inspired back-up plan. By the time an hour had passed, we were all clear on what would unfold should anything not go to plan, and where each of us should be. Levi was the only one without a specific task. It was a bit hard with him being the main act for the night, and even if he didn't like it much, he knew he was trapped, although as Dad pointed out, he was in the best position of all – elevated above all of us and able to see everything – as long as the house lights were up.

As we went over the details one last time, I felt Levi's hand on my back again, tapping out a rhythm I didn't recognize. I hoped he wouldn't stop. Mom announced supper and left for the kitchen, with Chad trailing her and Bailey trailing Chad. Fale, Harley, Marcus, and Dad were busy hunched over the plan making refinements when Levi and I snuck out the side door. Dad rolled his eyes in resignation, but did nothing to stop us. We ran away from the house, not stopping until we were two doors down, nearly at the waterfront, where Levi slid his arms around me from behind, abruptly halting our mad dash for freedom. His cool demeanor was in full form tonight, black jeans teamed with a vintage U2 t-shirt and a scruffy black hooded cardigan. He almost looked like a stranger, as if he had stepped from the pages of Rolling Stone Magazine into my tiny world, and I didn't know what to say.

"Did you guess the song?" he whispered over my shoulder, and I imagined his eyes sparking with the challenge, and turned to look into them again. I really was a hopeless addict now.

I cocked my head sideways, not understanding his question. "The song, I tapped the rhythm on your back."

"Oh … umm..." Brain freeze. "It has a fast beat, kinda catchy – something by 'NeverShoutNever!'?"

"Could be…" he smiled down at me. "But no. It was 'Can you tell me how to get to Sesame Street'."

I punched him at that point – trust him to go from the sublime to the ridiculous in a matter of seconds.

"Hey!" I remembered suddenly, "I brought some Joy bubbles with me. You ready for a blast?" I twirled out of his arms and danced a few feet in front of him, towards one of the nearby marina jetties. Slipping the small glass vial from my dress pocket, I undid the stopper. Levi observed with his hands thrust deep into his pockets, relaxed and amused at my childish enthusiasm.

"You try first." I held the vial out to him. "We want to see if other people can blow the bubbles and create Emospheres."

He took the bottle and blew a small steady stream of bubbles, right into my face.

"That tickles!" I giggled, but after waiting a few minutes, there was no sign of any unusual emotional reaction from either of us.

Taking the bottle back, I kept my eyes on him and gently blew the soft spheres in his direction. The light from the street lamps caught each bubble, creating an enhanced 3-D effect. As they fell I sashayed back to him, stirring up the avalanche of tiny fizzy balls and they began to implode all around our heads, landing on our arms, our backs, our legs. We stood, not touching, and I felt a ripple of happiness start at my shoulders, circle through my hips and surge to a tidal wave by the time it reached my feet. Levi looked giddy. His whole body swayed back and forth until the Joy could no longer be contained and had to exit through his shoes. He began to sing "Jeremiah was a Bullfrog" by Three Dog Night, and together we sung the lyrics: "*Joy to the world, all the boys and girls, joy to the fishes in the deep blue sea, joy to you and me,*" and we danced until our feet ached, before collapsing at the side of the jetty, throwing off our shoes and cooling our toes in the calm water. I rested my head on his shoulder as we swung our legs in time, and the Joy flowed through our conversation about our favorite things: open fires on the beach and tumbling down sand dunes; speed and roller coasters; cotton candy and full moons; music that stirs the soul and words that feed the mind.

"This Joy..." Levi mused, "It's so sweet, so pure, so... intense. It's like a key that unlocks any long, forgotten happy moments, rushing them into your head to explode into a million particles of Joy. My Mom used to sing me that Jeremiah song, you know…" He bent his face down towards me, and instinctively I looked up. "There is only one thing left to make my joy complete," he murmured softly, but before his lips could meet mine, we heard a familiar voice drift down the pier.

"They must be here somewhere," complained Harley, "I know that was them I heard singing earlier."

"Keep looking," Chad grumbled. "I wanna go home. It's past midnight."

"You sound like a Grandpa," quipped Fale. "The hour is just young like us, you old man you!"

I whispered to Levi as we scrambled up and he pulled me in behind one of the huge pier supports. "Wanna have some fun?"

His eyes sparkled and he nodded, already guessing what my intentions were. Whistling long and hard between his teeth, we stayed hidden, pressed up against the rough wood.

"Down here!" Fale's voice drifted towards us excitedly. "I think that's them sitting on that boat moored up to the left. Hey Jazz! Levi!"

Fale and Harley rushed up the pier together, maybe hopeful of catching us kissing or something; thereby providing them with some new ammunition. Chad was not far behind. As they drew close to where we were hidden, I dipped the bubble wand into the potion and blew, watching as the tiny spheres of euphoria cast their net out across the wharf. The boys ran bang smack right into Joy, and it was their turn to whoop and holler. As the three of them stumbled around like drunken clowns, Levi beckoned to me, and we snuck up on them from behind, shoving them off the edge into the black, dappled sea. Fits of laughter ensued, and as Levi slipped off his jacket he grabbed my hand, launching us off the edge to join them, his laughter now loud and hilarious.

I came to the surface gasping at the sudden cold plunge, only to find Levi's lips fiercely claiming mine, his arms tight around me as he kept us both afloat. I wanted that kiss to last forever, and I knew the next song I would have him guess was vintage U2 as the evocative lyrics flooded my mind: "*who's going to taste your salt water kisses?*"

I kissed back harder; the sensations of water, of salt, of skin, of utter joy were there for the taking, and we ignored the splashing, the wolf whistles and the chaos around us, creating a memory that no one could destroy.

Making our way back to the house dripping wet, my red dress began clinging more than in just the right places. The boys peeled off their t-shirts and wrung them out, walking home bare-chested in the balmy night air.

"Nice to be a guy," I grumbled inside, until I caught Levi eying me with undisguised admiration, and I blushed, changing my mind.

"Here," said Chad, who had run ahead to fetch towels for us all, "cover your chest up, Levi, before my sister falls into temptation, eh? You too, sis. You're like two love-sick puppies, you are!"

Fale stuck his finger down his throat in agreement. Levi and I just grinned, silly and soporific, riding too much of a high to care.

"That's some punch those Emo-thingies pack." Harley's muffled voice came from under the towel he was using to dry his hair. "I'll pay you for more of that stuff, Jazz." He looked half-pie serious as his head poked through the towel.

I held the bottle out to Harley. "Here, you try blowing them on Dad – he's still watching TV. See if they work when you try."

"Yo sis – you sure?" He grabbed the vial. "Well 'K then, if you insist," and ran inside towards the living room. We all crowded in behind to view the results, but even though he blew twice, the bubbles fell prettily, but nothing changed. Dad just lifted his eyelids enough to say, "Yeah, whatever, very nice, but does Jasmine know you've nicked her bubbles, Harls? Don't think she'll be happy. Now go to bed would you, before I have to yell!"

"Bummer!" whispered Levi, "it's all on your head now, Jazz. At least we all know what to expect on Saturday now I s'pose, not that I've experienced the love bubbles yet. I'm looking forward to that," added Levi, winking at me. "They really are something else,' he continued, looking at me proudly. "I don't know how you did it, but they're going to knock the stuffing out of any hate at the gig. I feel slightly less nervous about the plan now – only slightly, mind you." he added sternly, as I smiled a cocky grin at him.

And then came good night, with Chad hustling me to the car wrapped in a towel. "Where's Bailey?" I asked surprised.

"Already took her home – she was exhausted. The demand for Alien Potion is sky high and negotiating the deals for concert venues and tour dates has been a real headache for her."

My heart sank as I realized Levi would be gone soon, on the road and on the stage for at least three months. Our time together was running out, and with all my focus on Saturday's Emospherica debut, I hadn't thought any further ahead. Resolutely, I retrieved my ring from under the pillow and let it circle my finger again before I lay down – my need for time with Levi was greater than any need for sleep.

We danced in the desert that night. Bodies pressed together, eyes locked, lips parted. We danced, but we didn't move fast, and there was no need for words, no need for music – we were the words, our love was the music.

The following morning the sky was gray and foreboding, almost identical to my mood. Leaving the desert and Levi each night was getting harder and harder. Dan was insisting on coming to the meeting with Melinda. Apparently she had rung the night before to confirm, and Dan being Dan was not taking no for an answer. Chad was working anyway, as was Neville, so in line with their stepped-up security around me, I wasn't given any say in the matter. It wasn't until we were in the car that I told Dan that the meeting was being held at Levi's house now.

"It is Levi's concert, after all," I explained to him. "He's concerned about security for the President's daughters too. And he knows Melinda better than we do. I believe him when he says we can trust her."

"Yeah, yeah, yeah. Got all that. Let's just get it over with then, eh?" Dan sounded glum, and we fell into an uneasy silence.

When we arrived Dan just sat in the passenger seat unmoving. I looked over at him impatiently. "I still can't get my head around the fact that Levi is Chris from Alien Potion. Rock stars are so egotistical; I saw him on stage the other night, swaggering around like he owned the show ... and you." He didn't look back at me as he spoke.

I sighed. Maybe this was a Joy-withdrawal hangover I was having. I didn't have the time or the energy for Dan's gripes. "Let's go," I said firmly, ignoring his comment and opening my door. Dan reluctantly did the same.

Bailey greeted us at the door, smiling wanly. She still looked extremely tired. "Everyone's here," she said wearily, "would you like a drink?"

"Thanks – that would be lovely. Whatever everyone else is having will be fine, although I think Dan needs strong coffee with lots of sugar." I couldn't help sounding caustic, but I tried to soften my tone before adding,

"Hey Bailey? I.... I think you and Chad are great together. I hope you don't mind me saying."

She stopped and looked at me properly, for the first time ever, I thought.

"Your family ... it's ... you're lucky. And Chad's great." Her eyes were still difficult to read, but she did smile at me briefly before turning again and leading us through to the lounge.

Levi sat with sunglasses on, flanked by Jamal and Terrance. (That'll confirm Dan's opinion, I thought ruefully.) Melinda was pouring a cup of tea, looking just as avant-garde as last time.

"Sup, Jazz," Jamal nodded at me, "and Jazz's friend ..."

"Dan," Dan roughly rejoined.

Levi stood holding out his hand to shake Dan's, which Dan pointedly ignored, turning to find a vacant seat as far as he could from Levi.

"I don't think you've actually met Jamal and Terrance? Jamal: drums; Terrance: bass. Fraser, who plays guitar and keyboards, is at the venue already, overseeing the set-up. He's quite particular like that."

Terrance guffawed loudly, slapping his knees. "Fraser the Taser –our lethal weapon!"

Dan nodded at each of them in turn as Melinda passed him a cup of tea.

"Never guessed you'd be having morning tea with Alien Potion, eh?" Melinda teased. She leaned forward and whispered, "There are those who would kill to be in your shoes right now." Dan's eyes flickered to hers momentarily, but he didn't bother replying.

I wished Levi's eyes weren't hidden behind those glasses. It was as if we were mere acquaintances; there seemed to be no inkling of last night's passion evident. Turning to Melinda, I jumped right in, determined to focus on the task at hand rather than Levi's aloof, cool manner.

"Melinda, we talked on the phone about concerns in regard to the security around the president's daughters. What can you tell us?"

Launching into a whole lot of information, it was quickly evident that Melinda was meeting us without Vander's knowledge.

"I may be acting outside my jurisdiction here, but the safety of those girls is paramount." Terrance and Jamal were nodding furiously. Melinda picked some muffin crumbs off her paisley skirt as she continued. "I have met first hand with the FBI and they agree. They have been watching White extremist groups closely since Obama came to power, and have always maintained it was only a matter of time before they contrived something foolish – like this protest."

"Well we ain't gonna back down," interrupted Jamal.

"Hang on a minute guys," Levi was firm, "let's let Melinda finish and see how we can all work together on Saturday." I couldn't tell if he was looking at me or not.

Melinda was certainly efficient, and by the end of the meeting the level of confidence in the room had risen and all possible scenarios we could dream up had been covered. As we headed to the front door, I lingered until Melinda was free.

"Melinda," I whispered, "a couple of last things: Can I have a code word to text you if I'm in trouble? Not that I'm expecting any," I added hastily as her eyes narrowed. "I just want to be prepared, that's all. If I text you the word '*dragonfly*,' it means Plan B has swung into action – and I need you to follow the instructions in this sealed envelope. Can you do that?"

Melinda's eyes were still narrow as she thought for a moment before replying. "We are on the same team, aren't we Jasmine."

It was a statement rather than a question. "Team Reader," I replied, steadily holding her gaze. "The same team as Levi." My voice dropped to a mere whisper.

She nodded at me slowly, taking the envelope and slipping it into her jacket pocket. "Team Reader," she repeated, and I knew she understood.

"Have you found any suspects for those stupid threats yet?" I tossed my hair, feeling a little stupid for even asking. She would have said something if she had.

"No, I'm sorry to say. We've tried every lead possible, and nothing. It's so frustrating – and strange – and a Jagger knows that a Reader won't be intimidated by mere threats, but who else could it be?"

"Yeah, who knows? Well, thanks Melinda, for everything." I smiled, liking this bright, thoughtful lady more each time I saw her.

Jamal and Terrance swept me into a bear hug at that point, depositing me on the porch. Terrance winked at me. "Thanks for rescuing our brother Levi. You done good, girl." I blushed as he tapped his cheek for me to kiss, before he kissed my hand and followed Jamal back inside.

Slipping my shoes on, I stood looking around for Dan, and then realized he was already in the car, glaring at me. Turning to go, I felt rather than saw Levi behind me and mechanically rotated again to politely say goodbye. He had shut the front door behind him and taken his glasses off; his eyes told me all I needed to know.

"This is for you," he murmured, pressing me hard against the handrail of the porch and crushing his mouth to mine. The weight of his body set my flesh on fire, and my mouth burned in response. When he finally released me he whispered in my ear: "The glasses were for my protection – I wouldn't have been able to concentrate if our eyes had met. The kiss was to make up for it." We both jumped as the car horn tooted rudely. I sighed as I slammed the car door and saw Dan's knuckles were clenched and white... Why are guys so primal?

The sky seemed to lower from that point on and the gray day dragged on and even Chad was uncharacteristically on edge. The tension was slowly mounting and my mind wouldn't let me rest. Mental checklist after checklist played over and over like a bad sitcom rerun. Rather than resist it, after a while I decided to roll with the mood and lay on the lounge floor with iPod earphones on, listening to the heaviest rock and metal music I had. By 3pm I was wired, and I suggested to Chad and Dan that we go for a run along the beach to shake down the tension before Ali and Arabella arrived. Perhaps it would appease Dan too.

Mom and Dad were both busy, so Neville had offered to collect them from the airport and bring them to the beach house for dinner. Before he left, I updated everyone on my Emosphere experiment from the night before.

"Levi tried blowing the bubbles, and so did Harley, but nothing happened. I'm convinced the activation of the Emospheres is connected to my breath – the breath of a Reader. So there are no options, really – but I'm up for it. In fact, I'm quite looking forward to it."

"I thought as much," Neville said, folding his arms, "but don't worry, darlin'. I'll be there for you; we all will be."

"I just said I was up for it," I replied, strangely irritated by his reassurances, and as we made our way to the beach I raced ahead, trying to make Dan and Chad eat my dust, thinking instead of Ali and Arabella, and how much I was looking forward to seeing them. I realized fiercely that I wanted to make them proud; for them to realize after all the family hurt and separation over my gift as a Reader, that they had been right to want me to pursue my Destiny within the CFR, and that my discovery of Emospheres would be a success, celebrated in the world of scientific research and development.

I blocked out the threats of the past few days and focused instead on the mantra of the Seven Pillars, reciting them over and over, faster and faster, to match the rhythm of my feet. By the time we returned, I was still way out in front with sweat dripping from my brow in rivers, and my breath so fast I couldn't catch it.

"You are a maniac, Jazz," Dan panted as he dropped to his knees beside me on the sand.

"You know how you're amped before a big game of foot- ... I mean rugby," I gasped back, and he nodded. "That's how I feel right now; like I'm on the cusp of either life-changing success or epic failure, and I want the taste of victory more than I've ever wanted anything." I savagely swept back the loose tendrils of hair that had escaped from my ponytail and watched as Chad dived into the water, knowing he was feeling it too.

"We're all rooting for you Jazz, you know that; especially me," Dan said. He looked out at Chad as well, pausing before he spoke again. "Neville ... my dad ... he's never been a real father to me, and even though I've been here three weeks now, I still don't feel that I know him any better than when I arrived." His honest eyes looked straight into mine, his blond hair plastered down with sweat, and his expression confused. "I thought seeing him again would help me understand where I fit, but I still don't feel like I belong. Helping you, protecting you, is the first time I've felt useful, needed. I guess what I'm saying is that I'm with you Jazz, for better or for worse – and I know you can do this; I know it. I guess that's why I've been so black lately." He left the other reason unsaid.

I looked at him gratefully, knowing that he didn't find it easy to be this open. Leaning against him and pushing gently I smiled a sweet smile. "Thanks, kiwi boy. One last swim for the road? I'll race you."

"No, together," he replied, taking my hand in his and pulling us both to our feet. We ran down to the water to join Chad, and I knew without a doubt I was in very good hands indeed.

Back at the house I didn't bother with a shower. Throwing on a clean t-shirt, I ran to answer the front door as the bell rang. There on the door step stood Levi, his disheveled rock look complete, and it took all my self-control not to throw myself into his arms. Instead I stepped backwards to lessen the waves of electricity that sparked around us. It seemed as if we couldn't come within yards of each other without setting off power surges, and I had been taken by surprise once again.

"Your ring. The one from your parents. In my pocket. From when we dug the beach for the turtles." His words were mixed up as he held it out towards me. I stared at his hand, wondering if I touched it I would experience the same shock as I used to get when dismounting the trampoline on a sunny day. A shiver ran down my spine but I managed to reply.

"Thanks ... I … uh ... knew you'd keep it safe." He slipped it on the finger next to my Reader's ring before I could move, and leaned in to kiss my forehead gently.

"Got to go; boys are waiting for me at the arena. See you tonight?" There was really nothing else he could say – it just all had to happen now.

I was still swimming in the hydroelectric current his proximity had unleashed, when I became vaguely aware of a car door slamming, but Levi was still here, seemingly reluctant to let me go. So what was...?

A familiar voice made my eyes fly open, and there, on the other side of Neville's car, peacock blue jumpsuit screaming as loud as she was, stood Arabella effusively trying to catch my attention.

"Jasmine, darling! We're here at long last! Come give your

very young Granny a hug!"

Levi stepped aside and I smiled at him gratefully, then rushed down the front path as she first walked then lithely ran towards me in an effort to cover more ground and prove her youth. All at once there was a loud CRACK! Then CRACK CRACK! In quick succession; and just where we should have embraced my arms grasped thin air as Arabella collapsed in a heap at my feet. Pandemonium broke out. Levi lunged in front of me, shoving me to the ground and covering me with his body, whilst Neville and Ali dropped bags in the gutter and raced to Arabella's aid.

I heard footsteps and Dan shouting, "I'll carry her, I will!"

"I've got her, man," Levi replied savagely. "You help Arabella!"

All I could think was when did it start raining? I felt wet patches on my cheeks, which my fingers showed to my eyes, identifying them as blood. Then I was aware of a terrible noise and realized it was me wailing. Levi clutched me to him and sprinted inside, softly shushing me like he would a baby.

How can seconds take the place of hours in a matter of minutes? Why can't time move backwards as well as forwards? And when do questions become the battle cry for war? For even though I was caught in a maze of pain, deep down I knew that this pain was just the beginning – the catalyst to launch me into the heart of my Destiny.

22. EMOSPHERICA

NEVILLE, JOINED BY CHAD, WHO HAD HEARD THE commotion from inside, went racing across the road in an attempt to discover the gunman, using the neighbor's rubbish bin lids as shields. People out in their yards were running back into their houses, some peering through the windows clutching phones and ringing emergency services, some comforting small children startled by the loud noise. Neville yelled at them as he ran.

"Get back inside, all of you! Someone is armed and dangerous! I repeat: someone is armed and dangerous!"

I guessed the chase would be futile, my mood despairing as Levi slammed the front door with his foot. Whoever used us for target practice would be long gone by now.

Ali was distraught, clutching Arabella to his chest, making it difficult for Dan to assess her injuries, and across the room I could hear low moaning interspersed with raspy shallow breathing. Even as I was struggling to get up, Levi's hands were gentle on my shoulder, tearing away my t-shirt to reveal two contusions, already beginning to swell. One bullet had just grazed the top of my shoulder at the edge of my neck, and I could feel the blood trickling down into my ear. Pressing a clean tea towel firmly against it to stem the flow, I felt Levi examining the second wound, running his fingers over a bump under my skin.

"Damn!" he whispered, more to himself than me.

"I'm fine," I yelled at him, then realized my voice was little more than a whimper, but I still fought to stand, desperate to be near Arabella. I fell from the sofa to the floor with a soft thud, clutching my shoulder and gritting my teeth.

"The ambulance is taking too long," Dan panted as he tried to staunch the flow of blood from Arabella's back.

"Agreed," Levi growled. "We're taking my car –its right outside."

As he spoke I had used my one good hand and two knees to find my way towards the moaning, but just as I reached out to comfort Ali, I felt myself being lifted again, more roughly this time. Arabella and I were rushed into Levi's car. (He had a car too? I remember thinking vaguely.) Levi strapped me in the front seat and Ali and Dan supported Arabella in the back; her breathing sounding weaker.

Ali whispering over and over, "You can do it, Bella, you're stronger than me, you're the strongest woman I know. Stay strong, stay strong." His voice was beginning to break up.

Levi drove fast and furious, accelerating to speeds well beyond any I had ever experienced. The twenty-five-minute journey to Carteret General Hospital took just fifteen minutes, and screeching into the emergency entrance it was only seconds more before Arabella was ripped away from us by medical staff and I was laid out on a waiting room bed. The movement had caused the bleeding to begin again, and I stared at the red stain appearing somewhere down by my side – the white sheet as blank as my mind; the red as wild as my anger. I wished I could catch this emotion and unleash it on those who deserved it. If they wanted me, they knew where I was – but my grandmother? That was an abomination! If she was damaged beyond repair ... A kaleidoscope of red and white exploded in my mind, dragging me under, where I decided to stay for a while. Pain was definitely over-rated.

I awoke what seemed like minutes later with a crowd of faces hovering over me, and I let my eyes drift from head to head, identifying each in turn: Dan, Neville, Chad, Levi, Dad, and Mom ... Mom! I struggled to sit up, all of them reaching in together to help. If it didn't hurt so much I might have even laughed.

"I'm fine; I'm fine ... am I fine?" I suddenly thought to ask, giving myself the once over to check. "Granny! I mean Arabella ... is she ... she's OK?" Mom squeezed my hand tenderly.

"She's fine, though not quite as fine as you, but she will be in a few days, so don't worry yourself."

"She's a tough old bird," added Dad. "I remember this one time on the ski slopes at Wanaka; she broke her leg going over a jump, and still skied out on one ski, leaning on me for support with not a whimper till we made it back down. Then you should have heard her holler for attention!"

"The doc says she's real lucky," Chad added. "The bullet was rubber, but it still managed to penetrate the skin on her back, causing a rib to fracture and bruising her lung. That's why she was spitting up so much blood, but if the bullet hadn't glanced off her rib, it might have torn an artery."

I looked up at Chad, and then each of them in turn again. "If it weren't for her ..." I whispered, "She probably saved my life."

Looking at Neville now, I asked, "Did you and Chad find anyone? Anything? Did the police turn up? What did they say? You got any suspects in mind?"

"Whoa! Slow it down Lara Croft!" He shook his head, slowly explaining what had happened after we left. "Neither Chad nor I found anything helpful, but the police started a door to door inquiry, so maybe they'll come up with something. The policeman I spoke to said you were extremely lucky, that even though the bullets were only rubber, they could still be fatal at close range. He estimated the sniper to be located around fifty feet away, possibly around the side of a dwelling across the street – much less than the one hundred thirty feet recommended for such crowd control weapons. He was convinced this was an act of intimidation rather than someone with an outright murderous intent, and I would tend to agree. It fits with the previous two threats: aimed to scare you off. It was just unlucky that your grandmother got in the way."

I threw back the sheets and quickly stood, grasping the nearest arm for support. It happened to be Levi's. (That was no good; it would make my knees even weaker.)

"Take me home, eh? It's only 10pm and I've got some prep to do for tomorrow, plus I need a good night's sleep in my own bed if I'm going to be of any use. See? Look at me – I'm fine, just fine." I hastily let go of Levi, standing as tall as I could. There was silence as they all stared at me as if I were crazy. "What?" I argued irritably. "They took out the bullet and stitched me up, didn't they? It's no big deal; it was just a crowd control weapon with fake ammunition. I could have ended up with stitches just by falling down the front stairs." No one had responded yet. "At least I didn't break any bones. Look, I'm walking. Who's taking me home?"

Levi unceremoniously picked me up and dumped me back on the bed. "This is not negotiable. You … are staying put. Understood?"

Dan nodded, his arms folded with that bodyguard look on his face again. "I'm staying with you, Jazz. No arguments. Now take your pills." Opening my mouth he shoved them in, pinched my nose and poured water down my throat till I gagged. My eyes shot daggers into him in return.

"What about the concert? What about tomorrow?" Oh, heck, I thought, my voice sounds all whiny now.

Mom stroked my hair as I lay back in defeat. "We'll see how you are in the morning, dear. The best thing your body needs right now is sleep, so just relax, honey." She continued the soothing motion on my head, humming softly, and I shut my eyes, tears slipping slowly out from under my eyelids. I wouldn't let them win. Not like this. Whoever "they" were.

Levi leaned over me one last time, his lips soft and caressing on my forehead.

"I am truly fine," I grumped. "Just go – I know you need to – I'll see you tomorrow... *at the concert*."

He replied softly, talking quickly, taking the opportunity as everyone made their way towards Arabella, whose bed had just been wheeled into the room.

"I can't stand to see you crushed like this. The fury in my head is like…like an arctic anger, deep and lethal, and any Jagger out there responsible for hurting you will wish they *were* in Antarctica when I get my hands on them, BUT I fully expect to see you at the concert tomorrow. Your name *is* Jasmine, tenacious and tough, just like the wild vine, and you drive me crazier than even the sweetest jasmine. So, *we* will be there, together – it's our Destiny." In typical Levi fashion, he began to sing "Lean on Me," by Bill Withers. Not just the first verse either.

"I'm gonna kill you for getting that song trapped in my brain – but thanks." I realized again how good it felt that Levi didn't talk down to me, treat me like a child, or a feeble girl. He wanted a Reader he could not just fight *for*, but fight *with* – Carrying only if completely necessary. I cupped his face in my hands, knowing goodbye was coming. I stared into the stormy gray seas that were his eyes, fiercely loving him.

"Here's my spare cell phone. It's got all my numbers on it. Look under 'drivers' if you need an emergency eject button from this hospital." He winked at me, that crazy rebel twinkle in his eyes all over again. Damn those eyes! By the time my brain refocused, he was gone, and when Dan came back with another lot of pills to force feed me, I was still humming, "Lean on Me."

He slumped into a chair beside the bed, pulling his cap lower over his face and saying miserably, "They've all gone now ... except Ali. He's staying with Arabella. Chad and Neville are following things up with the police and staying at Nev's house tonight." He hung his head even lower. "I failed, Jazz. Failed you, failed Ali. He was counting on me, and look at the welcome they got! I feel like crap, total crap – and you must feel even worse. I'm so sorry, this just shouldn't have happened." His voice trailed out, and then five minutes later started the apology all over again.

"Shut up you moron!" I hissed at him, surprising even myself. "It's not your fault; you didn't fail, it just happened – and we're not dead. Levi was there too, and he couldn't save me from the shooting – and he's a Carrier! I don't blame him, so why would I blame you? Haven't you heard the saying that whatever can't kill you only makes you stronger? Now go get yourself a blanket and some sleep. I need to think. All sorts of things are swirling around in my mind, and I need time to mesh them together."

"But..."

"No! Go!"

He wrestled with himself for another moment or two, then dejectedly walked out, turning off the lights at my instruction, and I breathed a huge sigh, letting the medications do their work on the pain while I worked on the equation stuck in my brain.

With the strength of the drugs I was on, a visit to the desert was well and truly out of reach. I came to this realization in the same minute sleep took me under and the last thing I remember feeling was tears on my cheeks.

I awoke to find Ali sitting on the side of my bed and Dan still asleep in the chair beside the window. The early morning sunlight was just beginning to filter through the thick old glass, sending small prisms of light like tiny fairies around the room. I bet fairies are really out there I thought drowsily, wanting to stay in Never-never land, but knowing there was some important reason why I needed to wake up.

"Jazz," Ali was whispering softly, "can you wake up? Arabella wants to talk to you before anyone arrives. Come on honey; I know you're close to the surface, open your eyes." Open them I did, sitting up with a jerk. The shooting pain in my shoulder quickly reminded me where I was and what day it was. "That must have been some dream," Ali half smiled. "Your face was screwed up in concentration for at least ten minutes. Did you hear me at all?"

"Yes," I mumbled, "Granny's OK, isn't she?" I asked anxiously, swinging my legs over the side of the bed, feeling decidedly grubby and more than a little wobbly.

"Apart from the ring of purple roses on my back, I'm right as rain," Arabella's strained voice floated from the other side of the room, followed by a raspy cough. "And I want you to be my first visitor; we need to talk, missy."

"My first visit will be to the ladies, if you don't mind. Even keeping my legs crossed wouldn't help me now, if you get my drift." I clutched Ali's arm, giving him a peck on the cheek as I stabilized myself. "That's a 'hello' kiss and an 'I'm glad you're here' hug, since your arrival didn't go smoothly." I looked at him ruefully before shuffling my way across the room in search of the bathroom. I showered as fast as I could, and then gently padded back to Arabella's bedside.

I guessed that unlike mine, her eyes had looked in the mirror; she must have been awake for ages. Her deep gray hair was brushed carefully, curving around her face effortlessly against soft and gently lined skin, already enhanced with expertly applied make up, but her best feature as always was her smile. She looked much better than Ali, I thought, who seemed to have aged during the night. His hair and clothing were unkempt, partly from the ordeal of the last twelve hours and partly from the long flight from New Zealand.

Arabella grasped my hand tightly, and I raised it to my lips, kissing it tenderly.

"Wow, Arabella, you sure do know how to make an entrance," I weakly quipped, wondering why I felt like a school girl who was about to be reprimanded.

"Oh honey," she gushed, although I knew by now that her greatest skill in achieving her ends was in that sweet voice. "What an adventure – and we are so blessed, thank God; Ali would make an absolutely awful widower!" Her proclamation rung true and I smiled; trust Arabella to be thankful and funny in the same sentence. She leaned forward, indicating for Ali to place an extra pillow behind her back and continued. "Ali and I have talked, Jazz, and we know it is imperative for you to fulfill your mission today – you must go! We spoke with our dear old friend Neville in the car on our way from the airport, and he was saying how every eye in the FBI will be on you at the concert, waiting with bated breath to see if the last bastion of emotional warfare has been crossed, and your Emospheres do what you say they do: this is too important a demonstration to miss."

"It's more than just a demonstration," I protested. "These

skinheads might get out of control and people might get hurt if I don't dissipate their anger. And the president's daughters – I don't want them exposed to one iota of such gross racist fascist behavior, so you don't need to worry; wild horses couldn't stop me from going!"

"That's our girl," Ali said proudly, patting me on the shoulder. "We still have our doubts about Vander too. Nothing concrete; except that his father used to be the national director of The Knights Party, an off-shoot from the Ku Klux Klan. When Vander was a boy he attended the youth corps, but broke away when his father was sent to prison for corporate tax evasion. His older brother enlisted him in the Navy to get some discipline, and eventually he ended up at the FBI – goodness knows how. He has a spotless record from that time forward though."

"Well that at least gives me some understanding as to why Vander gives me the creeps. I've been trying to keep an open mind, but it's not easy, Ali. However, I do know those I can trust and Vander is not one of them – neither is Neville." I looked at them, trying to catch their first response.

"Oh dear," Arabella looked downcast. "You do know he is an old friend of ours; surely you put some weight on that?"

"Well of course, but you haven't been with him over the last few weeks. He is constantly preoccupied, seems to be living in past mistakes, and whenever he's around I feel like I'm being watched – and not in a good way – in a hair-standing-on-the-back-of-your-neck way." There was an uncomfortable silence, and I rose as if to leave, not sure what else to do.

Ali stood too, rather stiffly I thought, saying, "I suppose you have the independence to use your own judgment as a Reader to decide that, but don't write him off completely. He is Dan's father, after all."

I nodded, not wanting to hurt them any further, nor highlight the fact that Neville hadn't been much more of a father figure to Dan than Ali had been to my dad. "I'm glad you're OK, Granny," I whispered to Arabella softly. "I couldn't have borne losing you so soon after finding you. And thanks for coming to watch my big debut!"

By the time the family turned up to visit, I was well on my way to Raleigh, having used Levi's get-out-of-jail-free card, summoning his driver to the hospital door to collect me. I left a note for each one of them on separate hospital sick bags, giving a couple of last minute instructions and reminding them to stick to the plan. Ali and Arabella assured me they would talk them around to my way of thinking, and in all honesty, I didn't think it would take too much persuasion. My dad would just say that Blades were not characterized by "giving up," and it was time to take the bull by the horns. But I knew my mom would worry; she had always been the worrier for all of us, but something within was whispering to me, "*Don't stop. Keeping walking the path you are on; be brave and know that in making a seemingly foolish decision, you are pursuing wisdom.*" It was like a drum beat, throbbing in time with my wounds, and I was compelled to act.

Jerome, Levi's driver, made it clear that he would drive me wherever I asked, and like the doorman outside a night club, he had that "don't mess with me" appearance, although I knew I wouldn't require his services. It made me feel a little less alone as we approached the empty beach house, where, just hours before, the bizarre and surreal had outplayed itself.

As I walked up the garden path, I noticed that blood was still splayed on the concrete. I felt the taste of fear in my mouth, and was acutely aware of my back bared to any random sniper that might be waiting for my return. Step by step, I demanded the ordinary from my body, approaching the door without hurrying. Jerome sat in the car where I had asked him to wait, but had I turned around I would have been comforted to see him alert and on guard, watching my every move. After the pandemonium of the previous evening the house seemed ominously still; the scenes inside freeze-framed at the moment of chaos, and again, it was the evidence of blood that disturbed me the most. Perhaps no one had stayed here last night or maybe the police had asked them not to disturb anything, just in case. I shuddered, and then set aside my qualms, resolutely remembering why I was here – to collect the tools of my new trade. I had left a handbag hanging on my bedroom door containing everything I required for the concert: my collection of Emosphere bubble mixes, concert tickets, security I.D. tags, band aids. I smiled wryly as I thought of them. Perhaps I was underestimating that item – should have packed bandages instead! I stopped at the bathroom to gather a couple, thinking that like MacGyver, they might come in handy anyway. I shivered again. This house was way too quiet and I had told Jerome I would only be a few minutes. I needed to pick up the pace.

Shoving open the bedroom door, my quickened step came to an abrupt halt, and my eyes widened in shock. There, silhouetted against the window, with the gentle dunes and dull sea as his backdrop, stood a man – a man with a gun. Again, the scene went into pause mode as I froze with my hand still on the door handle, paralyzed at the sight of potential death. He stood still as a statue also, and bizarrely, I wondered what he was thinking. I heard my stomach rumble like thunder and wished I could eat one last meal before I died, then I told myself off for being so morbid. Was this guy going to introduce himself, or what?

The phone rang, but we both ignored it, too intent on the cat and mouse game unfolding. Games used to be fun, I thought ... duck, duck goose, duck ... duck ... goose. Was I the duck or the goose? I had no desire to be a sitting duck, and a wild goose chase didn't sound that appealing either. The sudden sound of his voice, nasally and tight knocked the "play" button, and the game was on as I jerked back into real time, my hunger dissipating into nauseas fear. I felt it in my throat, but resolutely swallowed in defiant bravery.

"I always thought Levi would go for blondes, like his mother. Now there was a gal who was blonde on both the outside and the inside. But I'm guessing you could be chocolate with a blonde center." He waved his gun at me as he laughed loudly at his own pathetic attempt at a joke. Who was this guy? And why was he in my bedroom? Come to think of it, how did he know I would come here? I felt the strap of the bag on the door handle under my fingers, and tightened my grip, but said nothing. "Chatty, aren't we?" he continued, his voice dripping with sarcasm. "I'm bored already. Listen here, darlin'. You, me, and those special bubbles you've made are going on a little journey, so start packing. And travel light, eh?"

I folded my arms and didn't move – gun or no gun – forcing myself to think of the recent Bible verses I had searched in relation to wisdom and growing wise as part of my girly-swat sessions: *Prudent people don't flaunt their knowledge; talkative fools broadcast their silliness. Escape quickly from the company of fools; they're a waste of your time, a waste of your words.* I was taking a bet that this guy was a fool – maybe a dangerous fool, but a fool nonetheless.

"Oh," he exhaled with mock exaggeration, "you're the type that wants an explanation for everything. I get it." He rolled his eyes in obvious distaste, and kicked a backpack from beside my work table across the floor. "Well, we'll work and talk, then. That suit you better Little Miss Sourpuss?" He cocked the gun and pointed it towards the wardrobe. "You've got two minutes."

Seizing the opportunity to grab a change of clothes – May as well die looking my best, I reasoned – I finally moved, but still refused to be goaded into a response.

"Carson C. Denver, my dear, at your service." I gritted my teeth at his continued mockery, but held my tongue. "I know of your status as a Reader," he said, giving a fake yawn, "but frankly, Readers are so last century, and I know people in this century that are prepared to sell their souls and pay me gold for your so called Emospheres – although I'm convinced it's all been a big stunt. It's ludicrous to think that science can capture emotions in a bottle. The very thought is childish and silly, if you ask me." I bit the side of my cheek, but didn't rise to the bait. I decided to let him think what he wanted, but then again, maybe I could capitalize on his foolishness. My brain ticked into overtime as he kept talking, the nausea lessening as I kept pretending to pack.

"I've been trying to scare you into doing something silly over the past few days. I though perhaps if you were intimidated enough you might run away, at which time I was going to befriend you and lead you astray – if you get my drift – but you threw away the fish, took on some extra security, and I couldn't use real Anthrax." He winked at me, obviously having fooled himself that he was abundantly clever. He was dressed respectably enough, and would blend easily into any environment, but his eyes were too close together and his nose was bent, as if he had been punched way too many times by high school seniors. His jaw line was slack and his hair, probably his only redeeming feature, fell down over his ears in an effort to soften the overall dismal effect of his face. It was his eyes that scared me the most; they were a recipe for wild evil, boiling anger, and sadistic cruelty.

He sighed. "But there were always too many people around you, bolstering you up, so I had to resort to this." He gestured disdainfully at the gun. "It would be so much nicer facing my Asian partners in a spirit of unity and friendship, wouldn't you agree? After all, you could profit nicely out of all of this as well," his eyes narrowed, "if you chose to cooperate. By the way, I trust your grandmother is recovering alright? If you see her again, please do pass on my apologies and condolences – quite unfortunate, really. Now, are you done? Two minutes is well and truly up!"

I zipped up the bag and slung it over my back, wincing as it dug into my shoulder inches from my wound and walked slowly towards the door. I finally spoke, focusing on keeping my voice steady, with no evidence of the tremors shaking through me, the anger and fear churning into a whirlpool of despair in the pit of my stomach. Time enough for that later.

"So, Carson," I turned when I reached the door and smiled at him, "perhaps if you are so convinced my Emospheres are fake, it would be helpful for me to demonstrate them to you before we go. After all, I can take a good guess at what Asian Triads do to White men who don't deliver. I'm sure I wouldn't be their only victim. It's a long way to go to be wrong. But then," I shrugged, "who am I to question you? You've obviously thought this through very carefully and know exactly what you're doing. And I am totally at your mercy. You've succeeded, Carson. After all, how did you even know I was here?" I made myself look as deflated and down-trodden as possible, while my heart was hammering in my throat. One chance and one chance only, I thought. Would he be fool enough to take it?

"I was just getting to that part before you so rudely interrupted," Carson postured arrogantly. "You obviously read my mind. I am not so foolish as to leave this room without a demonstration of your comic-book Emo-powers." He chuckled to himself at his clever reference to super hero powers. "I have nothing to lose here. They work, then we're on our way to money and glory; they fail, and we fake a terrible accident – not hard for someone with my abilities, not hard at all." His cruel eyes promised delivery, glowing at the thought of inflicting more pain on me. "And, of course I am not going to tell you who my informant was! A clever magician never gives away his tricks – you should know that, Reader. Now, what have you got for me? Bring it on!"

I had taken the other bag from the door handle and put the strap over my head carefully, twisting it around until I could open it easily in front of me. Reaching in, I looked Carson in the eye, my voice trembling slightly in response.

"Joy is the best example of my work, and you seem to be the sort of guy that enjoys a good laugh. That OK with you?"

He nodded, keeping a sharp eye on my every movement, but with the gun trained at my head. I purposefully kept my movements slow, so as not to startle him or give him reason to come any closer. Gently curling my hand around the bottle I was looking for, I raised it towards my face while removing the wand.

"Stop!" he barked nervously, before I had the chance to blow. His fingers tightened their grasp on the gun. "Have you used these on humans before?"

I observed him coolly, sensing the power shifting from his hands to mine, gun or no gun. "A few times now," I reassured him, "but if you're scared ..."

"I'm no chicken, honey." He hastily replied, jerking his head at me to continue "Just checking, that's all. Now get on with it!"

I shook the bottle and took a deep breath, blowing a hard yet gentle steady stream of air, enough to maximize the number of bubbles and ensure they would travel in his direction, as far away from me as possible. I was grateful the bedroom window was shut, and I knew I only had moments to make my move. His face had already begun to crumble, and as I turned the door knob his eyes dropped from me to the gun, and he dropped it as if he were burnt.

"Arrgh!" I heard him yell as I slipped out the door, shutting it firmly and grabbing a chair from the hallway to shove under the handle as a precaution. "I hate guns; they scare me. Daddy had a gun an' he shot Mammy. Don't leave me alone with a gun ... he said it was an accident." I heard him whimpering and rattling desperately on the handle as I sprinted for the front door, as far away from fear as I could get. If Carson wasn't scared before, he definitely was now!

Jerome started the car as I came running, and I threw myself in, panting, "Go, *go*!" feeling the taste of fear flowing through me, but laughing hysterically at the nature of my escape and the frightening fear I knew Carson would be swimming in for quite some time. Looking down at the Fear Emosphere I still clutched in my hand I shuddered, remembering my own fear of the possum attack in New Zealand, grateful that I had ignored my doubts at mixing a negative emotional Emosphere, and relieved that it had actually worked.

But as I sat in the back seat, surreptitiously changing my clothes as the limo roared its way up the highway to Raleigh, my mind was still racing. Who was Carson? A Jagger? And what was his association with Levi? The name sounded vaguely familiar, but what did Carson have to do with Vander, if anything? I tried phoning Levi, but got his answer service – he would be in the middle of rehearsals. Next I rang Ali, but his cell phone couldn't have been set to global roaming as it wouldn't even connect. Lastly I rang Dad, desperate to hear a voice that loved me; plus, he would know what to do about Carson. The fear Emosphere would wear off soon, and I didn't want him chasing my heels with that gun.

"Be careful, Dad," I pleaded as he expressed his fury while driving like a bat out of hell from the hospital to the beach house.

"It's OK, Jazz. It'll be no different from dealing with a terrified sea lion, and Chad's coming with me. We'll drive up to the concert from there. Chad's got just the place to dump the slimy skunk. Don't you worry; he'll still be terrified even when the bubbles wear off."

"Dad! I got a beep in my ear – I gotta go – see you at the venue rendezvous point at 6pm?"

"But your injuries? What do I tell your mom? She's frantic with worry over your safety as it is."

I clicked over to the other call, cutting him off and feeling guilty; I would text them both in a minute, but I needed to take this call.

"Jazz! You there?" I recognized Neville's voice, but the reception was not good; the crackling on the line made him sound thousands of miles away.

"Yep – got the supplies and on my way. Where are you?"

All I heard was distorted sounds, and after a few frustrating minutes I gave up, laying my head back against the seat and closing my eyes. Now I felt my shoulder throbbing and knew the blood was seeping through the unchanged dressings. Lucky I chose a red t-shirt, I thought, as I kept a lid on my emotions. Now was not the time to cry, to fear, or to despair. The worst was over, and the best was yet to come. The miles ticked over, taking me to Destiny's next meeting point.

23. OUT OF THE FRYING PAN

I CHECKED THE CONTENTS OF MY BAG ONE MORE time, just to be sure. Dan was at my shoulder, still going on at me for leaving him asleep at the hospital that morning.

"You just can't help it, can you Jazz? You chase down trouble like it's the last bus of the night. Don't you ever think before you act? You make me so crazy sometimes. Can't you just stop for a minute to include me?"

Taking a security tag and thrusting the lanyard over his head, I answered without thinking. "Destiny waits for no man, Dan, and I guess I had an appointment with Destiny. Just like I do right here; and you're with me now, aren't you? Besides, I'm fine. Jerome was there if I needed him." I didn't tell him about my episode with Carson – it would only freak him out further – Dad and Chad would take care of it, the less people worrying about it the better.

I shrugged, feeling more adrenalin than pain run through me, "I'm up for it." My eyes flashed excitedly as I thought about the concert. "This is my chance to actually feel like a Reader, to be on a real assignment with an actual task – kind of like a school field trip, but with a big exam thrown in. I'm good at sitting exams!"

I looped my arm through his as we made our way to meet

Neville, who had left Dan to wait for me while he got some cold drinks. "Come on, Danny-boy," I added as I elbowed him in the ribs, "the worst is over – we're on the home straight." He just glowered at me in response, so I nudged him in the ribs again. "It shouldn't be any different than at that rugby game of yours. You told me you've never seen your football mates behave so civilly on the pitch!"

After a while I stopped trying to cheer him up. He was determined to be glum, and I was determined to save the rest of my energy for what lay ahead. It was a long walk from where I had insisted Jerome drop me off up to the rendezvous spot, and my legs were soon protesting at the distance. I was feeling wobbly again, with my arm aching, and any last optimism was slipping slowly away. It was only 3pm: four long hours before the concert began and already I knew the waiting had the potential to be worse than the main event. The sky was settling into a sluggish white heaviness and the humidity was rising as if it could sense the tension mounting in my heart. Finally, I could see Neville loping towards us, sweat patches under his arms and a light film on his brow, but it looked like he was smiling, and I was relieved that it seemed he had no idea what had gone down at the beach house.

Gratefully taking the cans of coke Neville handed us, we collapsed under the nearest tree, in sight of the entry where we were to meet the others at 4pm. It was the sweetest thing; cold icy liquid in my parched mouth, flowing down my throat like a heavenly drug, slapping away the sugar slump I was in. Closing my eyes I lay back, and eased down slowly, focusing on relaxing every part of my body. I was so tense! I could feel cramped muscles screaming for release, but as hard as I concentrated, the tightness did not lessen, until I gave up in frustration, realizing that my body was responding to the adrenalin in my system, and that was not going to dissipate any time soon. Tapping my toes, I plugged in my iPod earphones and scrolled through my song library, searching for a beat that might help, but I could find no relief from the tension building in my body and my brain. I'm tired, but I'm wired, I thought distantly ... and a poet and I didn't know it. Lame, lame, lame. I listened as Neville and Dan tried to fill the time with conversation.

"So how long you gonna hang around, son?"

"Depends." I could feel his eyes lingering on me, but I didn't open mine.

"Depends on what?"

"On today; on whether Ali and Arabella want me to stay put – maybe even on you."

"On me? Whaddya mean? Thought you would have had enough of me by now."

"We might have spent some time together, Nev, but we haven't talked."

"Yeah we have! I asked you how your mom was doing; how life in kiwi land was. What more is there to say? Sorry?"

"Wouldn't hurt. Would be nice to know you were. Sorry, that is." Dan crushed his coke can till it was flat as a Frisbee and tossed it towards the nearest trash can, like he didn't care less. Watching underneath my lashes, I winced, knowing the pain he couldn't quite seem to speak of. There was a few minutes silence before Neville replied.

"I've done a lot of things I'm ashamed of – a lot of things I'm sorry about; still got things that are gonna need a sorry one day," he kept his head and his voice low, "but I've never been sorry about having you. Maybe I've been far away, but that don't change the way I feel. I love you man – we're flesh and blood, son, flesh and blood."

"Then tell me, Dad, where do your loyalties lie today? With me and Jazz? Or perhaps Vander? Or maybe only yourself? I guess by the end of today I'll know whether you really do love me, or like I've believed for the past twenty years, you only love yourself." He jumped to his feet and stalked off, leaving Neville scoffing Oreo cookies one after the other, chewing furiously, trying to restore his equilibrium by the only opiate he had on hand.

I didn't think it possible that the clouds could crush any more moisture into the atmosphere, but by the time Dad, Chad, Ali, and Marcus arrived, the heavy humidity was oppressive, and I felt the heat clutching my clothes and clawing nervous fingers of static electricity through my hair. But I hugged each of them long and hard, my relief at their arrival tangible, whispering that I was OK, and could we not discuss what happened until later please. There wasn't time, anyway. Our appointed security liaison officer-slash-FBI agent bustled us into the venue, where we were given the grand tour, plus introduced to other undercover security guards from the FBI. We were kitted out with a uniform and an ear piece, and learned that Vander would be set up in the sound booth with communication equipment, so he could track progress and results. The locations of all video cameras were detailed, and I observed carefully, but I was most concerned about the position of the fans. I walked and re-walked the perimeter, and requested they be turned on, so I could determine their force and flow paths. With my eyes closed I positioned myself by feeling the air movement, rather than by sight, and found that a whirlpool of air came together at one strategic point, before rising to the cavernous ceiling above. Looking upwards, I noticed that a remnant of old party streamers were swirling with the upward air movement, and committed the location to memory, glad I had a visual marker. I knew the air currents would differ slightly once the auditorium was full, but I was banking on the fans being powerful enough to find the path of least resistance towards the ceiling – right where the ground crew were laying out a roll of red carpet, which security were to keep clear for access through the middle of the crowd. Once the bubbles rose, they would then disperse before floating gently down upon the heads below. Perfect. I saw Bailey up on the stage and she gave me the thumbs up, which I silently returned. We were going to be great friends one day; I just knew it.

By 5.30 the place was buzzing, and final sound checks were underway. Scanning the stage every so often, I finally saw Levi appear, intent on directing the stage crew as they positioned extra speakers and following the instructions of the lighting team, who were checking the visual cues one last time. I stood and watched, feeling like an alien intruder, as if my relationship with Levi was nothing but a young girl's fantasy, stolen from some other chick that was more familiar with this world. He may as well have been on another planet, his focus was so intense. I wondered if Destiny was pulling us together or apart. The potential future use of Emospheres seemed so far removed from his success, his dream as a musician. And I could never stand in the way of that; his talent should be shared with the world, and the world, in return, should embrace him to heal the stolen and broken years of rejection and loneliness. He was laughing with Terrance now as they rehearsed a dance move, and he moved so naturally, so intuitively, his presence and physique a magnet on the stage to every girl's eye, making me wish he was all mine. The aches I had forgotten over the past hour came back with blistering intensity and my shoulders drooped as I turned to review procedure and tick checklists with my team.

I was too nervous to eat the burger Dad had bought me for dinner, and as we sat in one of the side rooms, I stared at it in distaste before getting up to pace around the floor.

"Sit!" Ordered Marcus firmly. "You're putting us all off our food – and some of us are hungry you know."

Fale nodded in agreement. "It's been a huge day of set-up, sis – another great learning curve for the Cajun Braves – but I think we're too lazy to ever work this hard for success. Levi fully cranks up the pace for professional gigs – he's a machine!"

Harley glanced at me sideways, shaking his head at my clenched fists and stern face. "Hey Jazz," he called out, "You heard the one about the man who went to the doctor complaining he had a strawberry stuck up his butt?"

Fale jumped in before I even looked up. "Don't worry said the doctor; I've got some cream for that!"

The boys dissolved into laughter and as even Dad and Ali joined in the joke-telling, I eventually had to crack, laughing stupidly at their ridiculous stories, and I suddenly felt like eating.

"Well," I said to everyone around the table between mouthfuls, as the laughter finally subsided, "anyone for strawberries and cream for supper after the gig?"

Later on, as the medical officer Dad had located checked my shoulder and changed the dressings on the wounds, I realized that my family was good at this. The times when tensions rose over some major or minor catastrophe to a family member were tempered by the eventual but inevitable arrival of laughter, breaking the heat out of the issue, enabling the heart of the problem to be reached and healed. A flood of love flowed through me, and I knew they were here for me, all of them, to see me succeed, to hold me should I stumble, to laugh and keep me humble. Waiting to prove yourself is never easy, I mused, whether it is the final minutes in the changing shed before a big game starts, back stage before the curtain rises, the last hours of study before an exam, or the nervous wait prior to a first date: to kiss or not to kiss? You soon learn that you have more fun on the roller coaster by relaxing; perform better in games, recitals and exams if nerves have been tempered by happy thoughts and words; and you should always put laughter at the top of the priority list for a first date.

Chad rushed into the room just as I had donned the black security uniform and was twisting my hair into a tight pony tail.

"Guys! Come! Finish your drinks! You have to see this!"

We sprinted after him (well, jogged really) down the labyrinth of back passages until we came to the main foyer, turning sharp left just short of the entrance and out a side exit then along for a few hundred meters behind a tall hedge. I raised my eyebrows at him, unsure of what he wanted us to look at and if I was allowed to speak or not. By this time we had reached the entrance to the State Fairgrounds themselves, where people were lining up to buy their tickets for the Alien Potion concert in the Dorton Arena. Ducking down, he thrust his hand into the hedge and pressed branches aside until you could see daylight out the other side.

"Quick," he whispered, "take a look for yourself."

At first, all we could see was a mass of people, but as Chad made the hole bigger, I realized the group directly in front of us were mostly skinheads and conservatively dressed White men – an unusual gathering, to say the least. Directly opposite them, and facing us, were a group of men and women wearing silly white dresses and clown makeup – an even stranger array.

The first group, that I quickly surmised were White supremacists, had begun chanting "WHITE POWER, WHITE POWER" over and over, stabbing the air with their fists in rhythm to the chant.

"Who are the clowns?" I whispered softly.

"They belong to the Anti-Racist Action Group. It's called a 'clown block.' Just watch and see." Chad bent down beside me and we both peered through the hedge.

The clowns were pretending that they couldn't understand, cupping their hands to their ears and looking confused. One finally yelled back.

"Oh, you mean WHITE FLOUR?" And several clowns held up signs with letters that spelt out "WHITE FLOUR" while others threw actual flour from baskets high in the air and ran round in circles under the white rain.

This infuriated the skinheads, who took it upon themselves to angrily shout even louder: "WHITE POWER!"

The clowns nodded wisely and yelled back: "WHITE FLOWERS!" This time they threw rose petals and white daisies into the air, while dancing wildly. The expressions of innocent bystanders flickered between distaste, bemusement and fear as they watched the drama unfold.

Those attending the hate rally moved menacingly closer to the clowns, trying once again to get their message through: "WHITE POWER!"

"Ohhhhh!" the clowns laughed, "TIGHT SHOWER!" and one of them held a solar shower in the air, the others crowding under and scrubbing themselves in obedience to the instruction given.

The rage was barely restrained now, as the angry mob raised their fists to the sky and screamed over and over: "WHITE POWER! WHITE POWER!"

When the police finally arrived and formed a human barrier between the two factions to avoid an all-out brawl, the clowns seized one last opportunity as the "WHITE POWER" chant died out, and yelled "Now we understand! WIFE POWER!" and they lifted the letters up in the air, the women picking up the men clowns and chanting merrily "WIFE

POWER! WIFE POWER! WIFE POWER!"

We all stared in amazement at the ludicrous scene being played out before us, loving the tongue-in-cheek cleverness of the clowns, but certain that it would fire up the White supremacists for blood once they made it through the gates and into the arena. As we watched, a couple of the more vocal skinheads were dragged off by police, having rushed at the clowns with raised fists and profanities. But the rest surged towards the gates, with bulging eyes and trembling hands, and veins nearly exploding out of their necks in white-hot anger, but determined to restrain their rage until the main course – in the Dorton Arena. We walked back to the main entry, shell shocked and silent.

"You know," I finally whispered, "we might just be able to use this to our advantage, Chad. Remember where I told you to stand as the concert ends, and who you need to watch? Well, think you can infiltrate the clowns? Recruit their assistance?"

He laughed a low hard laugh. "You are an evil genius, you know that?"

I grinned. "Learnt from the best, you know!"

It was almost time for action, and I began to feel adrenalin pump into my system, increasing my heart rate and oxygen supply, sending glucose to my brain and muscles. I already felt stronger, unaware now of my wounds, and focusing all my energy into the fight ahead. Just before we left the room to take up our positions, Ali called us into a huddle, and he prayed.

"May the God of all wisdom guide us all tonight, especially our Jasmine, your Reader, and may each of us know your presence with us, amen."

I held on tight to Dad and Ali, wondering what God really thought about all this, and if I was ready, if love really was stronger than hate, and if one bottle of Emospheres would be enough. Dan threw his arms around me and drew me to his chest, where I heard his heart beating firm and faithful – and then the back stage wait was over.

"Where's my bag?" I asked Dan. "I left it here on the chair, I know I did."

"It's on the table, silly girl; just over there." He pointed over to the remains of my hamburger.

"Oh…right. Nerves." I smiled apologetically as I glanced inside, just to be sure.

Taking up our stations was easy; watching the crowds grow was not. The Dorton Arena would be filled to capacity tonight, mostly with young folk, at my guess aged from about sixteen up to mid-twenties. There were plenty of hot blooded young men with their eyes on the pretty girls; a fair mix of nationalities – handsome strong African American lads, a smattering of Latinos and your usual American High School flavors: jocks, emo, punk, skaters, and rave – even the odd Goth. I kept my eyes sharply peeled for the group I had seen at the gate, but they must have split up, because other than one distinctive skinhead with a snake tattoo on the back of his skull and a couple of fair-headed boys that looked like Mormons in their white shirts and black slacks, I saw nothing and no-one out of the ordinary. The mood was upbeat despite the heavy humidity. After all, this was summer in the U.S.A., and *this* was Alien Potion: Live. I could feel a tangible taste of excitement in the thick air. The girls dressed up to please the boys; the boys dressed down to take their place in the savage mosh pit. A pool of saliva welled up under my tongue, and I quickly swallowed it, but not before recognizing the metallic flavor of fear. Was I missing something vital? Had we somehow forgotten something, or was there nothing here to worry about? I ran through my mental checklists and visually located my team, who were standing as I was, casual but alert. Checking my phone, I made sure the draft message to Melinda was ready to go with the word "*dragonfly*," and, satisfied it was, I placed my phone back in my pocket, where it immediately vibrated vigorously. New message: from Levi. My heart flip-flopped as I opened it and read two small but very important words: "*still falling*." My eyes flashed towards the stage, but he wasn't there, no surprise. A second text buzzed on the small screen: "*turn around and follow the guy in the red cap*." Mystified, I glanced over my shoulder, and sure enough there was a guy wearing a red cap with dark glasses on, and as I took a step towards him he turned and walked away, so I hurried along behind, both cautious and worried at the same time. Following the side access to the arena down towards the stage, passing security checkpoints on the way, the man turned hard left, then tapped three short knocks on a light green door, opened it up and stood back for me to enter. I couldn't help but be suspicious.

"After you," I smiled at him, indicating for him to go through the door first. It might buy me some time should this be some sort of trap. (Man, was I getting paranoid or what?) He shrugged, but stepped through into the room, and I waited for a couple of seconds, took a deep breath in, and followed.

The room was long and narrow, hugging the outside wall of the arena, with the ability to be segmented into smaller spaces by large bi-fold partitions. I heard the door shut gently behind me, but did not look back. At the far end of the room was a charcoal grey couch, but it was of no immediate consequence. All I saw was Levi, seated with his guitar casually across his knees, strumming gently. The early evening sun had fought its way through the thick clouds, and was streaming crepuscular rays down from high windows, adding an ethereal quality to the scene in front of me. I nearly knocked him off the couch in my hurry, and although he laughed, he too could sense the urgency behind my approach, and pulled us both back onto the sofa until I was lying on top of him, the guitar between us, neither of us seeming to notice.

I needed to see what was in his eyes this one last time, before the stage and the crowds devoured him, before I walked into a hate pit to plant seeds of love, before anything went wrong, before anything went right. Our eyes were hungry, and words unspoken passed between us, with mine filling with tears at the depth of love I felt for this man. Finally he kissed my trembling lips, and kissed the tiny tears that had escaped and were staining my cheeks, and kissed my eyes, my forehead, my hair. I had never felt so beloved, so precious. Sitting again, with only minutes left together, he played the tune I instinctively knew was the one I had heard in the desert, and I ached inside as the tender melody clutched my heart and tore at his. As he looked up his eyes were glistening too.

He whispered, "I only have one line for this song. It says, '*this is my forever love flowing to you my lovely*'." The music said it all, and his fingers caressed the strings of the candy-apple guitar, each note delivering a cherished memory, another invisible chord binding us together: our song; our love.

All too soon the magic of the moment was broken and he had to go. The suave, cool mask reappeared that made Levi so irresistible to girls and envied by guys, and I felt a thrill at knowing he loved me, had chosen me. As we parted, a sudden thought occurred, and I blurted it out without thinking.

"Carson ... Isn't that the name of the father you never knew?"

Levi was still intent on committing my face to memory, and I had to repeat my question, as his thumbs traced my features, making it hard to breathe, let alone talk.

"Carson ..." he absently repeated, his fingers weaving through my hair, tugging it backwards until my head was cradled in his hands. The pain was wanton and sweet.

"Carson is allegedly my father. What of it? Why the sudden mention?"

"He ... he ... I saw him today, that's all."

"Saw him? Where?" Levi stiffened suddenly and his hands ceased their exploration.

"Um ... at the beach house ... um ... he kind of asked me to come to Asia with him ... to sell Emospheres to the highest bidder ..." His hands clenched tightly back into my hair, forcing my face up towards his.

"Did he hurt you? Did he?" I had never heard his voice so fierce, as a wild passion gripped his eyes.

"No! No ... he ... I … actually, I tricked him into testing the Joy Emosphere, but then released Fear instead, and escaped. I tried to phone you. Dad and Chad took care of him I think, but I forgot to ask them what happened." My eyes looked deep into Levi's, searching to find his answer.

Slowly his grip loosened and his lips sought mine, crushing and bruising them with all the tragic passion he carried and I responded with a fierceness that shocked me to the core.

"He's not who he says he is," Levi eventually responded, his voice husky and broken. "He holds a key to my past, but he's dangerous, Jazz, lethal. I've felt him hovering in the background, but haven't gone near him for fear of what I might find – or not find. I need to know if they caught him, otherwise God help us all."

I rang Chad immediately to check, and Levi watched my face turn pale as I heard Chad's answer. Lowering the phone as Chad continued I stared at it blankly.

"I'm really sorry, Jazz, Dad did report it to the police, but there's nothing much they can do until he shows up again."

I dully repeated his first words to Levi: "He had gone by the time Dad or the police got there – vanished without a trace." I felt the increasingly familiar taste of fear rise like bile as I whispered, "He's a Jagger, isn't he?"

Levi gripped my shoulders and I winced in pain. "Listen, Jazz." He shook me, then realized my pain and gently pulled me into his arms, nuzzling his face into my sore shoulder and feathering it with soft kisses. "As soon as the second encore is called, come to this room. Follow Jake again, in the red cap. We can leave straight from here and head to the airport. I've been thinking about clearing up some mysteries in my past, starting in Saudi Arabia, where I know my mother first met Carson. He was serving in the Peace Corps based in Jordan at the time. I have access to a private jet a friend of Jarven's said I could loan at any time. He won't be able to find us, Jazz, I promise. Not until we want to find him, at least."

His eyes were pleading with me, and my mind was in turmoil. Run away – after Dad asked me never to again?

"But what about Mom? Dad? Chad and Bailey? And Dan for that matter. What about them? I can't just leave, not without explaining."

"There's no time to explain. If we wait to explain it might be too late… I don't know. Tell them to meet us here too, to come to the airport, to come on the jet if they want! Whatever it takes!"

I looked at the expression on his face and saw fear rising

– the same fear I was feeling. I had to know: "Why are you so afraid of him, Levi? What hold does he have over you?"

His eyes looked again like they belonged in a lost little boy; the poignancy pierced my soul. "I think he killed my mother ... Felicity ... for her money. He's been chasing it ever since, right to my doorstep, and now he's like a shadow feeding on my every move. I don't want to remember – and he can't be my father, he can't be!"

He buried his face into my neck again and I stroked his back, running my fingers over his disheveled hair, soothing us both with the calming action. It was my turn to clutch his hair, forcing his eyes up to mine, willing him to let me in, and he did.

"We're stronger than he is. We have Destiny on our side. Go where love is for you, Levi, you have to, you have to." I was almost whimpering; the fear was so tangible.

"You're right," he choked, looking more like the man I knew him to be. "But will you come? I can arrange for Jerome to locate your passports and travel gear, although you won't need much."

I nodded gravely. "I will come. I may or may not bring others, but I will come."

With one last desperate embrace I breathed in the heady scent that was Levi, and our time was up. Slipping out the door, I was immediately accosted by Dan.

"Where were you? I was worried! There you go, disappearing on me again – text, OK? Were you with him?"

"I'm fine, Dan and I don't have to tell you who I was with – but yes, because I know you won't drop it, I was with Levi. Can't you get it through your thick head that he is part of this plan too? Everything is not all about you!"

"No," he replied softly, "it is all about you, Jazz, all about you, and that's what scares me."

24. INTO THE FIRE

BACK AT MY POST I STARED BLANKLY AT THE SCENE in front of me. The opening support band, Scenic, were playing, and although a few brave souls were moshing, most were socializing, waiting for the main event to begin in thirty minutes' time. It was the longest half hour of my life. A buzzing in my head had begun as I went over and over how the evening might play out – and how it might end: on a jet plane. I kept nervously looking behind me, half expecting to see Carson's seedy eyes on me, waiting to pounce from the shadows.

Darkness was descending, and in the true nature of a rock concert, the only lights were focused on the stage, where flashes of green, red, and orange reminded me of traffic lights: Green for go; red for stop – what was I thinking! And orange for the twisting and turning of Destiny that I just couldn't keep pace with. The truth was, I was tired, exhausted really. Adrenalin was the only thing keeping me upright – that and the thought that this day couldn't possibly go on forever, despite my fears. I just wanted the action to begin, to release some love, and head home to bed. A text from Neville jolted me back to the present: "*Trouble brewing at three o'clock.*"

Where's three o'clock, I thought irritably; why couldn't he just say Stage Left or Exit Five or something. Visualizing a giant clock with twelve o'clock being the stage, I followed around to the right, a quarter turn, zeroing my eyes onto the back of the skinhead I had seen earlier, whose white skull glowed strangely with a blue tinge from the stage lights. He just looked like he was crumping to me – rather violently – but it was all part of the dance. Perhaps Neville was new to gigs like this, I thought, out of touch with my generation. "*Dance move*" I texted back, shifting from foot to foot and wondering if the president's daughters were here yet. Yep, they'd just arrived, right on cue. I hoped they enjoyed the show. I hoped they would be safe.

Everything went black momentarily as Scenic left the stage and the dry ice was given time to build up. An eerie electronica tune began to play, and tiny green pinpricks of light flashed on the dark stage, increasing in size and intensity with the flow of the music. Mystically, green letters slowly formed in the dry ice, making up the words "Alien Potion," and then melted away to the sound of tom-tom drums. Drifting into focus was a solitary figure, all in black: black skin, black clothing, with psychedelic green eyes and green gloves. Jamal! The auditorium was deathly still, mesmerized by the beat and the motion, which was rising in its urgency, taking us on a journey as if in a space ship, to a super nova. And just when your heart felt it couldn't stand another beat, when the vibrations had climaxed beyond any imagined expectation, an explosion of light burst into being, stunning the massive crowds into action. Moving as if one single living organism, the throng started jumping in unison to the strains of the opening song, and I found myself unable to stop from joining in, such was the level of hysteria building. Desperately, I wanted to see Levi, to know he was still near me, and so I jumped, as we all did, waiting, waiting, waiting … for the song to begin in earnest. And then he was there: white t-shirt with a glowing green cross on the front, black jeans ripped, bandana tight around each wrist and a microphone at his lips, the first lacerated gravel tones making us all want dance with reckless abandon.

I realized then that it was pointless to fight Destiny. It was like trying to climb backwards over a roller coaster at top speed, or trying to run up the down escalator: more energy is expended and less is achieved. If tonight was to succeed, I needed to embrace my calling, trust in my instincts, and forget my fears. I needed to feel my emotions deeply and all at once, allow them to flow through me and from me into the bubbles I blew. No holds barred, no distractions, no regrets; even fear would be my friend and anger my ally. The mantle of Readership had arrived, and I was ready.

At first it was just a few caterwauls when Jamal did another drum solo and a single "White Power" scream, which sounded like a jumble unless you knew what you were hearing. A little later, when Terrance laid down his guitar and busted some moves, another yell came quite clearly "Blood-sucking Black alien!" My palms started to sweat and my feet began to walk me towards the infiltrator, as if by remote sensor. Moving into the crowd, I realized that the hecklers were more spread out than I first thought. Calls were coming from across the floor of standing room only, where around fifteen-hundred people were crammed. I hesitated, looking for the air currents, but found none. Someone had turned the fans off! There was no airflow, nothing! Nothing apart from a growing core of White supremacists peppering the crowd. I didn't even have to see their faces to know, I could sense evil prickling the back of my neck and felt their anger rising.

"Alien Antichrist in the White House!" came another snarl.

I radioed Neville for help. "You better get over here quick. Five o'clock I think, but in towards the stage. I want you to turn the fans on and take me to them. I won't be able to blow enough bubbles; the rabble are too spread out!" I had my finger over my ear in order to hear him over "Fast Wine," which, I somehow managed to think, Levi was singing even faster than usual, with a worried undertone.

It was only seconds before Neville was next to me with Vander following close behind, and I was grateful to know that he had been observing, and was on his way even before I called. I was also thankful to him as he buffeted off the bigger guys around me who had smelt the fight and were closing in. We were standing just outside the worst of it, the fine line between mosh pit and observers, avoiding most of the hard core dancing. I shrugged anxiously at Neville, leaning in to ask him about the floor fans, but was caught by surprise when Vander pushed past, grabbed the bottle I held in my hand and shouted in my ear, "Here, let me try!"

"It won't work for you!" I yelled back. "It has to react with my breath. I think it's because I'm a Reader, or because of my DNA – I told you that!"

"It's OK," he shouted in my ear, "I made this!" He held up a contraption that looked much like a pump you use to blow up balloons. "Here, blow into this balloon – that way I can help you. I'll have your breath trapped, and can use this to force the air out to make the bubbles – blow into one for Neville as well; we'll work together seeing as the fans aren't working. It'll be much faster."

He held the pump in front of my nose, almost hitting me with it as a rather large man elbowed him from behind. It was a bit like being churned by huge surf, I thought, slightly hysterical – but not a bad idea. It would mean we could spread out and all blow – but why hadn't Neville shared Vander's idea earlier? We could have used more pumps, more people. I blew into two bright red balloons and handed them to Vander, who took off in the direction of Neville, busy working his way to the front. I tried to keep a visual, but it was just too difficult in the mayhem. I wasn't happy about Vander being in the thick of it, but I had no choice now. Besides, I had the extra love vial in the bag slung over my head, and I needed to start blowing, and fast. The anger gauge was rising, not falling; we were going to have to use every drop of ammunition.

Just as my hand closed around the bottle, a humongous fat White guy slammed into the side of me, knocking me off balance and I found myself on my knees surrounded in a sea of fast moving feet, kicking and leaping in feverish flight. Managing to stumble to a more upright position, I suddenly realized the mood *had* changed. Dramatically changed.

All around me were snarls and snapping, like I was caught in the middle of a hungry pack of wolves. I saw eyes roll back inside heads and men like bears ripping off their shirts and brandishing them over their heads. Blood curdling screams, profanities, and fists clenched around iron bars … iron bars? How the...? I blew furiously, but it wasn't making any difference; chaos had caught hold and my bubbles were simply a momentary distraction. Abruptly I found myself crowd surfing again, but this time I was not carried above heads by dancing hands, but through bodies with giant clawed paws, tearing at my clothes, shredding my shirt buttons and cotton until the remains sank to the ocean floor. I saw men with ink-branded metal stamps, slamming them into black foreheads, the imprint so hard it was mixing with the red blood that flowed; I saw African American girls screaming as their hair was brutally seized and they writhed in agony, some able to twist free, others ending up like me. I felt a vine of sweat-covered hatred wrap its tendrils around the hearts of decent men and excruciating pain as their fists hit my face as they lashed out at one another.

I tasted my own blood and the blood of others as I slithered through their hands. Fingernails bit into my flesh, blades sliced down to my bones, and even teeth sunk into my wrist, ripping away skin to my elbow – and yet still I held on to the vial, knowing it was my only hope. What had Vander done … what had my breath unleashed? For all our planning and strategizing, nothing could have prepared us for this. Everything depended on my Emosphere's working; and they weren't.

The stage looked empty from where my head screamed, in the crook of a black man's arm, locked in place as he tore at my hair and took his knee to meet my nose. Through a haze of pain I discerned that I was falling – not just to the ground, but from this earth. I felt ashes in my mouth. Destiny had the last laugh; it was all an illusion, this Emospherica. Although I knew somehow, somewhere, there was a missing piece of the puzzle, if only I could find it, if only my head would stop buzzing, if only the dismembering of my body might cease and let me think ... think.

Through blood-misted eyes I forced my hand to find my phone, each action a blur of agony, and awkwardly tried to squeeze the button pre-set to send out the mayday message "*Dragonfly*" to Melinda, Levi, Dan, and Chad ... before my phone tumbled, trampled in seconds. In my head swirled the last A-HA lyrics I would ever hear:

Don't ask how, don't ask why, just fly dragonfly, just fly dragonfly..."

Elle and I had talked about drowning one time on a lazy high school lunch break, lying on the green sandy grass under the blue ocean sky. Elle had said, "I don't want to drown. The claustrophobia I would feel as my lungs filled with water and my body was crushed by tons of liquid blue makes me cringe with dread – like being buried under gluggy toilet cleaner, really ..."

Then I interrupted before she got too silly and said, "The sensation of drowning appeals to me; being drowned in love, drowned in memories, drowned in beautiful blue. It seems romantic and tragic with flagrant disregard for the sanctity of life. Take The Titanic, for instance: Jack Dawson died a noble death by drowning to save his one true love Rose. Do you remember seeing Jack sinking into the icy blue depths? It was art, it was poetry. It was the greatest beauty known to mankind – voluntarily laying down one's life for another."

And then Elle had kicked me in the shin saying, "Don't be such an airhead, Jazz! Most drowning's are just stupid accidents that shouldn't happen in the first place. There's nothing noble about them at all."

Something was filling up my mouth so I couldn't breathe, and I realized I was on the sandy ground, forgotten in the eye of the storm. Funny how my head turned automatically to let the blood trickle onto the floor. There was an awful sound right near my ear, and it took a few moments to realize that it was a gurgling in my chest and a rattle every time I chose to take just one last breath ...

I remembered how my brothers would come into my bedroom to catch me snoring, and I would wake with a peg on my nose, or a mustache drawn above my lips. If they saw me now they might draw a smiley face with my blood on the way to the hospital – anything to make me mad, or make me grin. I pictured Mom and Dad briefly, but the pain I felt even remembering how deep their love ran for me stung, and I had to block them out. Glimpses of Dan, of Chad, of Ali, and of Arabella flashed in my head, mixed with photos of those already passed this way...

My head slipped under the imaginary water momentarily, the weight of cherished memories sweet and heavy like lead, dragging me to the bottom ... then nothing.

Then nothing.
Then nothing.

Then conflicting, consuming emotions exploded in the core of my being, ripping to shreds any last blockage to my heart. I knew an anger for evil that was raw and ravenous; a euphoric joy of victory despite death; a river of love flowing from the stage, parting in front of me, and I knew my Carrier was coming. The peace that unified my feelings came from the sound I heard in the distance, and it was traveling towards me – a melody so pure, a current so deep that its electricity was calming the stormy seas. The battle was done, and no one had won, although all would have a story to tell. Hands on me seemed soothing now, kind even. Tears were beginning all around me, contrite sobbing and the grief that flows in regret. I could hear words of a song rebounding off people, the voice sounding less like Levi and more like an electronic remix, ringing out in ever increasing circles, waves of sound unseen...

"*Glory, Gloria,*
Feel the euphoria..."

Over and over, each time richer, each time hacking hate into tiny pieces and creating a misty fog of peace over the raging waters. But where was that bright light coming from? It was hurting my eyes, my head! Peering through slits I managed to fathom that it was Levi, an incandescent beacon – and it was not light shining on him, but out of him. And he was shaking! With every word, every "*Glory,*" each "*Euphoria,*" a stab of light hit another target, breaking the hold of darkness. He was close now, and I saw his hands on his guitar, strumming, but his fingers were white hot and burning. It was almost as if it was he, not his guitar plugged into the amp, and the volts he was shooting were lightning bolts. But how could he sustain such powerful forces? Was that Dan next to him? Was Levi falling? He was! And now his eyes were burning into mine, and we were fused together as one; a laser pathway that came closer and closer and I felt his precious weight on me, jarring and sudden, then nothing.

Then nothing.
Then nothing.

Then hands tore him away as I tried to move my arms to clutch him, to keep him near – Levi, my Carrier, laying down his life in order to save me – no greater love has any man…

25. ALL THINGS

BLACK. ALL OF THEM DRESSED IN BLACK. ALI AND Arabella – designer black. Dan – black t-shirt and black jeans. Dad and Marcus – black shirts and dress pants. Chad, Fale, and Harley – black selection of random clothing. Mom – simple, elegant black dress, with pearls. Bailey – blacker than black short skirt and blouse, black tattoo. Something was wrong ... I was wrong! I was dressed in white, a gown of some sort, twisted around under me, and my body lay in a bed, circled by the people I loved ... in black. I don't think they realized I was looking at them through tiny slits as they talked in hushed somber tones that sounded like the buzz of an annoying blowfly. Oh how my head hurt; and my throat was parched! Perhaps I could just reach ... no, I couldn't. Was I dead? Was this my body laid out and they were paying their respects? I slammed down my lids and waited a few minutes, then re-opened and closed quickly, hoping something would make sense, and this time the movement caught Dan's eye, because he rushed over to the side of the bed yelling in a whisper, "I saw her eyes move! She's waking up!"

And then they all crowded in, a circle of black love around me, hands on the bed, on me, and my heart waited for the hand I knew would send a bolt of electricity through my veins, even through the sheets, but I knew it wasn't coming, not now, maybe not ever. A single tear slid from my eye to my ear, and the liquid pooled there, tickling me, and I wanted to scream: "Where is he? Where's Levi?" but as another tear joined the first I just couldn't; I just couldn't.

In gasps it came back to me, the black Sabbath, my final memory. I saw Levi fall on my broken body, cover me like a blanket of glory, then felt him ripped away by cruel hands, gone ... and I remembered that Dan had been there. I was aware of Mom's gentle cheek on my arm, wet sobs rising from her bowed head. Chad, with Bailey clinging to him like a child, bent his face down to mine and with a voice hoarse and broken spoke words I did not want to hear.

"We need you, Jazz; we all need you to come back. Can you hear me? Please," he pleaded, emitting a deep groan of anguish.

Each in turn added their support. "We love you, Jazz … Oh honey don't leave us. Jazzy, my angel, stay here, choose us ... Mate, I love you, I love you ... Stay strong my little Reader, stay strong ..." and so it went on, falling on deaf ears filled with tears. Would no one be honest?

As others pulled back into sweet embraces and bear hugs, a solitary figure bent down to my ear. It was Bailey, dabbing at the pool of salty sorrow with a tissue before whispering the truth in a tragic small voice.

"He's dead, Jasmine, dead. He paid the ultimate price for you, and now you ignore the pleas from your own family? I hate you for robbing him from me, for letting him die in your place, and I've come from his funeral to tell you that if you live, you will pay. But as I love Chad, should you choose to wake up, I will only show love from this point on, but know this ... I will *never* forgive you."

I didn't hear anything Bailey uttered after those first two words: "He's dead." My breathing stopped; maybe even my heart stopped. My soul took an empty bottle, writing down her words and squeezing the parchment into the narrow opening, along with my heart. Firmly jamming a cork in the spout, I threw it far into a distant ocean, and once I had watched it sink, I opened my eyes wide and sat up.

26. A TIME FOR EVERYTHING

IT TOOK ME A COUPLE OF WEEKS TO PIECE everything together. I had been unconscious for three days. The deep gashes and broken bones eventually began to heal and my punctured lung recovered. Apparently one of my ribs had taken an airline flight, by-passing my heart, but landing for a breath of fresh air on the next closest island: my lung. Harley told me my face looked like I had tried to give myself a face mask with a blender – so gentle with words, that brother. He offered to get a mirror, but I declined. I knew I would only look into dead eyes; dark shutters concealing my grief.

Many visitors stopped by with bits to add to the puzzle. Melinda, who had been appointed the new CFR Chairperson was somber but chatty, and sad that Levi ... you know. She explained that the code word "dragonfly,' never arrived, but that they had all flown into action anyway. Melinda had sent her off-siders to accost Neville for leaving me at the mercy of the mob, but he had disappeared from the arena altogether and was found hours later, lying in a drunken stupor behind one of the showground's bars, as if he had tried to blot out all memory of the past few days. He had played no part in the Emosphere melt-down.

In the meantime, Dad and Chad had managed to infiltrate the group of protesting clowns, convincing them to utilize their

Clown Block one last time – and they had spread a wide net around the arena, blocking every hole, enlisting any sympathizer Dad could find within the show grounds. Many of the extremists were caught in the blockade, held tightly by the merry smiles and raucous laughter of the clowns and subdued like a big white powder puff until security and the police arrived. But Vander was not to be found by the CFR until days after the event, and his accomplice was never found. From the description, I guessed it must have been Carson.

Melinda also told me that they had tested the blood in the "First Love" vial that must have been taken from me either sometime at the beach house or before the concert and used by Vander. It was a mix of Vander's and another's blood and spittle, and having interviewed Vander under duress, he confessed to switching the blood combination for mine one night at the beach house. He had also taken the serviette with my scrawled notes on it, describing how I needed to use blood, saliva, and skin cells to create Love. Vander (and the mysterious 'other' – my guess Carson) had simply concentrated all their hate for Blacks into their blood stream and spit, taken thumb prick samples, and then tricked Neville into exchanging the vials before I completed the formula. So the vine of hate I had seen winding its way through the crowd had been real. I shivered, not wanting to remember any more. If only Love had been released, how different things would be today. I could feel my heart beating wildly against the green glass bottle I had thrown into the deepest ocean, straining to wail with the winds on the wet desert sands, but no, no, no ... NO!

Neville confessed that he had thought Vander had just wanted proof the Emosphere formula actually existed, and had only agreed to show them to Vander because he thought Jasmine was being childish in keeping it so under wraps. He felt Vander had a right to know – and he had been promised a promotion. He was being held in custody by the CFR until a decision could be made about his future – the FBI had a few ideas for him, which they were keen to discuss, even though they wanted to cut ties with the CFR – they had difficulty explaining their way out of the media backlash from the concert, and felt that Emospheres, while obviously effective, were too risky to pursue. "*Fraught with ethical and moral dilemmas,*" was the summary of their verbose reply to Melinda's enquiries.

On the night of the concert, Marcus had been assigned to watch the president's daughters, and he had told me how at the first sign of trouble, he had handed the girls signed copies of Alien Potion CDs plus other merchandise before their bodyguards bustled them out of the arena through a rear entrance. The Emospheres had been released too far from their seats to affect them or anyone sitting nearby, and although one extremist had yelled profanities towards the girls, he was dragged away by another guard before the girls even realized he was shouting at them. Marcus had called in reinforcements, but any other troublemakers saw the folded arms and pepper spray and slunk off to the hornet's nest of hatred on the ground floor, where I was standing. Always with a head for numbers, he informed me that two others had been killed in the riot, both Black.

Dan didn't come to visit again. Ali told me he was still distraught, blaming himself for my injuries and Neville's defection ... and ... the other thing that had happened. He told me how Vander had approached him and Dan before they realized what he had done, and blew the hate straight into their faces. Ali had the good sense to flee outside and take his dark side out on unprotected bushes, ripping them out of the ground with wild abandon until the effects wore off. Dan on the other hand, went to attack his father, chasing him into the mêlée where he too was set upon. His rage knew no bounds, and his fists laid low several large men before he was hit from behind with a steel bar. The "*Euphoria*" song was weaving magic when he came around, and he had searched the crowd to find me. I stopped Ali there. I didn't want to hear anymore. I only really wanted Mom ... and sometimes Dad. I wanted to be five again, with Mom tucking me into bed and Dad telling me stories. Plus something just didn't make sense … I saw Dan just before Levi fell, I know I did!

I knew Levi must be dead, though, as I never found myself in the desert during the lonely nights. I dreamed of it constantly, but it was always empty and one dimensional, a shadow of the real thing. Knowing I would be leaving hospital the next morning, I gripped the sheets tightly and bitterly prayed a prayer I remembered my grandma saying with me when I was little, although I used some artistic license with the words: "*This night as I lay down to sleep, I pray dear Lord my soul to keep … **please let me die** before I wake, and take me to heaven for Jesus' sake.*" Amen, so let it be...

No such luck. At 10am Chad came to collect me, and waking from a state of fitful dozing, I saw his back to me, stuffing cards, letters, teddies, and junk into a large box angrily. I had known he was upset with me for days now. He had barely spoken a word in my hearing, throwing dark glances in my direction every so often, and I wondered if Bailey was slowly poisoning him against me, but I was too listless to care much.

"I'm ready," I offered dully, sitting on the edge of the bed and wondering where my shoes were. And then he was right in front of me.

"You are not ready, you are *so* not ready!" I blanched at the vehement tone of his voice, but stayed silent and somewhat wary. "You haven't even asked," he said between clenched teeth. "Don't you want to know? Don't you even care?" I stared at him blankly, my body temperature dropping, trying to freeze any last feelings. "I was there," he continued, "I saw everything. And you need to know, you have to hear, and I'm going to tell you right now ... I don't give a rat's arse for your feelings right now, for your tragic posturing. I know you better than that, Jazz; I know you're in there ... somewhere." He searched my eyes before he spoke again.

"I was at the side of the stage, having agreed to help Bailey in case things got out of hand, and I wanted a better view of what was about to happen. I was looking forward to seeing the mood of the crowd change, like a Mexican wave of Love, and when I became aware that something had gone terribly wrong I looked over at Levi." I winced at the mention of his name, but no more. "I saw that he realized it too, a look of sickening horror crossing his face as the thought occurred to him that you were in the middle of such violence, such base vitriol. All over the mosh pit pockets of hate were erupting, like boiling mud in a volcanic field of ash, and it was spreading fast, faster than the eye could follow. Skinheads were beginning to clamber over the barriers to the stage, bashing security guards with chains, belts – anything they could find. It was only a matter of seconds before they would breach the platform itself, and it seemed farcical. The band was still playing desperately, not knowing what else to do." Chad paused, a distant look in his eye that reflected the fear, futility, and dread he was remembering.

"But not Levi ... he seemed to know exactly what to do, Jazz. Without missing a beat I watched him grab a second quarter-inch instrument cable that was coiled on top of a huge stand-alone amplifier. The connector had been sliced off it, revealing the twisted wires inside. While Jamal drummed like his life depended on it, I saw Levi wind the wires around the strings of his guitar, but I still had no idea what he was doing until I grasped that he was about to switch the amp on. As I rushed over, out of the corner of my eye I saw that a skinhead was clambering up onto the stage, just beside Terrance, and before he got upright, I raced towards him ramming my heel into his throat, sending him flying back. By the time I turned around, Levi had disappeared. Searching wildly, I heard his voice, over and over, quiet and commanding, '*Glory, Gloria ... feel the Euphoria*,' and following the sound I saw him down in the crowd, and with each strum on his guitar, his body was convulsing, sending out sound waves that you could actually see, Jazz! You could see them! They were like pure gold strands of a spider web, bouncing off those they touched, creating an intricate mesh net; people falling under the electrical current. It travelled like the speed of light, and we watched from stage, astonished, frozen in disbelief. And I knew he would find you; I didn't know if he would live, but I knew he would not let you die."

His voice was barely a whisper, and his eyes brimmed with tears as he looked deep into mine. My back was stiff, aching; and it was all I could do to stop the dam from breaking, crashing under the weight of wet emotions. I could not, would not cry. But there was no way of stopping the mental pictures from spilling: Levi, near me, glowing like gold, fingers white from the burn, eyes like laser beams, falling, covering me with pure glory, that none may have me but him.

Then nothing.
Then nothing.

Then Dan.

"Dan?" I whispered.

"Dan is on suicide watch – won't sleep, hardly eats. You may as well know, sis, he threw the final blow that caused Levi to collapse and die. The doctor said that had Levi not been hit by an opposing force, a force that conflicted with the waves he was emanating through his guitar, his voice, and his hands, he might have survived. Kind of like sticking a fork in a toaster, or some such thing."

I stared up at Chad, aghast.

"Apparently our Dan met Carson – yes Carson," Chad repeated after he saw me flinch, "…after the first concert we went to at Raleigh – Carson was disguised as one of the media. Dan was livid at Levi stealing you up on to stage and then afterwards stealing you from right under his eyes, and then of all things attempting to kiss you! Carson picked up on it, stalked him and revealed his identity as Levi's father. He spun Dan a story about Levi stealing the fortune that was rightfully his, and promised he could help remove Levi from your life, in return for Dan's help."

"But the dead fish! The white powder! The shooting ..."

"He swears he knew nothing; that Carson had convinced him he was after Levi and Levi only. He never stopped to think that Carson might use you as bait. He actually thought Nev was responsible for 'arranging' those things. And it was Carson, not Neville, who worked with Vander spreading the hate Emosphere. And even Vander was just a lackey. It was Carson – fully bonafide Jagger – who was the mastermind of it all." Chad sighed heavily. "Dan didn't tell Ali the truth about what happened. When Vander blew hate over him, there was only one person he wanted to take that passion out on, and that was Levi. By the time he located him, Levi was already moving through the crowd with his guitar, singing that haunting song. Dan realized in that moment that Levi was playing the part of the 'hero' and the fading rage began to swell within him – after all, it had been *he* who had rescued you after the sting ray attack; *he* who had valiantly fought off the possum; *he* who had hardly slept over the past few weeks, guarding and protecting you. There was no way he was letting Levi steal his rightful role, the knight in shining armor rescuing the princess, whom the princess will then adore … You know the rest."

"I saw him … then Levi fell. I wondered … Chad …" I whispered brokenly, "I have locked away my heart; I can't do this, I just can't. Dan? A traitor?" My lips trembled as it all sunk in. Not only was I to lose Levi, but also now my dearest friend who betrayed me because I could not love him. A new ache, a new loneliness crept up on me, and I was desolate.

Closing my eyes, the first thing I saw, as if in 3-D, was Levi, strumming his guitar, and I heard his words:

"This is my forever love, flowing to you my lovely …"

I waited, sure there was more, and as I imagined looking into his eyes I read the words instinctively, like a song on the radio that you haven't heard for years, but still remember:

"Blue stars in the heavens
Sometime 'round eleven
Just look and see
Though they fall they are free
Search for me, search for me
This is my forever love, flowing to you my lovely …"

Looking down at my wrist I saw the blue star, my mark identifying me as a Reader, glowing of its own accord. In fact, it was throbbing and pulsating wildly, as if trying to tell me something. I could almost feel blue, noble blood travelling up my arm towards my heart, calling for me to rise, to fight, to believe. I clutched the blue star with my other hand, and feeling its power, forced my eyes up into Chad's, a small, tiny idea forming in the back of my mind, a nagging memory that hurt too much to open, but I had to peek to be sure.

"My Reader's Ring! It's gone! It was on my finger in the mosh-pit, I remember that much…the empty desert…no wonder…I know what I must do," I whispered in a strangled voice. Trembling all over, I clutched Chad's hands in mine, letting him feel my restraint. Then, as quickly as I dared, with only words and no pictures, I told him of my moments with Levi before the concert, his plan for us to run away to Saudi Arabia to chase his past, to find the truth about his father, about Carson. Shuddering, the old fear returned, but the feeling of Destiny was rising again, out of the ashes, prompting me, wooing me to action.

"I'm going to Saudi. I have to – for Levi. I need to do this for him, to track Carson and find the truth." I jumped up, wincing at the sudden unplanned movement. "And you can't stop me! Not you, not Bailey, not Mom and Dad – not anyone." I poked my finger angrily towards his face. "So back off, brother, you'd better not stand in my way!"

He folded his arms and gazed steadily at me, a slow grin forming on his face. "Stop you?" He replied sardonically, "Stop you? You'll be the one that has to stop *me* from coming with you. Ali told us to be patient; that Jasmine the Reader would know what to do. All we knew was that when you were ready, we would join you, whatever the quest, whatever the cost."

I rudely interrupted, barely able to contain my trembling, feeling it surge through my body causing chaos and uncontrollable muscle spasms.

"Who do you mean, *we*?"

"Me, Bailey, and Ali. It's all settled."

I stared at him aghast. "Over my dead body! This is my

pilgrimage, not yours, not theirs."

"No!" he hissed angrily. "We are all family now, joined by tragedy, by a common thread, and you need us as much as we need you!"

He threw his arms around me, drawing me roughly to him as only a brother would, and Destiny whispered through the words of George Eliot, words from an old English class coming back to haunt me:

"*What greater thing is there for human souls than to feel that they are joined for life –to be with each other in silent, unspeakable memories.*"

I wrapped my arms around Chad, and held on for dear life, faintly aware that my lips were somehow tingling.

The End

The story continues in

Emovescent

(The Destiny of Jasmine Blade: Part II)

Sequel to Emospherica

To be released 2014

Turn the page to read the first chapter…

"To every action there is always opposed an equal reaction: or, the mutual action of two bodies upon each other are always equal, and directed to contrary parts."

Sir Isaac Newton

1. THE OUTFIELD

I THINK I'LL STAY HERE AWHILE. THERE'S SOMETHING about the emptiness of this place that sits well with my soul. Watching the ball spinning towards my head I wonder each time if I'll catch it…but I always do, the familiar reflex never failing. There's a security in catching it that comforts me; warm soft leather cradled in my hand, knowing what goes up must come down – Newton's Law of Universal Gravitation told me so. This sphere will not float away on the breeze like a bubble, nor will it disappear into the heavens without a trace, ceasing to exist in my reality. No, as I lie in the greenest grass and aim the ball into the bluest sky, it will always, without fail, every time come back to me. Not like Emospheres. Not like Levi.

I throw higher and higher, knowing if my hands fail to catch the unforgiving orb, it will hurt. But I'm beyond hurt; untouchable, unbreakable. Life without Levi is like that - unbearably empty; catching in my throat, but no further, no further.

Suddenly, without prior warning, the ball disappeared before my eyes and I sat up with a start, searching for the untimely interruption. I had not heard Dan's approach, so deep was my introspection, and now he stood above me tossing the ball carelessly, daring me to rise and snatch it back. Scrambling to my feet I lunged towards him, but he danced backwards, just out of reach, taunting me. I had no desire to play games. I had nothing to bring, so I simply stood, waiting.

He paced further away from me, and then as I relaxed, threw hard and fast in the direction of my head. My body responded instinctively and the ball snapped into my hand, inches from my nose. I didn't even flinch, drawing my arm back and thrusting the ball through the air as hard as I was able. For ten minutes the pattern continued, back and forward, forward and back, each of us refusing to drop the ball, silently satisfied with the smacking sound of white leather in hand. Finally Dan spoke, his throws having become increasingly wild, as if trying to put me off balance, or smash through the glass-like barrier we both knew I had erected. I wasn't ready for it to shatter, not yet, so I focused on making sure I took each catch.

"You throw like a boy, Jazz. Guess that comes from having so many brothers…I s'pose your family used to play baseball in the back yard?" I pursed my lips, refusing to reply, speaking words unspoken with another hard throw, hoping to hurt him. Without taking his eyes off the ball, he continued, as if he didn't really expect me to reply anyway.

"Growing up in New Zealand we played back yard cricket when I was younger. Ever heard of cricket?" My eyes were stony as I caught his catch, feeling my fingers smarting at the impact.

"You have three sticks called 'stumps' behind the batter and the bowler – that's the pitcher – aims to hit the stumps and knock the bails off the top. The ball is very hard – a little smaller than this baseball and much, much harder. An international cricket match can take days to play…how long are we going to play this game, Jasmine Blade?" He sighed, the ball sailing high over his head, but he managed a jump catch without too much bother, his thick blonde hair falling across his eyes, long and disheveled. I could feel sweat droplets forming on my back with the exertion, but I was not ready to quit, nor to reply. It felt good, this rhythmic physical activity, requiring all my focus and energy; none left to waste on pointless thoughts and conversation.

Besides, Dan was wasting his gaming wordplays on me – I wasn't playing. If I let words out they would crush him like a melting mountain torrent crushes snow. I was ice cold.

Dan looked like an American now – baseball cap tossed on the grass, Abercrombie and Fitch t-shirt, jeans and sneakers. I guess it agreed with him – the all-American boy look, I mused scathingly, biting my lip. I had liked him as a kiwi boy; it took me to a much happier time and place, until that fateful day unfolded. Now, although my heart ached, I was still not sure he would ever feel my forgiveness.

A 'kuth-unk!' from behind caused me to involuntarily spin around, still vulnerable to sudden loud noises after the recent series of events. Unfortunately Dan had already thrown and the fast moving ball made contact with the back of my head, sounding a 'bunk' combined with another 'kuth-unk' and it seemed to be the only noise I could hear, over and over as I clutched my skull and fell to the ground. *When did it start raining?* I thought confusingly; *the sky is still blue…*

"It's the sprinkler system!" Dan yelled, rushing over. "You ok, Jazz? I'm sorry…jeez, I *still* can't do anything right. Gave me a shock too, but you have to admit, isn't it awesome? I've always wanted to get caught in one of these…it's kinda like the movies or something…"

He lay beside me and we watched the rainbows fizz through the misty spray, feeling the droplets nuzzle their way over our dusty skin and listened to the soft 'kuth-unks', breathing in the fresh scent of water soaked turf. Opening my mouth I let the water tickle me until I felt a remnant of joy, a weak thread of fun, and I laughed. And cried; mostly cried. It hurt to be this alive, but it was good, it was right. I felt the water wash away the hardness, the hopelessness, the heartbreak; even if it was only for a moment in time.

Finally I stood, and drenched from head to toe we walked together, but I kept my arms tightly hugged around me, trying to keep the avalanche in check. Part of me knew it was time, but part of me didn't want to admit it. I didn't really know what to say to Dan. He still thought Levi was dead, but I knew differently. I still felt Levi sing in my veins and heard him call me in my dreams. I hated the loneliness of his absence and I knew it was only a matter of time before my starving soul needed to find him. I had learned from my grandparents, Ali and Arabella, that the bond between Reader and Carrier was breakable only by death and the very fact that I still felt him near me refuted the state of his deadness. Sometimes the facts before you present one reality, but the truth speaks something else altogether. Intuition was calling me to challenge the facts in order to embrace truth. As we walked in silence, me pretending to listen to my iPod, I made a mental list of the facts:

1. My debut as a Reader went terribly wrong at Levi's concert and the emotion released created a hate Emospherica rather than one of love.
2. Two, no three (if you counted Levi) people died at the Alien Potion concert by the hands of neo-Nazi extremists with the added assistance of the Emospheres I had invented.
3. Government agencies in the US wanted nothing more to do with the Council of Carriers, Framers and Readers (CFR), or the Emospherica bubble mix I had created in line with my quest as a Reader.
4. What we had intended to be used for good had been hijacked by evil.
5. Bad dude Vander (ex-chairperson of the CFR) and Dan's Dad Neville (only he was not so much bad as he was stupid) had been caught and extradited; Carson was still on the loose.
6. There was no doubt that Levi had saved my life that night. The next fact made me shiver:
7. Dan had thrown the final blow to Levi's head in a jealous rage – the one that supposedly killed him…but they were only there because of me…

I baulked and stumbled, feeling bile rising in my throat at the ultimate betrayal of our friendship, my mind whipping past the guilt of my involvement…and yet here Dan was, grabbing my elbow to stop my fall. I pulled away as if burnt – he had asked for my forgiveness at least one hundred times by now, but I wasn't ready to give it. There was nothing more he could say, nothing that would bring Levi back. We both knew it, so we just walked silently through the asphalt desert until we came to Dan's car. I walked straight past; I had run here earlier, I could walk home now.

"Don't be silly, Jazz. I'll give you a lift." He jumped in front of me, his eyes pleading, mine stony.

The truth flickered through my mind, a fiery wick that refused to be extinguished. *He didn't mean it, he had no idea his blow to Levi would be fatal, maybe it's your fault for getting them involved…and anyhow…Levi isn't dead.* My lips, remembering Levi's kiss that bonded us together a Reader and Carrier, throbbed violently at the thought. Intuitively I stepped around Dan and opened the car door, listening to the voice of truth. Relieved, Dan hurried to the driver's side before I could change my mind, turned the key and headed for home.

'*Keep your friends close and your enemies even closer,*' I had learned whilst training to be a Reader with my Grandparents in New Zealand. Was Dan a friend or foe? Had he been truly tricked by Carson? Only time would tell, so for now I would watch, I would wait.

Leaning my head back against the seat I remembered the Dan I had first met in New Zealand – how we had surfed together, laughed and hung out. He had rescued me twice; once after the barb of a stingray pierced my ankle, the next from a possum clawing my back. I hadn't seen it coming, the fierce feelings he developed for me. He just reminded me of my brothers; I had always found it easier to relate to boys than girls. I had already been half in love with Levi anyway; Dan never stood a chance. And now we were together but alone, a wall of mistrust, mistakes and maligned emotion between us. I sighed heavily, my eyes closed, and heard an equally heavy sigh in reply. Then a third sigh, deep and long. I opened my eyes, looking over at Dan in annoyance.

"You don't have to overdo it, you know."

"What? That wasn't me; that was you! You don't say anything; you only sigh these days…" I interrupted before he could finish.

"It wasn't me, ok?" Silence. Another long sigh, one that sent prickles up my back as I felt warm air floating around my throat.

"No, it wasn't you, Reader. It was me."

The voice was deep, old and strong, causing me to freeze, not scared, but on guard. Dan jammed on the brakes but before he could turn around to rout the mysterious intruder, the voice continued, low and gritty.

"I wouldn't suggest trying anything much with a gun in your back. Feel that? That's a Cobra Shadow Revolver .38. Blow a nice hole straight through you if my finger slips. Now! Eyes ahead! Both of you!"

He must have caught my eyes trying to swivel sideways, and I saw Dan flinch as the barrel of the gun blackballed his back. His knuckles were white on the steering wheel and I could see the sweat on his forehead, but I didn't feel sorry for him – not much, anyway. More orders were barked.

"Do a U-turn. Stay on Price Street and then take the Ocean Highway north. Don't talk, not a word!" There was that jab again.

It was strange how I didn't really care if I died, or if Dan died for that matter. *No, actually*, come to think of it, *I didn't want Dan to die. Having one guy die because of me was enough; I wouldn't wish it to become two.*

"Knock-knock." My voice came out like I didn't care.

"Huh?" There was a grunt from behind.

"Knock-knock. You're supposed to say 'who's there?"

"Who's there?" Just like half the world, he couldn't help himself from replying.

"Ashley."

"Ashley who?"

"Ashley wish you would point that gun at me instead – it would be stupid to kill the driver – we'll all die!" I could hear the scowl in his voice now.

"I have two guns if you have that much of a death wish…now shut it!" Even looking straight ahead I could tell Dan was grinning.

We drove for at least forty-five minutes before the invisible wild card indicated for Dan to turn off the highway.

"Left!" He barked. "Now right! Right Again! Drive to the end of the road!" *Must be navigating by GPS*, I half-pie thought.

It was so very strange, I thought again, *how I wasn't really feeling anything. No anger, fear, distress…I just felt…like a passive observer, mostly disinterested, hardly curious.* That was life without Levi. That was life after failure.

ABOUT THE AUTHOR

I write to keep my sanity – living with five teenagers and a husband does that to you! Truthfully though, they are my inspiration. Life for the young is a book yet to be written and I love to watch the lives of my kids evolving; I also like to think that Karl & I are still young at heart and furiously writing each new chapter of our lives.

We live by the beach (actually everyone in New Zealand lives by the beach!) – 'Godzone', us kiwi's call it. My day job involves environmental planning and resource management consulting, my night job requires multi-tasking for a large family, and my in-between passion is writing. I like to write books I want to read – they write themselves, really; I just read as I go. Other stuff I love to squeeze in includes music 'n movies, poetry 'n painting, swimming 'n skiing, beaches 'n baking (especially when I'm stressed). But my most favorite thing of all is a Good Idea, and most days that is enough.

The books I love best are ones that make you feel happy inside; or one where you might learn something new; one that is full of passion and life; one that awakens the senses with a fresh pure light; or one that has adventure, romance and most of all – destiny!

Finally, the thing I value most in this world is a loving Father & friend: God, the ultimate story-teller.

Contact me via Facebook:
www.facebook.com/Emospherica or visit my blog:
pauapub.blogspot.co.nz/

AND if you liked/loved my book, please review on Amazon and spread the word – it will be just the inspiration I need to finish Book II!!

19550285R00221

Made in the USA
Charleston, SC
30 May 2013